Ohana

The Indigo Adventures, Book 2

- Published by Five Dimensions Press:
  - *Eye of a Fly* (Kindle edition), by Justin R. Smith.
  - *Introduction to Algebraic Geometry* (textbook), by Justin R. Smith.
  - *Abstract Algebra* (textbook), by Justin R. Smith.
- The Indigo Adventures:
  1. *The God Virus* (Kindle and paperback) Indigo Voyager.
  2. *Ohana*, by Justin R. Smith.

Five Dimensions web page:
http://www.five-dimensions.org
Email: indigo.voyager2@gmail.com

Ohana

by

Justin R. Smith

The Indigo Adventures, Book 2

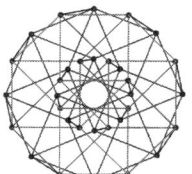

Five Dimensions Press

Ohana is a work of fiction. Any resemblance between its characters and real people (living or dead) is unintentional and purely coincidental.

©2017. Justin R. Smith All rights reserved.
ISBN-13: 978-1975678791
ISBN-10: 1975678796

Dedicated to my wonderful wife, Brigitte.

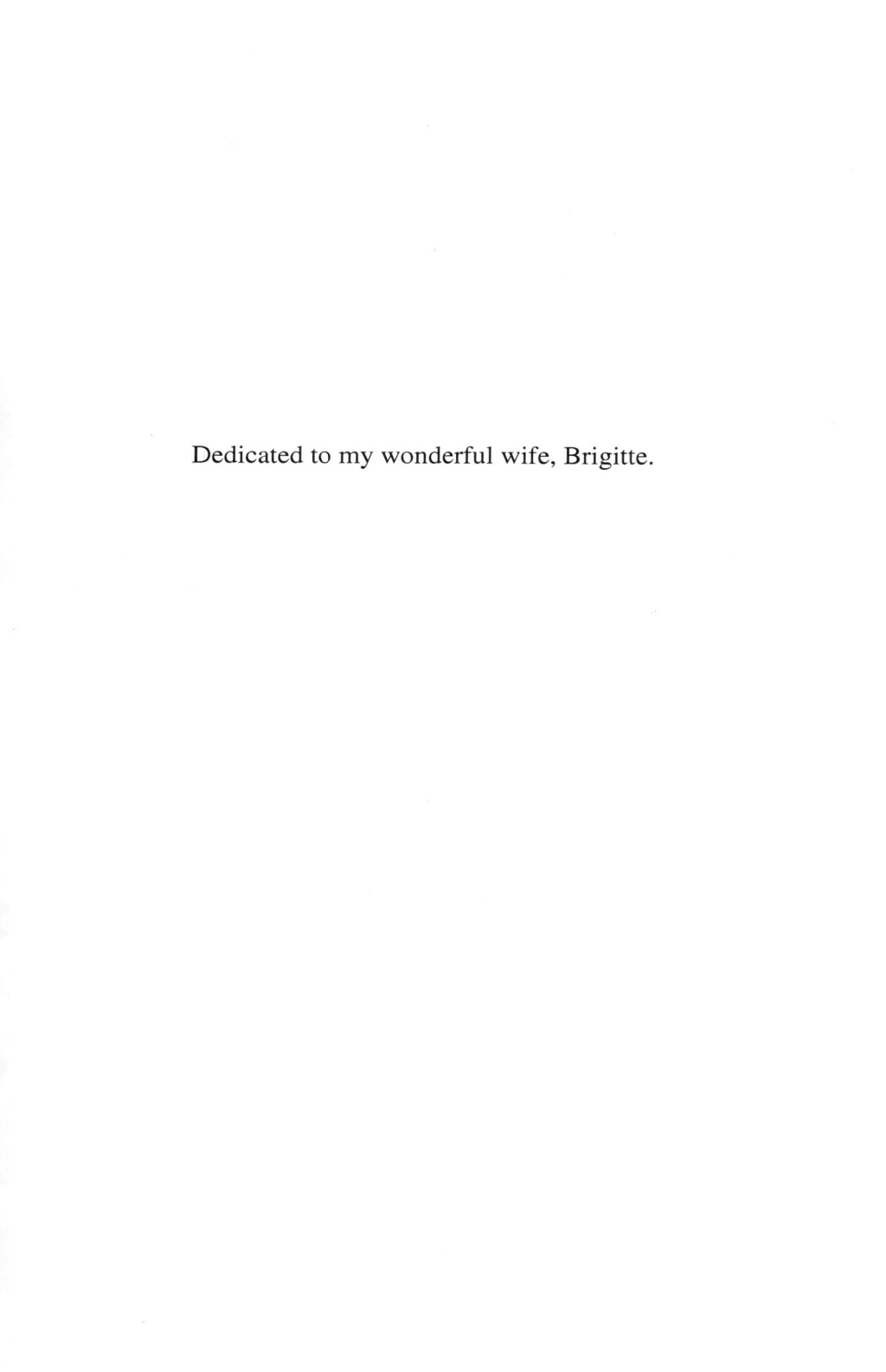

Ohana

"To see a World in a Grain of Sand,
And a Heaven in a Wild Flower,
Hold Infinity in the palm of your hand,
And Eternity in an hour."
— William Blake, from
Auguries of Innocence.

x

Chapter 1

"Isn't it a pain in the ass when people you murder come back?" Derek asked the lady who answered the door.

Confusion on her face gave way to mind-shattering terror.

"*I cremated you!*" she wailed, fleeing into the house as Derek ambled after her.

The place intrigued him.

Its exterior was nondescript weathered gray stone, its architectural style like that of an old church. One half-expected to see gargoyles squatting on downspouts.

Here, of course, the gargoyles lived *inside,* a middle-aged couple that had murdered dozens of street-people, students, their own son, and an unfortunate other version of Derek — all in their efforts to create a master-race.

They had succeeded.

Indeed, they had done so in ways they could never have imagined, ways that defied logic and the laws of physics.

Today, he would deliver a morsel of retribution.

Derek strolled down the long hallway past oil paintings of landscapes on the walls and entrances to the living room and dining room, the parquet floor creaking under his feet — until he reached the study's massive oak door.

He kicked it open.

Books in darkly stained walnut bookcases lined the room, and a walnut desk stood in front of the French doors that opened out to the garden.

Mrs. Pembroke cowered beneath it, sobbing.

He was *almost* tempted to give her an explanation of what was happening.

She didn't deserve one.

"Where are the red pills? The ones you created from my brain."

She howled.

Derek scanned her mind and learned the pills were stored in liquid nitrogen in the basement laboratory.

He teleported to the lab and spotted a cryogenic Dewar flask wrapped in mist on the workbench. He put on insulated gloves, grabbed it, and teleported home.

✳✳✳

Derek Evans was a husky, pale, six-foot four twenty-five-year old with brown hair and brown contact lenses.

He teleported to a restroom on the second floor of the University of Chicago's Oriental Institute and then joined Alessandra and Professor Andromeda Cole in her cluttered office.

Piles of papers and old books covered most of the floor-space. Massive wooden shelves behind the desk held stone tablets with Egyptian hieroglyphics, a human skull covered with arcane symbols, and decaying scrolls.

Derek's wife, Alessandra — Allie — was a petite brunette with an olive complexion and a beautiful face marred by a scar on her right jaw-line — and brown contacts.

Get the pills? Allie wordlessly beamed to him as he sat in the other guest chair.
Yes.
"Where is this site?" Professor Cole said. She was a middle aged woman with a rugged face in jeans and a blue denim blouse. Her gray hair was gathered in a ponytail.

One could easily picture her living out of a tent in the Middle East with a coiled whip hanging from her belt.

"It's in Southern Africa, sort of," Derek said.

"Sort of? What does that mean?"

"To explain that, I have to flip a coin," Allie said, throwing a quarter in the air.

She caught it and slapped it on the desk.

"What's the outcome?" she asked.

"It came up heads, of course," Professor Cole replied. "Why are we flipping coins? I thought you were going to explain..."

"Wrong," Allie said. "It came up heads *and* tails and, to a slight extent, landed on its edge."

"All in different universes," Derek continued. "When an event has multiple outcomes, all possibilities occur in multiple copies of the universe. You split into several Andromeda Coles, each one seeing a different outcome."

"If you'll excuse me," Professor Cole muttered. "I have an urgent meeting on uh ... Planet Earth."

Archaeologists are catnip for crackpots, she thought.

Allie and Derek laughed.

"Huh?"

"It's just that we have a cat named Norton," Derek said. "And we should plant catnip in ... at home."

"We're crackpots with money," Allie chuckled, fanning out a sheaf of hundred-dollar bills. "Just humor us a few more minutes."

Professor Cole stared at the money.

"Please join us in this corner of the room," Derek said, standing. "We want to demonstrate something."

Professor Cole eventually joined them, thinking, *The sooner they leave the better.*

A flash of ... discontinuity and ... ecstasy followed.

"What was that?" Professor Cole gasped. "It's like something I experienced ... long ago."

"The spirit world," Allie said. "We tunneled through it."

They stood in a corner of Professor Cole's office — and other versions of Derek and Allie sat in her guest chairs, while another Professor Cole sat at the desk.

The two Professor Coles stared at each other in shock.

"Tails," the seated Allie said, pointing to the coin on the desk.

"We have to return you to your original timeline," Derek said. "There are two of you here and *none* of you there."

There was another flicker and the office now held three people, huddled in the corner.

"Who ... *what* the *hell* are you two?" she muttered, shaking.

"You thought you need a drink," Allie said. "So let's get one, and we'll answer your questions."

Are they reading my mind? Professor Cole thought.

"Yes, we are telepaths," Derek said.

✳✳✳

They walked to the Wabash Pub on the corner of Woodlawn and East 59th street — bordering the Midway Plaisance Park, its trees blazing gold and yellow on this crisp fall day.

The place was almost empty.

It was a dark wood-paneled bar with tables opposite the bar and pool tables in the back. On one wall, a large poster announced a Halloween party and dance at the University of Chicago student union.

A jukebox blared *American Pie*.

Looking at the poster, Derek felt a twinge of nostalgia.

Longing for the days when we were young and foolish and full of hope? Allie beamed at him.

"Aren't we full of hope now, *me amuri?*" he said, his eyes tearing up.

"Oh *maniac,* I love it when you talk Sicilian to me," Allie sighed, tapping Derek on the shoulder. "You're right of course. Our time has come."

Get a room, guys! Professor Cole thought.

"We don't need a room," Allie whispered. "We have the Sea of Desire in the land of Oz."

"Believe it or not, that's a place," Derek said.

When their eyes had adjusted to the dim lighting, they took a table.

"God, I *hate* these things," Allie muttered, removing her brown contact lenses. "I can't imagine how people wear them all the time."

Professor Cole gasped when she saw Allie's Indigo eyes, with irises sparkling like diamonds.

Derek removed his contacts too.

"That's one of the most visible outward signs of Indigos like us," Derek said. "Besides having no fingernails or toenails."

"Indigos?"

"That's what we call our species," Allie said. *"Homo Sapiens Indicus."*

"Your *species?"*

"We are the result of genetic experiments," Derek said.

"In another timeline we call Origin," Allie said.

"Hi doc," the bartender said, waiting on them. "Balvenie neat?"

"You know me too well, Nick."

Derek and Allie ordered coffee, and Nick left.

"Three keys to happiness," Andy said. "True love, a good career, and a well-trained bartender."

"I can't wait to be able to drink again," Allie said, pointing to her pregnant belly.

"When are you due?"

"No idea," Allie said. "I don't know what our gestation period is. The funny part is I can see her being born."

Andromeda smiled.

"In most futures, she's born in the daytime and some, at night. Different times, different places."

"In *most futures?*" Andy said. "You literally *see* this?"

"All I know is it'll be *amazing* ... and *soon*. Somewhere between a day and a month from now. Most important, she'll be *healthy*."

"Our precognition doesn't sync with calendars or clocks," Derek said.

"Vittoria will be our first natural-born," Allie said. "Ever."

"You two weren't natural-born?"

"Doctor Pembroke gave me a DNA-altering virus," Derek said. "Part of a bogus drug-study."

"Pembroke?" Professor Cole said. "The name sounds familiar."

"In our timeline, he was nominated for a Nobel prize in biology," Derek said.

"I remember! My ex was a biologist and she was always going on about what a genius Pembroke was."

"He was a *monster,*" Allie muttered.

"He knew physics? I mean physics must be involved with going into timelines."

"No," Derek said. "All he knew for sure was that we'd be telepaths. His lab animals became agitated whenever he *thought* of torturing them, and calmed down when he changed his mind."

"That's horrible!"

Nick served their drinks.

"He got what he deserved in the end," Allie muttered. "In our world, he got it *after* infecting Derek. In yours, he got it before."

"How *do* you travel to different timelines?" Professor Cole said. "I mean, if Pembroke didn't know physics."

"We go to a place we call the spirit-world," Derek said. "The crossroads of existence. Every corner of every timeline is accessible from there."

"It's a place where thoughts are sounds," Allie said. "That's the basis of telepathy and ... everything else. Pembroke screwed with the human brain and got a *lot* more than he bargained for."

Professor Cole sipped her drink.

"What is your timeline like? What did you call it? Origin?"

"It looks a lot like yours," Derek said. "Except it's five years out of sync."

"And President Eakins is trying to turn America into a police state," Allie said.

"That lunatic is *president?*" she said. *"That's not possible!"*

"His two opponents despised each other," Derek said. "Each had supporters who hated the other. They stayed home on election day."

"A woman told me she couldn't vote for either of them in good conscience," Allie said. "She asked me whom she should write in: Mahatma Gandhi or Martin Luther King. That was Eakins's opposition."

"Jesus!" Professor Cole muttered, gulping her drink.

She ordered another.

"What do you call *this* timeline?" Professor Cole said, rapping on the table.

"The *Culinary* timeline," Derek said. "For personal reasons."

"So why did you guys pick me? You're not the typical loonies who want me to investigate ancient astronauts."

"It's your book *The Future of the Past,*" Allie said. "At the top of page 203, you said 'given advances in space travel, especially Eldon Trask's manned Mars missions, archaeologists must prepare to study alien cultures and artifacts.' As far as we know, you're the only archaeologist to say anything like that."

"I became a laughingstock. I've always been interested in the idea of first contact. My parents were astronomers."

"Hence your name Andromeda?" Allie chuckled.

"Call me Andy," she laughed. "Everyone does. I have a brother named Sirius and a sister named Ceres. And I don't believe for a minute that you know the exact page number in my book."

"We have good memories," Derek said.

"We'll see," Andromeda said. "What is it you want me to do?"

"Investigate ancient astronauts," Allie laughed.

"We don't know that they're astronauts," Derek said. "They are ancient — and not human. In a timeline we call Oz."

"How ancient?"

"A hundred thousand years," Allie said. "Maybe more."

"Most artifacts on the surface will be severely degraded,"

Andromeda said. "Even the Egyptian pyramids would be unrecognizable in that length of time."

"The surface has been scoured," Derek said. "Southern Africa in Oz has huge plains of fused black glass and a melted mountain. We think someone detonated a large number of atomic weapons."

"Is it radioactive?"

"Not at all," Derek said. "That's why we think it happened at least a hundred thousand years ago."

"Whatever happened there killed off these aliens *and* early humans," Allie said. "So the human race never evolved on Oz."

They sat in silence for a few minutes.

"I can't believe it," Andy Cole said. "I split into *two people?*"

"More than two," Derek muttered, beaming *Should we burden her with the truth?*

No, Allie beamed.

Professor Cole sighed and looked around.

"This has been fascinating," she finally said, standing. "But I've got ... papers to grade."

She left.

"Back to square one," Derek muttered.

"Maybe not."

✽✽✽

Back at her office, Professor Cole pulled out a copy of her book, *The Future of the Past,* and turned to page 203. Sure enough, Allie had quoted it verbatim.

She left the institute and strolled to the elegant Gothic cathedral-style building containing the Mathematics Department. Her partner, Llewellyn Masters, had her office on the second floor.

She chuckled at the poster hanging over the open door: "Infinity bottles of beer on the wall, infinity bottles of beer. If one of the bottles should happen to fall, infinity bottles of beer on the wall..."

"My goodness, Andy!" Professor Masters said. "You look like you've seen a ghost."

Llewellyn Masters was a petite brunette in her mid thirties wearing a white blouse, black skirt featuring a picture of R2D2, a colorful beaded necklace, and thick glasses on a red silk eyeglass-necklace.

Her office was a stark contrast to Professor Cole's: spotless with everything in its perfect place. Pens and pencils lined up on her shiny desk — parallel and equally-spaced.

A framed photo of her and Andromeda standing in front of Egypt's Great Pyramid hung on the wall.

"I just spent the most bizarre half-hour of my long... absurd life. On this ordinary fall day, an ordinary-looking couple came to my office and *showed* me ... portals to alternate worlds."

She related her encounter with Derek and Allie.

"Did you actually see *another version* of you?"

"Yes!"

"The Many-Worlds form of quantum mechanics postulates the existence of other timelines."

"You've mentioned it once or twice..."

"As far as I know, you can't visit them," Llewellyn said.

"Well, we did. Even the ... trip to this other ... timeline was strange. It was like that hermit's cave in Ethiopia."

"When you were looking for the Ark of the Covenant?"

"Yes, that uncanny feeling ... of ... of ecstasy or infinity. They said it was the *spirit world*. I've seen weird in my day, but aliens who can alter space and time is a whole different flavor of weird."

"Aliens? What did they want from you?"

She explained.

"Your absurd life?" Llewellyn smiled, hugging her. "You're my fearless Lara Croft."

"I'm not a cartoon character, honey. And I'm not feeling very fearless today."

"You've traveled the Middle East, Africa, Tibet," Llewellyn murmured. "Lived among Tuareg tribesmen in Mali and monks in the Himalayas. This could be the greatest adventure of your life. Of *our* lives."

"Our lives? Your idea of roughing it is slow room-service."

"Our sabbaticals are beginning soon. I want to go along and ... and see what you do, be *part* of it. If it means living in a tent and sleeping on the ground, so be it. I'll be your assistant. And I could work on p-adic Hilbert schemes without distractions."

"I'll never see those two ... people again," Andromeda sighed. "If I do, I'll say yes to them. We sure as *hell* could use the ten million dollars."

"They gave you ten thousand dollars just to *listen* to their pitch?" Llewellyn said.

"Yes. I say we go to the most obscenely expensive restaurant in town. A place with heel-clicking, French-speaking waiters in monkey suits."

"I have nothing to wear."

"We'll go as we are. Our money's as good as anyone's."

Chapter 2

In their spirit-bodies, Derek and Allie hovered near the Oval Office's ceiling.

They were in the Origin Timeline — the one where they had been born.

"Bastard!" President Pete Eakins muttered, slamming the phone down. "Daniel Ford!"

"Isn't he one of your biggest supporters, Mr. President?" Renard Moreau said. He was the former director of the CIA's Clandestine Service, and now President Eakins' right-hand man.

"He reminded me of a promise I made."

"You're not in a giving vein?" Mr. Moreau smiled.

"What the hell does that mean?"

"Never mind."

"Are you familiar with Hitler's Night of the Long Knives?"

"In one night, his people murdered all his political opponents," Mr. Moreau said. "Some eighty-five people."

"The real number was in the hundreds. The absolute fucking *genius* of that operation wasn't that he eliminated his enemies. Any idiot knows to do that. He also murdered his *friends*. People who put him where he was and felt it made them his equal. People who felt he *owed* them. A true leader has no equals ... and owes *nothing* to *anyone.*"

"You want to get rid of Mr. Ford?"

"*All* my early supporters," President Eakins nodded. "Treason against the human race — conspiring with Derek and Alessandra. I want *signed confessions.* Their property will form a nice revenue stream. Hmm..."

"What?"

"Accuse people of crimes and let them sign their estates over to us. In exchange, they get a subsistence pension. If they refuse, they go to prison. Incidentally — how's the search going?"

"Search?"

"*The* goddamn *search!* What, am I speaking a foreign language?"

"We've gone worldwide and found nothing. I still say..."

"Derek and Allie are *not* in another timeline!" President Eakins shouted. "Your own chief scientist says they don't exist. You were drugged and brainwashed."

Renard felt an aching nostalgia for the time he was Derek's prisoner on Maui in the Oz timeline. It had been more like a long-needed vacation than imprisonment — and he hadn't had to listen to lectures on Hitler's brilliance.

If that was drugs, where do I get more? Mr. Moreau thought.

"He's not the final authority," he said.

"That fucking Nobel prize winner. What's his name?"

"Korman, Mr. President."

"He said only atomic particles travel between timelines. Cancel that prick's research grants. He dissed me."

Mr. Moreau said nothing.

"Call it off," Eakins finally continued. "I know how to flush them out."

"OK."

"We execute everyone in Derek's hometown, one by one. All three thousand."

"Pardon me, Mr. President," Mr. Moreau said. "How far will Derek go to defend them? Your supporters there burned down his parents' house and blew up Chloe Teague's church. Derek's own Aunt Abigail is one of your more ... enthusiastic followers."

"Chloe Teague? Who the hell is she?"

"The Episcopal minister who performed Derek and Allie's wedding. A close friend of theirs."

"Right. Well, that's why we have to kill the children too. Those two are insanely sentimental when it come to children."

"They'll do anything to stop it, Mr. President."

How right you are, Derek said.

"They'll be sucking my dick."

We've got to stop him, Allie said.

He'll be alone soon, Derek said.

"The military won't do it," Mr. Moreau said. "Even my people won't believe American children are terrorists."

"One of these days," President Eakins sighed. "I'll have a military that *works*. Replace enough four-star generals with hungry second lieutenants. OK, do what you did with my secret service contingent."

"Prisoners?"

"People on death row or lifers. Assemble a force of ten thousand and give them state-of-the-art weapons and training. The President's Own."

"It'll be messy. Boothbay Harbor is rural and everyone has guns."

"I know," President Eakins said. "Begin by disbanding all local police. Your people can do that at least. Quarantine the area so people can't leave."

❋❋❋

Accompanied by a security detail in two cars, President Eakins's limo exited the White House complex onto Constitution Avenue NW and took I66 to Northern Virginia.

After twenty minutes, the motorcade entered the town of Hadleyville and pulled up to a small suburban ranch style home. The security detail fanned out and surrounded the property. When they had declared it all clear, President Eakins exited the limo.

His Secretary of the Interior, Mallory Keithley greeted him at the door with a smile. She was a middle-aged woman in a gray pants suit.

"I have a treat for you tonight," she said. "Six and seven and *stunning*. Brother and sister."

"Sedate them better than the last two," he said. "I don't want another wrestling match."

"As you wish, Mr. President."

They entered the living room where two blond, blue-eyed children sat on the sofa, yawning and barely able to keep their eyes open.

President Eakins looked them over.

"They are positively angelic!" he said, flushing and roughly stroking the boy's hair. "You have an artist's eye, Mallory. I'll wait in the bedroom."

Unbuttoning his shirt, President Eakins strolled down a long hallway to the master bedroom.

He shut the door and unfastened his belt.

Alessandra popped into existence beside him and zapped

him in the neck with a stun-gun, as Derek appeared and caught him slumping to the floor.

They vanished.

※※※

They appeared on a grimy city street in early afternoon. It looked a bit like New York except for the hundred-foot high posters of a smiling middle-aged man that covered every building.

The stench of rotting meat and shit hung in the air.

Building-mounted loudspeakers blared military music as a female announcer said, "Yet again has Sacred Leader led The Land of Peace to *glorious victory*. The invaders were *utterly* destroyed. It is the duty of every citizen to hate Sacred Leader's enemies."

On cue, three people down the street chanted, "Hate! Hate! Hate!" in unison, pumping their right fists into the air.

Derek and Allie deposited President Eakins on a garbage can as he came to.

"What third-world toilet is this?" he growled. "My people *will* find me, and everyone you know or love will die slowly and in the *utmost agony*."

"Geographically, we're in North America," Derek said.

"This is what a real police state looks like, Eakins," Allie said. "If you want to survive, keep your head down and your mouth shut."

They vanished.

Pete Eakins fastened his belt, buttoned his shirt, and staggered down the street to a man carrying a wicked-looking automatic weapon. The man wore a black helmet whose visor covered his face and heavy black body-armor emblazoned with the words *Safety Service*.

"Officer!" Eakins said. "I want to report a kidnapping."

"What is your citizens' welfare number?"

"I'm the fucking president of the United States! Don't you recognize me?"

"You have uttered a proscribed phrase! Show me your papers! Where's your barcode?"

"How dare you use that tone with me!"

The Safety Service officer punched Eakins in the gut, doubling him over.

As Eakins vomited, the officer cuffed his hands behind his back and threw him into a black windowless van that pulled up.

※※※

In the Oval Office, Renard Moreau answered the phone.

"President Eakins disappeared," Mrs. Kiethly sobbed. "Without a trace. We tore the house apart."

"Take the children home," Renard said.

"I can't. The security people ran off with the limo and the other two cars."

"That's what Eakins gets for using murderers as bodyguards," he muttered. "They clearly kidnapped him. I'll send a car for you."

He hung up, called the Secret Service, and gave them the house's address.

Afterward, Renard paced the Oval Office.

"OK you two," he said to the empty room. "Where did you stash him? Oz?"

"We wouldn't pollute Oz with scum like him," Derek said, materializing and making Renard jump. "All you need to know is he isn't coming back."

"We put him in a timeline we call Pembroke," Allie said, popping into view. "A police state."

"Pembroke? As in the Harry Pembroke who experimented on you two before he got murdered?"

Derek nodded.

"We wanted to ask his spirit how we would change over time," Allie said. "Since he'd created the virus that ... created us."

"We were afraid he was in hell, though," Derek said. "We didn't even want to *visit* there."

"I don't think Pembroke really knew what his virus could do," Allie said. "Besides telepathy."

"We finally got up the nerve to visit him," Derek said. "And found he'd already reincarnated."

"He's a she, now," Allie said. "Two months old ... with a barcode tattooed on her neck."

"Some government official's clone," Derek said. "To be used for spare parts."

"This is all very interesting," Renard Moreau said. *"Bizarre* but interesting. The big question: where's the nuclear football?"

This was the steel attaché case containing launch codes for the country's nuclear arsenal.

"Eakins was about to rape two small children," Allie said. "He barely had clothes on."

"He had the football with him when he left the White House," Renard said. "He dismissed the marine who usually carries it."

"Doesn't it have a GPS tracker?" Derek said. "It would make sense for something that important..."

"Eakins disabled it whenever he went to Hadleyville," Renard said. "Did he make any stops on the way?"

"I don't know," Allie said. "We didn't follow him. We knew how to find him."

"Right now, the US is unable to retaliate if attacked with nuclear weapons," Renard said. "This may or may not be serious. It all depends on where the football wound up."

"The *US?*" Derek snarled. "You mean the country that put out a kill-order against us and our friends? That elected a president who'd murder three thousand innocent civilians to get at us? *That* US?"

"I know we've treated you horribly," Renard groaned, rubbing his face. "And I'm responsible for a lot of it. You don't owe us a damn thing. Whether you help us or not, I'll try to make it possible for you to return. This country shot itself in the foot a hundred times when we drove you and your friends into exile."

"Yes," Allie said.

"I acted out of fear," Renard said. "With your abilities, you two could've committed devastating acts of terrorism. You've been useful enemies for Eakins. Anything that goes wrong gets blamed on you two."

"Like what?" Derek said.

"Last week they blamed you for an earthquake in California. They even made a geologist go on TV and say so."

"How'd they do that?" Allie snorted.

"The guy wanted to stay out of prison. Anyway, we provoked you, but you just stayed away."

"We have a home in Oz," Derek said.

"It's a wilderness," Renard said. "You don't strike me as people who'd be content watching grass grow. You could reopen your art gallery, Allie."

"Is that a *joke?*" Allie growled.

"What do you mean?"

"Your people *raided* my gallery," Allie sobbed, tears running down her face. "I see Jim Moretti's *Gotham Redux* hanging on the wall over there, so you must've liked *some* of the art. You never paid him a *dime* for it. You threatened him with *prison or death!"*

Renard sighed deeply.

"And that steel sculpture, *Land of Fire*. You ripped it to pieces and sold it for scrap. If you didn't like the art, you should've given it back to the artists!"

"We searched for embedded microchips," Renard muttered. "We couldn't believe it was just pieces of metal welded together."

"It was Lena Fairchild's *heart* and *soul,"* Allie said. "Six months of her life! I've heard people call art crap and ask why anyone would pay *anything* for it. We *need* it, though; it's our *soul*. It's what makes us *human."*

Curious, Renard thought. *From one who is definitely not human.*

"I'll have my assistant look into it," he muttered. "We'll compensate all your artists."

"I gave those *poor bastards* my *word* as a *businesswoman* and critic," Allie shouted. "I said I'd display their work and try to sell it. I failed them — completely! I'll *never* be able to show my face in the art world here. *Ever!"*

Allie broke down and cried.

"Let's go, honey," Derek said, hugging her.

They vanished.

"I heard shouting," an aid named Henry Martins said, running into the room. "What was that?"

"Oh, I just pissed off the last people ... in the entire universe ... any sane person would want to piss off."

"Huh?"

"Luckily they're not vindictive."

"President Eakins?"

"I said they're *not* vindictive."

✳✳✳

Derek and Allie arrived in a secluded grove of palm trees in Oz.

"I'm sorry," Allie said. "Moreau touched a raw nerve."

"We already paid our artists with gold bars," Derek said.

"Not easy to convert into cash," Allie said. "Especially when they can't say where the gold came from! Lena Fairchild wouldn't take any. Besides, Moreau *owes* them and should pay too! He and Eakins destroyed so many lives. Paying our artists is the *least* he can do."

✳✳✳

Two days later, Derek and Allie hovered in their spirit bodies near the ceiling of Andromeda's office.

"I feel like we're being watched," Llewellyn said, shivering in the guest chair and rubbing her hands together.

"Ah, Breasted's ghost!" Andy laughed. "There's a legend he hangs around here and haunts lazy grad students. Maybe he doesn't like mathematicians either."

"Was he the inspiration for Indiana Jones?"

"He founded this place," Andromeda nodded. "Probably the greatest Egyptologist of all time."

Derek and Allie materialized in nearby restrooms, went to the office, and knocked on the door.

"That was us in our spirit-bodies," Derek said. "Some people sense our presence."

"Your eyes!" Llewellyn said.

"I just can't stand these accursed contacts," Allie muttered.

"Have you considered our proposal?" Derek said.

"If you're telepathic, you already know the answer to that," Andy said.

"I was being polite and pretending not to."

"Our answer is yes," Andy said. "I'm just concerned..."

"It might be dangerous for Llewellyn?" Allie said.

"I *can* handle it," Llewellyn said. "I *want* to."

"We don't want this to be dangerous for either of you," Derek said. "At the first sign of danger, we'll call it off and give you all the money we promised."

"I'll have to acquire expedition gear," Andy said. "Tents, ropes... What do you think we'll need?"

"Just bring yourselves," Derek said. "We'll provide living quarters on site and everything else you need. We can always go shopping."

"There's shopping there?" Llewellyn said.

"There's shopping *here*," Derek said. "Travel is ... easy for us. It takes minutes."

"I normally have a bunch of graduate students assist me," Andy said.

"That will be a problem," Derek said. "But we have plenty of refugees in Oz who are bored out of their minds and eager to participate."

"Refugees?" Andy said.

"President Eakins and the government drove us and our friends out of the Origin timeline," Derek said. "They put out a kill-order against us.

"President Eakins?" Llewellyn said. "That has such a bizarre ring. If *he* could become president, I guess anything is possible."

"With our powers," Allie said. "We could steal a nuclear weapon and set it off in a big city. *Theoretically.* There's no defense against us. There's no prison that can hold us, either."

"We never lifted a finger to carry out this insane idea," Derek said. "We never even hinted that we were thinking of it. We even agreed to work with the CIA."

"Here's the speech Eakins gave on TV," Allie said, playing a video on her cell phone.

They watched intently.

"Space aliens from another galaxy?" Llewellyn said. "That's ridiculous. Even if you *were* extraterrestrials, it would be from another planet or a nearby star."

"Yeah," Derek said. "Eakins felt his followers were too dumb to understand *Earth*-aliens not from Mexico."

"Dumb?" Andy said. "That's for sure. I can't believe he told gun owners to kill anyone *suspected* of helping you guys."

"Yeah," Derek said. "People are getting shot in broad daylight. The death-toll's in the thousands..."

"And includes all of Eakins's political opponents," Allie added.

"If there's no defense against you," Andy said. "They felt they *had* to kill you."

"We're almost invulnerable," Derek said.

"Oh," Andy said. "So they had to threaten people close to you. Non Indigo people, I mean."

"They tried," Derek said.

"I hate to ask this," Andy said. "If you're refugees, how will you get ten million dollars to pay us? I mean, we'll probably do it for a lot less. Hell, if it's half as interesting as you say, we'll do it for free."

"We picked winning numbers in the MaxiMillion lottery," Allie said.

"Indigos are good at... acquiring money," Derek said. "We also have access to gold."

They agreed to meet in two days.

✳✳✳

Derek and Allie teleported into a gray concrete ten-by-ten cell with a metal chair bolted to the floor and a sink and bucket.

Wearing a gray jumpsuit, a barefoot Pete Eakins sat in the chair sobbing.

Ancient and fresh bloodstains decorated the walls.

Bruises closed Eakins's right eye and blood ran from his nose and mouth. A wall-mounted camera recorded everything.

Before guards could intervene, the Indigos teleported him to Volcano Island in Oz — its counterpart to the big island of Hawaii.

※※※

The sun blinded them, and the humid gale carried the scent of wild orchids and sulfur.

Miles away, a thundering lava fountain spewed liquid fire hundreds of feet into the clear blue sky, radiating heat that warmed their faces.

The ground shuddered.

Tiny plants bravely tried to poke through the black lava moonscape.

Eakins looked around and burst into tears.

"Please don't take me back there," he sobbed. "I'll do anything."

"Where's the nuclear football?" Derek said.

"Ah!" he smiled. "Take me back to the White House ... and I'll tell you."

"OK," Allie said. "I see what happened to it."

※※※

They returned him to a rural area of the Pembroke timeline. A sea of golden wheat swayed in the wind, and stacked sheaves stood every fifty feet.

"Maybe you'll be able to stay out of trouble now," Derek said.

They left.

Across the road, three men with pitchforks bundled hay into horse-drawn wagons. One pulled a tarp over his his wagon, tied it down, climbed aboard, and started to clop away.

"My God!" another whispered, pointing to Eakins. "You're wearing *starvation* garb!"

"Please don't turn me in," Eakins moaned.

"Quick! Jump in the back of my wagon!"

Eakins complied, the man covered him with a tarp, and the wagon lurched into motion.

"I recognize you from TV," the driver said through the tarp. "When they put you in the chamber."

Eakins cowered.

※※※

"He left it in the presidential limo," Derek said.

"Thank you," Renard said.

"We rescued him from a Starvation Chamber," Allie said.

"A *what?*"

"Yeah," Allie mumbled. "They film prisoners starving to death and televise a speeded-up version with the statement 'Thus do Sacred Leader's enemies perish'."

"He committed three crimes that carry death penalties," Derek said.

"Crimes?" Renard said.

"Uttering the phrase 'United States', lacking papers or a neck-barcode, and failing to drop to his knees when confronted by safety service officers," Derek said. "Oddly enough, people there have no idea what 'United States' means. They just know it's illegal to say."

"Bizarre!" Renard said.

"Hell, *they* don't even know," Allie said. "They have an agency that rewrites history. They don't even know what year it is. They restart their calendar with each new Sacred Leader."

"How strange!" Renard murmured. "A brain-damaged nation."

"What about the vice president?" Derek said. *"Here,* I mean."

"Leave Knox to me," Renard said. "He's a buffoon and total nonentity. We're close to finding the limo. The bodyguards will die in a shootout."

Derek and Allie registered shock.

"What? They're all *murderers!* On death row before Eakins recruited them."

Chapter 3

"This is *loony tunes!*" Joanne Fine screamed, attracting the attention of nearby patrons. "I went to your funerals. Both of them!"

They sat at an outdoor table at *La Fontaine,* a French and Thai fusion restaurant in New York City's Central Park. It was a warm, sunny fall day.

"Look honey," Joyce Pincus said. "It's complicated. There's more than one reality, one dimension where we exist. In one of these other dimensions, we never died."

"You're not my mom!" Joanne said. "How dare you claim to be her? I don't know what your scam is, but I'm calling the police."

"And say what?" Vaughn Williams said. He was a tall, thin soft-spoken African-American man. "What exactly are you accusing us of?"

"I don't know," she said. "That lunatic you ... I mean *mom* married ... blew his brains out, and now he's *sitting* right here? Why doesn't he *say* anything?"

"Reginald is on his meds," Joyce Pincus murmured.

"We can make you and your sister rich beyond your wildest dreams," Vaughn said. "If you allow us. We have a cold-fusion device called a *Pincus Generator*. It produces sixty kilowatts continuous power. Converting tiny amounts of hydrogen into helium."

"What are you?" Joanne said. "A Nigerian prince or something?

"We don't need this crap," Vaughn muttered.

"What *happened?*" Joyce mumbled, tears running down her face. "You and your sister were so imaginative once. You made a whole village out of pasta dolls, with clothes of construction paper. I admit it's hard to wrap your brain around what we're telling you, but you could try."

"Let it go, Joyce," Vaughn said, putting his arm around her. "You don't need this either. We've got the technology and the money."

"*Mom?* Is it really you?"

"The mother you buried is dead," Joyce said. "I'm a ... duplicate of her, from a few years back. I have her memories up to then and different ones from then on."

"Up to a few years ago?"

"Up to sometime before Eakins became president," Vaughn said.

"*President Eakins?*"

"That turned out about how you'd expect it to," Vaughn muttered.

"How can people be duplicated? Someone waved a magic wand?"

"It's a natural process," Vaughn said. "It happens all the time. Up to a few months ago, if anyone told me this, I'd have said they were crazy."

"You have thousands of duplicates, yourself," Joyce said.

"You don't meet them because they live in their own worlds. We found a way to travel between these ... worlds."

"You traveled here from another world? Why?"

"We're refugees," Vaughn said. "Mainly because Derek Evans invested in our business. All of his associates became enemies of the people."

"That timeline screwed itself royally," Joyce said. "We could've provided unlimited free energy. At the moment, all they care about is their ... political upheaval."

"Do *we* live in this other world?" Joanne said. "I mean duplicates of us?"

"Yes."

"You didn't bring us with you?" Joanne said. "Why *not?*"

Joyce sighed.

"What?"

"You have children ... and husbands with families and careers," Joyce mumbled. "They weren't willing to leave."

"What happened?"

"You did what you had to," Joyce said.

"What?"

"We *never* blamed you! Not a bit!"

"What did we *do?*" Joanne said.

"You publicly denounced us and turned us over to the police," Joyce said. "You knew we'd easily escape, which we did."

"We'd *never* do that! We're not *evil!*"

"Honey," Joyce said. "Life's choices are rarely between good and evil. They're good *versus* good. Your love for your mother versus your love for your husband and children. You wanted to survive; you wanted *them* to survive. We *told* you to turn us in."

A sobbing Joanne fled.

"Quite a bit to dump in her lap," Vaughn muttered. "Telling her she turned her mother in to the Nazis."

"She'll come around," Joyce said. "I hope. We should've gone to the Columbia timeline. We don't have counterparts there."

"The pollution would kill us," Vaughn said. "Me, anyway — with my asthma."

"I suppose Derek's parents could help us in the Nostalgia timeline," Joyce said.

"No," Vaughn said. "I'm never going anywhere with Eakins as president."

They ordered food.

"Besides," Vaughn said. "Things are gearing up now. I've got meetings with the navy, Daimler, and Oswego Power and Light."

***

The Pincus and the Williams families had adjoining brownstone buildings on a quiet, tree-lined street in Brooklyn Heights — two blocks away from their tiny prototyping factory and the East River.

Their living room's windows offered a view of the Manhattan skyline.

Vaughn and his wife Rosa put their children, Jacqueline and Trey to bed on the third floor.

"When are we going back to Oz?" twelve-year-old Jacqueline said. "We're in their Ohana."

"No more talk of Ohanas," Rosa said. "We're not Hawaiians."

"Ohana means *family*," Jacqueline said. "Family means nobody gets left behind, or forgotten."

"Lilo and Stitch," Vaughn chuckled. "That Disney movie."

"I miss Oz," ten-year-old Trey said. "I miss the Green Lady."

"We'll visit Oz again someday," Rosa said. "You guys have to go to school, like normal children."

"Time to go to sleep," Vaughn said, kissing them on the cheek.

"Eew!" Trey muttered, rubbing his cheek.

"Will we see the Green Lady, mom?" Jacqueline said. "She was so nice."

"That's enough about the Green Lady, honey," Rosa said. "Go to sleep now."

※※※

Returned to the living room and Vaughn opened a bottle of Pinot Noir.

"Jacky's Green Lady talk makes my skin crawl," Rosa said, sipping her wine. "Derek and Allie call her Glinda."

"The good witch of the North," Vaughn laughed. "The ancient Greeks thought the Earth had a spirit they called Gaia, and Oz has Glinda. I think I even saw her, once. About two months ago, I was hiking in Rainbow Valley with Ed and Heidi, and I saw a green lady in the distance. Then the wind shifted and the leaves and branches no longer formed the shape of a lady."

"An optical illusion."

"No. I felt a real presence there. As if someone was looking at me."

"Is that supposed to make me feel better?" Rosa said. "Some lady's ghost is haunting Oz?"

"No. I don't think it's human. It takes the shape of a lady to relate to us."

"That's even creepier."

"It always gives me the message that we're welcome in Oz. It's our home if we want it."

"Our home is where our *family* is!" Rosa said.

"We almost got killed there," Vaughn said. "I'm not going back unless..."

"We're *not becoming aliens!*" Rosa interrupted.

"It might help in my business dealings," Vaughn sighed. "Hell, in twenty years, there won't be a gasoline car on the road. And we'll be richer than Bill Gates."

"We don't need to become Indigos, then," she said. "We don't need to join some ... Ohana thing."

"They already regard us as being in it," Vaughn said. "That's why they gave us a hundred million in seed money. It bought this house."

✳✳✳

Someone pulled the burlap sack off Eakins's head. He was in a tool shed lit by a bare bulb hanging on a wire.

The smells of freshly cut grass and manure hung in the air.

"He's a plant!" the stocky farm-hand said.

"He has no *neck tattoo,* Skags!" the elderly farmer said, pointing to Eakins's neck. "It wasn't just removed. There's no sign he *ever* had one. You can't get rid of all traces of a bar-code. He's the One."

"Bullshit, Jeeter! He'll get us killed. Feed him to the wood-chipper and spread him over the back forty."

Eakins desperately searched his mind for a story to keep him alive.

"Skags is right," Eakins finally said. "I had a neck-tattoo just like you."

"No!" Jeeter said. "That's impossible!"

"I wound up in a starvation chamber because..."

Better make this good.

"You got caught in a security sweep?" Skags volunteered.

"Yes, a sweep," he said. "They locked me in the chamber, and I waited to meet my maker, expecting to languish unto death. I knew a better world awaited me."

They nodded.

"Then — ♪ radiant ♪ as the ♪ noonday sun — they appeared," Eakins sang out. "The angels Mishak and Schmedrik. In voices like ♪ thunder, they proclaimed that my time had not yet come."

"My God!" Jeeter said.

Maybe I'll survive.

"The Lord had further work for me," Eakins intoned. "They *raised me up* to heaven where Jesus touched my neck and took my bar-code."

"Took it?" Skags said. "What happened?"

"It appeared on his neck and then vanished, as nothing impure can remain with Jesus."

They nodded.

"They removed my contagion and made me pure as a newborn child. All in preparation for my *god-sent ministry, my great work.*"

I've eaten salads smarter than these people.

"What great work?" Skags said.

"To *lead you* out of *oppression.* Into the promised land. *Freedom Awaits!*"

The other chanted "Freedom Awaits" several times.

Dumbest slogan I ever heard, but good enough for these morons.

Chapter 4

At ten in the morning, Oz time, Derek and Allie teleported Andy, Llewellyn, and their luggage to Oz.

A cool breeze carried the scent of wild orchids, onions, and cranberry.

They landed on a seventy-foot-wide deck attached to Derek and Allie's house. It faced the sea with two sets of steps leading to the beach, and two large sets of French doors leading to the dining and living rooms.

The thundering surf made the beach shudder.

Heaven to Earth dominated the deck — a ten-foot-high glass sculpture of an angel descending to Earth and morphing into a tree. Allie had rescued it from the warehouse in Origin containing her gallery's confiscated art.

Sunlight shattered against it into kaleidoscope colors.

A patio table and six chairs occupied the deck's opposite corner.

"What a bizarre experience," Llewellyn murmured. "Pleasant but ... strange."

"Waikiki Beach without the hotels," Andy said, gazing down the beach.

Two-story brick houses divided the crescent beach from the rain forest behind them, and Diamond Head loomed in the distance.

"We went here last year," Andy added. "I mean *there.*"

"We call it Destiny Beach," Allie said.

"It's beautiful!" Llewellyn said.

"Actually," Andy said, looking at the row of houses lining the beach and waving her hand. "I half-expected to see a futuristic city with people flying around with jetpacks, not..."

"Catfish Row?" Derek laughed.

"Or the desert island in *Lost.* I mean, you guys can control space and time."

"We don't need jetpacks," Derek laughed. "My sister will bring the house where guys will stay."

"Bring? The house?" Llewellyn whispered. "What does that even mean?"

"Over there," Derek said, pointing to a cleared area among the palm trees.

The air above the lot shimmered and rippled, as if viewed through a water curtain. The shimmering became opaque fog — and the fog congealed into a spacious two-story red brick house with a patio and hot tub.

"My goodness!" Llewellyn exclaimed, almost fainting.

Her red hair in disarray and beads of sweat running down her freckled face, a nineteen-year-old, visibly pregnant Wendy popped into view next to Derek.

Llewellyn yelped.

"My sister, Wendy," Derek said.

"Wow!" Wendy grinned, shaking their hands. "Are you guys *real lesbians?*"

"Real lesbians?" Andy laughed, wrapping an arm around a blushing Llewellyn. "God knows I can't abide the fake ones."

"I never met *lesbians* before," Wendy said.

"We never met anyone who could move a house before," Andy said. "So I guess we're even."

"When you're ready to begin, she'll move it to the dig site in Africa," Derek said.

"I'll dig your well and septic tank now," Wendy said, vanishing.

"You make her do the dirty work around here?" Andy said.

"She does it better than anyone else," Derek said.

"I have a better imagination is all!" Wendy said, popping into view next to Andy. "You just make your spirit-body into a house-shape and teleport. It's not rocket-science, and the work isn't even dirty."

"Aloha!" Travis Howland smiled, appearing beside Wendy. Wendy's husband was a husky six-foot-two twenty-year-old with the golden complexion so many Hawaiian Islanders have — inherited from his Japanese, Caucasian and Hawaiian ancestors.

He shook the ladies' hands.

Next, a sandy-haired, thirty-something man of average build, a chiseled and angular face, and a twinkle in his gray eyes greeted them: *the* Eldon Trask, owner of Space Ventures corporation.

"The *rocket-man!*" Llewellyn exclaimed, covering her mouth with her hands. "I knew you were going to Mars but I didn't know you could visit other timelines!"

"I loved that piece on you in *Time Magazine!*" Andy said.

"Very pleased to meet you," Eldon Trask said. "I'm afraid I'm not the rocket man you know. I'm a refugee from the same timeline as Derek and Allie. Wait a minute; I *met* you. You're a physics professor. I offered you a job but you wouldn't leave Chicago."

"No," Llewellyn said. "I'm a math professor. I've always been interested in physics though."

"Eldon met your counterpart in *our* timeline," Allie said. "If you have a deep interest in something, chances are you have a counterpart pursuing it full-time. Somewhere."

"I'll install your Pincus generator," Derek said. "Then you'll have electricity."

"Pincus generator?" Andy said.

Derek pointed to a rectangular piece of machinery about two feet by two feet by one foot sporting two prominent electrodes and upper and lower vents.

"Cold fusion," he said. "Sixty kilowatts of power. It takes hydrogen from the air and turns it into helium."

"You could change the world with that!" Andy exclaimed.

"We were on the way to doing that when Eakins drove us out," Derek said. "Joyce and Reginald Pincus are trying to do that in *your* timeline, along with Vaughn Williams and his family."

"You'll meet them later," Allie said.

"We have an announcement folks!" Derek said. "Eakins isn't president anymore."

"What?" several people shouted at once.

"We'll go over it at the ceremony later," Derek said.

"Ceremony?" Llewellyn said.

Do we want to let these two into our heads? Allie beamed at him.

They seem like decent people, Derek said. *I scanned them carefully.*

Allie shut her eyes for a moment.

Looking forward, I see them contributing to our group, Allie said.

"You are welcome to sit in on it and even *participate* if you want," Derek said.

"Participate?" Andy said. "Do we have to sacrifice a goat and drink its boiled blood with milk? I did that once among the Maasai."

"Nothing that simple," Allie laughed. *"Participating* involves taking a pill and becoming . . . like us."

Chapter 5

At noon, under a cloudless turquoise sky they all gathered around a roaring bonfire on Destiny Beach.

A cool breeze blew off the ocean.

Norton joined them and stalked an exotic Oz bird with blue wings with purple rectangles on them.

"Are these all refugees from your world?" Andy said.

"Most of them," Derek said. "Some are friends from yours."

"That *house* you've provided is so much better than our condo in Chicago," Llewellyn gushed. "The Jacuzzis, the *hot* tub. I just *love* the foam king-sized mattress. We'll have to get one."

"Damn!" Andy said. "Our secret's out. We archaeologists are always telling people we crawl around in the dirt. Now you know we have Jacuzzis and hot tubs."

Carrying a silver tray with sandwiches made with dark brown bread, Culinary Derek and Culinary Allie joined them. Culinary Derek was heavyset and — due to the time difference between the Culinary and Origin timelines — five years older than Derek. Culinary Allie had just given birth to baby Travis and hadn't lost her pregnancy weight.

"I'm seeing double!" Andy said, staring at the couple.

"Ah yes!" Derek said. "These charming people are our counterparts in *your* timeline. It's the reason we call it the Culinary timeline. I've always had an interest in cooking, and *this* Derek is a master chef. He and his wife operate a fine Italian restaurant."

"Exploring timelines is like excavating your soul," Allie murmured. "As a girl, I had fantasies of running an Italian restaurant with my papa."

"And I had fantasies of being an artist," Culinary Allie said.

"Renovations are nearly complete," Culinary Derek said. "You're all invited to the Grand Opening."

"Where's baby Travis?" Allie said.

"Mom is watching the kids. I mean both moms. My mom and *Culinary* mom."

"This is getting confusing," Llewellyn laughed.

They all took sandwiches and ate.

"This bread," Derek said. "It reminds me of what we ate in Egypt, minus the bits of sand."

"It's from emmer wheat," Wendy said, launching into a lengthy discussion of the virtues of emmer wheat as opposed to the dwarf wheat more commonly planted.

"A botanist!" Llewellyn said.

"No!" Wendy said. "Three years ago, mom and I were in a restaurant called *The Happy Cormorant*. We were arguing about me getting a car."

"Happy Cormorant?" Andy chuckled. "Sounds like New England."

"At the next table, two guys from the U of Maine were talking about wheat."

"You remember that?" Llewellyn said.

"I wasn't paying attention but I remember every word they said. I remember everything about every day of my life since I was born. Which I remember, too. I remember things from before then too."

"Typical of Indigos," Allie said.

"My goodness!" Llewellyn said. "Were you *born* an Indigo?"

"No. I've only been one for a few months. I remember everything from *before* I became one."

"Long-term memories live in the soul," Derek said. "And the brain accesses them. Indigo brains do it better."

"Indigos tend to be walking encyclopedias," Allie said. "Without trying. In a normal life, the average person is drenched in knowledge and forgets it. We remember every bit of it and have at our fingertips."

"God, I could use that in my research!" Llewellyn said. "Not a memory of being born but ... the other stuff."

✳✳✳

Others joined them on the beach.

"We're all here," Derek said, introducing them to Andy and Llewellyn.

"Andy and Llewellyn will be observing and, maybe, participating," he added. "It's a big step to take."

Derek appeared with a vial of red pills and the ceremony began.

"Remember how Pembroke financed his research by borrowing from the Russian mafia?" Derek said. "He gave me a red pill and then the Russians got impatient and murdered him."

"He was the *dumbest smart* person ever!" Allie muttered. "Or maybe it was just arrogance."

"He'd planned to have me in for a followup meeting, knock me out, remove my brain, and make a hundred pills from it. Anyway, there are plenty of timelines where the Russians waited a couple days to kill Pembroke. He had time to murder the Derek living there and make the pills."

"So the virus is the *same strain* that infected us," Allie added.

"Are there others?" Llewellyn said.

"Yes, in other timelines," Derek replied, thinking of countless timelines in which the virus had turned out differently. In most cases, it caused severe brain damage. In a few, it did that *and* spread like wildfire — creating pandemics that nearly wiped out the human race. Worlds populated by zombies staggering around until they dropped.

In one — Ek-world, for ecstasy — it was contagious and aroused feelings of ecstasy so intense people saw no need to eat, sleep, or clean themselves. With beatific smiles, they wasted away in their own filth.

When you screw with the human brain, what can possibly go wrong? Derek mused. *Especially if you do it with a contagious virus.*

"There's bad karma attached to them?" the Reverend Chloe Teague said. She was a short, thirty-something former Episcopal minister with light brown hair, wearing a large silver cross on a necklace.

"A mountain of it," Allie said.

The *original* pill had bad karma," Derek said. "The Pembrokes murdered dozens of people to create this virus. They even tested it on their newborn son and put him down like a dog."

"Look, people," Allie said. "Here's something that might affect your decision."

She described President Eakins's plans for Boothbay Harbor and how she and Derek had removed him from the presidency.

"We can go back?" Eldon Trask said.

"Yes," Derek said. "With you gone, the US space industry's in the toilet. With the Pincus's gone, they missed out on a revolutionary power source. Eakins's reign of terror is making educated people flee the US."

"The real question," Allie said. "Is how much can Renard accomplish? It'll be hard to unring that bell. Eakins's supporters are way scarier than him."

"I'll never be able to go back," the Reverend Chloe Teague said. "There are a *lot* of Eakins followers back home. They dynamited my church, for God's sake!"

"I'm not going back to that hellhole unless I can leave under *my own power,*" Mr. Trask said. "I'm taking the damn pill."

"I can't wait to visit the spirit-world," Chloe breathed.

"As a scientist," a white haired petite lady with a slight German accent said. "And head of the Oz Institute of Philosophy, I also must take it."

Her husband, Ian Roberts also took one.

"Scientist?" Andy whispered to Derek.

"She was a biology professor at the Ludwig Maximilian University in Germany," Derek said. "Birgit Fischer. We hired her to test our DNA, and that made her an Eakins target. Basically — almost anyone we've known became a target."

Derek and Allie passed out red pills and bottles of water.

Llewellyn impulsively grabbed one.

"If she's doing it, so am I," Andy said, taking a red pill.

"Here's some light reading," Derek said, handing her a paperback book.

"The *God Virus?*" Andy said. "By Indigo Voyager?"

"That's what Pembroke called his virus," Derek said. "It's

an account I wrote of how we got started. I even published it under a pseudonym. It's part of Professor Fischer's Indigo Documentation Project."

"I strongly object to the title you gave it," Professor Fischer frowned. "It sounds like a trashy science fiction novel. Or even a *religious* book."

"What would you have called it?" Derek said.

"*A definitive account of the origin of the human subspecies, Homo Sapiens Indicus,* of course. I would've include scholarly references."

"Some things to keep in mind," Allie said. "In taking this pill, you are leaving the human race."

"You will have thirty pairs of chromosomes rather than twenty three," Professor Fischer said. "A new species unable to mate with standard humans and produce viable offspring."

"Honey," a thin middle-aged man in an Aloha shirt said — Ian Roberts. "You could get your old job back. You won't have the CIA trying to kidnap us. I'd love to live in Munich with you. Indigos learn languages very quickly."

Ian was a recently-retired New York City detective who'd investigated the Pembroke murder and become friends with Derek and Allie — and had married Birgit Fischer. His wife of thirty years had passed away ten years ago. Professor Fischer had never been married.

"Oh, *mein Schatz,*" she said, kissing him. "What of our grandchildren? My students? They are not safe unless they think we are both gone forever."

"OK, people!" Allie continued. "You'll be able to visit thousands of timelines. But if people there know your true nature, you may be persecuted. Of course you'll always be able to come home to Oz."

"We were persecuted *without* taking the damn pills," Eldon Trask muttered.

"I feel like we're converting to Judaism or something," Andy laughed.

"Are these pills safe?" Culinary Derek said.

"They're mad-scientist pills," Derek said. "*Seven* people have been infected without ill effects. Make of that what you will."

"I don't know," Culinary Derek said. "Leaving the human race? That's a pretty extreme step."

"Of course you're reluctant," Allie said. "You aren't refugees. You have wonderful lives in your timeline."

"Yes — thanks to you winning the lottery for us," Culinary Derek said. "I'm just thinking of our kids."

"Don't feel any obligation," Derek said. "You'll always be welcome here in Oz. We'll try to save some pills in case you change your minds."

"If you don't take the pills," Allie said. "You should stay away from the others for a couple days. It's a virus and slightly contagious."

Everyone except the Indigos and Culinary Derek and Allie took the pills.

"Now what?" Andy said.

"Nothing for a few hours," Derek said. "When you go to bed, you may find yourself in an out-of-body state."

"You'll be in the spirit-world," Allie said. "Solid matter has a ghostly appearance but thoughts and ideas appear rock-solid."

"How do you see an *idea?*" Andy said.

"You'll see," Derek said. "I suggest we all assemble here in our spirit-bodies,."

"How do we do that?" Professor Fischer said.

"Just think of us and you'll be wherever *we* are," Allie said.

"In the next few days, we'll teach you things we learned the hard way," Derek said. "Some of them in ... combat situations that nearly ended us."

"Remind me again, why Pembroke created these pills," Andy said.

"To create a master race and take over the world," Derek said.

"Did it work?" Andy said. "Is there a timeline where it did?"

"Oddly enough — no!" Allie said. "In most, the Russian mafia kills him and his wife."

"The pills get lost in the chaos," Derek said. "And — if you kill someone in cold blood, your Indigo powers disappear."

"Wow!" Andy said. "If you use your powers...?"

"If you kill someone, period," Derek said. "Anyone who isn't an immediate threat. Self-defense is OK."

"God takes away your car-keys," Chloe said.

"As good an explanation as any," Derek said. "Or killing damages your soul."

"Maybe the soul heals," Andy said.

"It must," Derek said.

"Derek and I were soldiers in the first world war," Allie said. "We killed lots of people."

"You believe in reincarnation," Andy said. "Interesting."

They walked through the sand toward Derek and Allie's house.

"Oh!" Allie moaned. "Baby Vittoria's on her way. It has been ten months, and she's coming out *now*."

"You're having a baby?" Llewellyn said.

"I can help," Andromeda said. "I delivered a Tuareg baby in Mali once."

Allie teleported to her bedroom as the rest trotted to the house.

"Maybe she should teleport to a hospital," Llewellyn said.

"She said only as a last resort," Derek said. "She seems to think she won't need one."

***

Andy went into the bedroom and staggered out, whispering, "Oh my God!"

"Is she OK?" Derek said.

"She's fine," Andy moaned, taking a swig from a hip-flask.

"Will somebody help me with the umbilical cord?" Allie's voice called out.

"You're having your *baby?*" Culinary Allie said, running out of the house's guest quarters where her family stayed. "Derek! *The baby's coming!* I'll ... uh ... boil some water."

Derek ran into the room to see a bloody baby Vittoria and her placenta lying on Allie's stomach.

Blood and amniotic fluid drenched her dress and the bedspread.

"I can teleport-cut it," Allie said. "But I need to tie it off first."

Derek found twine in the kitchen, returned, and tied a knot in the umbilical cord. Then Allie cut it.

"Welcome to Oz, Vittoria!" Allie and Derek said with one voice.

The pink, hairless Baby Vittoria stared at them with her diamond Indigo eyes and — lifting a quivering nail-less hand — touched Allie and then Derek.

"I'm so glad you were born here," Allie murmured, kissing her.

"A true citizen of Oz," Derek wept.

Vittoria made a mewing sound and then beamed, "Hi mom and dad!" into their minds. "Say hi to the lady who ran away."

"We need a bath," Allie said, getting out of bed. "Why don't you give the placenta a proper burial?"

A foot-wide bloody sack of tissue that looked like calf's liver trailing three feet of white umbilical cord lay beside her.

"Don't you need to rest?"

"No, honey. I only had *one* labor pain and then it was over. Maybe I need a little rest to let my belly shrink, but that's all."

Derek scooped up the placenta and cord in the bloody bedspread and left.

✳✳✳

"She's doing fine," he told Andy, Llewellyn, and Culinary Allie. "She and Vittoria are taking a bath."

"It's already *over?*" Culinary Allie said.

"Vittoria teleported out of the womb," Derek said. "Labor took about thirty seconds."

"I'm sorry I . . . I lost it in there," Andy stammered. "I never saw anything like. . ."

"You tried to help and we're grateful," Derek interrupted. "Incidentally, Vittoria says hi."

"*Vittoria?*" Llewellyn said. "She's the baby, right?"

"She can't talk yet but she can beam thoughts."

"What's that?" Llewellyn said, pointing to Derek's bundle.

"It's the bedspread and placenta. Allie wants to give it a proper burial. We have a . . . little cemetery on the mainland. I can take you guys there."

Wendy appeared and said, "I'll spot for you."

They teleported.

✳✳✳

Under a clear dusky sky, they stood at the edge of the world — a two-mile-deep chasm so vast it had no opposite side. To the south, a wall of black clouds glittered with lightning bolts, some hitting rocky pillars rising from the canyon floor.

They stood in a grassy clearing bordering the canyon with a dense forest to the north.

Its trees sighed in a steady wind from the south that carried the scent of spruce and ozone.

"Magnificent!" Andy exclaimed.

"I can't believe you guys own this *whole world,*" Culinary Allie said.

"It's our Indigo homeland," Derek said. "And now it's yours too, Andy and Llewellyn."

"Don't forget the dolphins," Wendy said. "They own this planet too. They're our friends."

"Being an Indigo would've helped when I had baby Travis," Culinary Allie said. "But Derek wants our kids to be normal."

Andy stared at her.

"My Derek, she laughed. *"Culinary* Derek. He wants them to be trust-fund kids. The toast of high society."

"Is this what the Grand Canyon on Earth looks like?" Wendy said.

"Yes," Derek said. "We're on the north rim. On Earth, there'd hotels and campgrounds all over the place."

"My goodness," Llewellyn said, looking away from the canyon and pointing.

Ten enormous creatures grazed a half mile away, oddly-shaped elephants with curled tusks and long brown fur that blended with the tall grass.

They softly trumpeted.

"Oz's mainland is very wild," Derek said. "Millions of bison, woolly mammoths, wolves ... and smilodons."

"Smilodons?" Andy said.

"Sabertooth tigers," Wendy said. "I'll teleport-dig a hole."

A five-foot-deep hole appeared in the concrete-like soil as Wendy popped to the right with a pile of dirt beside her.

"How did you do that?" Culinary Allie said.

"I imagined my spirit-body had a shape that included that hole," Wendy said. "If you have a good imagination, your spirit-body's like an amoeba. Then I teleported and carried the dirt with me."

Derek dropped the wrapped placenta in the hole, and the pile of soil reappeared on top of it.

Distant thunder rumbled.

"Oz..." Llewellyn breathed. "This is the greatest treasure imaginable. Are you sure it's uninhabited?"

"On Earth," Derek said. *"Either* of our Earths — cave men killed off the mammoths. I don't think humans ever evolved here."

"Maybe they just didn't kill them off here," Llewellyn said. "Maybe they were environmentally conscious."

Andy laughed.

"We haven't seen any villages or any other signs of human life. The only place that isn't in a natural wild state is part of Africa."

"Why?"

"That's what we hope you'll tell us," Derek said.

The dark clouds to the south advanced, and heavy drops of water hit their faces.

They returned to Destiny Beach.

***

"Why did you go all the way to the Grand Canyon?" Andy said. "It's thousands of miles away."

"We have a different sense of distances," Wendy said. "You'll see."

"You have to admit, it's a beautiful location," Derek said.

As a cool breeze caressed them, they walked to the ocean-facing patio at Derek and Allie's house with the roar of pounding surf in the distance.

They sat.

"When do we start on the project?" Andy finally said. "I love hanging out here, but I vaguely recall we were supposed to *do* something... What was it again?"

Llewellyn laughed.

"Originally, you were to start immediately," Derek said. "Since you've taken the pills, I think you should hold off a while to get used to your new abilities."

Wendy joined them.

With Culinary Derek, Allie came out the door carrying baby Vittoria. She tried to wave.

Allie sat, opened her blouse, and breastfed Vittoria.

"Childbirth is a *lot* easier for us," Allie said.

"That's a relief!" Wendy sighed. "Mine will be born soon."

Derek's parents, Liz and Thomas, materialized — followed by Allie's mother, Renata.

The visibly pregnant Liz was a middle-aged heavyset woman and Thomas was a thin, white haired man. Both had been schoolteachers in Boothbay Harbor, Maine before President Eakins drove them out.

Now they lived in the Nostalgia timeline's version of Boothbay Harbor, one in which neither of them had counterparts.

Renata was a frail, thin, fifty-something woman wearing jeans and a white blouse.

All were Indigos.

"She's *so beautiful!*" Liz gushed. "Look Tom. Our *granddaughter!* Her eyes are silvery and ... and slightly ... *Asian.*"

Like a touch of Downs' Syndrome, she thought.

Trying to be tactful by not saying it out loud? Allie beamed at Liz, smiling. *I guess that's the natural Indigo look.*

"It's looks like ten months does it," Allie said.

"Tom!" Liz said. "We have to stay with Allie for a while. When it comes to babies, we're *experts*."

"Sure."

Is every woman in this place expecting? Andy thought.

"Ah ... yes," Allie smiled. "Indigos are fertile. And ... um ... horny."

"My goodness!" Llewellyn said.

"Is it OK to be around you guys?" Culinary Derek said.

"Sure," Allie said. "Until the sneezing stage."

Vittoria yawned and fell asleep as they chatted for another half hour.

Then Llewellyn stifled a sneeze and they all retired to their houses.

Chapter 6

In their translucent spirit-bodies, Derek and Allie hovered over the campfire site. As usual, solid matter had a ghostly appearance — semi-transparent with washed-out colors.

The spirit-world pulsated with its own colors and soft musical sounds, with tiny organic shapes forming in space and dissipating.

Andy and Llewellyn joined them.

"It's like swimming in an ocean of enthusiasm!" Llewellyn said.

"I've *seen* those things before!" Andy said, pointing to the glowing shapes winking in and out of existence. We're *in Dreamtime!*"

"Dreamtime?" Allie said.

"I went to an exhibition of Australian Aboriginal Art last December," Andy said. "There were paintings that looked *exactly* like those things! It can't be a coincidence. The Aborigines had a myth of a dream universe they called Dreamtime. Eons ago, part of it awakened to form our physical universe."

"So the Aborigines did what we're doing now?" Derek said. "They weren't Indigos, were they?"

"*Songlines!*" Andy exclaimed. "The Aborigines knew *timelines* too. They thought the gods flew through dreamtime *singing* worlds into existence."

"So poetic!" Llewellyn sighed.

"Songlines remind me of *Dreamfall Chapters*," Derek said. "We've *got* to meet some Aborigine shamans."

"Dreamfall... what?" Andy said.

"A computer game."

"My thoughts are so quick and clear!" Chloe Teague said.

"I just imagine an equation," Llewellyn said. "And it appears."

Mathematical equations hovered in the air, glowing as though made of neon lights.

"Ah, that's the spirit world for you," Derek said. "Ideas look real and solid matter looks like smoke."

Eldon Trask zipped through space, soaring and dipping to the ground.

"I've never felt so *awake* in my life," Andy said. "Where's the campfire? I can hardly see it."

"I think you're seeing it as it really is," Derek said. "Solid matter is mostly empty space."

"No!" Andy said.

"Yes," Eldon said. "There are electrons and protons and a whole lot of empty space in between. Even the electrons and protons aren't all that solid. They're tiny force-fields."

"What you see in *waking* life is like a file-icon on a computer desktop," Derek said.

"The icon *is* a file!" Andy said.

"No," Llewellyn said. "The file's a pattern of magnetized

dots on a hard drive. What are you saying, Derek? The world is software?"

"I always thought we were characters in a computer game," Eldon said. "Remember my statement that there was a one in a billion chance we *weren't* living in one?"

"Your spirit body is the player and your physical body is your avatar," Derek said. "Computer program is too strong a word. It's something more organic, like an idea in a mind. We and our world are ideas in a vast mind."

"The spirit-world around us is the computer where the simulation runs," Allie said.

"Or Dreamtime," Andy insisted. "When the Aborigines said it awakened to form this world, your computer simulation started to run. It's just semantics."

"So beautiful!" Chloe murmured, joining them. "The mind of God!"

"I can *manipulate* equations too," Llewellyn said. "It's like a magic blackboard. I think that quadratic term belongs on the other side of the equation."

Sections of the glowing equation in the air dutifully slid over to the other side, other terms making room for them. The part of the equation where they had come from closed ranks.

"Now those two terms clearly cancel out," Llewellyn said, pointing.

The terms she'd pointed to vanished and the rest of the equation closed up the space they had left.

Vittoria darted around, giggling.

"You belong in bed, young lady," Allie said. "I can't have the *unborn* babies flying around when people materialize."

Allie corralled Vittoria, and they both vanished.

"Your powers will slowly increase over the next few months as the new DNA takes hold," Derek said. "For instance, we recently developed the ability to project thoughts into people's minds."

"Mind control?" Andy said.

"No," Derek said. "When we beam thoughts at people, they hear us in their heads. We were always able to do it with dolphins."

"So you can hold telepathic conversations with non Indigos?" Llewellyn said.

"Yes," Derek added. "Like the one we're having now."

"We're having a telepathic conversation?" Llewellyn said.

"You think we're making sounds? Derek said. "Vibrating air molecules?"

"They *sound* like ... sounds," Llewellyn said.

"Yes," Chloe said. "In the spirit-world, thoughts *are* sounds."

A glowing bird flew by.

"Why does it glow so brightly?" Llewellyn said.

"We think that's *life-force*," Derek said. "Living things *glow* in the spirit world, even though their physical bodies are shadowy outlines."

"The spirit-world is *so fascinating!*" Chloe said. "So all living things have *souls?*"

"Derek has found living things *on other planets,*" Birgit nodded. "Where life-chemistry is so alien, I wouldn't have recognized it as life."

"When you get really good," Derek said, "Not only can you read people's minds. You can read the minds of people *they* met, and people *those* people met. I did that once with a Chinese spy applying for a job. A company we owned in Origin."

"It's defunct now," Allie muttered. "Like everything else we had there."

"I was able to scan *him,* then his *supervisor,* etc. The entire Chinese intelligence apparatus. It was amazing."

"Like plugging into a mental Internet," Allie said. "Pretty overwhelming."

"OK, people!" Derek said. "Focus on the dead campfire. Try to see it *clearly* — the way it looks in waking life."

"Be sure you're close to the ground," Allie said. "Gravity's a vindictive bitch!"

Everyone fell to the sand in a heap.

Under a full moon, a shadowy Destiny Beach had replaced the spirit world.

The campfire still smoldered.

"That's the first two lessons," Derek said. "Out of body travel and teleportation. We should try to get some sleep."

They walked back to the houses where they were staying.

✳✳✳

Derek went for his usual morning swim.

On the deck, Allie sipped coffee as she nursed Vittoria. An easel in front of her held a impressionistic painting of the Koolau mountains.

Andy, Llewellyn, and Wendy popped into view.

"Wow," Andy said. "This teleportation thing is wonderful. I could go on a dig in Egypt and sleep in my bed in Chicago each night."

"Waking life takes on a dreamlike quality," Allie said. "In a dream, you're in one place and then another — without traveling."

"I'm going to pick some coffee," Wendy said. "Anyone wanna come with me?"

"Pick ... coffee?" Llewellyn mumbled. "Oh, what the hell? I'll go with you. Where is it?"

"On another island. In your world, it would be on Mount Waialeale on Kauai."

"That sounds ... far away, and I'm not really sure about mountain-climbing."

"Nothing's far away now," Wendy said, picking up a wicker basket. "It's wet though. I'll go first, you go out-of-body, and then think of me."

She vanished.

"Try going inside and lying down," Allie said. "It's easier to get out of body when you're half asleep."

Llewellyn took her advice.

"Is is dangerous?" Andy said.

"In your world, it is," Allie said. "I've read it's a tough climb, and they have wild hogs that eat people."

"What?"

"We don't have them here, and she doesn't have to climb anything."

"Any sneezing going on?" Culinary Derek said, coming out the door.

"Not at the moment," Allie said.

The Culinary Evans children, five-year-old Tony and four-year-old Loretta, bolted out the door and sprinted down the beach to the chicken coop.

"Our little egg-gatherers," Culinary Allie said, feeding baby Travis with a bottle.

Andy laughed.

"This place is heaven for them," Culinary Allie continued. "We spent two weeks here last summer."

✼✼✼

Her ears popped as Llewellyn materialized in a wind-whipped cloud-forest.

A cool mist drenched her.

"Stay close to me," Wendy said. "I fell off a cliff around here once."

"My goodness! What did you do?"

"I teleported back up."

"You can do that? While you're in *free-fall?*"

"Believe me, you'll get a *lot* better at teleporting. My crazy husband dumps our garbage by teleporting above an active volcano and letting it fall in."

"Why did you plant coffee *here?*" Llewellyn said.

"The TV commercials always say mountain-grown is best."

Llewellyn laughed.

Wendy pointed out the coffee plants and said, "The ripe berries are red. They all ripen at different times."

They spent fifteen minutes picking red berries until the basket was almost full.

In distance, they heard a bird call.

"So beautiful and haunting!" Llewellyn said. "I never heard anything like it."

"Professor Fischer says it's the *Kauai 'o'o*. Not much to look at, but it sings like an angel. In our world, it went extinct in the 1980's."

"That's a *tragedy!*"

"Yeah, we've destroyed a lot of beautiful things," Wendy sighed. "Well ... what do you say we start back?"

"I'm scared!" Llewellyn said. "I don't think I can teleport back, and I know I can't *climb* down."

"No problem!" Wendy said. "I'll take you. Travis will spot for us."

Travis appeared and said, "No *huhu*, ladies! Good to go."

※※※

They rejoined the others on the deck.

Derek and Allie's tabby, Norton, joined them.

"What do we do with the berries?" Llewellyn said.

"We dry them in the sun," Wendy said. "When they turn into raisins, we peel off the outside to expose the beans. Those are coffee seeds. We plant some of them and roast the rest."

"Lot of trouble for a cup of joe," Andy said.

"Have you tasted it?" Culinary Allie said. "It's way better than Jamaican Blue Mountain, which goes for 50 bucks a pound back home. We'd serve it in our restaurant if we could get enough of it. We save some for a few select customers."

"Yeah," Wendy said. "Maybe someday we can talk our kids into picking berries. Now I've got to get some onions, garlic, and basil."

"I'll help," Llewellyn said.

"I'm curious, too," Andy said.

Wendy disappeared.

Andy and Llewellyn shut their eyes and vanished, too.

✸✸✸

They all found themselves on a flat plain between two mountains. Jungle growth covered one and the other had the distinctive look of a volcano caldera. Several miles to the south, the land sloped downward to the sea.

"In our world, this would be Maui," Wendy said. "Either of our worlds. We call it Valley Island."

She pointed to neat rows of two-foot tall stalks with bundles of microscopic white flowers on their tops, and started to pull some of them out of the ground.

"Onions!" Llewellyn said. "Why do you grow them here?"

"In our world, Maui onions are supposed to be the best," Wendy said. "When they flower like this, they spread more seeds. You constantly get onions coming up."

Llewellyn laughed.

A light mist started to fall, forming a double rainbow.

Holding a bunch of onion plants in one hand, Wendy hiked about a hundred feet away to a patch of small green shoots coming out of the soil.

"Garlic," she said.

Llewellyn picked two heads of garlic.

"Now we go to Spice Island for some basil," Wendy said. "In your world, that would be Lanai."

"Basil?" Andy said.

"Culinary Derek usually needs it when he cooks Italian food," Wendy said. "Whatever he doesn't use here goes to his restaurant in New York."

She vanished.

Andy and Llewellyn followed.

✷✷✷

They found themselves on a hill overlooking a crescent beach under a cloudless sky. Palm trees gave them some shade.

Wendy motioned them over to a patch of leafy plants and said, "Smell."

The aromatic scent of fresh basil filled the air.

She picked a few plants and handed them to Andy.

"Over there, I have pepper plants," Wendy said, pointing inland.

They returned to Destiny Beach.

✷✷✷

Tony and Loretta staggered down the beach, lugging a basket full of colored eggs — white, brown, red, and blue.

"Are these from ... Indigo chickens?" Llewellyn said.

"They're from *Easter chickens!*" Loretta shouted, jumping up and down.

"Careful honey, you're going to break the eggs," Culinary Allie said.

"We have breeds of chickens most American farmers don't use," Wendy chuckled. "Black Copper Marans, Araucana, and others. They're beautiful pets."

"How do they taste?" Andy said.

"Like fresh eggs," Culinary Allie said. "Delicious! The other day, we had green eggs and ham."

"They'll make good eggs Benedict and pancakes," Culinary Derek said, taking the basket of eggs and going into the house.

"He does the cooking here?" Andy said.

"When anyone else cooks, he nitpicks it to death," Culinary Allie said. "Yeah we're talking about *you*, Culinary Derek. 'You should've carved *exes* on the pearl onions before putting them in the beef bourguignon.' We all take turns as dishwashers and cleaners. That's a lot of work because he always uses every pot in the place."

"When their vacation ends, you'll have to put up with our cooking," Derek said. "Or Chinese takeout."

"Or fast food," Allie said.

"Scary," Culinary Allie laughed.

Vittoria stopped nursing, yawned, and vanished.

"What happened to her?" Culinary Allie said.

"She went back to her crib," Allie said. "She's asleep now."

"You *know* that?"

"Yep," Allie said. "One thing about being an Indigo is you *always* know where your kids are."

"She's so low-maintenance," Liz murmured. "Nothing like you were, Derek."

Norton jumped into Allie's now-empty lap and purred.

"Vittoria sleeps a lot," Travis said. "Is that normal?"

"It takes a lot of energy to grow a body from scratch," Allie said. "Think back to the weeks after you were born, Travis."

"Oh, yeah."

"She was much more active earlier," Allie said. "We used to have long talks. She had many past lives in ancient China."

"Our *keikis* don't say much," Wendy said. "They won't talk about their past lives."

"They want to be farmers," Travis said. "Live quietly. No *huhu*. No *pilikia*."

These people get stranger by the minute, Llewellyn thought. *What have we gotten ourselves into?*

No kidding, Andy thought. *Wait a minute! Your lips aren't moving.*

You're reading my mind? Llewellyn said.

You have no idea how deep this rabbit hole goes, my friends, Allie thought, smiling.

"I have an announcement," Culinary Renata said. "I've decided to become an Indigo."

"Mom!" Culinary Allie said. "Are you sure?"

"You guys want to have normal lives and that's OK. My normal life is playing mahjong with cranky old ladies who whine and cheat. At my age, I'm not an adventurer but there's got to be more to life than that."

"I talked her into it," Renata said, hugging her. "We have more in common than you have with the other Derek and Allie. We've lived ninety percent of our lives before the split."

"Split?" Culinary Allie said.

"In your timeline, your father stood up to your grandfather and refused to go on collection-rounds," Renata said. "In mine, he took little Tony along, and they were murdered."

"I can't even imagine what that was like for you," Culinary Allie muttered, hugging Allie. "You should meet my brother

Tony. If we decide to let him in on the Indigo-thing. *My* Derek wants to keep it our secret."

"I'll change Vittoria's diaper and get you an Indigo pill," Derek said, vanishing.

"I can't believe all these gardens you have, Wendy," Andy said.

"It's so strange," Wendy murmured. "I'm a farmer in this life."

"What's so strange?" Llewellyn said.

"They tried to force me to farm in my last life."

"Huh?" Andy said.

"I was a !Kung ... named Tashay," Wendy said, clicking her tongue for the '!' sound.

"A Kung?" Travis said.

"A Kalahari bushman," Andy said, uttering a series of odd syllables punctuated by tongue-clicks and tsk-sounds.

Wendy responded in kind.

"You speak better !Kung than I do," Andy said.

"I had more practice. I also spoke Tswana, and a little Oshiwambo."

"You must've lived in Botswana or Namibia then," Andy said.

"We lived in huts in the desert. We didn't know about countries. I hunted. Every once in a while, we'd move to a new place and build new huts."

"You were a man?" Culinary Allie said.

"Were you an *African warrior?*" Travis said.

"No," Wendy sighed. "Our biggest battle was finding water and game. A day when we could find water was a good day. We drilled holes in the ground and tried to sip water from them. When I came home with an animal, my little daughter would run around shouting 'Ho, ho, daddy brought meat!' Hearing that felt so good."

"Then men came wearing strange clothes," Wendy added. "All dressed the same."

"Uniforms," Andy said.

"They rounded us up," Wendy said. "They beat us with sticks and shot some of us."

"Botswana!" Andy said. "Prospectors found diamonds on bushmen lands. Then the government brutally relocated them to reservations. Many of them died."

"They stole your land?" Llewellyn said.

"Our land?" Wendy said. "How can you own land? It's like owning a piece of the sky or the air. It always seemed odd to me when people talked about buying land. Even in Boothbay Harbor."

"Maybe you didn't own the land but they still forced you away from your watering holes," Andy said.

Wendy nodded.

"Is that how you died?" Culinary Allie said.

"No," Allie said. "At some point, I got very tired. An aid worker took me to a place called Gaborone."

"The capital of Botswana," Andy said.

"In one glance, I saw more people than ever before in my whole life," Wendy said. "It terrified me! One of the doctors was very kind. An American man, black like Vaughn Williams. He spoke Tswana and reassured me. He told me about a magical place where water stretched as *wide as the sky*. I didn't believe that was possible but... That image filled my mind as I slipped away. The sea... and America."

"And then you were reborn on the coast of Maine," Llewellyn said. "You *chose* where you'd reincarnate!"

"Yeah," Allie said. "But why isn't everyone born a billionaire?"

Llewellyn shrugged.

"Whenever we went fishing and caught something, you whispered to it," Thomas said.

"I apologized for killing it," Wendy said "I said it would become part of us when we ate it. It would see the world through our eyes."

"A bushman custom," Andy said. "They were some of the most humble and gentle people on Earth."

"Oh, come on," Wendy said. "We had lots of fights. Usually men fighting over women or women fighting over men."

"The way the Bantus and Zulus treated them was obscene," Andy said. "The Zulus even hunted them for sport."

"We could contact Culinary Wendy and tell her about it," Travis said.

"No," Wendy said. "We don't need to complicate her life. She's living her dream. She has a wonderful relationship and her own lobster boat."

"What about *your* dreams?" Culinary Allie said.

"I have a wonderful relationship," Wendy said, hugging Travis. "This is the strangest life I ever lived and so ... so complicated. Even before I became Indigo. I dream of raising my children and seeing them raise theirs. Of living a thousand lives here. Building our Indigo world ... making it even more beautiful than it is."

"Mom," Culinary Allie said. "Are you planning to *move* to Oz?"

"I don't know. Maybe. I'll be able to travel back and forth whenever I want. I might move here and spend my days in Brooklyn."

"To change the subject," Andy said. "What's next on our training agenda?"

"Memory, I think," Derek said. "And regeneration."

"Regeneration is important," Wendy said. "Travis got a leg bit off by a great white shark once. The dolphins *told* him not to go into the water, but did he *listen? No!"*

"What happened?" Llewellyn said. "He seems OK now."

"He regenerated. Good as new."

"How long did that take?" Andy said.

"A few seconds."

Andy and Llewellyn stared at her in shock, and Andy said, "You're telling the truth!"

"One great thing about being an Indigo," Derek said, popping into view. "You always know when people are lying to you.

"And when they're telling the truth," Allie added.

He handed Culinary Renata a red pill and glass of water.

"Here goes nothing," she said, downing the pill. "Maybe I'll take an Oz name, like Ozma."

"Call yourself Glinda, mom," Culinary Allie said. "The good witch of the north."

"That what we call the spirit that lives here," Derek said.

"I remember *The Marvelous Land of Oz,"* Allie said. "I was reading it in the school library once. It said of Princess Ozma, 'Her eyes sparkled as two diamonds.' That's how your eyes will look in a couple days, mom. Uh, other mom."

Allie's mother chuckled.

"You could take the name *Ga*linda, like in the show *Wicked,"* Culinary Allie said. "It sounds Italian."

"What sounds Italian?" Culinary Derek said, bringing out plates of pancakes for the children and eggs Benedict for the adults.

Chapter 7

After breakfast, Derek conducted another Indigo lesson.

Derek, Andy, Chloe, Llewellyn, and Eldon hovered in their spirit-bodies over Destiny Beach.

"Since you're fascinated with memory," Derek said. "I'll recall something from my college days."

※※※

Without any transition, they hovered in a university lab class. All but Derek were invisible, but saw and experienced everything as if they were present.

It was a muggy summer day and the air conditioning had broken down, so the windows were open and powerful oscillating fans swept the room.

They couldn't dispel the formaldehyde stench.

Standing at a gray stone bench, Derek dissected the head of a two-foot-long dogfish shark — pulling back its sandpaper-like skin and exposing rows of tiny pods filled with clear jelly — its ampullae of Lorenzini.

Other students at other tables did similar things.

Something's off, Derek thought. *This isn't what it appears to be. I'm forgetting something important.*

"Good clean dissection," Julie Chen, the twenty-year-old teaching assistant said — rubbing a breast against Derek.

His body responded.

She's always accidentally doing that.

The dead shark turned its head, opened its mouth and — in Allie's voice — said, "You're getting lost in your memories again, honey."

"Oh, this is just a *memory!*" Derek exclaimed, and the scene vanished.

✳✳✳

"Very good, maniac," Allie said, joining them. "This time you were aware something was off. I hope we reach the point where we can experience memories and never get lost in them."

"My God!" Eldon Trask exclaimed. "A 3D movie complete with touch, smell, and sensation. I was sweating!"

"The soul's memory is *perfect,*" Derek said. "Every detail of every life is recorded. Every sensation, every feeling and thought. For all we know, it records the whole state of the universe."

"So the brain *waters down* memories," Eldon said. "It has to. We couldn't drive a car if we relived yesterday every time we thought of it."

"What are those?" Eldon Trask said, pointing to glowing orange wisps of cigarette smoke.

"Ah, you *see* them now," Derek said. "They're our thoughts. Every time you think something, you generate mental energy in the spirit-world. You shed a tiny portion of your soul when you think something."

"That sounds bad," Allie laughed. "But it isn't. Your physical body sheds skin cells without you missing them. They go on to nourish other life on Earth."

"Something eats our thoughts?" Andy said.

"No!" Derek said. "They're tiny souls or ... soul-atoms. They grow and develop. Eternally."

"These thoughts," Chloe said. "Do they know what they mean?"

"Does a clock know what time it is?" Allie said. "No. Our thoughts mean something to *us* — tiny words in our mind's language. They're life-forms, too simple to have memories or thoughts of their own."

"Maybe we got our start from two ancient aliens arguing with each other," Chloe laughed. "Over eons, their curse-words turned into us."

"I like that," Andy chuckled.

"What I'm wondering is what *that* is," Chloe said, pointing to a pulsating green cloud.

"I don't see anything," Andy said. "Oh, OK."

"Someone's *watching* us," Derek said. "And *thinking* about us."

※※※

They found themselves floating near a large chamber's ceiling. Six-foot long ghostly cockroaches operated many small machines whose purpose was impossible to determine.

"Don't focus on them," Derek said.

"God no!" Chloe muttered. "They're disgusting enough in their *ghostly* form."

"The sentinel was right," Katalluwana said to Kef. "A new manufactured dwelling appeared on the last differential."

"We have the *entire system* on long-range scan!" Kef protested. "The transport *couldn't* have gotten past us!"

"They must have a cloaking device. Or underground factories. Now we see the creatures themselves."

"They're so ugly! And oddly dormant."

"They're molting," Katalluwana said. "Look at the sheets of tissue around them."

How can we possibly understand him? Chloe said. *He's speaking English.*

We're picking up pure thought-forms, Derek said. *Our souls, minds, or whatever word you want to use — translate them into terms we understand. Even their so-called names are our minds' interpretation of their identities.*

Sheets of tissue? Allie said.

Our bathrobes, Derek replied.

"I don't care," Kef replied. "I only see *vermin* to be cleansed!"

What the hell does he mean? Eldon said. *Cleansing?*

Then they knew.

A thermonuclear bomb? Chloe said. *Or an asteroid?*

One of the spirit-world's many strange features, Derek said. *You wonder something and knowledge just comes to you.*

"Patience," the first one said. "If we cleanse these few creatures, we accomplish nothing. It's the *hives* that we must cleanse, and the *queens.* Do you know why this planet *has* a sentinel orbiting it?"

"No."

"Check the database and *educate* yourself," Katalluwana said. "Go back two million cycles."

"Two million cycles? We existed that long ago?"

"Of course," Katalluwana said. "The age of the Nine Presences. This cluster of manufactured dwellings is clearly a distant outpost of a vast infestation. We must locate it before we take action. This will be the last place we cleanse."

They want to kill us? Andy said. *Why?*
Because we exist, apparently, Chloe said.
Another thing you'll notice is that we'll always be able to locate these creatures from now on, Derek said. *Every soul in the universe has a unique identity.*

The Indigos drifted through the chamber's walls, through many layers of conduits and devices until they exited a large shell — part of a rapidly rotating wheel-shape. The wheel's hub connected to it via radial struts.

A space ship, Eldon said.

I can trace these creatures to others they've met, Derek said. *Follow me.*

✳✳✳

They floated outside a huge rectangular object. Cockroach-creatures scurried in all directions, three of whom were Kef's colleagues.

This must be their home planet, Eldon said.

Birgit Fischer joined them.

They flew over an array of translucent rectangular shapes — probably a city that stretched to the horizon and searched for its city limits.

They found none.

Indeed, the city covered most of the planet, with parts of it under the oceans.

After what seemed like an hour, they found an enormous low rectangular building with many creatures operating machines that loomed hundreds of feet high.

They processed some sort of sludge that included solid chunks that looked like pieces of dead giant cockroaches.

"Dirtiest job I ever had!" one of the creatures muttered. "One more cycle and I'm out of here!"

"It looks better on the other end," another replied.

"Thank you *Professor Obvious*. The sun hangs fixed in the sky. Maybe you'd like to tell me that too."

They're processing their waste products into food, Birgit Fischer said.

They returned to Destiny Beach.

❋❋❋

Allie nursed Vittoria while Norton struggled to stay in her lap. Culinary Allie sat beside her feeding baby Travis.

"How was it, guys?" Allie said. "Have fun?"

"Unheimlich!" Birgit Fischer muttered.

"Huh?" Culinary Allie said.

"Beyond strange," Professor Fischer added. "Giant intelligent insects with a sense of humor."

"He wasn't that funny," Derek said. "They want to destroy us."

"What?" Culinary Allie said. "Oh, you're joking. Not funny!"

"No," Derek said. "There's an alien spacecraft overhead that plans to destroy us. If we had a good telescope, we could probably see it from here."

"What did we ever do to them?" Culinary Allie said.

"They called us sentient vermin," Birgit said. "They're on a mission to rid the universe of anything different from themselves."

"You guys are taking this awfully well!" Culinary Allie said.

"We're not in any immediate danger," Derek said. "Not for a while — maybe weeks. They're headed out, looking for our 'hives'."

"What do we call these things?" Eldon muttered. "Giant roach-thing doesn't seem right."

"*Archy!*" Allie said. "When I was a kid, my grandpa read an odd old book to me called *Archy and Mehitabel*. It was about Archy, the poet-cockroach, and Mehitabel the alley-cat."

"I *remember* that book!" Culinary Allie exclaimed. "I loved the cute pictures!"

"Poet-cockroach?" Eldon said.

"Something I understand *now*," Allie said. "I didn't at the time. Archy was a failed poet who killed himself and came back as a cockroach. Mehitabel was a cat who thought she was Cleopatra in a past life."

"*All* cats think that!" Culinary Allie laughed.

"But what is our alien creature's *correct* name?" Birgit said.

"Maybe a smelly fart," Derek said. "If they communicate with pheromones."

"OK," Birgit muttered. "Archies is better than nothing."

"Too cute for an enemy, but OK, I'll go along with it," Derek muttered. "We *must* get rid of that sentinel satellite."

"Good luck with that," Eldon Trask said. "It's probably no bigger than a compact car."

"I thought satellites fall out of orbit after a while," Llewellyn said.

"Not if it's high enough," Eldon said. "If it's above forty thousand miles, it'll stay there forever. We'd need hundred-foot radar dishes and months to find it."

"How far away is their planet?" Chloe said.

"Light years," Eldon said. "It has to be."

"We traveled *light-years?*" Andromeda said.

"Distances don't mean much in the spirit-world," Derek said. "We could've teleported there."

"Why didn't we?" Andromeda said.

"Is their atmosphere breathable?" Derek said.

"That's easily tested," Eldon said, referring to the space suit at the Oz Institute — from Trask's Space Ventures Corporation in Origin. It had instruments that could analyze the air.

"I say we scan the *shit* out of them and visit them in the flesh," Derek said. "I want to know these creatures better than they know themselves."

"How will we find them again?" Chloe said. "We can't even locate their satellite."

"Like I said," Derek smiled. "Once you've been anyplace or met anyone, you can always revisit them. It's almost as if you have a bookmark in your ... soul ... or wherever. Just think of them and you'll be there."

"They must have faster-than-light travel," Eldon said.

"*We* have that," Derek said. "Better than theirs. We don't even need spaceships."

"They understand how theirs works and we don't," Eldon insisted.

They sat and had lunch, while Derek explained to the others what had happened.

"I'm going inside and lying down," Eldon said, standing and leaving.

"He's going to study the Archies' technology," Allie said.

"Good," Derek said.

"I should take air and water samples from that planet," Professor Fischer said.

"You've got to get better at teleporting," Allie said.

Vittoria appeared in Allie's lap.

"Tori wants lunch too," Allie said, opening her blouse and letting Tori nurse.

"I'll collect the samples, Professor," Derek said. "I've used our space suit before."

***

After lunch, Derek and Professor Fischer went to the Oz Institute of Philosophy — a four-story brick building at the end of the beach.

"We could move the Institute anyplace you want," Derek said. "Maybe give it its own island, like Kauai."

"Philosophy Island?" Professor Fischer smiled. "There's a little voice in the back of my head. It says we should *claim* this world."

"Huh?"

"Build in the *wild places!* Places with wolf packs, smilodons, and mammoths. As Indigos, we have no natural enemies — *anywhere.* These beautiful islands are a gateway, but we need to move beyond."

"You have a point there."

They went through the building's glass doors into its heavily air-conditioned lobby. Professor Fischer's office — with the only computer in Oz — lay to the right and her lab was on the left.

The Infirmary lay in the back.

It had an examining room, an X-ray machine, a refrigerator with a stockpile of drugs, and a well-equipped operating room.

Professor Fischer had insisted on the last item.

When they had moved to tropical Destiny Beach, Derek and Allie had developed the worst acne of their lives — and Derek's red and swollen nose had looked like a clown's.

In the tropics, antibiotics always come in handy.

The X-ray machine had also been useful, too. Professor Fischer had used it to study "seed pods" they had found on the mainland, which turned out to be insects in cocoons.

The cocoons blossomed into a previously unknown species they had named Scarlet Demons — foot-wide, bright red, venomous butterflies that squealed like pigs.

That had been an adventure.

Luckily, they had never needed the operating room — no one in Oz had the faintest idea how to do surgery.

Now that all of Oz's residents were Indigos, the whole Infirmary was probably unnecessary.

Brilliant pastel drawings of birds and animals covered the walls — part of Birgit and Allie's long-term project to document the flora and fauna of Oz.

They firmly believed that well-executed drawings showed more useful information than any photograph could.

Professor Fischer went into the lab and returned with a test-tube with a rubber stopper and a metal cannister with a tight-fitting lid which she handed to Derek.

"Right out of the autoclave," she said. "We don't want to introduce contamination. With the cannister, just open it for a minute and close it again."

"I'll try to be back within the hour."

"Good luck!"

✸✸✸

Derek teleported to the Institute's second floor where the space suit was stored. It was a striking red, blue, and polished stainless steel contraption with the Space Ventures logo on it. One of Trask's design requirements was that it look "cool."

After checking its batteries, he put it on and activated it. One of its unique features is that it was "one size fits all": Motors and artificial muscles contracted the suit until it fit Derek like a glove.

Then he staggered into a disinfectant shower.

✸✸✸

In his spirit-body, Derek flew over the Archies' city for what seemed like half an hour, looking for a secluded area.

He never quite found one.

He finally settled for a spot beside a cluster of buildings. A depression in the ground promised the possibility of standing water, and a scan of the area showed that there were only three Archies nearby.

Fighting off waves of vertigo and a feeling of impending doom, he materialized.

Gravity crushed him against the ground.

My God! It must be three G's.

The G-forces drained blood from his brain, making him very dizzy.

Putting his head against the ground seemed to help.

Can't pass out, he thought, cursing himself for underestimating this place. *I'll die here.*

Mustering every iota of willpower he had, he forced himself to look around.

Under a red orb of a sun that glared like a merciless eye, scattered red clouds zipped across a glittering violet sky that roared like thunder.

A vast mountain range rose in the distance — bristling with gray buildings.

Derek's space suit analyzed the air around him: 80% oxygen, 19% carbon dioxide and traces of other gases. The strangest aspect of the alien atmosphere was its pressure: five kilograms per square centimeter as opposed Earth's one.

It was 20 degrees Celsius — room temperature.

As he'd hoped, the depression in the ground contained water with mounds of brown sludge. He crawled over to the depression, scooped water and sludge into the test tube, and stoppered it.

Then he opened the cannister.

It hissed as alien air filled it, and he resealed it.

From a nearby gray building, an Archy spotted him — a cockroach covered with a riot of swirling red, blue, green, and yellow.

It's almost pretty, Derek thought. *Like an insect-clown on mescaline. The Archies' world is also beautiful in its own ... way.*

A new scavenger robot? the Archy wondered. *Looks like it's malfunctioning. Nothing works right these days. I'll call Maintenance — for the tenth time this cycle!*

When it looked away, Derek vanished.

The Institute's decontamination unit sprayed disinfectant liquid all over his suit and rinsed it off.

He staggered out of it and teleported to the lobby.

✳✳✳

Derek handed the sample containers to Professor Fischer.

"One of the Archies spotted me," he said. "These pressure and oxygen readings are off the scale. I'm glad the space suit didn't implode or something."

"Earth insects have no lungs at all," Birgit Fischer said. "These creatures probably have primitive lungs, and they need all the oxygen they can get. This brown sludge might tell us something about their organic nature."

"Could we learn their DNA from it?"

"Or whether they use DNA," Birgit Fischer said.

"What?"

"The creatures on Triton don't use it," she said.

"Ah, yes," Derek said, recalling his explorations of Saturn's sixth moon in this timeline. Oceans of methane covered its surface, harboring living creatures whose souls he'd seen.

He had no idea what they looked like in the flesh.

Maybe — someday — he'd have a space suit able to withstand the conditions there and physically visit them.

"In the past few months, we've learned so many strange things," Derek sighed. "You'd win three Nobel Prizes if we could present them to our old world."

She smiled.

"I can't believe I flew *light years* in a few seconds," Derek said.

"I wonder how far you could go," she said.

"There's one way to find out."

"Where will you go?" she said.

"Away. As far as I can."

"If you're not going to a planet, you should mark the location somehow."

"Suppose I take this," Derek said, picking up a conch shell holding down a stack of papers. "I'll get you another."

"You had better," she chuckled.

✹✹✹

Derek returned to the room with the space suit, put it on, lay on the floor, and went out-of-body.

Pulsating colors surrounded him in the spirit-world and he tried to fly as fast and far as he could. He visualized a place where the colors were sparse almost to the point of vanishing. After what seemed like an eternity, they indeed faded.

How do I feel about materializing? he asked himself, recalling the premonitions he'd had at the Archy planet. *OK, I guess.*

He did it.

Blackness surrounded him and he felt an overpowering sense of emptiness.

"Where are the stars?"

As his eyes adjusted to the darkness, he became aware of nearly invisible smudges of light — tiny ovals, and spots.

They were few and far between.

He turned on his space suit's helmet light to see the conch shell floating nearby, slowly rotating.

"This is literally the middle of nowhere," he said aloud, his voice echoing in his helmet.

Maybe matter never formed here. It's capable of existing, though.

He began to panic, wondering whether he'd be able to return home.

To his relief, this presented no problem.

Chapter 8

As the dusk fell, and heavy surf pounded the beach, Culinary Derek brought out plates of veal francese and said, "This is your last supper. We've got to get back."

"Last supper?" Allie chuckled. "Sounds ominous."

Culinary Renata had reached the God Virus's sneezing phase so Renata took a plate of food to her in her bedroom and rejoined the group.

"I don't get it," Llewellyn said. "You predicted the winning lottery numbers?"

"They sure did," Culinary Allie said.

"Every time try to look into the future and see the outcome of flipping a coin, I see heads *and* tails," Llewellyn said. "When I roll a die, I see 1, 2, 3, 4, 5, *and* 6."

"Yet you saw the winning numbers?" Andy said.

"Yes," Derek said. "You could scan us, but why don't you figure it out for yourself?"

"I can see *all* possible outcomes?" Llewellyn said.

"Absolutely," Allie said.

"So there was only *one possible* outcome of the drawing?" Andy said.

"That would mean the drawing was *rigged!*" Llewellyn said.

"Bingo!" Derek said.

"I always wondered about those big lotteries," Andy said. "You know who rigged it?"

"A money manager," Derek nodded. "He can't win for himself because winners are under a microscope."

"Are they *ever!*" Culinary Allie said. "After we won, the FBI questioned Derek and grandpa for hours."

"My goodness," Llewellyn said. "Why would they do that?"

"The grandpa in question is Don Carlo Giancana," Allie said. "Head of the New York mafia. Retired in the Culinary timeline."

Andy let out a low whistle.

"What's it like being related to the mafia?" Llewellyn said.

"It got my brother and father murdered," Allie growled.

"My father refused to go into the family business," Culinary Allie said, hugging her. "Grandpa threatened to kill him, at first. Then he gave in and accepted it."

"My father never had the nerve to do that," Allie said.

"You and your children *have* to become Indigos!" Renata said.

"We want normal lives," Culinary Derek said.

"That ship sailed when you won the lottery," Renata said. "Your phone's ringing off the hook from crackpots with get rich quick schemes."

"How do you know?" Culinary Allie said.

Renata frowned at her.

"Telepathy," Culinary Allie sighed.

"No — common *sense!*" Renata muttered.

Meet me, Eldon said in Derek's mind. *You've got to see this.*

"I'm being paged," Derek said, vanishing.

※※※

Derek teleported to his and Allie's bedroom on their house's second floor — an airy room decorated in pastel greens and blues with a sepia-toned painting hanging over the bed of a hula dancer on a beach.

Allie's work.

Vittoria's crib sat beside the bed.

"Sleep well, sweet Tori," he whispered, kissing her forehead.

He lay down.

※※※

As always, the spirit-world flickered and pulsated with colors that seemed alive.

He thought of Eldon Trask.

A structure larger than a building surrounded them, nearly transparent. Its straight lines and smooth bulkheads showed that it was artificial.

"What did you learn?" Derek said.

"I scanned a passenger vessel and the people — creatures — operating it. It was all push-button stuff to them. When the red light goes on, push the green button. Then I scanned the go-to people when things go wrong. They knew how to trigger the self-diagnosing and self-repair features but that's it."

"Maybe they're just not scientists."

"Last January, I was on a Saudi prince's yacht and chatted with the engineer," Eldon said. "He not only knew the general principles behind an engine; he could've built one from scratch. That's how engineers *are.* One of these alien so-called 'engineers' asked another what happens when self-repair doesn't work. He said 'pray to the nine gods who built the ship'."

"Pray to the *gods?*"

"Check out this place," Eldon said, indicating the structure that surrounded them. "Tell me what you think of it."

Derek scanned the enormous structure. He flew through what seemed like an endless series of decks and levels — containing chambers lined with equipment.

"No detectable signs of life," Derek said.

"Exactly! I needed to hear that from you. This place is a *space ship* in orbit around the aliens' planet. There appears to be hundreds of them, all deserted. They don't look anything like the passenger ships."

"I supposed we could steal it."

"It's my ticket back!" Eldon said. *"One,* reverse-engineer the engines. *Two,* offer the technology to Culinary Me. *Three,* become his long-lost twin brother. *Four,* explore the solar system."

"You don't want to go home?"

"Origin is dead to me. My employees are scattered to the four winds — the ones who are still alive. How do you teleport something like this to Oz?"

"If it's a warship, it might have dangerous weapons. It might also have a homing device that alerts the aliens."

"They already know we exist. You said it's uninhabited."

"I can't tell if it has active electronics. I'll revisit it in a spacesuit."

✳✳✳

They returned to Derek and Allie's deck on Destiny Beach, joining Andy, Llewellyn, Chloe and Renata.

"What's it like to have a counterpart?" Andy asked Renata.

"It's like discovering you have an identical twin sister," Renata said. "Whose life turned out a bit differently."

"You have the same DNA?" Llewellyn said.

"Before I became an Indigo, we did."

"You want to bring an *alien warship here?*" Chloe exclaimed. *"Are you out of your mind?"*

"Just a thought, honey," Trask said. "The main thing is to put it somewhere where we can study it."

"Weird goddamn planet, the Archies have," Derek muttered. "I almost *died* there. The G-forces almost made me pass out."

"What?" Chloe exclaimed.

"I would've become an alien relic, rotting under their monstrous red sun."

"Red sun?" Eldon said. "Are you sure?"

"Is that significant?" Derek said, as a purring Norton jumped into his lap.

"It sure as hell is! It means their sun is smaller and cooler than ours."

"It looked huge," Derek said. "I was barely conscious but I'm sure of that."

"For the Archy planet to be as warm as ours, it has to orbit its sun very closely," Eldon said.

"So?" Derek said.

"That means it's tidally locked," Eldon said. "One side permanently faces the sun and the other faces away."

"I was on the day side, then. But it should have been *incredibly* hot, then, hot enough to melt my spacesuit. God, I was so *goddamn reckless!* I'm lucky to be alive."

"Was the atmosphere dense?" Eldon said.

"You could eat it with a spoon."

"OK," Eldon said. "The dense atmosphere transports heat from the bright side to the dark side. With *very* high winds — hurricane-force, even."

"The purple sky roared like thunder. You get all this from the sun being red?"

"What a bizarre place," Andy muttered.

"I participated in a UCLA seminar," Eldon said. "On exotic planetary climates. We did computer-studies of all sorts of weird scenarios."

Norton jumped down and stalked a bird perched on the railing.

"Their planet's dark side is cooler so it rains constantly," Eldon continued. "Since water accumulates there, huge rivers must carry it back to the bright side."

"Their civilization must've started on the day side," Andy murmured. "The night side was their 'new frontier'."

※※※

It was time for Culinary Derek and Allie to go home.

Tony and Loretta whined and complained, while baby Travis slept.

After many hugs and kisses, Culinary Allie said, "Who's going to babysit for us? My mom is still sneezing."

"I can babysit," Renata said.

"Sparkly grandma!" Tony said, clapping.

Derek pulled Culinary Derek aside and said, "We know why you're afraid of becoming an Indigo. You cheated on Allie once, and fantasize being a celebrity chef and doing it again."

"She knows more than you think," Allie said, materializing beside them. "It's not totally your fault. You should clear the air with her."

"We don't need to bother sparkly grandma," Culinary Derek said, blushing. "We'll *hire* a babysitter."

"It's no bother at all," Renata said. "They're the most beautiful kids in this and *any other universe*."

"We've spent too much time here," Culinary Derek said. ". Our kids have to go back to reality, and be among their own kind."

Culinary Allie registered shock.

As Derek, Allie, and Wendy ferried them and their children back to their home in Queens, New York, Culinary Allie glared at her husband.

✳✳✳

Lying in bed, Derek and Allie couldn't sleep.

"How could he do that to her?" Derek growled.

"He craves success and acceptance," Allie said. "His self-esteem is below zero, and she even calls him a failure. She loves him but she's terrified of them winding up on the street. She just loses it sometimes."

"Their restaurant *was* failing," Derek muttered.

"He's running it way better than papa did," Allie said. "He's even a better chef. I guess it's hard to succeed in the restaurant business. Especially when Grandpa badmouths it to anyone who will listen."

"Being an Indigo is so strange," Derek murmured.

"Yes. We might've lived our entire lives without knowing these wonderful people existed. Their triumphs, their beautiful children. Their problems."

"Ignorance is not an option," Derek said. "And their problems are our problems."

"That's another thing. Culinary Derek is genuinely terrified of being an Indigo. Remember — your father tried to *kill* himself when he became one. The Culinaries are more Earth-oriented than we *ever* were. That restaurant is their lives. That and their beautiful children."

"I was a total asshole," Derek muttered. "Now he feels they can't trust us, and they have no privacy around us."

"Yes, you were. We all were. We ganged up on him."
"So what do we do now?" he said.
"Nothing. Just hope they work it out. They love each other too much not to."
"I hope they forgive us."
They drifted off to sleep.

Chapter 9

At three in the morning, Derek and Allie awoke and removed their nightgowns.

In their spirit-bodies, they flew to the Sea of Desire — Oz's version of the Caribbean — scanned an area for threats, and satisfied themselves that none existed.

Squinting in the morning light, they dropped naked into the bath-warm water.

They made love.

Caressed by the placid water's ripples, they floated on their backs, listening to whale songs and the squawking of black and white birds perched on the sea near them.

A shadow cut off the sun.

An enormous albatross drifted overhead, landed on the water twenty feet away, and fed on small fish.

A naked Vittoria appeared on Allie's belly.

"Hi baby girl!" Allie said, kissing her and giving her a breast.

"Hi mom and dad!" Vittoria beamed at them, giggling.

After a while, they treaded water, holding Vittoria between

them, and she pooped. They rinsed her off and teleported home. There, they took turns washing off the salt water and went back to bed.

"God, I hope we don't have to abandon Oz," Allie sighed as they drifted off to sleep. "I love Columbia, but we need Oz too."

"You've foreseen our descendants living here," Derek said.

"Yes, that's one possible future."

※※※

Andromeda and Llewellyn stirred in bed, daylight streaming through their pale blue bedroom.

"How did you sleep?" Llewellyn said.

"Not well," Andy said.

"Why?"

"I can't turn my brain off. The last few years I've done nothing but chase phantoms, the Ark of the Covenant, the lost city of Ubar. They call me *Illinois Jane* behind my back, and it's *not* a compliment. I'm a laughingstock."

"You're in a slump, honey. You wouldn't be at the Oriental Institute if you hadn't done first-rate work."

"It's just that we're living the greatest adventure of our lives," Andy said. "The beginning of a ... a new *Atlantis,* and we *we're there*. But I can't report on it to anyone."

"Write a book!"

Andy frowned.

"OK, they won't believe us at *first*. We can prove it, though! We're Indigos."

"You can say that after what happened to Derek and Allie?"

You don't smell like mommie, a small voice said in their minds. *Please lick me like mommie does.*

"Huh?" Andy said.

"It's *Norton!*"

Norton carefully padded over them.

"I can't believe we can *hear* a *cat!*" Llewellyn said, petting him.

"I draw the line at licking you, pal," Andy chuckled, petting him too. "Travis did say all animals think."

Norton purred.

✳✳✳

Derek teleported to the men's room in Lew's Diner in Flushing, Queens in the Origin Timeline. Since he and Allie had been there before, it was easy to locate in the spirit world.

It was a cozy, stainless-steel 1950's style place with booths and advertisement-covered paper placemats.

It was late afternoon, there, but they served breakfast all day.

He ordered eight breakfasts to go: pancakes and various styles of eggs and hash browns.

The owner and two patrons stared as he carried the bundle of wrapped packages back into the men's room.

"Is he the guy from TV?" one asked. "The one who causes earthquakes?"

"Yup," Lew said.

"He coming out of there?"

"Nope."

"Why didn't we call the cops?"

"If he's really that shit-all powerful, why are they even messing with him?" Lou said.

✳✳✳

They began breakfast on the deck but moved everything into the dining room when clouds drifted in and misted the beach.

Pale yellow walls gave the dining room a regal quality, and a large oak table with six chairs dominated it.

On one wall, a bay window framed Diamond Head, and Allie's radiant oil paintings of the island's beaches and mountains covered the others.

As Derek opened the packages from Lew's, Eldon and Chloe appeared.

"*We need to steal spacesuits!*" Eldon exclaimed. "Ideally, one for each of us — with backups."

When Chloe elbowed him, he added, "Uh, good morning."

Chloe sneezed and gave her nose a wet blow.

"Good morning," Allie said. "The sneezing phase doesn't last long."

Andy and Llewellyn hovered in their spirit bodies.

"May as well join us," Allie said. "Be our guests."

They materialized.

"*Ooh,*" Llewellyn cooed. "Trashy breakfast food. Where did you get it?"

"A New York diner," Derek said. "In Origin."

"Why do you keep going back there?" Allie said. "You could get killed."

"I guess I feel sentimental about Origin. We lived most of our lives there."

"Chicago has the best trashy food anywhere," Andy said. "Cheezborgers. Pizza pot pies."

"You and your pizza pot pies," Llewellyn muttered. "Pastry-wrapped *heart attacks* is what they are! I *worry* about you."

"Who are we stealing these spacesuits from?" Derek said.

"Me, of course," Eldon said.

"Did he say stealing spacesuits?" Llewellyn whispered to Andy.

Andy nodded.

"Culinary you?" Allie said.

"*Him* him," Chloe Teague said.

"I found a heavily-guarded warehouse with two dozen of them. I estimate ten are functional."

"Those Eakins *bastards* impounded them!" Chloe growled.

"My dear Reverend Chloe!" Eldon chuckled. "Such language! I'm shocked, shocked!"

"It's not stealing when you already own them," she blushed.

"Why do you need ... spacesuits?" Andy said.

"Can't battle the Archies in our spirit-bodies," Allie said.

"Breakfast with you guys is an adventure," Llewellyn said.

"Speaking of adventures," Andy said. "We had the weirdest experience this morning."

She described their experience with Norton.

"We *have* to get a cat, Andy," Llewellyn said. "We can *talk* to it."

"Yes," Derek said. You can't debate Wittgenstein, but you can talk. That's why we want to become vegans."

"We're devout hypocrites for now," Wendy said, appearing with a basket of coffee berries.

"Oh God," Allie sighed. "I just realized I've got an announcement to make."

"You're pregnant?" Chloe said.

"You could've at least waited for me to say it."

"Sorry! I'm also pregnant."

"You can't *possibly* know that," Eldon Trask exclaimed.

"Indigos know when they're pregnant," Allie said. "Almost immediately. We don't need pregnancy tests. I'm having a son."

"I'm having a daughter," Chloe said.

Ian Roberts appeared.

"I can't tear Birgit away from analyzing those samples you brought, Derek. I'll take her some breakfast and *make* her eat it. I'll hold a gun to her head, if I have to."

He picked up a paper plate of scrambled eggs and hashbrowns and vanished.

Chapter 10

All the new Indigos joined Derek and Wendy in their spirit-bodies.

Your spirit-bodies look like your clothed physical bodies now, but this is a psychological fact only, Derek said.

Clothed? Andy said. *Is that why we teleport with our clothes?*

Yes, Derek said. *You identify with your clothing so it's effectively part of you. When Vittoria teleports, she's naked because she doesn't identify with clothing. We'll have to teach her that.*

You better, Wendy chuckled.

You can make your spirit body any shape you want, Wendy continued, as her spirit-body took the shape of an enormous sphere. *Use your imagination. Remember when you were children and played make-believe?*

Meow! Chloe said, as her spirit body took the shape of a cat — and then smoothly morphed into an enormous roaring lion.

Trask turned into one of his Raptor rockets.

So shall it be written, so shall it be done! Andy intoned in a deep, throbbing voice, taking the shape of a sixty-foot granite statue of Ramses II.

What's that? Travis said, appearing in their midst. *It hurts to look at.*

I imagined I was a seven-dimensional p-adic lens space, Llewellyn said. *Over the prime thirteen, with a twist of three.*

Why are you guys so much better at this than I am? Derek muttered.

You flunked make-believe 101, Wendy said. *To teleport an object, engulf it with your spirit body.*

How do we do that? Andy said. *Physical things are almost invisible, they're ghosts!*

Focus on the outlines, Wendy said. *I almost clipped off part of your house because I didn't see it at first.*

They practiced teleporting masses of beach sand from one place to another.

Now we practice regeneration, Derek said. *That's something I'm good at. When you materialize, picture yourself when you woke up in the morning.*

Really? Andy said.

After you got dressed, Wendy added.

✶✶✶

They all appeared, standing on Destiny Beach.

"What the hell?" Eldon said. "I'm getting dressed and suddenly, I'm ... here."

"We *spontaneously* teleported!" Chloe said. "Does this happen often?"

"Just wait," Derek said. "And you'll understand..."

"Oh," Andy said. "It's coming back to me. We were practicing teleporting things."

Derek filled them in on what happened next.

"The price you pay for regeneration is a few minutes of amnesia," he said. "But it'll save you even if you're fatally wounded."

"Teleport and imagine yourself *before* you were wounded," Wendy said. "Even your clothes get fixed. The bullet hole in your shirt disappears."

"Why the amnesia?" Andy said.

"Short term memories are stored in your brain," Derek said. "And long term memories are in your soul. That's my theory, anyway."

"We discovered this by accident," Allie said. "We wondered if, in our *nineties,* we could become young again,"

"The answer is, *probably,"* Wendy said.

"You mean we could live forever?" Eldon said.

"Probably," Wendy repeated.

"Do you really want to?" Chloe said. "Sometimes one needs a new beginning."

"Dammit, Chloe, you can be so starry-eyed," Eldon snapped. "Death is not a beginning!"

"It's not an end either," Chloe murmured. "After all we've been through, you still doubt the soul's existence?"

"If I could live to be three hundred, I could put a colony on Mars! I could see it prosper."

"So live to be three hundred," Chloe said. "Outlive your loved ones, if that's what you want."

"God, I can't talk to you sometimes!" Eldon muttered, vanishing.

"I can't believe I'm having a child with this man."

"He'll ... uh probably be a good father," Derek murmured.

"How do you know?" Chloe snapped. "How can you *possibly* know him as well as I do?"

"Come on, honey," Allie said, appearing next to them and putting her arm around Chloe. "Let's talk."

They vanished.

"Trouble in paradise?" Andy said.

"Those two are the most unlikely people to hook up," Derek muttered. "I see it but I don't believe it."

"Opposites attract?" Llewellyn said.

"They *repel,* too," Derek said. "I still think they'll both be good parents. They're responsible people."

"Whether they are or not, their children are *our* responsibility," Wendy said. "This Indigo life is ... so familiar. It's déjà vu."

"Huh?" Derek said.

"Before I was a !Kung," Wendy murmured. "I was cold. *Always* cold. In a place with ice and snow ... cruel winds. Summers were never warm. We wore furs, and there were so *few* of us. Maybe twenty in our group."

"Another past life?" Andy said.

"In my whole life, we only met other groups like us five times," she continued, a dreamy look in her eyes. "We'd sing and dance ... feast and fuck for days. Then the other group would go away ... or we would. In the months afterward, our women would become goddesses."

"Goddesses?" Andy said.

"When a woman was pregnant, we worshiped her as a goddess. She kept our people from vanishing. We carried pregnant-woman amulets when we hunted. They had healing powers. At least we believed they did."

"What did you look like?" Andy said.

"*Look* like?" Wendy said. "We had black skin, darker than the !Kung. And long black hair. And blue eyes."

"Cro-magnon!" Andy exclaimed.

"My greatest accomplishment was killing a mammoth," Wendy said. "It charged, and the others ran. My spear crunched into its head. We had meat for days. It could've fed us for months, but it went bad. Afterward, I became arrogant and hunted alone. I told them they slowed me down. I got lost in the snow."

"Is that how you died?" Llewellyn said.

"I became sleepy. I couldn't make a fire. I fell asleep dreaming of a warm place. Where it's *never* cold."

"Why did you say déjà vu?" Derek said.

"Because there are so few of us, like then. When I was a ... what did you call me? ... cro-magnon — we helped each other, we celebrated our ... lives. We *must* do that now. A child of *one* is the child of *all!*"

I'm ready to make my report, Professor Fischer's voice echoed in their minds.

✳✳✳

The sacks of grass-seed Wendy had scattered around the Oz Institute of Philosophy three months ago had grown into a thick, lush carpet.

They sat on it.

"One," Birgit Fischer said. "The water samples were *completely devoid* of microscopic life. This is an amazing contrast to water here."

A vivid image formed in their minds of water under a microscope crawling with countless organisms.

"Wow," Derek said. "You don't need a projector or anything. You just blast images into our minds."

"This will be important when we educate our children," Birgit said.

"The brown sludge in the water is cast-off alien cells mixed with dirt," she continued, projecting images of cells into their minds. There is no decay since there are *no bacteria.* The cells have nuclei containing DNA."

"What about the air sample?" Derek said.

"High in oxygen," Birgit said. "Four times the concentration as our air. Also five times the pressure, so their bodies 'see' *twenty* times as much oxygen as ours. *No* spores!"

"No spores?" Andy said. "Does that mean something?"

"Every breath you take contains about 200,000 spores," Birgit said. "From bacteria, fungi, etc. This alien planet has none."

"200,000?" Llewellyn said. "That's creepy!"

"Life is creepier than that," Birgit said. "The human body contains ten times as many bacteria as somatic cells."

"What?" Derek exclaimed.

"They're tiny but there are many of them, and they perform vital functions. They keep harmful bacteria in check and digest our food for us."

"How's that?" Allie said.

Tori appeared on her chest and nursed.

"When you eat food, the bacteria in your gut digest it. Then you digest *them.* That's why some antibiotics cause terrible stomach cramps and indigestion. They kill off your gut-bacteria."

"So we're walking bacteria colonies?" Llewellyn said.

"Exactly. Our immune systems keep them in check. The aliens have no bacteria in their environment *or* their bodies."

"So they have no immune systems?" Ian said.

"Yes, my dear detective!" she said. "Nature gets rid of what's unnecessary. If these aliens had immune systems once, they lost them long ago."

"So they're incredibly vulnerable!" Derek said.

"Yes, their chirality is even the same as ours," Birgit said.

"Chirality?" Andy said.

"It means our bacteria can *probably* infect the aliens. In fact, Oz bacteria are rotting Derek's samples as we speak."

"Derek, your samples violate *every principle of biology I know!*" Birgit muttered. "*Simple* life-forms evolve *first* and *then* become complex. Here, we have complex life forms and no *simple* ones. No bacteria, no viruses, no spores. The lack of spores suggests no *plants* or *molds,* either. It doesn't make any sense. It is a great mystery."

"You could do major surgery in the open without any danger of infection?" Derek said.

"*Genau!*" Birgit nodded.

"Destroying them might be easy," Llewellyn mused. "Find a rotting deer-carcass somewhere and dump it on their planet."

"Easier said than done," Derek said. "Dropping it from space won't work. We'd have to set it gently on the surface."

"Which almost killed you," Andy said.

"In addition," Birgit said. "Their planet's high-oxygen atmosphere would kill most Earth bacteria."

Chapter 11

"Why the hell did you *say* that?" Culinary Allie screamed at her husband as they opened up a dark *Ristorante Alberto's* in the morning. "They're our best friends. Alberto's was circling the drain before they saved it!"

"They're not even human for God's sake," Culinary Derek said. "Our children have to live in this world. What do we say when they watch people teleport and ask why they can't?"

Allie switched on the lights to see two men seated in front of the maitre d' podium.

"Grandpa!" Culinary Allie said. "What are you doing here? Did you break in?"

"I'm having a chat with my new best friend," Don Carlo said, indicating an Asian man in a pinstripe gray suit next to him. "Jonas Nakatomi. He's a goddamn genius who figured out how to fix the lottery."

"At first, I assumed your picking my numbers was sheer luck," Nakatomi said. "Then I discovered you were related to Don Carlo Giancana. So luck had nothing to do it. I contacted him."

"*I* didn't pick the numbers," Don Carlo said. "The gangster business is not for amateurs, Derek *Evans*. Being a chef should've been enough. On the bright side, I persuaded Jonas to cut me in on his action. In exchange for one thing."

"What?" Culinary Derek said.

"You."

Two thugs stepped from the shadows and grabbed Culinary Derek.

Jonas punched him in the stomach, doubling him up.

"Do what you want with him," Don Carlo said. "Leave my granddaughter and her children alone."

"Of course, Don Carlo."

"He's family!" Culinary Allie shouted.

"*Family?*" Carlo roared. "Not from Taormina, not even *Italian*. You disgrace my son's memory by operating this place in his name. I should've done this long ago."

Barefoot and in pajamas, the Indigo Derek and Allie appeared beside the thugs and zapped their necks with stun-guns.

"We're their guardian *fucking* angels," Allie snarled, as they tied up the men.

Culinary Derek coughed and vomited on the floor. His wife hugged him.

Nakatomi whipped out a pistol and fired at Allie, and her image blurred briefly as she regenerated.

Derek charged at him, regenerating twice as Nakatomi fired at him. When Derek reached him, he pummeled Nakatomi to the floor.

Carlo stared, his mouth silently working.

"I'll get the children," Allie said. "The nanny you hired works for this asshole."

She vanished.

"Huuuh?" Carlo moaned.

"Your schlong's hanging out," Culinary Allie chuckled.

"Oh shit!" Derek muttered, tightening up his pajamas. "You guys caught us with our pants down."

"Don't worry. You're my almost semi-husband."

She gasped as Nakatomi grabbed Derek from behind with a knife at his throat.

"Back off," Derek said. "You're in the splash zone."

"Splash zone?" Culinary Derek said.

"Kill him," Carlo growled between clenched teeth.

As Nakatomi's knife pressed into Derek's throat, Derek teleported a foot to the right — taking Nakatomi's forearms with him and sending fountains of blood gushing from the stumps.

Culinary Allie screamed, and Carlo gasped.

"If we get him to a hospital soon, they can reattach them," Derek said. "I know an emergency room I can reach quickly. Want to come?"

Culinary Derek and Allie nodded.

"Each of you grab an arm."

✳✳✳

There was a transition and they almost fell to the floor as their surroundings changed to a busy emergency room. They stood on a bloody circular panel of wood almost a foot thick.

The hospital's intake area rang with the sound of bells, medical monitors, and doctors' pages. Nurses, doctors, and orderlies ran to and fro — and nobody noticed the new arrivals.

"I had to take some of your floor with me to be sure to get all of you," Derek said.

He dragged the now-unconscious Nakatomi to a nurse's station and lifted him onto a gurney.

Dazed, Culinary Allie stared at a TV report on the search for the missing President Eakins.

"Put his arms on the gurney next to him," Derek said.

Culinary Allie and Derek came to their senses and complied. A nurse spotted Nakatomi and called a doctor and security.

"Let's get out of here," Derek said, tugging on Culinary Allie's arm.

They teleported back to the restaurant, taking a circular section of the hospital's floor with them.

✳✳✳

"The TV mentioned *President Eakins*," Culinary Allie said.

"I had to go to the Origin timeline," Derek said. "The only place I've been hospitalized. I spent a night in the psych ward there."

"The *psych* ward?" Culinary Derek said.

"The first time I ever teleported, I went to bed and woke up standing in a crowded restaurant," Derek said. "In my *pajamas!* Like one of those embarrassing dreams of being naked, but it wasn't a dream. Seems to be my destiny with that hospital. Whenever I go there, I'm in pajamas."

"That was the most horrible thing I ever saw," Culinary Allie muttered. "Chopping that man's arms off."

"That's how we fight when we're forced to," Derek sighed. "If he didn't have a knife at my throat, I could've just punched him."

Nakatomi's thugs writhed in their bonds.

"I suggest you two leave while you can," Derek said, untying them. "Your boss is not coming back."

They fled.

"I zapped the nanny," Allie said, appearing with Tony, Loretta, and carrying baby Travis — and standing on a six-inch circular section of plywood floor.

"That lady tied *tape* on us," Tony shouted. "We couldn't even *move*."

"Watch out for the hole in the floor," Derek said, pointing to a four-foot-wide cutout. The basement was visible through it.

"I see it," Culinary Allie said, running over and scooping up Tony and Loretta.

"Sorry about your floor," Derek said.

"No big deal," Culinary Derek said. "One more job for the carpenters. I'll say it was dry rot or something."

"Who..." Carlo groaned. *"What are you two?"*

"Shut up!" Allie snapped. "You don't deserve an answer. Maybe if you ask them *incredibly nicely,* they might give you one. Just know — clothed or naked — we'll *always* have their backs."

"If you ever succeed in harming them," Derek said. "You could lock yourself in *goddamn Fort Knox's* deepest vault, and we'd get to you — and escort you to *hell. Ahead* of schedule."

Don Carlo staggered out the front door.

"Can you forgive a meddling asshole?" Derek said to Culinary Derek. "I'm sorry for what I said."

"It's OK," Culinary Derek said, hugging him.

"What will become of that *poor man?*" Culinary Allie said.

"Poor man?" Culinary Derek said.

Derek shut his eyes briefly and said, "They stopped his bleeding and packed his arms in ice. They're prepping an operating room."

"They think they can reattach his arms," Allie said. "He *might* get the use of his hands back."

"When he wakes up, he'll think he's lost his mind. I mean, he's in an alternate reality."

"That nanny you hired," Allie said. "Sharon. She's trying to call him and won't call 911 until she gets him."

"Of course his phone's in another dimension," Derek said. "She may look you guys up."

"If she shows her sorry ass around here, I'll punch her *lights out*," Culinary Allie said, swinging her fist.

"I can look after the kids," Renata said, popping into view.

"*Sparkly* grandma!" Loretta said, clapping.

"*Both* of us will be sparkly soon," Renata said.

"We should get back to bed," Allie yawned, handing Travis to his mother. "Maybe we can get some sleep."

"It's morning here," Culinary Allie said.

"Our timelines are out of sync," Derek said. "It's two AM back on Destiny Beach. Or it's just the six-hour time difference between Hawaii and here."

"Maybe you're right about us becoming Indigos," Culinary Derek said, yawning. "We'll think long and hard about it."

"*Please* come to our grand opening," Culinary Allie said. "Bring *everyone*. You'll have the place to yourselves."

"It's a date," Allie said, hugging her.

Derek and Allie vanished.

Chapter 12

Under a cloudless blue sky, they stood on a black fused glass shoreline bordering a mirrored plain that blazed like a furnace. The sun-glare blinded them.

Waves thundered against the black sand beach.

"In our world, this would be central western Namibia," Derek said to Andy and Llewellyn.

"Then that's the Swakop River," Andy said, pointing to a stream flowing into the ocean. "The town of Swakopmund should be on the other side, to the north. Odd, though."

"What?" Derek said.

"In our world the river's dry most of the time," Andy said. "It only flows a couple days every few years."

"Maybe it's wetter here," Derek said. "Or the fused glass doesn't absorb the water."

"There are *ruins* around here?" Andy said.

"About two hundred meters below the surface."

"But ... but," Andy sputtered. "How would one *get* to the ruins? How did anyone *place* them there?"

"I think there was a tunnel once, but it got melted shut."

"Melted shut?" Llewellyn whispered.

"So we have to visit this place in an out of body state," Andy said. "How do we do that? I'm not lying on the ground here. Our shoes are disintegrating!"

Indeed, their rubber-soled shoes stuck to the glassy surface, leaving sticky footprints behind.

"We return to Destiny Beach. Now that you've been here, it'll be easy to come back."

❋❋❋

"OK," Andy said, waving a Shadowhawk Tactical flashlight. "I guess the air here is breathable. I'm breathing it, anyway. It smells musty but that's all."

She stood in a long circular tunnel littered with dirt and small rocks. An arrow on a wall had vaguely Chinese-like symbols carved under it.

She followed it.

She came to a circular chamber lined with what looked like dead video monitors and other equipment.

"A skeleton!"

"What does it look like?" Derek beamed into her mind.

"Look for yourself!"

She stared at it, and the others saw through her eyes.

A large skull mounted on a thick bony stump sat atop a circular bony plate that had six bony projections extending out from it in all directions, like a starfish.

"My god!" Birgit said. "That would be a two-meter wide octopus, if they had bones."

"Maybe octopuses on land need bones?" Derek said.

"Indeed," Birgit said, vanishing.

She joined Andy in the chamber.

"The cranium is human sized," Birgit said, gathering the bones into a cloth sack. "Or a bit larger."

Ian Roberts appeared and took the sack of bones.

"Don't you want to photograph that first?" Andy said.

"I've memorized the layout. I'll mount them on a board at the Institute."

She and Ian vanished.

※※※

"I rummaged around and found stacks of ... stuff," Andy said, pointing to flat sheets of what looked like plastic. "I don't know what they are."

They all shivered in the Institute laboratory's air-conditioning.

"I don't understand the electronic equipment at all," she added. "Really, Trask would be better suited to this than me."

"I'll look at them but I'm not promising anything," Eldon Trask said.

"Could you decipher the inscriptions?" Birgit said.

"Of course not. Hieroglyphics were only deciphered when they found the Rosetta Stone. Cuneiform took decades longer, and those were *human* languages, with *human* activities and body-parts."

Allie joined them and examined the sheets of plastic.

"There are faint lines on these things," she said. "Maybe they're faded photographs, or diagrams."

They scanned the sheets of plastic and computer-enhanced the images, but nothing interesting showed up.

Trask and Andy teleported to the circular chamber.

※※※

"We'll have to make a ventilation-shaft at least," Eldon said.

"I know," Andy said.

"If this was human equipment, I'd say these are monitors,"

Eldon said, examining the electronic equipment. "I don't know what the hell those other things are."

"Can't you attach a computer and ... hack it? You know, like in the movie *Independence Day*."

"Ah, my *esteemed* colleague," Eldon chuckled.

"You're about to say I'm full of shit."

"Exactly. People who hack Windows spend *every waking moment* of their lives studying the software's dirty little details. They find obscure flaws the people who *developed* windows weren't aware of."

"So hacking is as hard as deciphering alien inscriptions?"

"For the same reasons," he nodded. "Alien thought-processes, alien languages, etc. Even alien computer-design. Our computers use base two, but some early machines used base ten. Some Soviet computers used base three."

"Damn!" she muttered, strolling over to what looked like a large disk on the wall. A portal perhaps?

She tripped over a thick cable, ripping it loose from the wall.

"Shit," she growled. "Some archaeologist I am, destroying artifacts."

"Wait!" Trask said, examining the severed end. "This has three thick wires. Like a power cable."

"Doesn't look like copper," Andy said.

"Could be tarnished silver," Eldon said. "Silver's a better conductor than copper. If we back a couple inches away from the cut end..."

His image flickered and the cable split, exposing silvery wires.

"Teleport-cutting works!" he exclaimed. "And we have *silver wires*."

Trask traced the cable to a metal box with a cover held in place by four screws.

He vanished for a moment and reappeared with a screwdriver and wire strippers.

"They look like human screws," Andy said.

"Form follows function. They're threaded the opposite of human screws."

He finally removed the metal cover to reveal a forest of wires and a small box.

"I'm impressed," he murmured.

"Why?"

"The stuff we use to insulate wires would crumble in a *hundred* years and this has lasted thousands. It even protected the silver."

"They don't really know how old this place is," Andy muttered.

"It's still probably old. What do you want to bet that's a transformer? Two of the three wires go into it and the third is attached to its outside, like a ground."

"So?"

"Maybe we can't hack this equipment but we might be able to *turn it on.* Then we push random buttons and see what happens."

"How scientific!"

"All we can do. God, it's getting stuffy in here."

At that, a circular section of wall vanished, and loose gravel poured through the hole.

Andy and Eldon peered through it to see a spot of daylight at the end of a long inclined tunnel.

"Wow!" Wendy said, materializing behind them. "The *octopuses* built this?"

"Probably," Andy smiled.

"We should give them a name," Eldon said.

"In the tradition Allie established," Andy said. "I hereby dub them Squidwards, from *Spongebob Squarepants.*"

"It'll piss Birgit off," Eldon muttered. "So, sure."

✸✸✸

At the edge of the 12th District's Agri-Unit 371, they had gathered for a secret meeting.

The smoke of smoldering torches stung Eakins's eyes.

Their flickering light cast dancing shadows on the cave-walls.

"My name is Tung," the young man said. "That was an amazing speech, Prophet Eakins! We can only hope the Time Lords hear our prayers."

He looked to be twenty-something and had a military build and bearing that belied his ragged farm attire.

"Pleased to meet you," Eakins said, thinking, *Another moron!* "They spoke through me. I can't take credit for it."

"I used to be in the Safety Service."

Eakins's eyebrows shot up.

The people here seem to trust him.

"How did you...?"

"End up here?" Tung chuckled. "It's a long story. I grew tired of terrorizing innocent civilians, so I volunteered for the army."

"Interesting," Eakins said, wondering, *Where's he going with this?*

"They said I tested well," Tung said. "And they put me in the battle of Lake Trasimene."

"The vids of that were ... astonishing," Eakins muttered. "So intense!"

"Yeah, the director made us do twenty takes of the main firefight before he was satisfied."

"It was *staged?*" Eakins said.

"We did two versions, too," Tung smiled. "One where we won, and the other where Europolis won."

"Were there Europolitans ... involved?"

"Of course," Tung said. "Nice fellows. Some of them spoke English."

"So the war is ... is *fake?*"

"All the wars are fake. Good thing, too. Our army couldn't fight its way out of a wet paper bag."

"Did you run away from military service?"

"Not at all," Tung said. "I have a lot more free time now than I ever did in the Safety Service. I have to hone my acting skills."

"What do people in the Safety Service think of you?"

"I'm a war-hero. It's a secret that the army's phony, a *starvation-level* secret."

Chapter 13

Eldon, Derek, and Birgit floated in their spirit-bodies outside a city-block-sized building in a suburb of Los Angeles — in the Origin timeline.
The space suits are in there, Eldon said.
Is this where you kept them? Derek said.
No. They got moved.
They're booby-trapped, Derek said. *When I picture myself entering the building and running time forward, I see an explosion.*
I scanned the guards, Birgit said. *They've been told to never enter the building. One of them, named Frank, asked what to do if they heard someone inside, and his boss said to run like hell.*
Follow me, Derek said. *We'll have a little chat with Renard Moreau. He can fix this.*

***

Ian Roberts joined them.
I put the bone marrow in the furnace like you told me, he said.

Oh, thank you, my dear, Birgit said. *I'm going to do a carbon-fourteen analysis on it.*

The four hovered near the ceiling of a huge conference room in the Senate Office Building. Senators and representatives of Eakins's America First organization had grilled Renard Moreau for three hours with no indication of stopping anytime soon.

A section of the room had been cordoned off for spectators, including Renard's nineteen-year-old daughter, Marie.

Renard asked for a bathroom break.

"Departure from this room *for any reason* constitutes contempt of congress," Senator Mary Rubinstein said. "Tell us again why you replaced Eakins's secret service detail by convicted murderers."

I'm surfing a mile-high tsunami, she thought. *Stay on top or be crushed.*

"I *didn't* replace them; *Eakins* did!" Renard said. "I *opposed* it. I've told you that ninety-three times already."

"We have yet to hear the *truth,* though," Senator Rubinstein said. "Admit you released those men from death row to murder the greatest president of all time!"

"I *couldn't* have," Renard said. "Only a *president* can pardon convicted murderers. Eakins wanted bodyguards who'd overlook his ... nocturnal activities."

"Do *not* repeat those slanders," Senator Rubinstein snapped. "The parents of the *so-called* victims are paying a harsh price for their lies."

Renard urinated where he sat.

He is truly and royally screwed, Ian said.

Can't say I feel much sympathy for him, Eldon said. *He gave the order that killed my security team and my pilot — my friend.*

He sincerely felt we were a threat to the US and the human race, Derek said. *He felt he was doing what had to be done,*

I see that but I still can't forgive him.
It's painful to watch this.

"The constitution..." Renard began.

"Legalistic bullshit!" President Henderson Knox snapped, yanking his signature Desert Eagle .5 pistol from its holster, hefting it in both hands, and waving it around. "By the authority vested in me by the Council of True Patriots, I declare this a *People's* Court."

"Excellent idea," Senator Rubinstein said, thinking, *What the hell is a People's Court?*

People's Court? Birgit said. *That's what they called them during Robspierre's Reign of Terror — in the French Revolution.*

"I wasn't told this would be a trial or given any chance to prepare a defense," Renard said. "I request legal representation."

"In a *People's* court," Mr. Knox said. "We don't allow *lying lawyers* or any of that *I swear, you swear* bullshit. *Common sense* is all any real court ever needs."

Renard tried to call witnesses.

"If they're willing to testify on your behalf," Senator Rubinstein said. "They must be as guilty as you."

"It's time to reach a verdict," President Knox said, thinking *Did you really kill Eakins? If so, you did me a big favor. Doesn't matter. You'll die, soon, and Eakins is gone.*

"Verdict?" Renard said. "There hasn't been anything resembling a trial!"

The room must've shouted something because Senator Rubinstein said, "Guilty by acclamation. What's the sentence?"

The room shouted again.

Mr. Knox handed Senator Rubinstein a slip of paper.

"In three days," Senator Rubinstein read, choking back tears. "You'll be taken to a place of execution and hung by the neck until dead."

Marie Moreau broke down and cried.

"Do you have anything to say for yourself?" President Knox said.

"I deserve to die," Renard said, tearfully regarding his daughter. "Not because I betrayed President Eakins, but because I *served* him. I murdered innocents on his orders. If I'd been a better person and patriot, I would've *killed* him."

"Stop!" Mr. Knox snapped. "You may not turn this sacred proceeding into a soapbox for treason."

You want to rescue him, Eldon said to Derek.

I agree he was a bastard, Derek said. *He tried to do the right thing in the end.*

Don't bring him to Oz, Eldon said. *That's my only request. My only demand.*

Done.

"Where lies and rumors can kill a man who's not allowed to defend himself, *no one* is safe," Renard said. "Keep that in mind, Senator."

Oh, I will, she thought, shouting, "Take him away!"

Shit! Eldon said. *I can think of a plan B but it involves putting us at risk, maybe even getting us killed. We reveal ourselves to some non-Indigos.*

There must be other ways to get space suits, Derek said.

Not easily, Eldon said, hesitating. *OK, fuck it! Follow me!*

❋❋❋

This is the culinary timeline, Derek said.

Exactly, Eldon said.

They hovered in the air in a large conference room with four people in it, one of whom was Culinary Eldon Trask.

The meeting had apparently ended and two of the people left.

"Got a minute?" a man named Amit Chatterji said.

"OK," Culinary Trask said.

Mr. Chatterji launched into a presentation on why his company's optic sensors were better than the ones Trask was using.

"Minute's up," Culinary Trask snapped, turning away from Chatterji and sitting at his desk.

"I've barely begun," Chatterji protested.

Culinary Trask pushed a button on his phone and said, "Susan, please send security and the Hawthorn Police to my office. A man named Amit Chatterji is trespassing."

I've fantasized doing that! Eldon laughed.

After Chatterji fled, Derek, Birgit, Ian, and Eldon materialized in front of Culinary Trask's desk.

He stared at them, his jaw hanging.

Muffled sounds of the factory floor assaulted their ears.

Three large globes on stands stood beside the desk: one of the Earth, one of Mars, and one of Venus. Push-pin-mounted engineering diagrams covered one wall.

"This may take more than a minute," Derek said.

Culinary Trask slowly regarded them, one by one, his eyes widening at the sight of Eldon.

His hands shaking, he summoned his secretary and stammered, "S ... S ... Susan, c... cancel security and the police and c ... clear my schedule for the rest of the day. No, I'm OK. I'm fine. *Really.* Something ... uh something came up."

Two hours later — after many questions, answers, and demonstrations — Culinary Trask walked over to the picture window that overlooked his factory's Wizard rocket assembly area and pressed his forehead against the glass.

"I believe you."

"Fantastic," Derek said.

"I can't sell you any spacesuits, though. We need them all."

"You want to resupply your Mars colony and rescue Greg Jones, who had a heart attack," Derek said.

"How ... ?" Culinary Trask said. "Oh — you're telepathic. Look, I've lost *two whole hours* of precious time listening to your story. It takes months to prepare a Mars launch, but I have two weeks."

"It takes nine months to reach Mars," Eldon said. "Jones will be dead by then. We can do the resupply and rescue *this afternoon.*"

"Mars is *nine light-minutes* away. One hundred and twenty-two million miles."

"We can go in nine minutes," Birgit said. *"Hin und zurück!"*

"There and back," Ian explained.

"Don't be ridiculous."

"Try us," Derek said. "You have something outside pointing to Mars's current location in relation to Earth?"

"I *fired* the idiot who suggested that!" Culinary Trask said. "Waste of time and money."

"Just *great!*" Eldon growled. "Is extracting your head from your anus for *five minutes* too much to ask?"

"You can't talk to him like that," Derek said.

"Of course I can! He's *me* — an obsessive, tunnel-visioned version of me."

"Get out of here!" Culinary Trask shouted.

They vanished.

✳✳✳

They stood outside Space Ventures headquarters on the sidewalk along Galaxy Boulevard. It was a sunny, clear day.

A nearby bus-shelter had a bench.

"That went well," Derek said.

"I have an app on my phone that shows stars and planets,"

Birgit said. "Astro-finder. I can hold up my arm in that direction."

"I want to go!" Eldon said. "You already visited Mars in Origin. Besides, the astronauts there will regard me as their boss."

"OK, but we'll assist in teleporting Greg Jones."

"Try to keep people from sitting on me, " Eldon said, lying on the bus-shelter bench.

He went out-of-body.

Birgit started the Astro-finder app.

It showed a window on a simulated "night sky," or how the sky would look if the sun weren't blotting everything out — with labels naming every planet and constellation.

Birgit rotated her phone until Mars swam into view on the screen.

"Not very accurate," Derek muttered.

Birgit moved her arm until Mars was centered and then she pointed.

Derek also pointed in what he thought was the right direction.

Great! Eldon thought. *They're pointing to places million of miles apart.*

He soared into the spirit world, dazzled by its scintillating colors, and traveled a long distance.

Where the hell am I? he thought.

Allie joined him.

See that tiny translucent disk? she said.

Barely! Is that Mars?

I don't know, but it's worth a closer look.

How do I do that?

Just imagine yourself approaching it, she said.

The disk expanded until it filled their field of view.

Lightly-etched outlines of craters and mountains appeared on it.
Now what?
Now we look for life-forms. Allie said. *Glowing areas.*
They scanned the globe and found many faintly glowing areas nestled in rocks — none looking like a human outpost.
I think this is an asteroid, Allie said. *You went too far.*
There can't be life out here! Eldon said. *There's no atmosphere!*
Not life as we know it. You'd be amazed at where life exists.
If its biology is that different, how do you know it's alive?
The glow they give off is their souls. Anything with a soul is alive.

They moved back toward Earth and spotted another tiny disk.

This time, a close inspection revealed a brightly glowing area consisting of three low buildings nestled in a cliff's shadow.
That has to be it, Eldon said.

He entered one of the buildings and materialized in front of Ellen Morgan and Ricky Steen — two athletic-looking twenty-somethings wearing Space Ventures jumpsuits.

"This is classified at the *highest level*," Eldon said. *"Quantum teleportation."*

He introduced himself to the others and found Greg Jones.
I'll spot for you, Allie said.

Trask attempted to engulf Greg Jones with his spirit-body,

No! Allie said. *You're overlapping an exterior bulkhead. You'll break the seal and kill everyone.*

After several unsuccessful attempts, Eldon gave up and let Derek take over.

✳✳✳

They materialized in Culinary Trask's office, making him leap from his desk and almost fall down.

"Proof that quantum teleportation works," Derek said, indicating Greg Jones. "I suggest you call an ambulance."

Greg looked about wildly.

"Is that what he was told?" Culinary Trask said.

"As *you recall,* when you teleported to the Mars base — that's what you said."

"Oh, of course!" Culinary Trask stammered. "What happened to you is a corporate secret, classified at the highest possible level! It's um ... a *variation* on quantum teleportation. When the paramedics come, your name is Walter ... uh Williams."

"Yes, sir."

"I'll be leaving now," Derek said.

"How ... fast did you ... uh, *we* go?" Culinary Trask said.

"At least thirty times the speed of light."

"Wow!" Greg Jones said.

"I'll consider your ... other request," Culinary Trask said.

✳✳✳

Back at Destiny Beach, Derek lay in bed and visited Kef and Katalluwana.

They had scanned the solar system and concluded that none of the other planets had a technological civilization. Now they were headed out to the nearest other star.

Alpha Centauri, Derek thought. *Four and a half light-years away. I wonder how long it will take them to get there.*

He got up and joined Andy, Llewellyn, Wendy, and Allie on the deck.

"Can you guys survive without us for a week?" Wendy said.

"I think so," Derek said. "The Archies are headed for another star-system. Why do you ask?"

"Travis's mom is going through hell," she said, vanishing.
"Where does she live?" Andy said.
"In Maui, in the Origin timeline," Allie said. "She's staying at her sister's farm."
"Huh?" Andy said.
"Not all our friends became refugees. Some stayed under the radar."
"Travis's parents are going through an ugly divorce?" Andy said.
Travis's father, Kurt, had bitterly opposed his marriage to Wendy. In a heated moment, Travis had used his newly acquired Indigo powers to scan Kurt — and blurt out his mistress's name.
Derek nodded.
"I'm sorry," Llewellyn said. "We didn't mean to violate your privacy."
"Don't worry," Allie said. "We don't think of privacy the way others do."
"Their last name is Howland?" Llewellyn said. "I seem to recall seeing that name on a building in Hawaii once. *Oh!*"
Andy let out a low whistle.
"So, besides the divorce, they lead normal lives?" Llewellyn said.
"As normal as anyone's life is there," Allie said. "We would've had to leave even if they weren't trying to kill us. I don't know how Derek's parents stand it."
"They live in Origin?" Llewellyn said.
"No," Allie said. "They live in a timeline *like* it ... pre-Indigos. We call it Nostalgia. They don't have counterparts there, either."
"Nostalgia?"
"They — mainly Derek's father, Thomas — are trying to rebuild the lives they used to have. They even managed to buy the

exact same house they owned in Boothbay Harbor and decorated it the same way."

"Homebodies," Andy said.

"The images in Thomas's mind," Allie said. "I just *love* them. A beloved pillar of a small, beautiful community — where he raised two magnificent children."

"Is this your *Indigo*-self talking?" Andy said.

"Of course," Allie said. "If I were not an Indigo, I'd have regarded Thomas as nothing but a pompous ass. He used to lecture people constantly."

Andy and Llewellyn laughed.

"I like to think of myself as an artist," Allie said.

"You are," Llewellyn said, gesturing at her painting.

"Derek's parents are the ultimate artists, though," Allie said. "They created a home full of love, and their family was their living artwork. I hope I do as well by Tori and her younger brother as they did with Derek and Wendy."

"The thing is," Andy said. "Children grow up."

"I wish we could have children!" Llewellyn sighed. "I *know* we'd be good parents. The amazing things you could teach them, Andy!"

"We could probably adopt," Andy sighed. "It's a *huge* responsibility."

"Ironic!" Allie said.

"What?" Llewellyn said.

"I relate to people *so much better* now that I'm an *alien*," Allie said. "I see their souls ... their unique places in the universe. I relate to *animals* too. It's amazing."

You guys need to see something, Eldon beamed at them.

✳✳✳

They joined him in the underground chamber in Africa.

A hose running the length of the Wendy's tunnel spouted hot dry air from the surface.

"I didn't mean *all* of you," Trask muttered. "But OK."

He'd rigged a Pincus generator and other circuitry to the alien power cable.

"The inverter is set to sixty hertz, and I ramped up the voltage slowly," he said. "I wish I knew how old this stuff is."

They waited.

Suddenly, lights flickered on the alien console and one of the monitors lit up.

"I'll increase the voltage by ten percent," Eldon said. "So we're not at the bottom operating range."

Eldon gingerly pushed a button on the console and several lights turned on and others turned off. Cryptic symbols appeared on the monitor before them.

"Like the symbols on the plastic sheets," Andy said. "And just as incomprehensible."

"Watch," he said, pushing another button.

A movie sprang to life on the monitor.

It showed a vast city of cloud-piercing cylindrical buildings. Helicopters flew in the distance and two moons hung in the sky, one the size of Earth's and the other tiny.

Without warning, fireballs erupted all over the city and coalesced into glowing mushroom clouds.

The image pulled away from the surface into space — showing the entire planet writhing under a bombardment by asteroids and atomic weapons. Massive spaceships fired on smaller spaceships departing the larger moon, destroying some of them.

The scene shifted.

A spaceship circled a planet that was recognizably Earth. Finally, it approached the Earth and landed in southern Africa.

The landscape differed considerably from Oz's fused-glass

landscape: Although there was a desert, plants flourished and elephants and giant cats roamed the area.

"So the Squidwards were refugees themselves," Allie said.

"The Archies caught up with them here," Andy said.

"I wish I could locate their satellite and rip it to pieces," Eldon muttered.

"A radio direction finder?" Andy said.

"That would make sense if it used radio waves," Eldon muttered. "It's using something much faster than light. Entangled photons maybe."

"An *Ansible!*" Llewellyn exclaimed.

"Ansible?" Andy said.

"Like in sci-fi books. It sends messages instantaneously."

"The damned Archies are no help either," Eldon muttered. "I have yet to find one with any idea how their technology works."

Vittoria appeared in Allie's arms.

"I'll leave you to your research," she said, vanishing.

Chapter 14

Rescuing Renard Moreau was easier than rescuing President Eakins from a execution chamber: his prison cell didn't even have surveillance cameras.

Why are we doing this? Derek wondered. *Aside from his being treated horribly and trying to do the right thing in the end?*

I have a feeling we'll benefit from it, Allie replied.

I have that feeling too, Derek beamed. *Can't argue with a premonition.*

"Ready to leave?" Allie said.

"I've never been more ready in my life!" Renard muttered.

※※※

The three of them appeared on a tree-lined city street in mid-afternoon — the sun a purple orb bravely trying to penetrate a stinking haze.

Derek coughed.

Three-story brownstone buildings with elegant *art nouveau* wrought-iron doors lined the street. Skyscrapers loomed in the distance below a glowering black cloud.

An ornate brass steam-powered bus chugged along, belching clouds of thick black smoke.

"The worst thing about this place is the pollution," Allie said. "They desperately need Pincus generators."

"It looks like New York City," Renard said. "An upscale neighborhood."

"Yes, but it's called Knickerbocker," Allie said. "We hope to make this one of our homes. Oz is our ultimate home, but this will be where we'll go when we're sick of watching grass grow. I'd love to open an art gallery here."

"America is called Columbia in this timeline," Derek said. "They speak English, but probably have local slang."

A horse-drawn carriage with two passengers clopped by, pulling up to one of the buildings. Candles flickered in its polished brass lanterns.

"How strange!" Renard said.

"We don't have any local currency," Allie said, handing him a gold bar stamped 'Credit Suisse,' '1 kilo,' and '999.9.' "But you should be able to pawn this. Afterward, I suggest you go to a haberdashery shop and buy local clothes."

"Haberdashery?" Renard said. "An odd term. I've heard *of* it, but I've never heard anyone *say* it."

"Yes," Allie chuckled. "That's what they call a mens' clothing store here."

"Then go to a public library and read up on this place's history," Derek said. "We'd like to hire you as our local contact. Show us how to survive here."

"Assuming *I* can survive here," Renard muttered.

"It's civilized," Derek said. "A lot more so than Origin. What little we've seen of it implies that. World Wars one and two never happened here."

"Origin?"

"The lunatic timeline we all came from," Derek said. "We call this place Columbia."

"America was *almost* named Columbia," Renard murmured.

"Columbia desperately needs technology," Allie said. "So we could do well here, *all* of us. We'll all probably become wealthy public figures, so your job is to make that feasible."

"What do you mean?"

"Give us fake identities that stand up to scrutiny," Derek said. *"Unlimited* amounts of it."

"Back-filled legends," Renard murmured. "You need new names?"

"No," Derek said. "I don't want to have to remember a new name."

"This place has no Internet or anything like it," Allie smiled. "Documents are paper and getting information involves *talking* ... to actual humans."

"Give me time to get settled," Renard said. "I might need your help in ... placing documents. And stealing them."

"Of course," Derek said.

A naked Vittoria appeared in Allie's arms.

"My God," Renard gasped.

"Hello, honey," Allie said, kissing her.

"She pops up all the time," Derek laughed.

"A daughter who can teleport," Renard mumbled. "Amazing."

"She's a lot less work than I thought she'd be," Allie said. "When she's tired, she teleports to her crib and goes to sleep. I need to feed her now."

Allie and Tori vanished.

"The only thing I'll miss about ... Origin you called it?" Renard said. "Is my daughter Marie."

Derek didn't ask why Renard wouldn't miss his *wife:* She'd conspired with Senator Rubinstein to try and convict him.

"Thanking you seems ... *horribly* inadequate. All I can say is you won't regret this."

"Good luck," Derek said, shaking his hand.

He vanished.

✳✳✳

Derek joined Allie and Tori at their deck on Destiny Beach.

Dense clouds rolled in, and heavy droplets began to pelt them.

They retreated through French doors into their living room and closed the doors behind them.

An archway connected the living room to the dining room, and a concert grand piano stood in a corner opposite the French doors. A thick floral-print area rug covered the cream-colored tile floor, and a long polynesian-themed batik couch occupied the wall opposite the archway. It contrasted with the room's dark green walls.

Tori slept.

Allie wrapped Tori in a shawl, handed her to Derek on the couch, walked over to the piano, and played a soft and haunting Erik Satie melody.

Tori woke.

Her eyes glittering like diamonds, she tried to wave her quivering arms in time to the music as rain beat against the French doors.

Ghost-dancing! Tori beamed at them.

Poop is wonderful, she added, pooping into the shawl. *It feels so good when it comes out.*

Chuckling, Derek put the shawl in the wash and changed her.

You've got to see this, Andromeda Cole beamed at them.

※※※

They and Birgit Fischer joined Andy, Llewellyn, and Eldon Trask in the underground archeology site, making the chamber crowded.

"I seem to have located historical records," Eldon said to them, pushing a button on a console.

The monitor sprang to life and showed a space ship parked on a sandy plain surrounded by huts and tents. Octopuses scrambled around it, operating fork-lift-like machines that unloaded large crates from the spaceship.

"Fast-forward a bit," Eldon said, pushing other buttons.

The scene shifted to one of buildings under construction with many vehicles dashing about.

"A little further," he added.

The scene now showed a small — oddly human-looking — city with a helicopter flying overhead. The scene shifted and showed Squidwards swimming in the ocean and sitting on the beach.

The scene shifted and showed Squidwards meeting hairless apes and offering them food. Another scene showed thousands of human ancestors living around the octopus city.

"Apparently they tried to make friends with early human ancestors," Eldon said. "Fast-forward a little more."

The scene showed Squidwards going about their daily activities with smiling primitive humans following them, carrying things.

"They *enslaved* them?" Allie said.

"No," Derek said. "It looks more like the relation between dogs and their masters. With their hands and intelligence, primitive humans were more useful than dogs."

"I'm sure they'd never evolve *full* intelligence," Birgit said. "They became too domesticated. Those creatures were killing them with kindness."

"The records continue for some fifty years more, and then they stop," Eldon said.

"What do you mean?" Derek said.

"One day, everything's fine," Andy said. "A thriving community of Squidwards and their pet humans. And the next day... Well, there *is* no next day. There aren't any more records. I wish I could decipher their written language. It might explain."

"Someone hit them hard and fast," Derek said. "Probably the Archies. How long ago was this?"

"I've done carbon fourteen analysis of the skeleton's bone m arrow," Birgit Fischer said. "All I can say is it's *at least* fifty thousand years old. Carbon fourteen doesn't work on things older than that."

"You know what's disturbing?" Derek said. "These octopus-creatures escaped their enemies for *fifty years* and *still* got wiped out. The Archies have a long memory."

"Only from a modern perspective," Birgit said. "There was a hundred-years war between England and France. A thirty-years war that bled the German people white. The Shiite and Sunni Muslims have been at each other's throats for a thousand years."

Allie left with Tori.

Chapter 15

I'll treat this like my first overseas assignment, Renard Moreau thought. *When I retired Constantine Iliescu.*

Renard had been so cocky, so stupid then, confident his skills made him invulnerable against a man whose reputation for feeding his enemies' children to hogs had earned him the nickname Butcher of Bucharest.

The assignment had almost ended him.

What strange creatures, these Indigos are, he mused. He marveled at quick and dispassionate way they had pardoned him for the crimes he had committed against them. There was a childlike quality to them.

Summoning a lifetime of trained instincts, he scanned his surroundings for potential threats.

He didn't find any.

The brownstone buildings lining the street had elegant black wrought iron gates in front of their doors. Each building had tiny colored glass tiles embedded in the sidewalk in front of it, spelling out the house-number.

One iron gate looked like a spider web with a grinning iron spider in the lower right.

Another house had what looked like a willow tree in front of it. This turned out to be a green-patinaed copper statue with corroded green copper chains hanging from it.

I know why Allie likes this place. Everything has an artistry to it, an 'unnecessary' elegance.

He walked in the general direction of the distant skyscrapers, coughing as the pollution burned his eyes.

Pedestrians gave him odd stares.

An automobile passed by.

It was enormous — easily twice the size of cars he knew — and had a stack belching black smoke. Polished brass accents contrasted with its gleaming black paint.

He found a shop with the familiar three brass balls in front of it and stepped inside.

❋❋❋

Display-cases lined the dimly-lit room's walls. One held violins, guitars, clarinets, and a large, ornate hammered dulcimer. Another held jewelry, pairs of polished brass goggles, and pocket-watches.

The place seemed deserted.

Renard walked up to a counter and rang a bell next to a cash-register.

A white-haired man pushed through a beaded curtain and staggered to the counter.

"Who the hell are you?" he muttered, looking Renard up and down.

"Someone with gold to sell," Renard replied, plunking the gold ingot onto the counter.

The pawnbroker's eyes widened and he carefully examined the bar.

"Where did you get it?"

"Part of a large inheritance. From Europe."

"I see," the pawnbroker winked. "May I drill a hole in it?"

"Knock yourself out."

"Knock me out?"

"You have my permission to drill a hole."

The pawnbroker rummaged in the back and reappeared with a power drill. He drilled a hole through the ingot and examined the gold-shavings it produced.

He brushed them onto a piece of paper and weighed it.

"I'll give you three thousand for it," he said. "An outright purchase, not a pawn."

"I'll take it."

The pawnbroker counted out thirty purple and red hundred-dollar bills and said, "Give my regards to Black Bart."

"Black Bart?"

The pawnbroker smiled and winked.

❋❋❋

Renard left the pawn shop and continued down Mercer Street.

"My God," Renard exclaimed, spotting a sign that said *Nilus Haberdashery Shoppy*. "They really do call them that."

He went in.

Fabric samples covered the walls and racks of odd coats and pants filled the space.

"Greetings," an obese man said. "Hond Nilus at your service."

He looked like a roly-poly toy that rights itself when pushed over, and strands of his thinning black hair valiantly struggled to cover his balding head.

His hair and mustache glistened with pomade.

Time to change that oil!

"I'm recently arrived from ... France," Renard said. "And I'm looking for Amer..., I mean Columbian clothing."

Technically being from France wasn't a lie: his parents had brought him to America when he was five. He even spoke French, having learned it at the CIA.

"France?" Hond said. "Ah, I've always wanted to travel but forever lacked the time or money. The age-old problem! The one time I had both, the missus declined. Afraid of exploding airships, see? Even though we haven't had an explosion in twenty years. If God meant us to fly, he would have given us wings, she always says. Gets seasick on the ocean, too."

Renard smiled.

"So what do you need? Frock coats, trousers, underbritches, shoes? We have them all."

"Everything. I'd like to look like ... a gentleman. "

"That costs money."

"I have $2000 to spend," Renard lied. "I hope that's enough."

Hond's eyes widened.

"I trust your judgment completely," Renard added. "Pick out whatever you think I need."

"I wish all my patrons were like you!" Hond chuckled.

He measured Renard in a dozen ways and picked out clothes, chatting nonstop the entire time. An hour later and $1571 poorer, Renard left the Nilus Haberdashery Shoppy looking like a citizen of Knickerbocker — in the United States of Columbia.

He straightened the feather in his eight-sided black velvet Christopher Columbus hat, draped his folded black cape over his right shoulder, and wrapped his black leather purse's strap around his body.

I feel like an escapee from a Shakespearian play.

"Sorry, Sir," a ragged man who'd bumped him said. He scraped piles of what looked manure off the street into a large cloth sack.

At least nobody's laughing at me.

"*Black Bart Strikes Again!*" a fourteen year old boy shouted, holding up a sheaf of newspapers — the *Knickerbocker Scrutineer.*

He bought one for five cents.

As Renard tried to read it while walking, the sky darkened — plunging the world into dusk if not total darkness.

He looked up.

An enormous shape blotted out the sun — the Goodyear Blimp times a hundred — bearing the name *LS Luisa, №. 129,* and a globe-logo.

Rows of windows punctured its gray underside, some wide open.

A young couple waved from one of them.

Although the airship reminded him of the 1930's, Renard's newspaper's date was current.

A vibrant world of industry and prosperity. I could make a life here. Not everyone gets to start over.

Renard's stomach growled.

He noticed *Jor's Gustatorium* across the street.

What the hell is a gustatorium? he wondered, looking in the window.

It had people eating so he went in.

It was a standard diner, with a row of round stools in front of a long counter and with coffee machines and a refrigerator full of massive pies and cakes piled high with whipped cream.

Renard sat, putting his purse on the counter.

A waitress named "Meg" handed him a menu and poured

him a glass of water. The menu items had names like *Queen Margot's Complaint* and *The Kaiser's Monocle* with no further explanations.

"Do you have uh ... hamburgers?" he asked.

"Hamburgers, Sir?" she said. "I'm uh ... afraid we don't serve no uh ... German food."

"Sorry," he said. "I just arrived from France, so I'm not familiar with things ... around here."

"*France?*" Meg exclaimed, her eyes widening as she fluffed her hair. "You don't see many foreigners around here. Especially a gentleman like you. My great grandmater was from France."

Meg launched into a lengthy discussion of things she'd heard about France, barely giving Renard a chance to show his ignorance by replying.

At least he spoke French.

He finally ordered pork chops and mashed potatoes.

The headline story involved a 'pirate' named Black Bart robbing First Kingsport Bank in broad daylight. His henchmen also robbed the bank's customers of their cash and jewelry.

He made the police look like incompetent fools. Some regarded him as a folk hero.

Black Bart again? Sounds like an old western.

Aside from the robbery, the paper's front page featured odd international news: Kaiser Johann II condemned the British Empire's crushing a rebellion in southern India; a hundred British warships hovered ten miles outside Rio de Janeiro bay, and President Martin Binder threatened economic sanctions if they attacked.

A section called Potomac Beat reported that the Lakota Sioux Nation's application for statehood had been approved — as the *state* of Lakota — forty-fifth in the US.

Lord Cornwallis, governor-general of British Columbia, called this a 'deliberate provocation'. Three British Columbian cavalry divisions massed along the border.

Cavalry?

"As always," Lord Cornwallis had said. "We are the *Empire's Pointed Sword.*"

Celebrations with firework-displays were scheduled for next week in Potomac and the future Lakota state capital, Laramie.

Allie came out of the ladies' room and sat next to him, startling him.

"You've got a *Phantom of the Opera* thing going on!" she said. *"Love* it! I'll send Derek to Mr. Nilus. I only wish I could find a shop like that for me."

Renard laughed.

"You feel like a freak," she added. "But everyone else thinks you look like a judge or senator."

Allie looked at the menu and ordered *The Kaiser's Monocle.*

"Remind me again why you chose this timeline," Renard said. "I'm not complaining but it seems rather odd."

"I never said," she replied. "This place drew me to itself, like a magnet. And I felt we'd have a good future here."

"I burned through quite a bit of money," Renard said.

"We don't pinch pennies. And an elegant image opens doors."

She handed him another gold bar.

Renard's eyes widened and he shoved it into in his purse.

"It'll give you some walking-around money," she said. "If you can figure out how to turn it into cash. Probably not at a crooked pawnshop."

Renard opened the newspaper to the financial section.

"At least Wall Street is still called that," he said.

The Financial section had two pages of conventional-looking stock listings. He found an ad for Matheson and Silver, Purveyors of Precious Metals.

"Gold is valuable here," he said. "But there's always the..."

"Provenance question," Allie interrupted. "Proving that you're not doing money-laundering or something like that."

"Could you come with me, when I try to sell this gold? Scan people?"

"Sure."

Ten minutes later, Meg served their meals.

The *Kaiser's Monocle* turned out to be an egg poached in chicken noodle soup and served in it.

They ate.

"How do you like your food?" Meg asked.

"Best *Kaiser's Monocle* I ever had!"

"It's really good," Renard said. "Is is organic?"

"I... I guess so, Sir," Meg muttered. "Uh... it's not metal or glass."

I've got to watch what I blurt out, Renard thought.

Allie laughed.

When they finished, Renard paid and left a generous tip.

"Meg," he said. "Do you know where we can get a taxi?"

"Taxi?" she muttered. "I don't know no French words, Sir."

"Cab?" Allie volunteered.

"Oh, a *cab*. You see them in the streets sometime. Not around here so much. I can call one for you."

"Thanks!" Allie said.

They left.

❋❋❋

After they waited in front of the diner for fifteen minutes, a horse-drawn carriage pulled up.

The driver was a middle-aged lady wearing a voluminous blue dress and a hat covered with what looked like fresh flowers.
"Someone call for a cab?" she said.
"That would be us," Renard said.
They climbed aboard and spent the next half hour riding through the tree-lined streets, as the driver Edna Millay complained constantly about calls to ban horses from city streets.
"Unsanitary, my ass," she growled. "We've been together a lotta years, Dobbins and I. What'll we do?"
"We've got to start a foundation to help people like you," Allie said. "When we get settled."
They merged onto a bigger road, and a steam-powered car cut them off.
"Beef-brained maggot-pie!" Edna yelled.
They reached the East River.
"I'm from France," Renard said. "Is that Manhattan Island?"
"Yes," Edna replied. "We're going to cross the Manhattan Bridge."
So that's what they call the Brooklyn Bridge, Renard thought.
"Ah, the City is still the mighty City," Allie breathed like the true New Yorker she was, as they crossed the bridge. Dozens of boats of all varieties and sizes plied the river as an airship drifted overhead.
It was the *LS Mercedes,* № 76.
Manhattan's buildings formed a man-made cliff lining the water's edge and stretching to the horizon.
A large sign atop a cylindrical building said *Ellis Hippodrome.*
"Is that a *racetrack?*" Renard said. "In *Manhattan?*"
"My dearly departed Hank's home away from home," Edna sighed. "Tragically, his passion for the ponies was forever un-

requited. On Saturday mornings, like clockwork, mystery bags and eggs. Then off to the Hippo. Evening come, we'd be in the morbs and dragging our feet."

"Mystery bags?" Renard whispered to Allie.

"Sausages."

"In the morbs?" he whispered

"Sad or depressed. I guess from the word morbid."

In lower Manhattan, the carriage negotiated concrete canyons between high rises that almost closed off the sky.

∗∗∗

A half hour later, they entered the Wall Street offices of Matheson and Silver.

Since Allie's attire elicited stares from the clerks and others, Renard took the lead.

He presented the gold bar to an elderly, balding clerk in a white shirt with ribbon-armbands who examined it carefully using a magnifying glass.

The clerk disappeared into the back offices.

Ten minutes later, he reappeared with a middle-aged, emaciated-looking man in a pinstripe suit with a short trim beard who introduced himself as Daniel Silver.

"I thought I knew all the European metal men," he said. "Never heard of *Credit Suisse,* though. Are they based in Zurique?"

"We're not sure," Allie replied. "The ingots are part of a ... substantial inheritance."

"Fascinating," Mr. Silver said. "I'm afraid we'll have to assay it. There's a $100 fee for that, payable in advance and refundable on our verification of its purity."

"Of course," Renard said.

Mr. Silver produced a legal document.

"This states that you consent to our melting down and assaying the ingot," Mr. Silver said. "Something that will consume a small portion of it."

Renard and Allie both signed it.

"Excellent," Mr. Silver said. "This will take fifteen to twenty minutes."

After Renard paid, they both accepted a secretary's offer of coffee and waited.

"Switzerland is part of *France?*" Allie said. "That's what I picked up from him."

"We *really* have to learn this place's history," Renard said. "I'll hit the libraries. As soon as I get an apartment and bank account. Are they ... suspicious of us?"

"A little but they don't care," Allie said. "Money laundering is not a thing here — and melting down the ingot hides its origin."

"If we were dishonest..." he muttered.

"Yes, but we aren't. And as a certain President told you..."

"Don't shit where you live," Renard said. "So you were listening in on that. The fact is, I'd *love* to live here."

Allie smiled.

Mr. Silver returned and flashed them a thumbs up.

"Your mysterious gold bar is every bit as pure as its label claims," he said. "I've never seen such purity before. For that matter, I never heard of the term 'kilo'. Do you know what it means?"

Allie smiled and shrugged.

The gold merchant paid them $18,121 for the bar. Allie and Renard each took $3000 in cash and left the balance in an account at Matheson and Silver.

"My husband's an inventor," Allie said. "We plan to finance his work with gold bars. I also want to open an art gallery."

"Keep us in mind," Mr. Silver said, shaking their hands again. "It has been a distinct pleasure doing business with you."

They left.

✻✻✻

"Mr. Silver thinks we were in the military!" Allie exclaimed, as they strolled down Wall Street.

"Why?"

"The way we talk. Our sentences are short and to the point. He likes that."

"Really?"

"Our timeline saw two world wars," Allie said. "I guess it rubbed off on us. He's *burning* with curiosity about our gold bar. He's going to be on the phone all... Oops! Tori's about to join us. So long for now."

Chapter 16

At the *Kula Alii* Farm in Origin, Wendy and Travis sipped lemonade on Taka Matson's lanai with her and Travis's mother, Grace.

Grace Howland was a petite, forty-something Japanese-American woman with a kind face who wore an ankle-length, floral-print *muu-muu* that looked like a cotton nightgown.

Grace's older sister, Taka, owned the farm. Wrinkles covered her weathered, dark-brown face, and she wore a light green blouse, khaki shorts, and work-boots.

They sat in wicker chairs around a glass, wicker-framed table. The remnant of fast food hamburgers and French fries littered the table next to Taka's pith helmet.

The lanai wrapped around her sprawling farmhouse, with its low sloped roof and thin, algae-covered walls.

A dirt road ran up to the lanai, bisecting fifty acres of three-foot-high Maui onion plants in neat rows.

Flowering plumeria trees surrounded the lanai, providing shade — indeed almost cutting off the sun and cloudy sky. Black mynah birds perched in the trees, swooping down and stealing fries when people weren't looking.

Maui's iconic mist-shrouded extinct volcano, Haleakala — "House of the Sun" — soared in the distance.

"Ready to harvest section three," a thirty-something Hawaiian man said to Taka. "I've got eight pickers."

"Good."

After he left, Taka said, "That's Jab Kekoa, my foreman."

"This is harvest season?" Wendy said.

"It's always harvest season in Hawaii. Different sections at different times."

"It's such a *miracle*," Grace said, shaking her head.

"Really?" Taka said.

"I wish Travis and Wendy were here with me ... and then I run into them ... like magic. I didn't even know you guys were *in* the Islands."

Wendy smiled.

"Can these mynah birds talk?" she said, pointing to the black birds in the trees. "I heard they talk better than parrots."

"Not dese *wild* birds," Taka chuckled, thinking, *Except by the Kuakini house down the road, where they spew profanities so vile mothers keep their kids away. Which suits Old Man Kuakini just fine.*

Travis and Wendy laughed.

"So," Grace said to Wendy. "You're giving me grandchildren?"

"A boy and a girl," Travis replied. "We're naming our daughter Kaiulani, after the princess. Our son will be named Roger."

"Speaking of *keikis*," Wendy said, briefly shutting her eyes. "My mom just gave birth to my new baby brother, Kile."

"*Some ono!*" Travis said. "We should visit them."

He beamed congratulations at Wendy's mother, Liz.

"Oh?" Grace said.

"It went as smoothly as Tori's birth," Wendy said.

Grace and Taka stared at them, confused.

"There's something we should've told you long ago," Wendy said.

Twenty minutes later, Taka stared at them in shock and Grace said, "So you *are* aliens! Eakins said you're monsters."

"Like *Invasion of the Body Snatchers!*" Taka said.

"No," Wendy said.

"Eakins is *one liar kine!*" Travis growled.

After a poisonous silence, Taka said, "What's it like on your planet?"

"This is our planet!" Travis said. "We grew up here and never lived anywhere else."

Shouldn't we tell them about timelines? Wendy beamed at him.

No way they'll understand, Travis replied.

"Uh, you were worried about your divorce hearing, mom," Wendy said, trying to change the subject. "That's one reason we came. When is it?"

"Tomorrow morning. The Howland building."

"Isn't that in Honolulu?" Wendy said. "Got an early flight?"

"We don't need to be there," Taka said. "My nephew, Spencer, went to the UH law school and just passed the bar. He'll handle it."

"For something that important," Wendy said. "You should be there. People will think you don't care."

"Too late to book a plane," Grace sighed.

"We can get you there tomorrow morning," Wendy said.

"It take not even five minutes!" Travis said.

Grace and Taka looked at each other and timidly nodded.

✴✴✴

That evening, Wendy and Travis treated Grace and Taka to dinner at *Mokie's Grinds,* a seafood restaurant on Lahaina Harbor.

The view was breathtaking.

As they finished their *Broke Da' Mouth* specials, night fell and fog rolled in.

"Never used to see fog," Taka mused. "Or lightning. Or hurricanes. Keola Kekepania's *kahuna* said it mean the world is ending."

"You guys?" Grace said, looking at Wendy and Travis pointedly.

"Blaming that on us?" Wendy said. "No! It's global warming. Hurricane *Iniki* happened *years* before we became Indigos."

Wendy gazed up at the mist-shrouded full moon.

"I remember," she whispered. "So ... so long ago, but I remember. When the moon looked like that..."

"We would say 'she is putting on her furs'," Travis murmured.

"It's really you, Ragna?" Wendy said.

"Your alien name?" Grace said.

"No," Wendy murmured. "A past life ... long ... long ago. We were hunters. We hunted mammoths ... deer ... anything we could find. Once we even killed a cave bear."

"You were our best hunter, Krakar," Travis said.

"It got me killed," Wendy said, beaming, *This is getting too weird for them.*

Yes, we should tone it down.

They had dessert.

✸✸✸

At seven in the morning, they stood on the walkway off the front porch.

Terrified, Grace Howland and Taka Matson wore their finest Sunday *muu-muus* and sandals.

Travis wore an aloha shirt, shorts, and flip-flops. Wendy wore a voluminous *muu-muu* that hung over her pregnant belly.

"Will it hurt?" Grace said.

"No!" Wendy said. "It might help if you close your eyes and count to five."

They landed in a large room with wooden walls, floor, and many tables with upside-down chairs on them. To the right was a bar with beer-taps and pizza ovens.

"This is the Howland building?" Taka said.

"No," Travis said. "It's *da kine* pizza place by U of Hawaii."

"It's easier to teleport to a place where we've been before," Wendy said. "Now we get out of here before Sayako shows up. She's *da kine* owner."

After looking around for a few minutes, they found a back door they could open.

It led to an alley with a stinking dumpster covered with four-inch-long cockroaches.

"*Pilau!*" Taka muttered, holding her nose.

"I'm never having pizza here again!" Travis said.

"I feel like a criminal," Grace said.

"I'm sorry, mom," Wendy moaned. "We should've found a better place to land."

"No time, *ke aloha*," Travis said.

The alley opened out onto Dole Street.

Wendy called Aloha Taxi.

✳✳✳

After their taxi spent twenty minutes battling rush-hour traffic in congested central Honolulu, they arrived at the ten-story Howland Building.

As one of Hawaii's wealthiest families, the Howlands owned most of the state's undeveloped land and collected land-leases from half the population.

Their building towered over the adjacent Iolani Palace — the Hawaiian monarchs' last residence.

"We're early," Grace said, checking her watch.

"Let's have breakfast," Wendy said, pointing to the *Island Dreams Cafe* on the building's ground floor. "I need my coffee. Even though it makes the *keikis* ... active."

She patted her pregnant belly.

They went in.

✻✻✻

They took a table by the crowded cafe's picture windows onto Richard Street and sipped Kona coffee.

Wendy plowed through a plate of eggs over easy, hash-browns, toast, and a short stack of pancakes.

"I'm eating for three," she said.

"You seem like ... normal people," Taka murmured.

"We *are* normal people," Wendy said. "Normal people who can read minds and teleport. And do other stuff."

"*Mami*," Travis said. "We don't need Howland money. They can shove it up their fat *okoles!*"

"It's your money too. You're a Howland. You need it for college and your babies."

"Not really, mom," Wendy said. "The Evans family has lots of money, and we look out for our own. Which includes Travis and you guys."

"Hey!" Taka said, standing. "There's Spencer!"

She ran out the door and accosted a disheveled twenty-something man in an aloha shirt and sandals carrying a bundle of file-folders.

He almost fainted at the sight of Taka.

"Come," Taka said, all but dragging a terrified Spencer into the cafe. "Meet my sister and her family."

"You're really not supposed to be here," he said to Grace.

"Why not? The proceedings are about me."

"I *represent* you, *sistah*. Leave every*ting* to me!"

"I want to see my favorite nephew in action," Taka said, patting his arm. "I'm so proud!"

"Got to go now, aunty," he said. "The proceedings start in five minutes."

"You said they began at *nine*," Taka said.

"It ... uh got ... um changed."

"Let's go up with him," Wendy said. "We can't let him out of our sight."

Travis asked for the check.

※※※

In the elevator, Grace asked Wendy what was happening.

"I read his mind," she whispered. "He's working for Matheson, Ford, Baron, and Howland."

"That's the Howland Trust's law firm. He's working for *us*. We paid him."

"You should get your money back. They promised him a partnership if he signed the release forms *without* reading the prenup."

"Don't believe her," Spencer mumbled.

"Partnership?" Grace said. "I'm not an expert but doesn't it take *years* for a lawyer to become a partner?"

Taka was at the verge of tears.

※※※

A large polished *koa* wood table dominated the twenty- by forty-foot conference room. Picture windows onto Richard street overlooked downtown Honolulu and perfectly framed a distant Diamond Head.

Three white-haired men sat at the table's far end: Luther Howland and his brother Kurt — Travis's father — and Matthew Jamison, a senior partner of Matheson, Ford, Baron, and Howland.

Luther Howland was the Howland Trust's managing trustee.

A law clerk named Dennis Stendhal and a junior attorney in the firm named Abe Simpson sat to their right.

The two Howlands wore faded aloha shirts, shorts, and flip-flops — and Matthew and the other attorneys wore gray pinstripe suits.

Exotic attire in Hawaii.

A legal secretary in a navy-blue pants suit and a wizened, white-haired stenographer named Jessie Saganami in a floral-print dress sat to their left.

Jessie set up her stenotype machine.

Banker-boxes of legal files covered the table, with two more in a wheeled rack that looked like a rolling suitcase cart.

What the hell are they doing here? Luther thought. *Spencer was supposed to keep them away.*

"I have power of attorney," Spencer said. "I can sign the release forms right now."

"Only if Grace is *absent*," Wendy said. "Since she's here, your power of attorney doesn't apply."

Luther glared at her, and tears formed in Spencer's eyes.

A disheveled and breathless Travis stumbled through the door.

"I hope I gave enough tip," he said. "I never know how much is right."

"I read their minds," Wendy whispered to Grace, indicating

the people at the other end of the room. "There's something wrong with the prenup. You want to do the honors, Travis?"

"Sure," he said. *"Mami, I'm going to tell some lies now but we will win."*

Grace faintly nodded, putting her arm around a weeping Taka.

"OK," Travis began, standing. "I studied the *da kine* prenuptial agreement *very carefully."*

"You?" Luther laughed, as Kurt's jaw dropped. *You never studied anything in your life.*

Oh you delicious surfer boy, Jessie thought, typing on her machine. *I could just eat you up.*

Travis shot her an anxious glance.

Hope it's quick, Matthew thought. *I tee off at one. No way this ape knows about the 1925 contract.*

Travis paused as he carefully scanned Matthew Jamison, Abe Simpson — and his father.

"It was based on a prenuptial agreement drawn up in 1925," he said.

Matthew Jamison let out a long sigh and mopped his brow with a handkerchief.

"... for the wedding of Travis Howland to Lucy Maitland Channing," Travis continued. "My namesake was a playboy — they said he was wilder than King Kalakaua."

Oh baby, I could rip those shorts off you with my teeth, Jessie thought, grinning at Travis and licking her lips as she typed.

He fought the urge to flee.

King Kalakaua? Abe Simpson thought. *Oh — the so-called Merry Monarch.*

"The 1925 agreement was referenced without modifications or addenda," Travis said, scanning the attorneys for the exact wording. "At Lucy's insistence, it had a morality clause. If her husband *publicly flaunted* his infidelities ... the agreement became *null and void*."

"Publicly flaunted?" Kurt muttered. "What does that even mean?"

"*Da kine* contract *said* what it means. It means cheating in public, and a major newspaper reporting it. Dad — you took Leilani Kam to this year's Hibiscus Banquet. The Honolulu Star-Advertiser had a *picture* of you two. You even *told them* you were trading mom in for Leilani. You called her a younger model."

Did Wilfred mention that damned morality thing? Kurt wondered of the attorney who'd drawn up the prenup. It was too late to ask: Wilfred Chang had passed away three years ago.

"We're invoking *da kine* morality clause," Travis concluded.

Well played! Abe Simpson thought, nodding in admiration. *In his shoes, I'd demand half the estate as a starting position.*

"Mom gets half the Howland estate," Travis added.

A stunned silence followed.

"I warned you about this, Luther," Mr. Jamison muttered. "That demand is unsupportable, of course. We'll come up with a counter offer."

"Shut the *fuck up!*" Luther snapped, stunning everyone.

The stenographer looked up at Mr. Jamison inquiringly, and he shook his head.

"So the *piece of meat on a surfboard* grew a *brain*," Luther roared.

Travis lunged across the table, and Wendy and Grace restrained him, shouting, "He's not worth it!"

Kurt came over and shook Travis's hand.

"I'm ... I'm proud of you, son. You remind me of that Kipling poem that goes, uh ... I don't remember how it goes.

But it ends 'now you're a *man* my son'. Sorry I missed your wedding."

"You didn't just miss it, dad. You refused to come."

Kurt rubbed his face and nodded.

"You've won this battle, Grace," Luther growled. "But you've lost the war. Here's *my* counter offer: Sign the release forms within twenty-four hours!"

"Or what?" Travis said.

"You'll see what," Luther muttered.

"Telling the *newspapers* you're trading me in for a *younger model?*" Grace sobbed. "I'm not signing *anything!*"

Mr. Jamison and the other law firm representatives packed up their boxes of documents.

"I guess this is over for now," Mr. Jamison said, shaking Travis's hand and thinking, *You have the makings of a good lawyer.*

"Do I get a partnership?" Spencer said. "I did everything you asked."

"Partnership?" Mr. Jamison sneered. "We wouldn't hire you to *clean toilets."*

Taka slapped Spencer's face.

"Grace Howland," he continued. "We'll reopen negotiations when you've acquired *proper* legal representation."

"No negotiations!" Luther said. "The Howland Trust has never been split before, and it won't be on my watch."

"Let's leave," Wendy said.

"Do we have to go back to *da kine* pizza place?" Grace said.

"No, mom," Travis said.

"Twenty-four hours!" Luther repeated. "Or else!"

As they rode the elevator down, Travis examined it carefully and observed, "No video cameras."

They vanished.

***

They materialized in front of Taka's farmhouse. None of the farm hands were around.

It was raining so they went into her dining room and sat around the table.

"What do I tell Spencer's mother?" Taka sobbed.

"He's young," Wendy said. "He learned a painful lesson. Maybe it'll make him a better person."

"What'll happen now?" Taka moaned.

Wendy shut her eyes briefly and said, "The lawyers are discussing counter offers."

"You can read their minds from *here?*" Taka said.

"Once we meet people, we can read their minds from *anywhere,*" Wendy said.

"I see why they're so afraid of you," Grace said. "Why did you ask for so much, Travis?"

He explained.

"They are *sweating!*" Grace laughed. "After the *hell* they put me through, I *love* it."

"What are they ... saying?" Taka said. *"Da kine* lawyers, I mean?"

"They can offer you money, *mami,*" Travis said. "Millions. And give you your land, Taka."

"So I could own my farm *fee simple?*"

"Yeah," Wendy muttered. "Like every farm on *Earth* except in Hawaii."

"Come on," Grace laughed. "What else are they saying?"

"Luther doesn't want to give an *inch,*" Travis said. "It's his pride. He's also afraid of other lawsuits. Other ex-wives and mistresses."

"Maybe you should just sign the papers," Wendy said. "This

could get a lot uglier than it already is. We don't need their money."

"Oh I feel better than I have in *ages!*" Grace exclaimed. "I owe it all to you two *wonderful kids.* If you hadn't come along, Spencer would've sold me out. I'd never know any better."

Taka served iced tea and leftover spam fried rice for lunch.

In the middle of lunch, Travis said, "Now dad reminded them that you're pregnant, *ke aloha.* He said we may be the only people keeping the Howland name going."

"Oh, the precious Howland name!" Grace muttered. "The cousins have no time for *keikis.* Too busy being rich."

"You'll inherit anyway, Travis," Taka said. "Why so much *pilikia?"*

"I don't know, aunty."

Chapter 17

Andy paced the Squidwards' chamber, while Llewellyn examined the electronic consoles.

"I don't know what I can contribute," Andy said. "My skills are completely unsuited to this job. They need a linguist and computer specialist."

She pushed a blue button on the console.

"We need Eldon," Llewellyn said.

"His last idea was pushing buttons at random," Andy said. "Like monkeys pounding on typewriters."

"The ones that type out Shakespeare's works?"

"I may not be a rocket scientist, but I can punch buttons as well as the next monkey."

Andy pushed another button.

The screens flashed and filled with symbols like those inscribed on the tunnel wall.

"Well," Andy said, examining them carefully. "They don't mean a damned thing to me."

She snapped a picture of the screen with her phone.

Then she pushed the button again and the symbols changed.

She pushed it again and the screens flickered and rapidly flashed a pages and pages of symbols. Occasionally, pictures or diagrams appeared on them instead of symbols.

"Shit!" Andy exclaimed, trying to record a movie on her phone.

Her phone's battery died.

Llewellyn pushed other buttons and, if anything, the pages flashed more rapidly.

After twenty minutes, the screens went blank.

"My eyeballs are fried," Andy said, "and I've got to recharge my phone."

They returned to their house on Destiny Beach.

✵✵✵

Andy went upstairs to their bedroom, while Llewellyn changed into a bathing suit and went swimming.

Andy closed the shades, lay on the bed, and drifted off to sleep.

She floated above the bed in an out-of-body state and marveled at the shifting colors of the spirit-world.

Professor Fischer joined her.

How can I see anything? Andy thought. *My eyes are closed in a darkened room.*

You're not seeing light, Birgit replied. *An organism in an environment must have sense-organs that allow it to experience its environment.*

Huh?

The soul is an organism and its natural environment is the spirit-world. It experiences the spirit world in several ways. One is like seeing, and another is like hearing. When we're in our physical bodies, our eyes and brain translate light-waves into impulses the soul experiences as seeing.

I see colors that don't correspond to any standard... colors, Andy said. *I don't have names for them.*

I've counted over three thousand of these exotic colors so far, Birgit said. *Our inner eyes respond to some sort of energy that comes in many more flavors than physical light. Look directly up.*

It's a tiny kaleidoscope, Andy said. *Beautiful!*

That's the sun, Birgit said. *You're seeing through your house's roof.*

It doesn't hurt my eyes at all! Andy exclaimed.

Look at the dots around it.

What about them?

They're stars — not blotted out by the sun. Physical eyes obey the laws of optics; inner eyes are not so constrained.

Llewellyn joined them.

A dolphin named Squee-eet told me they were battling a tiger shark in the area, she muttered. *Then it started raining.*

It rains every day here, Andy said. *Wait — how the hell do dolphins fight sharks?*

Very well! Llewellyn said. *They rammed its gill-slits from opposite directions. This ruptured major arteries, and it's bleeding to death. Now they're pushing it out to sea so it won't attract more sharks.*

As always, Birgit said. *Brute strength is no match for intelligence.*

Anyway, Andy said. *I think I burned out the Squidward electronics.*

I hate that word, Birgit muttered. *We should come up with a proper scientific term.*

I wish we'd captured the images, Llewellyn said.

Andy tried to recall the images from the screens, they appeared floating in front of them.

Wow, Andy, Llewellyn said. *That's all 12,051 of them! How did I know how many there were?*
It just looks like 12,051 images, Birgit said. *Ganz fantastisch!*
There are seventeen distinct symbols, Andy said. *If we read each screen from left to right and top to bottom...*
And pick the first two symbols, Llewellyn said. *That pair appears forty-one times. Which is what you'd get by sheer chance.*
It's incredible, Andy said. *How we can count these... combinations... instantly. It's as if we're supercomputers.*
They continued scanning the screen-images with different symbol-combinations. Each combination occurred between thirty-eight and forty-two times — implying randomness.
So that's not how to read them, Andy finally said. *How about up and down?*
That turned out to be more promising: some symbol-combinations occurred hundreds of times and others not at all — implying coherent patterns.
In the end, they decided the screens should be read bottom-to-top and right-to-left.
I see thousands of patterns here, Andy said. *All we need is a tiny clue and everything will fall into place.*
Eldon might make something of the diagrams, Professor Fischer said.

✸✸✸

With Eakins wedged beneath a false floor, they had been traveling all night in covered carts bouncing along rutted roads.
The stench was unbearable.
Jeeter had insisted that a manure wagon was less likely to be searched.
Five rallies in five days, Eakins thought. *Grueling, but I'm still alive.*

The cart slowed.

Another damned checkpoint! Can't wait to get into a bed.

"Citizen's Welfare 116743-65367," a voice said. "Stone-Bound to sector 9 and on assignment to sector 10. For harvest."

"Yes, your Honor."

He's scanning Jeeter's fake barcode, Eakins thought, hoping the Safety Service officer wouldn't notice the tape covering Jeeter's barcode that contained the new one.

Eakins recalled the four levels of binding: Stone, iron, copper, and wood. Each limited the bound person's travel privileges to varying degrees. Stone allowed one to travel to adjacent agricultural regions but never a city.

What a pathetic world. Got to get out of here.

After a few more minutes, the voice said, "Authorized. Hail Sacred Leader."

"Hail Sacred Leader," Jeeter repeated.

The cart continued on its bumpy way.

After another hour, the cart stopped and Jeeter pulled up the false floor, freeing Eakins.

A tall, wiry man with long sideburns stood beside Jeeter.

He wore a loose gray tunic, baggy gray pants held up by rope belt, and cone-shaped hat.

"Dale Grogan, your host for tonight."

The man knelt at Eakins's feet and muttered, "I am unfit to wash your feet, Holiness."

"Rise, son of the world," Eakins said, and the man stood. "Freedom awaits."

"Freedom awaits," Dale repeated.

They ushered Eakins into a small room lit by oil lanterns with a charcoal grill in one corner, a table, and a large straw bed in the back. Dale's wife cooked, and two children stood beside the bed staring at Eakins solemnly.

"What angelic children!" Eakins breathed.

He walked over to them and stroked their cheeks with the back of his right hand.

Mustn't shit where I live! he thought, jerking his hand back as if stung. *I'd give anything to get back home, to be president again!*

After a small supper and prayers, Eakins slept on the Grogan family's communal bed while they slept on the dirt floor.

Chapter 18

Derek, Allie, and Eldon teleported to Culinary Trask in his bedroom.

Drawn curtains darkened the nearly empty room, which stank of urine and sweat. Its furnishings consisted of a chair, a desk-lamp on the floor, and a mattress covered with sheets and a blanket — also on the floor.

Culinary Trask lay there.

Blood from his wrists soaked the sheets.

"Leave me alone, you bastards!" he moaned. "You made my life-work *irrelevant!* You made *me* irrelevant!"

Chloe appeared.

"You disgust me!" Eldon yelled. "You're a distillation of every neurosis I ever had!"

"How can you say that?" Chloe snapped, kneeling and kissing Culinary Trask. "This poor man's in *agony*. If you can't be constructive, *leave*."

"Yeah," Allie said.

"He's *me!* A twisted version of me. If he was a stranger, it wouldn't bother me half as much,"

"Then show compassion for yourself," Derek said.

"I can't even *kill* myself properly," Culinary Trask sobbed. "If I had, you could've just taken over my life."

"Believe it or not, I have a life of my own," Eldon said.

Allie glared at him.

"Dear sweet Eldon, remember Matthew 11:28," Chloe murmured, stroking Culinary Trask's face. "Come unto Me all ye that labor and are heavy laden, and I will give you rest."

"I see it in your mind, Mr. Trask," Derek said. "Years of the most complex engineering imaginable. The countless near misses and explosions."

"You know, he has a meeting at two," Eldon said.

"Take it for him," Chloe said. "Do something constructive."

Eldon vanished.

"Who *are* you?" Culinary Trask said, looking at Chloe.

"A friend," she replied with tears in her eyes. "A dear friend."

"Just leave me alone," he moaned, burying his head in the pillows. "I'll call the *cops.*"

Derek closed his eyes and imagined all versions of himself — a universe of Derek Evanses, pulsating with life-force — living in an infinite number of timelines. Then he imagined all this energy focused on Culinary Trask, filling every corner of his body — bathing him in life-force.

Culinary Trask's spirit-body briefly glowed brighter than the sun.

"Huh?" he mumbled, lifting up his head, blinking, and looking around.

"Come on, buddy," Derek said. "Let's clean you up."

Urine had soaked through his pajamas and the mattress.

✼✼✼

They helped Culinary Trask off the mattress and into the bathroom. Its pale blue walls and marble floor framed an elaborate shower with twenty jets that sprayed from all directions.

Allie vanished briefly and reappeared with two rolls of gauze and betadine, and they cleaned and bandaged his wrists in the blue marble sink.

Chloe handed Derek underwear, a sweat shirt, and sweat pants, and left while Culinary Trask changed into them.

***

They returned to the bedroom.

"I feel a *lot* better!" Culinary Trask muttered. "I can't *believe* how good I feel. But there's no goddamn reason for it!"

"Why?" Chloe asked, beaming, *I saw what you did for him, Derek. Why isn't it working?*

He has free will. He has decided that launching rockets is his sole reason for living.

"My life's work is still *ruined!*" Culinary Trask said. "You guys come along and teleport."

"We had to save Greg Jones," Allie said. "Speaking of him, it looks as though he'll pull through. They're closing up his chest now. He won't be in any shape for space travel."

"Thank God."

"We can make you one of us," Chloe said. "You'd have our ability to teleport."

"That doesn't help me a *bit!*" he moaned. "I want to sell launch services and put colonies on planets."

"Study *yourself* teleporting," Derek said. "Something *we've* never done. You might learn how to build a teleportation machine."

"Really?"

"Your mattress and sheets are goners," Allie said. "I'll put them in the trash."

"No!" Culinary Trask shouted. "People are always stealing my garbage."

"Yes," Chloe nodded. "My Eldon had that problem."

"*Seriously?*" Allie said.

"Investigative reporters, corporate spies, *foreign* spies..." Culinary Trask said. "You name it."

"Those idiots call themselves garbologists," Chloe said.

"I threw away a memo on Comsys flow sensors," Culinary Trask continued. "And the next day it was a lead story in *Aerospace Perspectives*. I hadn't told *anyone*. Nowadays, I throw away *phony* memos, and they *always* turn up on the Internet."

"Alright!" Allie said. "I'll bury them on Oz. Incidentally, how would *you* like to visit, Eldon? You'd have some really beautiful beaches all to yourself."

"You'd *like* that wouldn't you?" Culinary Trask snapped. "Stash me where I'm incommunicado."

"Suit yourself."

Allie walked over to the urine- and blood-soaked bed and shut her eyes.

It vanished with her.

"When our Eldon learned about teleportation, it upset him too," Derek said.

"What'd he do?"

"He took it as a challenge and studied the *crap* out of quantum mechanics. He even hired professors at UC Berkeley and Stanford. Then everything went to hell."

"I don't believe what you said about Eakins!"

"I could take you to Origin," Derek muttered. "There's a kill-order on us, but it takes people a few minutes to recognize us."

"You're wanted by the police?"

"No," Chloe said. "A kill-order's different. So-called *patriots* are told to shoot us on sight, and Eakins gives them presidential pardons. Killing us is still illegal."

"Most police are *opposed* to the kill-order," Derek said. "Except for the Eakins supporters."

Culinary Trask numbly stared at them and shook his head.

"People are getting shot every day," Derek said. "Some don't look anything like us."

✳✳✳

Culinary Trask put on shoes and socks, and they went into the living room — made cavernous by the almost complete absence of furniture.

A chair stood in one corner and a pile of books and papers covered another — next to a lamp on the floor.

Walls were off-white and the two sets of French doors led out to an empty deck and wilted garden.

"I always dreamed of seeing an elegant Beverly Hills house!" Derek muttered. "Who's your gardener?"

"I don't like strangers poking around. When I moved in, I got rid of the gaudy, overstuffed furniture. I *hate* distractions!"

"There's nothing personal here," Chloe muttered. "Family photos, pictures of friends. Art."

"I have no time for that bullshit!" Culinary Trask snapped.

"I could decorate this place for you," Chloe said. "I'd love to."

"Short meeting!" Eldon said, popping into view, making the other Trask yelp. "Everything's on track for a launch in two weeks. I really love how you've organized your company. It's a well-oiled machine. Unfortunately, the launch will probably fail with loss of your crew."

"*What?*" the others exclaimed.

"You've got the technical bases covered," Eldon said. "A Mr. Jon Mercouri will sabotage certain cameras and telemetry devices."

"He's my chief of security!"

"Why?" Derek said.

"For ten million dollars of course," Eldon said. "I'll back up a bit. I spent the meeting pretending to listen to people and scanning him. A year ago, he received an anonymous note inviting him to check an account in Banco BBG in the Cayman Islands."

"You got this from reading his mind?" Culinary Trask said.

"It's one of our abilities," Chloe said. "You could have it too."

"The account contained a hundred thousand dollars in his name," Eldon nodded. "Then he received a burner phone with more offers. He's taken over two million dollars for various jobs. Like infecting your systems with the Doknet virus."

"Doknet made our lathes spin themselves to pieces!" Culinary Trask said. "Someone *died!*"

"That's why Mercouri can't turn down this or any other assignment," Eldon said. "The bad guys kept records of *everything*: Everything they paid him, everything he did. They can put him away for life."

"Who are these people?" Culinary Trask said.

"A cartoon-voice on a phone. Mercouri *speculates* your competitors gave up on trying to compete legitimately."

"It's not *my* fault they don't build better rockets!"

"That's a nerd's reasoning," Derek said. "To the *suits,* there are cheaper ways to compete — like lobbying for exclusive contracts."

"Yes, they tried that. We sued and won."

"Suits generally draw the line at physical violence," Eldon murmured. "That's what's so puzzling."

"Why do they want to disable those cameras?" Chloe said.

"Since we're not in a movie, they didn't explain," Eldon smiled. "We only have Mercouri's speculations. He noticed those sensors face *north* from the launch pad — to a wildlife preserve with lots of underbrush. Perfect cover for a sniper in a ghillie suit with an XM500, whatever that is. Some kind of gun I guess. He figures the rocket'll explode and burn up the evidence."

"Ghillie suit?" Allie said, popping into view with Tori in her arms. "Oh — suits covered with foliage."

"It's take our daughter to work day?"

Tori giggled and tried to wave to the others.

"Cute!" Culinary Trask grinned and stroked her cheek.

"Tori's hungry," Allie said. "And this news can't wait. *Wow* — this *living room!* It's like a Zen Buddhist retreat! Minus the visual poetry and uh ... cleanliness."

"What news?" Culinary Trask said.

"It's fan-and-feces time," Allie said. "An orderly at Cedars of Lebanon recognized Greg Jones and called his reporter friend at the LA Observer."

"I guess that was inevitable," Culinary Trask sighed. "It's OK as long as he sticks to his fake identity."

"About that," Allie muttered. "That's kinda hard to do when you're coming out of anesthesia and semi-comatose. Greg mumbled *everything*. The LA Observer wants to keep it exclusive, but their employees are leaking it everywhere. The Internet will be on fire if it isn't already."

"Questioning him was *so illegal!*" Culinary Trask growled, as his cell phone and landline both started ringing.

"Don't answer!" Eldon said. "We have to figure out how to handle this."

Then they heard pounding on the front door.

"Someone's in there," a voice said through the door, and the pounding continued. "I heard voices."

"It can't be Trask," another voice said. "He was just at a meeting."

"I think I just heard someone scream," the first voice said. "As responsible citizens, it's our duty to break down the door."

"Oh yeah, I heard it too," the other voice said.

The pounding became harder.

"We should leave," Derek said.

"They're going to steal my stuff!" Culinary Trask said.

"*What* stuff?" Chloe said.

"I don't want to be trapped in Oz!"

"I won't let you be trapped anywhere, darling," Chloe said.

"Somehow I believe you."

※※※

After showing Culinary Trask around, they all gathered on Derek and Allie's deck.

Derek vanished for fifteen minutes and returned carrying drink in an ornate glass with an umbrella in it.

"A Mai-Tai," he said, handing it to Culinary Trask. "From the Piikoi Palace in Honolulu. You need it."

In a daze, Culinary Trask sipped the drink and regarded his surroundings.

On the deck's railing, Norton stalked a tiny green lizard. When he pounced, the lizard's tail dropped off and continued to wiggle.

The lizard escaped as Norton played with the tail.

"I have an idea," Eldon said. "From the *Dune* movie of all things."

"That movie sucked rancid swampwater!" Culinary Trask muttered.

"Of course it did," Derek said.

"Build Heighliners!" Eldon continued. "You know — those gigantic metal shells people drove their spaceships into."

"Then a creepy, vagina-faced creature teleports the whole mess somewhere?" Culinary Trask said.

"Yeah. You'll be the creepy creature."

"Think of it!" Derek said. "Spaceships with a hundred seats, cargo holds, life support. And *no engines!* You'll pretend to *operate* the engines but you'll actually *be* the engines."

"It's really possible to teleport large objects?" Culinary Trask said.

"When you get good at it," Chloe said.

"My sister, Wendy, is *fantastic* at it," Derek said. "She claims she could teleport an *entire planet* if she had to."

"Which is more than a little scary," Allie muttered. "Not that she's evil or anything."

"I still won't need my rockets," Culinary Trask said.

"Yes you will," Derek said. "Teleporting swaps *volumes*. Let that sink in a moment..."

"OK," Culinary Trask said. "If I park a mile-long spaceship in front of my factory and teleport it to Mars."

"It gets swapped with a mile-long *vacuum*," Trask said. "The implosion would annihilate your factory. Probably half of LA, too."

"So my heighliners stay in orbit," Culinary Trask murmured. "At first, anyway. Until I build giant vacuum chambers."

"That's the spirit!" Trask said, beaming. *I feel responsible for him.*

We're all responsible, Chloe replied. *We interfered in his life.*

Allie and I feel that way about our Culinary counterparts, and their kids, Derek beamed.

"I've got work to do!" Culinary Trask said. "We already have a vacuum chamber for testing spacesuits and the Mars rover. We could build a *small* spaceship that fits inside it."

"If you become an Indigo," Chloe said. "You should stay here a couple days while your body ... changes. Eldon and I will look after you. *Right,* Eldon?"

"Of course, pal," Eldon replied. "I'm getting jealous of you." Chloe laughed.

"Leaving the human race is pretty drastic," Culinary Trask said, taking a sip of his drink. "This drink is intense."

"Cutting your wrists is drastic!" Chloe sputtered. "Next to that, becoming an Indigo is trying a new flavor of *ice cream."*

"Could you guys fly my spaceships for me?" Culinary Trask said. "I'll think about the Indigo thing."

"You *said* you wanted to be his long lost twin brother," Derek laughed.

"Thank you *so much* for reminding me," Eldon muttered. "Yeah, I guess I could. Chloe would join me. The other Indigos also could, for money. Hell, we could train the *kids* to do it when they're older."

"Slow down, guys!" Allie said. "We're not talking paper routes!"

"My competitors will go out of their *minds,"* Culinary Trask murmured. "We're undercutting them at sixty million a launch. We'll be able to launch for *ten million,* and even that will mostly be profit."

"I hate to rain on your parade," Allie said. "But teleportation got us run out of Origin. It scares the *shit* out of people."

"Unlike you, I had a *life* in Origin," Eldon said. "So I've thought long and hard about what we could've done differently."

"That's not fair!" Allie said. "I opened a wonderful art gallery."

"I'm sorry things went to shit," Derek said.

"Not your fault," Eldon said. "Anyway — you didn't have powerful politicians behind you."

"You will?" Allie said.

"I knew a few," Eldon said.

"Senator Rubinstein can't even protect herself," Derek muttered.

"From scanning you," Eldon said, nodding to Culinary Trask. "I've seen lots of others who could be bribed or blackmailed to support us. We have to build up to it — *slowly*. We'd become untouchable."

"Senator Wilmer?" Culinary Trask said, drinking more of the Mai-Tai. "I told him to go to hell when he asked for a 'contribution'."

"Him and others," Trask said. "We keep our ability to *personally* teleport a secret. That's what scares people. We say a giant *machine* is involved — using lots of power, flashing lights. You might've been able to do that in Origin, you know."

"We weren't politically savvy," Allie said.

"The bad guys knew we could personally teleport from *day one*," Derek muttered. "Then things went south in a hurry."

Culinary Trask finished his drink.

"Want another?" Derek said, taking his glass.

"No. This is going straight to my head."

"You needed it," Chloe said. "How are you feeling now?"

"Better. There's something about this place. It's so peaceful. It feels ... welcoming."

"Gotta return this glass," Derek said, taking the glass and vanishing.

"Your house was a black hole!" Chloe said. "I'd slash my wrists if I was stuck in that pit with *no one* to confide in."

"I never had time for friends," Culinary Trask said.

"Well, you have them now," Derek said, popping into view.

"Like it or not," Chloe laughed.

"Oh God, I'm getting *ideas!*" Culinary Trask said. *"Cancel the upcoming launch. Take the Mars landing module off the rocket and park it in front of my factory. Then build an airtight steel shell around it. Later, build a giant vacuum chamber like NASA's Plum Brook facility."

"That'll *work!*" Eldon said. "It doesn't have to be a hard vacuum. We'll call it a *teleportation chamber* and post armed guards around it."

"Then we put the crew in the landing module, and you teleport it to Mars."

Not to spoil things, Derek beamed at Eldon. *But if we do this for real, there will be overwhelming pressure to reveal our new 'technology'.*

At least he's not thinking of suicide anymore, Eldon replied. *One day at a time.*

"We should get Wendy involved," Eldon said. "I hope she's available."

Both Trasks vanished.

Chapter 19

In an out of body state, Derek spied on Kef and Katalluwana.
Another crew member handed Kef a document.
"Travel time to the closest system is one cycle," Kef said. "It appears to be a binary with a third sun that distantly orbits the two."
"Planets?"
"Impossible to determine from this distance."
I wonder how long a cycle is, Derek wondered.
"I've been looking at the databases," Kef said. *"Two million cycles ago* is ... is bordering on Forbidden. I know you flout ... Prohibitions, but I'm hesitant."
"I won't tell if you don't."

***

In Culinary Trask's living room, the two Eldon Trasks pondered how to introduce Origin Trask as Culinary Trask's long-lost identical twin brother.
This was theoretically possible since Eldon Trask had been abandoned as a baby and his birth mother had never been found.

"I'll take the name Jefferson," Eldon said. "Now we find fake adoptive parents for me who can't be tracked down."

"A couple that died years ago with no known family?" Culinary Trask said. "Shouldn't be too hard."

Developing a headache, Origin Eldon started a computer search.

"Something's wrong," he muttered.

"What?" Culinary Trask said.

"I don't know, and it's maddening. It's like fingernails scratching a chalkboard."

Congratulations on your new name, Jefferson! Andromeda beamed at Eldon. *You have to look at these Squidward diagrams!*

"The archaeologist wants me to look at some technical diagrams," Eldon said. "A working *Alcubierre drive?*"

"What?"

"It looks as though the Squidwards had one."

"That's *amazing!* Our ticket to the *stars!* I would've given my *right arm* for one. Check it out! I'll keep looking for fake parents."

✳✳✳

Trask joined Andy and Llewellyn at their patio on Destiny Beach.

"An Alcubierre drive is a *legal* way to travel faster than light," Eldon exclaimed. "I've been studying it for years."

"Like our teleporting?" Andy said.

"No," Trask said. "When it comes to the laws of physics, we Indigos are complete outlaws. We violate them all the time: conservation of mass-energy, momentum, you name it. I can teleport from a *sitting position* to orbiting the Archy's planet at thirty thousand miles per hour."

"So?" Andy said.

"Physics says you can't do that without expending a *lot* of energy," Eldon said. "Using a *rather* large rocket. This tells me Derek's right. Space and time are *programmed into* our world, and we bypass that programming when we're in the spirit-world. We're all players in a vast computer game. Indigos can leave it and reinsert themselves in different locations."

"What's the big deal about this ... what did you call it?" Andy said.

"The Alcubierre drive is like an ingenious lawyer, bending laws without *quite* breaking them," Eldon said.

"How so?" Andy said.

"If you can't reach your destination, rearrange the universe so it comes to you."

"Huh?" Andy said.

"Space and time are flexible," Llewellyn said.

"That's general relativity's explanation for gravity," Eldon said. "An object tries to move through time in a straight line. The path of least resistance. The Earth *curves* space and time around it so moving in a straight line means falling to the ground."

"That's just a theory, isn't it?" Andy said.

"No, honey," Llewellyn said. "Astronomers have *seen* the curvature of space. *Parentheses in space.*"

"Yeah," Eldon said. "They spotted a distant galaxy with curved images of another galaxy to its left and right, mirror images of each other. Like parentheses. They were images of another galaxy *behind* it. The galaxy's gravity curved space so much, the light of the other galaxy shone *around* it, highly distorted."

"Like a fun-house mirror?" Andy said.

"They've found lots of galaxies like this," Eldon said. "They call it..."

"Gravitational lensing," Llewellyn interrupted. "You can't travel *through* space faster than light. Imagine it's a viscous liquid. There's no limit to how fast *space itself* can expand and contract, though."

"During the big bang's expansion phase," Eldon said. "Space expanded billions of times faster than the speed of light. So a Mexican physicist..."

"Miguel Alcubierre!" Llewellyn shouted.

"You want to take over?" Eldon said.

"Sorry. Go ahead."

"So," Eldon said. *"Contract* space in front of your spaceship and *expand* it behind it. Technically, your spaceship *hasn't moved.* The geometry around it has changed so much, it's *as if* it traveled a light-year."

"But ... but that requires more energy than the entire universe has!" Llewellyn said.

"Early calculations suggested that," Eldon nodded. "But they've refined them a lot. I funded a group at Caltech. They reduced the energy-requirement to the point it might almost be doable. One thing we have *no idea* how to provide is *negative energy.*"

"What's *that?*" Andy said.

"Nobody knows," Eldon said. "Or I should say no *human* knows. You plug a negative value for energy into the equations and you get the right geometry. That doesn't mean negative energy *exists.* The math is more flexible than the physics."

"Culinary Trask!" Andy said, pointing. "Did you become an Indigo?"

My garden looked so sad, Culinary Trask's spirit said. *I took a break from my computer search and went out on the patio. Then something stung my head, and I was floating here.*

***

They teleported to Culinary Trask's house and found his body sprawled on the patio — with a bullet hole in the middle of his forehead.

Someone shot you, Eldon said.

I'm dead? I feel more alive than ever!

That's the spirit world, pal, Eldon said.

I'm drifting, Culinary Trask said. *They're telling me ... telling me it's time ...*

I'm so sorry to see you go, Eldon said. *I looked forward to being your long-lost twin brother. We could've been a fantastic team.*

You barely gave yourself a chance to live, Chloe sobbed, materializing beside Eldon.

I built my company and got my people to Mars, Culinary Trask said. *The only things that ever really mattered to me. Please don't let it all die with me! Promise you'll keep it going!*

I promise, Eldon said.

We both do, Chloe said.

I don't know why, but I feel safer and more at ease than ever before. I worry about you two! You have to deal with the bastards who killed me. Take care!

He departed.

"We have to give him a funeral," Eldon moaned, holding a weeping Chloe.

They teleported his body to the Indigo Graveyard in Oz.

***

A brisk wind blew under a sapphire sky, and a golden eagle rode thermals over the Grand Canyon, which looked as though it could swallow up the universe.

A nice day to bury a friend.

All the Indigos in existence appeared and stood around Culinary Trask's body.

Derek and Allie looped ropes under it, and Wendy dug a grave.

Chloe recited Isaiah 25:6-9: *He will swallow up death forever.* Under her telepathic direction, they sang the hymn *Love's redeeming work is done.*

An honored guest — Culinary Trask's spirit — appeared in their midst.

I'd cry if I could. You were my friends ... I see that, now — I see so many things clearly now. If I am reborn, it will be among you — in your tribe of angels.

"At the rate we have babies, you'll get plenty of chances," Allie chuckled.

They tearfully laughed.

Culinary Trask's spirit receeded.

They lowered his body into the grave, and Wendy closed it.

"I'll carve a granite obelisk," Allie said, putting a temporary marker on the grave. "An old inscription comes to mind, suitable for ... for a rocket man."

> "Culinary Eldon Trask looks on the rising sun's beauty without blinking. Higher than the height of Orion soars his soul — and it is united with the underworld."

"Use it," Eldon croaked, hugging a sobbing Chloe.

"We failed him," Allie moaned.

"*I* failed him," Eldon said.

The brief ceremony over, they took turns holding and welcoming Baby Kile to the world, and Chloe murmured a prayer of blessing.

Thomas and Liz took Kile back to Nostalgia; Wendy and Travis returned to Maui in Origin.

"Think the sniper saw us remove his body?" Chloe said.

"I hope he did what they do in the movies," Eldon said. "Pack up his gun and leave."

Derek shut his eyes briefly and said, "Two men are searching Trask's house for his body. Someone's afraid he survived."

"Oh, let's clear that up," Eldon growled.

※※※

Chloe and Eldon went to their bedroom in Oz — a spacious room painted pale violet with a framed copy of *Desiderata* on one wall and a large cross on another.

It radiated serenity.

The two lay on the bed and went out-of-body.

In their spirit-bodies, they followed the two men — Ridley Nazariy and Amos Lesley. A third, Michael Chang, sat in a getaway car humming and tapping the dashboard with his fingers.

Eldon retrieved a wire-cutter from the Squidward dig-site.

Chloe materialized by the driver-side window and zapped Chang in the neck with a stun-gun, as Eldon opened the hood and cut the battery-cables.

Chloe called the police.

※※※

They teleported to Eldon's office at Space Ventures Corporation and, lying on the floor, watched the proceedings in their spirit-bodies.

Afterward, they paced.

"It'll be easy to slide into his life," Eldon muttered, putting on his contact-lenses. "He barely had one. Poor bastard didn't have a friend in the world."

Jon Mercouri entered the office and gasped.

"Seen a ghost?" Eldon said.

"I ... I ... I didn't know you were here, Mr. Trask," Mr. Mercouri stammered.

"What's the problem then?" Chloe snapped.

"I ... I had four-alarm chili for breakfast and it's repeating on me," he replied, thinking, *Who the hell is this woman?*

He fled.

"He doesn't know the shooter," Chloe said. "But he knew it was happening. He gave the those three men information on Trask's alarm system. *Your* alarm system."

"I want to kick the shit out of him!" Eldon Trask snarled.

"So do I," Chloe said. "But he used to be a marine and police detective."

"I wonder how well he fights without arms or legs."

"No amputations! It'll raise too many questions."

"I suppose the smart thing to do would be to keep him around. Keep your enemies closer..."

"*Fuck that!* I don't want a goddamn murderer breathing down our necks."

"You're getting rather foul-mouthed, my dear priestess," Eldon smiled, hugging her. "I *love* it."

They kissed and hugged for a few minutes, and Chloe breathed, "Maybe it's my Indigo hormones ... or because of your funeral, but I feel we should get married."

"I thought you'd *never* ask."

"It'll be the most *amazing* ... and momentous marriage of all time," she murmured. "If we can figure out how to not kill each other."

I feel the need ... to merge our souls, Eldon beamed. *As did Derek and Allie. I guess it's an Indigo thing.*
Me too.
They went out of body and briefly allowed their spirit-bodies to overlap.
Memories, images, and feelings howled through their minds, giving each of them a complete understanding of the other.
They sat in stunned silence.
"Your adoptive father beat you *every day?*" Chloe finally said. "I could *feel* his fists! Your mother said it was to toughen you up? Then you worked your way through engineering school? You overcame so much, my love!"
She hugged Eldon.
"When you were a girl," Eldon said. "The images you had of God were so ... transcendent. You *had* to become a minister. I see that now. Your parents died in a car crash when you were seven. Your uncle raised you."
"I wish you could've met him."
"I feel I have," Eldon said. "You spent a year in Jerusalem ... for your divinity program. And had an affair with a *Rabbinical student?*"
Chloe sighed deeply.
"Strangest affair ever," Eldon continued. "You and Avram would meet at the Damascus Gate ... and skulk around the Arab Quarter ... like guilty cheating spouses."
"It could've gotten me thrown out of the program. And his community would've shunned him forever."
"You argued *theology* in *cafés?*" Eldon said.
"He confessed a haunting sin on his conscience: The feeling that Jesus really was the Messiah."
"Then you lost your virginity to him in a hotel in Rehovot. The desk clerk smirked."

"TMI!" Chloe muttered.

"Your dirty little secrets are *charming,*" he breathed, embracing her. "I wish I had dirty secrets like that."

"We'll work on it," Chloe smiled.

"Mine are just techy."

"Rocket engines operate at temperatures above their own melting points?" Chloe murmured. "How's that even *possible?*"

"Quite a trick, isn't it?" Eldon smiled. "I have so many bibles in my head, now — word for word. The King James."

"My favorite."

"The Latin Vulgate, a Koine Greek bible, and the Masoretic text," Eldon continued. "And now I understand Latin, ancient Greek, Hebrew, and Aramaic."

"Rocket explosions are called *RUD's?*" Chloe said. *"Rapid unscheduled disassemblies?"*

Eldon laughed.

They sat there, arms entwined.

"Department heads' meeting," the intercom squawked, making them jump. "In forty-five minutes. You told me to remind you."

"Thanks, Susan."

"So what do we do about Mercouri?" Chloe sighed.

"A bit of online banking, I think. We need to find an Internet Cafe."

I know one we've used in New York, Derek beamed at them.

I know one in Sicily, Allie added. *No surveillance cameras.*

※※※

They met Allie.

"Wow," Eldon breathed, as they exited restrooms.

A large round table ringed with laptop computers filled the cramped shop, and an ornate brass espresso machine topped by a brass eagle dominated its coffee bar. Posters of the Sicilian coastline covered its walls — golden beaches, castles atop white seaside cliffs, and Taormina's famed Blue Grotto.

Scents of almond and roses filled the air.

Eldon stepped outside the cafe and looked around, stunned. The others followed him.

Low buildings with boutiques, cafés, and wine bars lined the *Corso Umberto*, a narrow tiled walkway jammed with tourists — as vines and potted plants spilled over and through ornate wrought-iron railings on balconies above them.

It was early evening.

An elderly gentleman with a mandolin played a Sicilian song of lost love as people dropped donations into a bucket at his feet.

"*Taormina*," Allie smiled.

"Huh?" Eldon said.

"My family's ancestral home," she added, giving them a handful of Euro coins and folding money. "A charming place for a *honeymoon*."

She vanished into the café's ladies' room.

Eldon mopped his brow, and they returned to the *Mønte ©arlø Nët* cafe.

Luxuriating in its air-conditioning, they ordered cappuccinos and *Bacione di Taormina* — "Taormina kisses" — almond-cocoa tarts dusted with powdered pistachios.

The barista spoke American English with a Brooklyn accent. They sat at a computer.

This is almost too easy, Eldon beamed, typing.

I didn't know you could hack computers, Chloe replied.

I can't. I know all of Mercouri's account numbers and passwords. Telepathy, baby! Our killer app!

Before you rape his finances, Chloe beamed. *Does he have a wife and children?*

Good point! Eldon replied, scanning Mercouri again. *No, he dumped his wife and two sons for his executive assistant. Ream him a new one!*

Eldon transferred the funds from all of Mercouri's bank accounts — including the Cayman Island one — to a new one he created in Banco BBG under the name 'Rollo Tomasi'."

It had three million and change.

"*Rollo Tomasi?*" Chloe chuckled.

"From *L. A. Confidential,*" Eldon said. "Loved that movie. Rollo is to be identified by the password: '$TXiL7YM7RL6ew75XqYzuu4$'."

"Memorized!"

He logged off the computer.

They paid, entered restrooms, and returned to his office in Los Angeles.

※※※

"God that was strange!" Chloe smiled. "Beautiful but strange. From this sterile office to ... Sicily ... and back. In *seconds.*"

"Our lives have become lucid dreams."

Trask called Drax Security Services of Los Angeles with several requests, and Chloe and Trask slipped cotton gloves on their hands.

Fifteen minutes later, the meeting began.

With the exception of Jon Mercouri, Department heads carrying computer tablets filed into the office and took seats: Ray Cristóbal from Strength of Materials, Marjorie Corcoran from Hypergolic Propulsion Systems, Aaron David from Avionics, Gene Krupa from Cryogenic Propulsion Systems, and Lin Wong from Research and Development.

Derek and Allie attended the meeting in their spirit bodies.

One of the office's walls slid up into the ceiling to reveal a wall-sized monitor.

"While we wait for Mr. Mercouri, I'd like you to meet Chloe, my fiancée."

A round of puzzled congratulations followed.

You always said relationships are bullshit! Marjorie thought. *And here you are with a woman, an actual carbon-based human unit. I expected you to settle down with a nice android.*

Chloe suppressed a chuckle.

Why is he introducing her at a business meeting? Gene thought.

He seems different somehow, more youthful and animated, Marjorie thought. *Being engaged agrees with him.*

"Sorry I'm late," a breathless Mercouri said, stumbling into the room and sitting. "Damned ATM in the lobby's acting up."

"You *are* my head of security, are you not?"

"Uh, yes."

"Yet you don't make me feel especially secure," Eldon frowned. "Why is that?"

"I'm not sure, Sir," Mercouri said, thinking, *Where's he going with this?*

"Could it be your giving three thugs my home security passcodes?"

"I ... uh ... don't know what you're talking about."

"They broke into my house this morning. They're under arrest now."

Mercouri paled.

"Guess why they were there."

A fly buzzed around Eldon's desk — making the loudest sound in the room.

"They were looking for my *corpse*. After a sniper tried to kill me."

The fly's wings beat against the office window.
What the fuck? Ray Cristóbal thought.
Best meeting ever! Marjorie Corcoran grinned, rubbing her hands together. *They're usually so boring!*
Mercouri's eyes darted from side to side.
"Now how did I know that?" Eldon continued. "Maybe it was a voice on a burner phone. Sound familiar? I thought it was a scam until today. For the right price, they'll prove you infected our systems with Doknet. You know — the virus that spun our lathes to pieces. And killed poor Mike Roque. Think I should pay?"
You're a facile liar! Chloe beamed at him.
Can't tell them it was telepathy, can I?
Two burly men in black suits from Drax Security appeared at the door.
"These men will escort you from the building," Eldon said. "We'll mail your personal effects to your home. If you ever show up at a Space Ventures facility, you'll be arrested for trespassing."
"You'll probably be arrested anyway," Chloe added.
"I didn't know Doknet would *kill* anyone," Mercouri muttered. "You've got to believe that."
"Tell it to the police."
"You have *no idea* what you're up against," he added, as they dragged him out the door.
How melodramatic! Aaron David thought.
"He has no idea what *he's* up against," Chloe whispered.
Eldon pulled Chloe to him.
"We'll continue with preparations for the next launch," he said. "With the possibility of postponing or canceling it."
The department heads protested that they were 'ready.'

"Of course you are," Eldon said. "But are you ready for an armor-piercing round hitting a fuel tank?"

A shocked silence followed.

I wondered how long it would take for competition to get truly ugly, Lin Wong thought. *Who's behind it?*

"Look, we have technical holds on launches all the time. Now we have one more reason for a hold: security. Space travel is dangerous enough without putting our astronauts in combat situations."

"How can we ... function?" Marjorie said. "We're *engineers*, not soldiers."

Eldon sighed and rubbed his face.

"What about the rumors...?" Lin Wong said. "Greg Jones. Quantum teleportation."

Greg's condition is stable now, Chloe beamed. *We can quietly ship him back to Mars and deny, deny, deny. Or we can go all in.*

Greg's presence on Earth is known, Allie said. *You can't pull an Eakins and utter obvious lies: You don't have his fanatical followers.*

We'll support whatever you decide, Derek beamed.

I may regret this, but I'm going all in. Life is going to get complicated. Or more complicated...

I feel timelines splitting, Chloe beamed.

Really? Eldon beamed. *I guess we'll know which decision was the right one. We'll have Oz to fall back on if everything goes to hell.*

"The rumors are true," Eldon finally said.

An audible gasp rose in the room.

That's impossible! Lin Wong thought. *Except that Greg is here — and he was on Mars. Or was he? Maybe it was a scam, and he never went to Mars. Maybe Trask wants us to believe he has quantum teleportation. What's his agenda?*

"We haven't decided how to handle ... disclosure, so I'd appreciate it if you didn't repeat what I'm about to tell you. We have an off-site, ultra-secret mad-monk unit exploring ... exotic technologies. They include a variation on quantum teleportation and an Alcubierre drive. Chloe's the project director."

Rockets were your life! Marjorie thought. *You were the most rigid person I ever met!*

Why didn't they invite me to participate? Lin Wong thought. *Do they know I'm spying for China?*

"*Holy shit!*" Marjorie shouted. "Pardon my language, Sir. *An Alcubierre drive?*"

"That's what I said. Bringing Mr. Jones home was a Hail Mary operation. He was dying and we took a chance. Thank God it worked. The technology's nowhere near ready for prime time."

No one said a word.

"In theory, it could solve our security problems. We could launch satellites and Mars missions *from inside our factory.* Until we decide ... how to proceed, we should carry on as if nothing unusual happened."

Maybe it is real, Lin Wong thought. *It can't be quantum teleportation, though. I must tell my handlers about this 'Chloe' person.*

In a subdued meeting, they all made their reports — displaying them on the wall-sized monitor. They resolved to prepare for next week's launch as scheduled.

"I almost forgot," Eldon said. "A New York City startup has developed a successful cold-fusion generator."

Can this day get any stranger? Lin Wong thought.

"It's about four cubic feet and weighs about fifty kilos," Eldon continued. "I want you to evaluate this power-source and determine how you could incorporate it into your projects. It strikes me as a useful replacement for the batteries and atomic power plants we use now."

Then he gave them contact information for Vaughn Williams, thinking, *I hope I haven't painted a target on you guys.*

Eldon also told them to design a "quantum transport device."

"Basically, it's a space shuttle minus wings, heat-resistant tiles, and engines," he said. "It must have power, life-support, an airlock, crew quarters, and a cargo bay. It must have a sealed cockpit with a cubic space for the quantum device. There must also be an airtight chamber big enough to enclose the entire spaceship."

"What kinds of materials should we use?" Ray Cristóbal said.

"Weight is not a factor," Eldon replied. "In principle, you could make it out of concrete."

This drew gasps from everyone.

"Make it of steel or titanium with lead shielding," Eldon continued. "It'll still have to withstand the temperature extremes of space. Doesn't have to be aerodynamic or fly through the atmosphere."

The meeting ended.

✳✳✳

They joined Derek and Allie.

Under an azure sky dotted with cheerful clouds, a grassy sea stretched to the horizon around them — as they sat on a blanket beside a copse of trees.

Bison grazed in the distance.

"Where are we?" Chloe said.

"In Origin, this would be Nebraska," Allie said, offering them sandwiches from a picnic basket, champagne in paper cups, and a bowl of buttered popcorn.

"Popcorn and champagne!" Chloe moaned, grabbing a handful and sipping her drink.

"Birgit Fischer thinks we should get away from the islands when we can," Derek said.

"Beautiful," Chloe said. "In its own way."

A gentle wind rose, creating ripples in the grass.

"So the Chinese aren't behind Culinary Trask's murder," Eldon said, sipping his drink. "Or they didn't tell Lin Wong about it if they were."

Storm clouds appeared on the horizon to the north.

"Why would they?" Allie said. "He never needed to know."

"I wonder what their investigation of me will uncover," Chloe said, licking butter from fingers. "I have a counterpart in Portland, Oregon. She's five years older than me and had a nose job. We could be sisters, but we're not *identical* twins anymore."

"God, this has been a long day!" Eldon sighed.

"It's why you get the big bucks, honey."

"After we left Origin, I dreamed of running Space Ventures again. I wanted it so much I could *taste* it. But not like this ... never like this. That poor bastard would've been better off if we'd never contacted him."

"We'll never know, honey."

"Nonsense!" Allie said. "You're Indigos! Think back to the moment you contacted him and imagine yourself acting differently."

"This is so ... bizarre," Eldon whispered, shutting his eyes.

Allie smiled.

"What?" Chloe said.

"Images exploding in my mind, like a strange movie. We *don't* contact Culinary Trask; we buy space suits from a tech-startup called Wonderland Frontiers instead. Not nearly as good as mine! Greg Jones dies, and they bury him there — the first human buried on another planet. Flags fly at half-staff around the world. Eulogies and receptions at the White House and the UN. Culinary Trask never attempts suicide but still vanishes without a trace. Space Ventures is so well-organized they conduct next week's launch without him. The rocket explodes, killing everyone. The company disappears."

"We did good, honey! What about the people already *on* Mars? In that timeline, I mean."

"NASA and the ESA try to mount a heroic rescue mission. In some timelines it succeeds. Where it doesn't, we step in and teleport the whole damned Mars base to Cape Canaveral — people and all. It appears to be magic."

"How does that turn out?"

"Conspiracy theories galore. The main one is that the Mars mission was a hoax from the beginning. Others speculate that Mars is inhabited by a super advanced race, and *they* sent the astronauts home."

"Well, I'm glad we rescue them," Chloe said. "It's what we do."

"What I can't figure out is why the *hell* I wouldn't contact Culinary Trask."

Chapter 20

Wendy, Travis, Grace and Taka watched a quiz show on TV in Taka's living room.

"I should go on one quiz show *kine*," Travis said. "I'd win every time."

A special report interrupted the program.

"As most viewers know," the renowned TV anchor, Ellen Caulfield said. "A People's Court determined that President Eakins's most trusted advisor, Renard Moreau, murdered him. They sentenced him to death."

"Eakins isn't dead," Wendy muttered.

"He's alive?" Grace said.

"They should bring him back," Travis said. "That would show them."

"He wanted to kill everyone in my home town," Wendy said. "Including the *keikis*."

"Unfortunately," Ellen Caulfield continued. "Mr. Moreau escaped, probably with the help of his CIA associates. The Council of True Patriots has resolved to *compel* Mr. Moreau to justice. Blood shall answer for blood. Who ... who *wrote* this stuff?"

"Just read it!" an off-camera man's voice snapped.

Two men dragged a struggling nineteen-year-old woman in a gray sweater and blue jeans — Renard's daughter, Marie — onto the scene.

"I haven't done *anything*. What are the charges? I never broke the law in my life!"

One man produced a hypodermic needle and injected Marie in the arm with it. Then they shoved her into a jail cell and locked it.

She staggered around her tiny cell until she finally slumped onto the cot.

"Be on notice, Renard Moreau!" Ellen Caulfield continued. "We ... we have your daughter in a secret location. Unless you turn yourself in by eight PM tomorrow, we will ... will ex... execute her in your place."

"Ex...e...cute?" Marie slurred and started wailing.

"The q...question," Ellen stammered. "How much does America's most hated man love his only daughter? T...Tune in tomorrow... This is *barbaric!* I ... I can't do this..."

A "Technical Difficulties" screen replaced the video feed.

After a minute, one of the technicians came on and said *an execution* — of Renard or Marie — would be broadcast live at eight PM tomorrow.

"President Knox has designated this execution *Mandated Viewing*," the technician said. "Video of it will download to all cell-phones in the US, and the phones will not function until someone views it."

Wendy contacted Allie and Derek.

I sort of met her, Derek beamed at her. *I'm sure we can find her.*

"Got to get rid of my TV," Taka sobbed, turning it off. "It take up too much space. Why don't we play Hearts?"

✳✳✳

At two in the morning, an elderly security guard approached Marie's cell.

"Can't sleep, sister?" he said.

"No," she sobbed, her eyes red and swollen.

"We're praying for you," he said. "I'm Brother Ulasovich. We know your dad didn't kill Eakins."

"You *know* that?"

"Of course. Eakins is alive and well."

"He *is?* You've *got* to tell the authorities!"

"They don't believe us. You'll see, though. Your innocent blood will cry out to Heaven. And then you'll meet Eakins."

This confused Marie but she said, "I'd love to meet him! When?"

"After your martyrdom tomorrow," Mr. Ulasovich said. "Then you will sit at Eakins's right hand ... in Paradise. He is Jesus reborn and has risen again ... as he did so many years ago."

"Oh my God!" Marie moaned. "You're *crazy!*"

Allie appeared behind Mr. Ulasovich and zapped him in the neck with a stun gun.

He slumped to the floor.

Derek appeared with a roll of duct tape and a towel. He threw the towel over Mr. Ulasovich's head and taped his arms and legs.

✳✳✳

Allie and Marie appeared in a white marble-lined ladies' room and Allie led her out into an anteroom.

Polished marble statues of The Nine Muses of Greek mythology stood in front of a massive bronze door.

They walked through it.

Malachite pillars with gold accents lined marble walls with packed built-in bookcases. Surrounded by open books, Renard sat at a massive polished wooden table.

"How did I get here?" Marie said. "Where *is* this?"

"It's magic, honey," Allie said. "Remember the Harry Potter books?"

At the sound of Marie's voice, Renard looked up.

"Marie!" he exclaimed, jumping up and hugging her.

"They were going to *execute* me," she sobbed.

"You're safe now," Allie said. "That's all that matters."

"It's like a dream," Marie said. "They pulled me out of a chem exam and took me to Campus Security. Then they said I'd be *executed* ... and now I'm ... I'm here."

"I never imagined things could get so crazy they'd go after *you*," Renard muttered. "Your mother couldn't protect you?"

"She *suggested* they take me," Marie sobbed. "She said I deserved it because I wouldn't condemn you as a murderer."

They all left.

※※※

Gaslights and lanterns gave the concrete canyon of Fifth Avenue a warm glow, as a light rain fell.

Steam-powered buses shared the crowded street with horse-drawn carriages, and pedestrians thronged the sidewalks.

With Allie and Renard holding her hands, Marie stumbled like an automaton, staring blankly at the sights.

They decided to dine at The Colonnades Gustatorium.

It was a large restaurant lit by candles and brass oil-lamps. A plush red carpet covered the floor and there were many empty tables.

Two young ladies in flowing pale blue dresses played soothing but unidentifiable music — one played a harp and the other a flute.

The Maitre d' stared at Derek, Allie, and Marie.

"They're from the cast of *A Streetcar Named Desire*," Renard lied. "Still in costume."

"Show folk?" he laughed. "Never heard of *A Streetcar Named Desire*. Odd title!"

He seated them at a table beside windows that looked out onto Fifth Avenue and gave them menus.

Marie stared out the window.

"Pigeon breasts with *lavender sauce?*" Derek muttered, studying the menu.

"I'm sure everything's good," Allie said. "We have to get used to the food here."

Renard ordered Marie a dish called *Norman Conquest*.

"Getting you two birth certificates will be easier than I thought," Renard said. "They're written in *pencil* on *cardboard* sheets! Tomorrow I'll make you natural born citizens of Knickerbocker. It's easy to be anonymous in a city this big."

"Knicker...bocker?" Marie mumbled.

"The city we're in," Renard said.

"Not New York?"

"No," Renard said. "Ironically, there *is* a New York City in this world. It's a tiny village in Canada — which is called British Columbia. I mean *all* of Canada is called British Columbia. They call themselves The Empire's Pointed Sword and have a bizarre flag. The Union Jack with a sword running it through."

The waiter set a wicker basket of steaming rolls wrapped in cloth on the table.

"Can't have rolls without butter and *krell*," he chuckled, setting two white ceramic cups of ... stuff beside the basket.

"Norman Conquest?" Derek chuckled. "Odd name for a dish."

"Amusing story," Renard chuckled. "It's based on a *play* called *The Norman Conquest*, where a man named Norman is in love with ..."

"It's ... a dream!" Marie exclaimed. "It's ... all just a ... dream, and I'll wake up in my dorm room ... and everything will be ... normal again."

"Your daughter's having a nervous breakdown," Allie snapped. "That's the main thing now. You have a place for her?"

His top priority is ingratiating himself with his bosses, Derek beamed. *Just as with Eakins.*

"I have an apartment with a guest bedroom."

Allie handed Renard two more gold bars.

"Maybe she needs professional counseling," Derek said.

"Can't take her to a psychologist *here*," Allie said.

"Ma chérie," Renard said, tearfully hugging Marie. "You just lay low for a few days ... or weeks ... however long you need. We'll get through this."

"I understand you're studying art, Marie," Allie said.

"Art?"

"I'll be opening an art gallery here. I'd really appreciate it if you could help me set it up."

"If you can't stand this world, we'll take you to Culinary," Derek said. "It's a lot like your home except it has no Eakins in charge of anything."

The waiter served the rest of their meals.

"Krell?" Marie mumbled.

"It's a spicy cheese spread," Allie said. "That's what I got from reading his mind."

Marie buttered one of the steaming rolls and tasted it. Then she quickly finished off the rest of the basket, spreading rolls with butter and *krell*.

She ignored her *Norman Conquest,* which turned out to be a rack of lamb with a thick red wine sauce and artichokes.

※※※

After dinner, they took a steam-powered cab to Renard's apartment.

It was on the third floor of a brownstone building overlooking the East river. Its six spacious rooms were furnished in a Victorian style, with oriental rugs on parquet floors, inlaid antique cabinets, and Tiffany lamps.

Renard led Marie into the guest bedroom where she collapsed onto the bed and passed out.

Derek repeated what he'd done with Culinary Trask — visualizing a galaxy of Derek-versions streaming their life-force into Marie — making her spirit-body momentarily flare with energy.

She stirred.

※※※

They let her sleep and went into the living room.

"They call this a drawing room here," Renard said.

Blue floral-print wallpaper covered the walls, and a sofa and chairs surrounded an ornate coffee table beside a fireplace. An antique corner-cabinet housed a tube-based TV with a rabbit-ears antenna.

They sat.

"I wonder who they'll execute in Marie's place," Allie said.

Renard sighed and rubbed his face.

"Pembroke may experience a population explosion," Derek muttered. "I have an idea. Do you have paper and pen handy?"

"Sure," Renard said.

"When they — *you* — drove us out of Origin," Derek muttered. "I said good riddance. I'd hoped to wash my hands of it, but that seems impossible."

Chapter 21

In his spirit-body, Derek hovered over the control room of Columbia University Campus Security.

"You want me to pick out a random student to *murder?*" Spiro Lefteris said — he was head of Campus Security.

"*You* set the Renard girl free, so *you* find her replacement," James Knox said, gesturing at a computer listing of female students.

"I didn't set her free! I don't know how she escaped. It was probably Moreau and his CIA people."

"Makes no difference," Mr. Knox said.

"People will still know you didn't execute Marie Moreau," Mr. Lefteris said. "They'll know she escaped."

"One way or another, a statement will be made. I want your pick by the time I get back."

Flanked by two bodyguards, Mr. Knox went to the Mens' Room down the hall and locked the door.

An half hour later, the bodyguards and Campus Security broke it down to find the room empty except for a handwritten note:

> Hell's demons feast on another,
> The acting president's vile brother
> Not shielded by privileged birth
> He no longer defiles our beloved Earth
> We watch and wait
>   Our list is long...
>   — Renard Moreau's Army

They slid the note into an evidence bag and called the NYPD, the FBI, and the Council of True Patriots.

Spiro Lefteris tossed the listing of students' names into the trash.

✺✺✺

Eldon and Chloe sat in an odd red sedan that had cameras and radar-units on its roof.

"Remind me why we're wasting our time in traffic?" Chloe said.

"We've never been there before," Eldon replied. "After today, we'll be able to teleport to it. Besides, I want to see how my self-driving car works."

"It drives like my grandmother."

"I'm thinking of restarting the Joule Auto company," Eldon said.

The car finally arrived at the white three-story art-deco building that housed the Beverly Hills Police Department.

Looks like an Aztec Temple, Trask thought. *Or a movie set. Which movie though?*

Indiana Jones and the Temple of Doom? Chloe replied.

They got out.

Trask punched the 'Park' button on his remote control, and the car searched for a parking space and parked itself.

BHPD Detective Vic Martens greeted them at the door and ushered them into his office, a quiet airy room with a big desk, white walls, and a potted palm.

A bonsai tree occupied a corner of the desk.

They sat.

"I tripped over a loose patio tile and a bullet dinged the ground," Eldon lied. "Barely missed me."

"Yes, we found it and a little of your blood," Detective Martens said, thinking, *Not how I expected a tech billionaire to live.*

"Here's the burner phone I found in my mailbox two weeks ago," Eldon lied, handing it to the detective. "I wish I'd taken its threats more seriously."

Can they trace it? Chloe beamed.

Can't trace stuff from other timelines.

"The men we arrested haven't said a word," Detective Martens said. "Haven't even asked for lawyers. We've got them dead to rights on breaking and entering. Oddly enough, someone vandalized their car so they couldn't flee."

"Interesting! What else did you find out?"

"I can't discuss details. It's an ongoing investigation."

Eldon scanned Detective Martens.

The three men had a slip of paper with my home security passcodes and Mercouri's fingerprints, he beamed at Chloe. *They've issued a warrant for his arrest but can't find him.*

Let's scan Mercouri the first chance we get, Chloe beamed.

He's on a flight to Orlando, Eldon replied. *I don't think it's to visit Disney World. His handlers told him to await further instructions there.*

"You guys love staring contests?" Detective Martens chuckled.

"She has an angel's face," Eldon sighed. "I could stare at it all day."

"When's the wedding?" Detective Martens smiled.

"Soon," Chloe said. "After we do some redecorating. Of course that implies it was decorated in the *first place*."

Detective Martens laughed.

"OK, I'll cut you lovebirds loose. Stay in the area in case we have more questions. Good luck on your launch next week."

"We'll need it. The caller on that phone said a sniper would sabotage it."

"Any idea who might want your company to fail?"

"Three nations and six large corporations? Just off the top of my head. I'm sure I could think of more."

"Good luck, again," Detective Martens sighed, shaking his head.

They stepped out the police station entrance and Eldon pulled out his remote control.

He was about to push the 'Summon' button.

"Feel that?" Eldon said. "It's like before Culinary me was murdered."

"Yes, an excruciating tension in the air. The calm before the storm."

"I'm *never* going to ignore that feeling again," Eldon muttered.

They reentered the police station, and Eldon faked a heart attack.

"Help!" Chloe shouted.

✳✳✳

Chloe hung on for dear life as the ambulance carrying Eldon careened and bounced its way to Cedars-Sinai Medical Center.

They had strapped him down to a gurney.

He was able to get out-of-body and detected thoughts directed at him and Chloe. He followed them to their source: a man named Erasyl Timur in a coffee shop with a cell-phone and a pair of binoculars.

He'd planted a tiny bomb on their car's gas tank.

When his cell-phone signal detonated the bomb, it would look as though the tank had exploded on its own.

That had been the plan, anyway.

"In a police parking lot?" Eldon said, waking. "Very ballsy indeed."

✳✳✳

After spending two hours in the hospital getting EKG's and X-rays, they released Eldon with a diagnosis of "muscle spasm."

He and Chloe teleported back to restrooms at the Beverly Hills police station, and he went out to the parking lot.

Eldon felt under his car and found the bomb.

They returned to Detective Martens's office, and Eldon played dumb, saying, "I saw someone messing with my car and found this GPS thing stuck to it."

"That's no GPS!" Detective Marten's exclaimed. "Set it on my desk. *Slowly!* God, I hope it doesn't blow up my Herbert."

He named his bonsai tree? Chloe beamed at Eldon.

They reviewed surveillance videos, and spotted Erasyl Timur placing the bomb. Eldon resisted the temptation to give them Timur's name.

Chapter 22

In their Destiny Beach house, Derek went to the bedroom, lay down, and went out-of-body.

He visited Katalluwana and Kef.

"Two million cycles ago," Kef said. "We cleansed a species called G-thong Stith."

"Go on."

"We studied their hive-structures for four cycles. We mapped them meticulously while hiding our own presence. Then we proceeded with the cleansing. The Grand Fleet impelled four asteroids at their planet and attacked fleeing ships."

"Yes?" Katalluwana said.

"Despite these efforts, a portion of the infestation escaped. It took a thousand cycles to trace their hyperdrive trail. They expected to find dying remnants of the escapees. Or corpses."

"And?"

"Instead they found a small but thriving hive. The scout ship cleansed it with atomics and planted the sentinel that contacted us twenty cycles ago."

"How would you account for their survival?" Katalluwana said.

"They obviously took a Queen and at least three Destroying Consorts with them."

What the hell are they?

Then the answer came to Derek: The queens and consorts were the only Archies capable of reproducing. The consorts fought each other to the death, wreaking havoc on their surroundings — in one case, they had disabled the spaceship carrying them and caused several hundred deaths. The survivor — there was never more than one — impregnated the queen and died.

Then the queen laid eggs for the rest of her life, based on that single sex-act.

"How could they *possibly* have three consorts on a *single ship?*" Kef said.

"Quite a mystery, isn't it?"

"The creatures we saw there are *not* G-thong Stith! Their physical nature is completely different."

"That's why we need to find their hive."

They can't conceive of creatures reproducing differently than themselves, Derek mused.

※※※

Marie Moreau blinked in the light streaming through the window.

Boat-horns honked and moaned in the distance.

She looked around, slowly regarding the room's blue-green walls with a chair-rail and mother-of-pearl inlaid wooden dresser.

Carved animals writhed around her bed's four large darkly-stained bedposts.

Where the hell am I? Looks like some old lady's boudoir.

She looked out the window beside the bed and saw a river with boats of all sizes sailing back and forth. Like a parade-float, an airship drifted in the distance.

"Good morning, sleepyhead!" a hoarse voice said, making her jump.

"Huh?"

"I'm Miss Weena Fion," the voice added. "Mr. Moreau's maidservant. Your *pater* said to be lettin you sleep as *long* as you want."

My pater?

Weena was a pale, freckled girl her own age, wearing a white lace cap and a gray dress with a white apron.

"Nice to meet you, Weena. I'm ... uh ... Miss Marie Moreau."

"Nice to meet you. I'll be drawin your bath, now."

Drawing my bath?

✳✳✳

The bathroom had the usual implements but seascapes decorated its walls — some with lighthouses, and one with water-nymphs.

Purple towels embroidered with gold threads hung on polished brass towel racks.

Marie climbed into the white claw-footed porcelain tub, turning its brass mermaid-shaped knobs to let in more hot water.

As she bathed, the previous day's events came back to her.

It wasn't just some insane nightmare.

She lay in the tub for fifteen minutes with her eyes closed.

She sighed, dried off, and dressed in the smelly clothes she'd taken off.

✽✽✽

"You have leftover *Norman Conquest* in the ice-shronk," Weena coughed. "Me *Kaiser's Spectacles* are good too. Here's today's scroot."

"*Kaiser's Spectacles?*" Marie said, taking the bizarre newspaper from her.

"Like *Kaiser's Monocle* but with *two* eggs. Lamb broth gives it a nice flavor."

"Oh, OK."

Weena clattered with pots and pans.

"Weena," Marie said. "Are you from Ireland?"

"Ireland?" Weena laughed. "No, more's the pity. Knickerbocker born and raised. I was always wantin to travel. Maybe someday. What's it like to ride in an airship?"

"An airship?"

"It sounds so ... so *primo.*"

"Um, it was."

Marie tasted the food.

"How are you likin it?" Weena said.

"My compliments to the Kaiser."

"I'm not knowin the *Kaiser.* Oh, a *joke!*"

Weena doubled over with laughter for several minutes, ending with a sickening coughing fit.

Renard Moreau came through the door.

"Oh dad," Marie exclaimed, jumping up and hugging him.

"Sorry I couldn't be here when you woke up," he said. "I had some business that couldn't wait."

"What's that *costume* you're wearing?" Marie said. "You look like *Hamlet.* And how did I get here? Where *is* here?"

"Let's go shopping. I'll answer all your questions. Miss Weena, we'll be going out for a while."

"Sure thing, Mr. Moreau."

***

They took a horse-drawn cab to a department store.

On the way, Renard told his daughter everything.

"We're in another *universe?*"

"A nice one. Nobody's trying to *kill* us — a feature I find especially charming."

"So Eakins's speech was right?"

"No," Renard said. "Derek and Allie *are* aliens of a sort. Their plans to take over the world are truly fiendish: Opening art galleries and setting up charities."

They arrived at *The Elegant Pony Unishoppy* — a twelve-story city-block-sized building decorated in an art-deco style.

One window display showed an elegant lady in a top hat and long flowing dress riding a horse through an enchanted forest, with elves and fairies peeking out from behind trees and leering. Another showed gentlemen dressed like Renard playing billiards.

The motorized manikins' slow motion was creepy.

Real and artificial pumpkins were everywhere.

A huge poster advertised the store's annual *Pumpkin Parade Fashion Festival,* and a reporter in front of a huge TV camera gave a running commentary.

Renard and Marie shoved and elbowed their way through the crush of people into the store.

"This was the wrong day to shop here," Renard muttered.

***

In one corner of the store, laughing children rode brilliantly colored ponies to cheerful music from two violinists.

Another corner had a display called *The Wonderful World of Electric Lighting,* with impossibly ornate lamps and chandeliers.

An eight-story high atrium with organ pipes on its walls filled the store's center. At its base, a fountain surrounded a ten-foot-high bronze statue of a pony as colored lights played on it.

A sign said *Horse of a different color.*

"This is magical!" Marie sighed.

They stumbled through the mob to the Perfume Counter, where the *L'Étoile de Paris Parfumerie* had an exhibit showing how perfume was made. Master perfumers pressed flower petals into wax and — over six months to a year — the scents diffused into the wax, which was refined into perfume.

There's got to be a better way to do that, Renard thought.

He and Marie took an elevator to Women's Fashions on the seventh floor.

※※※

After a puzzling hour of shopping, Marie wore a long black skirt and a lacy white blouse with an amethyst brooch. Over the blouse, she wore a burgundy tailcoat, open in the front with an ornate brass chain connecting the flaps.

She wore a black-tulle-wrapped cylindrical top hat on her head.

The two of them found a crowded cafe on the second floor called *Lord Crittendon's Cozy.* Circular tables filled the place — each having four chairs and odd brass racks around it.

A middle-aged man in a white suit and white turban played a gleaming white piano.

They found an empty table and sat.

"I feel so silly in this ... costume," Marie said. "Everyone else seems to be wearing them, though."

"You are the height of elegance, my dear," Allie said, joining them. "Glad to see you're up and about."

She wore a long burgundy dress with a gold chain and a top hat like Marie's.

The air crackled with ten thousand stray thoughts, making Allie wince.

Like a swarm of angry wasps, she mused.

Online shopping was the only thing she missed from the Origin timeline.

"As you see, I've been shopping here too," Allie said, taking off her hat and setting it on the brass rack beside their table.

Marie did the same.

"It's odd," Allie continued. "Top hats were nineteenth century *men's* clothing, and they're worn exclusively by *women* here."

"I've made an appointment for Derek with the Halifax Fused Glass Concern," Renard said.

"Excellent," she said, and then looked at Marie and added, "Derek's about to invent Pyrex glass. Oh, you're thinking of how perfume's made here. I'll print out the Wikipedia page on that."

"Thanks!" Renard said.

A waiter arrived and they all ordered cappuccinos.

"Cappu...what?" the waiter said.

"Coffee for us all," Allie said.

The waiter left.

Marie thought for a moment and said, "I can't ever go back to school or see my friends again?"

"I'm sorry," Allie said. "But it looks that way."

"Knickerbocker University has a great reputation," Renard said. "I can forge whatever documents you need to get in. Hell, I could even get you into Miskatonic."

"*Miskatonic?*"

"One of the most highly respected universities in this world," Renard said.

"Let me guess," Marie said. "It's in Arkham, Massachusetts on the Miskatonic River."

"As a matter of fact, it is. How did you know?"

"This is so *bizarre!*" Allie muttered. "Tell your father."

"I'm in a coma and all of this is a *dream!*" Marie shouted. "Any minute they'll wake me up and *execute* me!"

People at nearby tables looked up.

"OK, I'll tell him," Allie said, hugging Marie.

"Tell me what?"

"Heard of H. P. Lovecraft?" Allie said.

"Yes," Renard said. "He wrote horror stories. Really nightmarish as I recall."

The waiter served their coffees.

"Miskatonic University is a *fictional* place in his novels," Allie said. *"The Dunwich Horror. At the Mountains of Madness.* All his Cthulu books. Marie had to read them for a course: *Gothic Novel and Horror Fiction."*

"Miskatonic?" Renard said. "That can't be a coincidence. It's too long a word."

"That's why Marie thinks this is a dream. Things from her *mind* are appearing in this *world.* There's only one possible explanation."

"It's all a dream," Marie said.

"Two explanations, then. Lovecraft was able to travel to *other timelines,* like we Indigos can. Or pick up ideas from them, at least. The Australian Aborigines..."

A gunshot rang out, and several women screamed.

"Black Bart!" a man at the table to their right muttered. "This is *outrageous! The Elegant Pony?"*

Dressed in a black jumpsuit, a thirty-something bald man with a bushy brown mustache waved a pistol at the patrons.

"Ladies and gentlemen!" the man announced, like a circus ringmaster. "I am doing you a *great honor*. Giving you stories to tell your children and grandchildren. How the *boldest* pirate of *all time* robbed you. *Your money or your lives!*"

"Down on the floor!" one of Bart's "associates" shouted. "Everyone! Empty your pockets and open your purses!"

People complied, some women weeping.

"Did you get our birth certificates filed?" Allie whispered to Renard.

"Yes, this morning."

Allie stood up and said, "Black Bart? *Seriously?* That the *dumbest cliché* I ever heard!"

"Get down or I'll *put* you down."

Gripping a stun-gun in her purse, Allie continued walking toward Black Bart.

He fired.

Several women screamed.

"Missed me," she chuckled, resetting.

When she reached him, she stunned him in the neck, Black Bart fell to the floor in convulsions, and she slipped the device back into her purse.

With both hands, she hefted Bart's pistol and aimed it at his henchmen.

"Will someone help me tie them up?"

Several men jumped up, pulled off their neckties, and tied the criminals' hands behind their backs.

One man ran to a nearby sporting goods department and returned with coiled rope.

Everyone applauded, and Allie curtseyed and set the gun on a table.

"Jolly good show!" a man with a British accent said. "The Empire could use women like you."

Police arrived.

"Better late than never!" one man shouted.

"I would've stepped in but you were doing great on your own," Derek said, approaching Allie and hugging her.

"This is you keeping a low profile?" Renard muttered.

"I couldn't have them searching my purse," Allie said, indicating the stun-gun.

"He *shot* you!" Marie said. "He didn't miss."

"Indigos are hard to kill," Allie said.

A breathless thirty-something lady ran up to Allie, dressed somewhat like Marie, except that her tailcoat was forest-green — wearing a press-pass that said "Elaine Hickey."

"I'm covering the Pumpkin Parade for the Scrutineer. Could I have ... a short interview?"

"Sure. I'm pressed for time now. I'm Alessandra Evans."

She spelled her name.

Ms. Hickey motioned for a man lugging a gigantic box camera with a tripod to come over and take Allie's picture.

"The City Desk and the Crime Desk can eat their hearts out! A *fashion* reporter with the scoop of a lifetime: A *lady* capturing the Black Bart gang!"

A crowd gathered around them.

"My first question to you: why did you do it, Alessandra?"

"I couldn't bear to see these good people victimized," Allie said, waving at the crowd. "Something snapped. I had to take action."

"How did you subdue Black Bart?" Ms. Hickey said. "That was the most amazing thing I ever saw."

Allie scanned everyone everyone around her, searching for a believable lie.

Here goes nothing.

"I hesitate to reply because I was sworn to *profound secrecy*. My husband and I traveled extensively through the Chinese Empire and Tibet. In Tibet's most remote and hidden monastery, we learned the Vulcan Death Grip. I will not answer further questions on it."

Marie stifled a laugh.

"Now we're home and hope to settle in this *magnificent* city. That's all I can say for now. I'll give you an exclusive on any future interviews."

"Thanks!"

To further applause, they left.

✱✱✱

In a light drizzle, they stood outside the store's Fifty-first street entrance, jostled by people scurrying about on ten thousand nameless errands.

"I've got to create back-stories for you two," Renard said. "High-schools, university graduations. You're about to become major celebrities. I'll look into where you could've traveled in Asia, too."

"This *has* to be a coma-dream," Marie said. "Things like that *just don't happen.*"

"If it's a dream," Allie said. "It's a one that'll last as long as you want."

"Life itself is a kind of dream," Derek said. "A shared mass-hallucination. You see that when you travel through the spirit-world."

"So apply to Miskatonic University," Allie said. "This world may be exotic, but it's a good world — my every instinct tells me so. It's at your fingertips, Marie. Use it."

"I'll send away for brochures," Renard said. "For Miskatonic *and* Knickerbocker. Just in case you want to stay near me."

"I doubt *this* Miskatonic has a demonology department," Derek muttered.

Chapter 23

At nine in the morning, Grace, Wendy, and Travis ate breakfast on Taka's lanai — eggs over easy on white rice with two pieces of fried spam.

"Dese flies," Travis muttered, swatting the air. "We should go back inside."

"The Howland Family Trust is having one of their big meetings," Wendy said, shutting her eyes. "The whole family is there with their attorneys. They're almost fist-fighting."

"We're Howlands," Travis said. "We belong there."

"I can't face those ... people," Grace said. "I know what they think of me. You kids go. Tell me what happens."

When no field hands were visible, Wendy and Travis vanished.

"I don't know if I'll *ever* get used to that!" Grace exclaimed.

✳✳✳

Wendy and Travis landed in the Howland Building's fifth floor restrooms, and entered the main auditorium.

"Speak of the devil!" Luther shouted. "What makes you think you're welcome here?"

Twenty white-haired men and women turned to Wendy and Travis.

"This is a Howland family meeting," Travis said. "We're Howlands."

"I'm carrying Roger and Kaiulani Howland," Wendy said. "In a couple years, we'll *be* the Howland family. *All* of it!"

Several voices muttered that she had a point.

"They are the future," Luther agreed. "It's a case of the future battling the present."

"We just want my mother to get..." Travis said.

"By opening the floodgates to *lawsuits!*" Luther shouted. "Mr. Jamison here tells me you have the law on your side."

"You don't tell your *adversaries* that," Mr. Jamison muttered.

"Doesn't matter," Luther said. "When the law fails us, we transcend it."

The crowd became restive.

"What the *hell* does that mean?" Mr. Jamison glared at him.

Travis scanned the attorney and said, "Without the law, you wouldn't be *allowed* to own so much of Hawaii."

Luther motioned to two men wearing combat fatigues standing just outside the auditorium doors.

They came forward.

"I represent the Council of True Patriots and the acting President Knox," one man said. "We have a kill-order against these dangerous aliens and anyone harboring them."

"That's my *son* you're talking about!" Kurt Howland shouted.

"Luther, you *crazy bastard!*" Mr. Jamison muttered.

"In addition," the man in fatigues continued. "All property of said traitors shall be subject to expropriation."

"The state government doesn't recognize any of these so-called 'orders'," Mr. Jamison said.

"Which is why we're putting the state of Hawaii under martial law. President Knox has activated the marines at Pearl Harbor and Kaneohe. They have taken the Hawaiian governor into custody."

Four other uniformed men came forward.

"Arrest these two," the first man said, pointing to Travis and Wendy.

They vanished.

✳✳✳

"They're coming for us, auntie," Travis said on Taka's lanai. "Luther called the Eakins people."

Grace started wailing.

"We can take you where we took our home," Wendy said.

"Will they come for me too?" Taka said.

"They go after their enemies' families," Grace said. "They executed that poor girl."

"No *mami*," Travis said. "Derek and Allie rescued her."

"We can take your house with us," Wendy said. "Even your farm."

"My farm hands live in cabins at the south end," Taka said.

Wendy vanished.

Fifteen minutes later, she returned.

"I found a place at the end of Destiny Beach," she said. "I can take the house and maybe ten acres of land. No farm hands on it. How deep should I go?"

"How ... deep?" Taka mumbled, dazed.

"Five feet, I guess," Wendy said, vanishing.

Ten minutes later, she reappeared.

"It's easier if I lie down," she said.

Taka and Grace stared blankly.

Wendy went into the house and stretched out on the sofa.

"We go already," Travis said, pointing.

Ripples ran across the sky and distant mountains — as if they were painted on a canvas fluttering in a breeze.

Taka and Grace looked about anxiously.

Ripples also ran through the military truck filled with troops that rumbled down the road that paralleled the property line.

The ripples became more intense and finer until it looked as though a translucent white dome had settled over the house and land around it.

The ground shuddered as the dome became more transparent, and then it cleared completely.

***

A dense rain-forest had replaced the road paralleling the property. To the right, a beach had appeared.

"Welcome to Oz," Wendy said, coming out to the lanai.

"Wh...where's Haleakala?" Taka said, referring to Maui's iconic landmark.

"We're not on Maui, auntie," Travis said.

Derek and Allie appeared and said, "Aloha!"

"Aloha," the sisters mumbled.

"As Governor-General of Oz, I hereby grant you *full ownership* of the land your farm occupies," he said. "And any additional land you may require. *Fee simple.*"

***

On Derek and Allie's deck, Wendy introduced Grace and Taka to all the others.

"We're going to hook up electricity, water, and a cesspool," Derek said.

He and Travis vanished.

"What happened after we left?" Grace said.

"The army guys watched us disappear," Wendy said. "Leaving a ten-acre jungle in its place. They posted guards around it."

"They're testing for radiation or something," Allie said. "A waste of time."

"The Eakins people have expropriated the whole Howland Trust," Wendy said.

"Expropriated?" Taka said.

"It means 'take it away'," Wendy said. "They're taking lots of rich people's money. They didn't know about the Howlands until Luther called them."

"That *stupid, stupid* man," Grace muttered, shaking her head.

"Soldiers just told Travis's dad he had ten minutes to move out of his house," Wendy said.

"The house where Travis grew up?" Grace said.

"Kurt hopes to move in with Leilani," Wendy nodded. "She has a one-room apartment in Makiki."

"She won't want him anymore," Grace murmured. "He's old, unemployed, and broke."

"Oh my God!" Wendy exclaimed. "Luther Howland just put a gun in his mouth and shot himself."

"Wait by the river long enough, and you'll see the body of your enemy floating by," Andy sighed.

"Huh?" Grace said.

"Old Japanese saying."

Allie tried to explain timelines to Grace and Taka, but lost them completely.

"So complicated," Taka sighed. "Got to go home."

"I can take you," Allie said.

"No. I want to walk with my own feet."

Taka stood and slowly walked down the beach.

"They've got the electric working, Taka," Allie said. "But not the water."

***

An hour later, Derek and Travis reappeared.

"Taka's house has all its utilities working," Derek said. "And roaches."

"Oh shit," Wendy muttered. "I couldn't take them to another island because they'd be trapped there."

"Everyplace in Hawaii has roaches," Grace said.

"Not our Hawaii," Allie said. "We'll just have to live with them."

"Geckos and birds eat roaches," Birgit Fischer said. "We have plenty of those. The roaches won't overrun the place."

"At least we have ten acres of the world's best onions," Wendy said. "Taka won prizes."

"Harvesting them will be a problem," Derek said.

"You have no imagination," Wendy said. "We have to find out which areas are ready for harvest."

"I'll ask her," Llewellyn said and teleported to Taka's lanai.

***

Llewellyn entered Taka's house to find her lying on the sofa listening to a scratchy vinyl record playing *Aloha 'oe*.

"Hawaiian blues," Taka muttered.

"Queen Liliuokalani wrote it? I had no *idea* that song was so sad."

"You read my mind?"

"I'm sorry," Llewellyn said. "I didn't mean to invade your privacy. Sometimes I can't help it."

"It's OK. Just an old farmer's mind; not much in there."

"Oh, Taka! It's filled with beautiful memories!"

"*Aloha 'oe* is about farewell. End of a way of life."

"You could become one of us! The end could be a beginning."

"Too old," Taka sighed.

"You've had a *wonderful life*," Llewellyn said, summoning Andy. "Thirty-two years with *Davis* on a farm in paradise. You still have your house with all its memories — and *part* of your farm."

Andy appeared with three beers.

They spent a hour drinking beer and listening to Taka recount her life — how she and Davis had tried to have children, how they had all but adopted her sisters' children and children from the neighborhood — and how he'd passed away two years ago from lung cancer.

"The Eakins people say you're monsters. Monsters wouldn't take an hour — listening to an old ... onion farmer. "

"When you read minds," Llewellyn said. "You realize what a shining treasure every person is. Every soul is a *universe*. It sparkles with life in ways ... no other possibly could."

"Maybe my sparkles are used up," Taka yawned.

"It's getting late, Taka," Andy said, patting her on the shoulder. "Sleep well. Things will look better in the morning."

Chapter 24

Derek checked on the Archy's again.

Katalluwana's space ship shut off its hyperdrive and engaged its rockets to fly around the cloud of debris that had accumulated in front of it. Every hundred millions miles or so, it had to do this.

"We are able to image our destination," Kef said. "Eight planets and two within the habitable zone."

"Any signs of life?" Katalluwana said.

"The planets in the zone have large quantities of oxygen in their atmosphere. Almost a sure sign of life."

"Excellent! This may be easier than I thought."

✸✸✸

Vaughn Williams and Ed Brocklesby had just demonstrated the Pincus generator in a corner of the Space Venture factory floor.

The department heads had ordered fifty of the devices.

Afterward, Eldon asked to meet them in his office.

"I'm thinking of restarting the Joule Motorcar Company," he said. "Your generators worked well with Joules in Origin."

"You're from Origin?" Ed asked. "Where's the Trask from … here?"

Trask explained.

"Why did they kill you?" Ed asked.

"A bullet's cheaper than building better rockets," Vaughn said.

"My first thought, too," Eldon said. "It doesn't make sense, though. Better rockets are an aerospace company's *business*. It's in their interests to improve their product. The same is true for a *nation's* space program."

"So why are they getting violent?" Ed asked.

"I don't know, but you should become Indigos — for your own safety. Derek has the pills."

"Count me and Heidi in," Ed remarked.

"Rosa is dead set against it," Vaughn sighed. "We get into a fight every time I bring it up."

"*You* could become one," Eldon said.

"We're a package deal," Vaughn replied. "I'm not becoming an alien unless my family joins me."

Derek appeared and hugged Vaughn.

Eldon Trask shut his eyes for a moment and said, "Wendy's having her babies now."

"When?" Ed asked.

"It's over," Eldon said. "Two more Indigos have drawn their first breaths. Roger and Kaiulani."

"Anyway," Derek said. "We found out why humans never evolved on Oz. We have enemies."

"If you need to evacuate," Vaughn said. "Please stay with us."

"Thank you."

"Well, I guess I should go now," Vaughn said. "My flight leaves in an hour."

"I could teleport you to New York," Derek said.

"No thanks," Vaughn laughed. "I worked eighty hours last week, and next week is shaping up to be busier."

"Wow!" Eldon said, although he knew the reason.

"We're building a mile-long factory in Dayton and a smaller one in Aberdeen, Maryland. Any down-time I get is worth its weight in gold. I'd take a *slow blimp* if I could."

"I know a place where you could do that," Derek laughed.

"At first, we had problems with Joyce's kids in this timeline," Vaughn said. "Putting a million into their bank accounts soothed that over. Then we had to deal with *our* counterparts."

"How'd that work out?" Derek said.

"Culinary me is running our factory operations and ... the Rosas, well they'll come around eventually."

"Say hi to them for me," Derek said.

Eldon led Derek out to the factory floor.

❊❊❊

In spacesuits, Derek and Eldon orbited above the Archy planet's dark side.

"Weightlessness *sucks!*" Eldon said, choking back a load of vomit.

"It's worse on the surface," Derek said. "I almost died there."

Vast areas of the planet below them glowed reddish-orange, and a billion strobe lights flashed blue-white, some forming jagged streaks.

"The orange must be urban areas," Eldon said. "Red is natural daylight to them."

"Some of those cities are a thousand miles wide," Derek said. "The flashes must be lightning, *constant* lightning."

"I never thought I'd say this, but their planet is beautiful," Eldon said. "The day-side must've been a tropical paradise, and the night-side is the mother of all thunderstorms."

"Look!" Derek said, pointing to a perfect arc of orange light extending over half the planet.

"It's got to be man-made. Archy-made, I mean."

"It must be ten thousand miles long," Derek said. "Makes the Great Wall of China look like a picket fence."

They turned to the reason for their visit: Row upon row of dark, giant hulks floated beside them — the Archy's genocidal fleet.

As their orbit took them to the planet's day side, its sun's searing red orb heated up their spacesuits.

They teleported into one of the space ships.

"No atmosphere," Derek noted, looking at his heads-up display.

"Makes sense. If I wanted to mothball a fleet, I'd leave it without air."

They shone their helmet-lights on the corridor's featureless gray walls.

Then they teleported to a succession of rooms, all empty, with cryptic markings on the walls.

They finally ended up in a cavernous chamber that seemed to stretch for miles. Rows of house-sized machines covered the deck.

"My suit says they're radioactive," Derek said. "Maybe they're the atomic bombs or reactors."

"We should sabotage these ships. Even if the Archies don't attack us, it would be a public service."

Over the next hour, they destroyed twenty of the ships, half-engulfing them with their spirit-bodies and teleporting away.

"Only a thousand to go," Eldon said, as the twenty-minute oxygen-alarm on his spacesuit sounded.

They returned to the Space Ventures factory.

"Wait!" Eldon said, pointing to wisps of light circling his spirit-body. "Thoughts about me."

They followed the thoughts to their source, a man in a one-room apartment.

✳✳✳

The man's name was Mladko Radic — a former Serbian soldier wanted by Interpol for multiple assassinations. He was proud of their code name for him: The Mongoose.

"I *never* miss!" Radic shouted into a phone. "Could there be *two* of them?"

An attache case next to him contained his sniper rifle in pieces.

He's the sniper who killed Culinary me. Where are we?

No way to find out, Derek said. *Until we materialize.*

They drifted out of the room and materialized in an empty outdoor corridor. Peeling paint hung off stucco walls and gaping cracks in the concrete floor made it look sketchy.

A rusted iron railing kept them from falling into the nearly-empty parking lot below.

"Unit 2B," Eldon said.

It appeared to be a motel room.

"Now we go down and figure out the address," he added.

Walking down stairs in spacesuits turned out to be far more difficult than they had thought.

Twice, Derek almost fell.

"Security cameras with cut wires," he pointed out. "Radic must've done that. Or junkies."

They briefly stepped out onto Fraser Avenue, and noted the building number and name of the hotel: The Stardust Dreams Inn.

It looked more like Gangrene Nightmares.

A vacant lot overgrown with weeds bordered it, and a street-person pushing a baby-carriage full of garbage hobbled by.

He stared at their spacesuits for a moment and continued on his way.

They returned to the parking lot and teleported to the Space Ventures factory, where they stowed the spacesuits.

***

Back in Trask's office, they debated how to give the police an anonymous tip without a burner-phone.

"Damn!" Eldon said. "I should've gotten a bunch of them in Origin."

They finally teleported to an empty office in the Beverley Hills Police Department.

It had a massive bare walnut desk, white walls, and a big window overlooking the parking lot.

They put on cotton gloves and locked the door.

Eldon called Detective Martens on a desk phone, and Derek told Detective Martens everything they knew.

The office door-handle rattled, and a voice said, "They're in here."

Eldon and Derek vanished.

***

Since it was raining hard on Destiny Beach, they gathered in Derek and Allie's house at the end of Destiny Beach closest to Diamond Head.

Chloe popped into view.

"As I furniture-shopped, two men followed me," she said. "A Chinese intelligence officer named Fen Yazhu. And another man named Borislav Pedja."

"What about Pedja?" Derek said.

"A Serbian thug, working for a voice on a burner phone. Hell, I know his whole loathsome life-story. It doesn't tell us a damn thing."

"Lots of Serbians," Derek muttered. "I wonder if that means anything."

"Losing those tails was so easy," Chloe said. "As Eldy would say, *teleportation, baby!* When they realized they'd lost me, the Chinese spy followed the *other* guy."

Eldon laughed.

"So the Chinese are *not* the ones behind this," Allie said.

"Can't you just use telepathy to resolve the whole mystery?" Heidi said.

"I could, if Mr. Big would just *think* about me," Eldon said. "He must be a busy man doing a lot of things unrelated to Space Ventures."

"Mr. Big?" Allie laughed.

"At least we found the guy who murdered me."

"What's happening with that?" Ed asked.

"The LA County Sheriff's office and Detective Martens have surrounded the motel," Derek said. "They're ready to make their move. Radic is still in his room."

Chapter 25

In Origin, Travis appeared in a deserted and silent Kapiolani Park at the foot of Diamond Head.

It was six A.M.

Gusting over the Koolau Mountains, damp, orchid-scented Trade Winds whistled through trees and sent old paper scraps rustling across the plush grass carpet.

Seeing the Waikiki Shell and the seats around it brought back memories of happier times, times they had enjoyed concerts there — when he had been young, and his parents had loved each other.

Christmas pageants had been his favorites.

A lion roared in the Honolulu Zoo, across the street.

Travis found what he was looking for: an emaciated white-haired man covered with newspapers, sleeping on a park bench.

"Dad?"

"Huh?" Kurt Howland mumbled. "Travis? Is that you?"

He stirred on the bench and struggled to sit up. His newspaper-blanket flew away, revealing his torn and grimy clothes. Purple bruises covered his face and almost closed one eye.

He glanced at his bare wrist.

"They took my watch ... and wallet."

"Come to Oz, dad."

"Got to contact Luther. He always knows what to do. It's all a big mistake. He'll fix it."

"He killed himself, dad."

"You're mistaken. Luther will know what to do."

"The Howland Trust is *pau,* dad. All gone. Come to Oz with me."

※※※

They appeared in front of Taka's house standing on a divot of earth Travis had brought with them.

On the lanai, Grace and Taka lounged and bottle-fed Wendy's children — Grace with Roger and Taka with Kaiulani.

"I wanted to punch you and slap your face," Grace muttered. "But someone beat me to it. You *are* Travis's father, though."

Kaiulani stopped nursing, yawned, and vanished.

"God!" Taka said. "I'll never get used to that. Wendy said not to worry though."

"She put herself to bed," Travis said. "Uh oh! She pooped."

Travis vanished.

"I haven't eaten in days," Kurt said.

"Here," Taka said, pushing a plate of sandwiches toward him. "Then clean up. Travis got clean clothes from a thrift store. That's about your speed."

"How can you be that broke?" Grace exclaimed. "You could've sold your car!"

"They said the car goes with the house," Kurt said, grabbing a sandwich.

"I had *jewelry!* You could've pawned it."

Kurt finished his sandwich and grabbed another.

"I called the police, but they never showed up," he said, between bites. "Then the soldiers said my ten minutes were up and shot at my feet. I hitchhiked to Honolulu."

"Meet your grandson," Grace said. "Roger Howland."

"Eyes like diamonds," Kurt murmured. "So creepy."

"The *keikis* are beautiful," Grace muttered. "Your grandson's the happiest baby I ever saw."

"Howlands are *aliens!* Except for me and you, Grace."

Allie popped into view.

"We may be aliens," she said. "But we're not the ones who stole your house or wallet."

Should we invite him to join us? she beamed to Derek. *Our Ohana?*

Hell no! Derek replied. *I don't trust him. For that matter, I don't like him, either. I'm fine with Grace and Taka joining us. What do you think, Travis?*

I don't want him inside our heads. I don't want him teleporting into our bedroom anytime he wants.

※※※

That evening, they all met on Derek and Allie's deck.

Taka, Grace, Wendy, and Travis had just returned from another shopping trip on Maui in Origin.

"We can't shop there anymore, Taka," Travis said. "The locals love you, but there are too many soldiers."

"We should shop in Culinary," Grace said.

"No! I might meet another ... me. What would I say to her?"

"We'll figure something out," Wendy sighed.

Derek brought Ed and Heidi, and Renata brought Culinary Derek and Allie.

"My mom's watching the kids," Culinary Allie said.

"Keep them home with you for a couple days," Allie said. "It's a virus so they'll catch it from you."

"We'll all lay low for a week," Culinary Derek said. "We stocked up at home, and I told the contractors what we want done. By week's end, we'll almost be ready for our grand opening."

Derek handed them red pills.

"That's all there is to it?" Grace said.

"Want one?" Allie said.

Grace and Taka timidly shook their heads. Luckily, Kurt Howland didn't ask for a pill.

"You're not *required* to take them," Allie smiled.

With a flourish, the Culinary couple took their pills.

"The next time you visit us," Derek said. "It'll be under your own power."

Chapter 26

As Vittoria slept, Eldon Trask, Chloe, Derek and Allie attacked Archy spaceships.

In two hours they managed to destroy another three hundred of them.

They stopped when Vittoria beamed that she was hungry.

"They still seem unaware of what we're doing!" Chloe said. "Amazing!"

※※※

Derek and Allie teleported to Knickerbocker — to restrooms outside the offices of Milton, Harris, Bennington, and Tweed — Attorneys at Law.

Renard awaited them there.

Jora Milton, Esq., greeted them. He was a gray-haired short man wearing a brown wool waistcoat and red cape.

He presented them with several contracts.

"This forms the *Indigo Concern*," he said. "A concern to serve as a shirm organization owning other concerns."

Shirm? Allie thought. *Oh, it's an umbrella*

They signed and the attorney notarized it.

Milton then produced a stack of documents.

"These contracts create Limited Collaborative Concerns," he explained. "You can create inventions in collaboration with others, and your interests are protected. It has non-disclosure provisions and allows you to fill in the percent of profit you wish to share with your collaborators. When you use one of these, it must be notarized."

Allie gave one of these to Renard, and a printout of web pages on the Butaflor process for extracting essential oils.

***

As a dense fog rolled in, Derek, Allie, and Renard took a steam cab to the offices of the Halifax Fused Glass Concern.

"Remind me again why you're inventing Pyrex," Renard said. "Not that it isn't valuable on its own."

"A crucial part of Pincus Generator is made of Pyrex," Derek said. "I'd love to be able to just buy it, but it doesn't exist in this timeline."

After a twenty-minute ride, they arrived at an imposing fifteen-story art-deco building on the corner of 86th street and 3rd avenue.

Colorful glass sculptures and mobiles filled the building's lobby, and a series of glass busts depicted the company's top executives over the years.

"It's an *art gallery,*" Allie said.

They took the elevator to the tenth floor.

***

In a spacious oak-paneled office, they met the company's Chief Engineer, Hondo Michalis, and its attorney, June Foster.

The attorney examined the contract carefully for fifteen minutes.

"It appears to be in order," she said. "In exchange for manufacturing your glass product, the concern gets $500 now and 5 percent of future profits."

They signed, and she notarized it.

Derek handed her $500 in cash and she wrote up a receipt.

"So, what's your big idea?" Mr. Michalis said.

"Manufacture glass in the usual way, except that you add 13% boron trioxide to the mix," Derek said.

Mr. Michalis raised his eyebrows.

"Will this be a problem?" Derek continued.

"Not at all," Mr. Michalis said. "We have a chemical supplier that should be able to provide the boron trioxide in quantity. What do you expect to happen?"

"I expect the resulting glass to have a thermal expansion coefficient comparable to that of fused quartz," Derek said.

"Extraordinary!"

"You could make glass cookware," Derek said. "Durable laboratory glassware. Mirrors for reflecting telescopes."

"The possibilities are endless," Mr. Michalis said. "I'm intrigued. I'll work on it personally. I should be able to produce a sample by tomorrow."

※※※

Derek and Allie took turns teleporting to the bathroom in Renard Moreau's apartment.

He handed them thick folders of papers.

"These are your life-stories," Renard explained. "Schools attended, places lived. Take some time to memorize everything."

"You've got to go to a doctor!" Marie said to Weena, who looked pale and faint.

"No money," she mumbled. "Got to finish cleanin..."

Weena collapsed.

"She's burning up!" Allie said.

"There's a hospital two blocks away," Renard said. "It's supposed to be good."

As night fell, they took her in a cab to the hospital.

"You can barely read street signs in this fog," Allie muttered.

They finally arrived at a granite-faced building with a sign proclaiming, "Knickerbocker University Medical Center."

They followed an arrow labeled "Emergency Room" to the right, and Derek noticed an odd bronze plaque on the building's side:

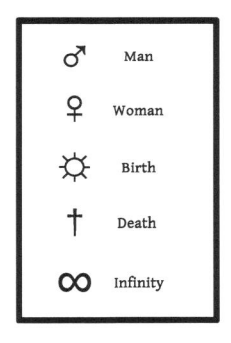

♂	Man
♀	Woman
☼	Birth
†	Death
∞	Infinity

※※※

The hospital looked much like ones in Origin or Culinary, except for the lack of electronics.

Derek told the Check-In Coordinator they would cover all of Weena's medical expenses and gave him $10,000 as an advance against future charges.

After a half hour, a man who introduced himself as Professor Doctor Willis Jordan came out and said his examination and the "Roentgen-gram" confirmed that she had "severe bacterial pneumonia."

Prof. Dr. Jordan was a clean-shaven short trim fifty-something man.

"I wish I could give you better news," he said. "Bacterial infections are devastating. A nurse will sit by her side through the night on Death Watch. I doubt she'll make it to morning."

"I wonder whether we could be alone with her for a few minutes," Derek said.

"Of course!" Prof. Dr. Jordan said.

***

Derek, Allie and a sobbing Marie went into Weena's room — a dimly lit room like a monk's cell with a black window opposite the door.

Piled high with blankets, she slept.

A glass bottle of saline slowly dripped into her IV line.

Weena's eyelids fluttered.

Professor Fischer popped into existence holding a hypodermic needle.

"This is maximum dose of azithromycin and a corticosteroid," she said. "If she's allergic, it'll kill her."

"She's dying anyway," Derek said.

Professor Fischer was able to slowly inject the drugs into Weena's IV line and gave Marie a small envelope of pills, saying, "Augmentin tablets and prednisone."

Weena stirred in bed and opened her eyes.

Professor Fischer smiled, bowed, and vanished.

A nurse and priest entered the room and pulled up chairs beside Weena's bed.

***

"Does she have family?" Allie said, as they left the hospital and flagged a cab.

"She has a mother — a mater — and a younger brother, Micah," Marie said. "I don't know how to contact them."

"I'm sure they'll contact you," Derek said. "After she doesn't come home."

"I'll visit her tomorrow morning," Marie said.

"I guess I have to 'discover' penicillin," Derek said as they made their way through the dense fog back to Renard's apartment.

A policeman awaited them and asked about Weena.

❋❋❋

At eight in the morning, Derek, Allie and Marie visited Weena at the hospital.

By the light of day, her room had white walls, a white marble floor, and a large window that overlooked the East River.

She sat up in her bed chatting with her mother, Clarice, and brother, Micah.

She broke into a fit of horrible gurgling coughs.

The nurse on duty captured her gobs of green sputum in a stainless steel bowl.

Prof. Dr. Jordan came in and examined her.

"I've never seen anything like it," he said. "She's doing remarkably well. The active disease process seems to have halted *completely*. She'll need several more days to make a full recovery."

"We can't afford no private room," Clarice Fionn said.

"All taken care of, madame," Prof. Dr. Jordan said, pointing to Derek and Allie. "Thanks to these two."

"We'll pay her full salary while she's in the hospital," Allie said.

"Thank you," Clarice sobbed, kissing Allie's hand.

"I was dreamin the *strangest dream*," Weena murmured. "An angel visited me and then bowed and *disappeared*."

"The feverish mind plays tricks on us, my dear," Prof. Dr. Jordan smiled.

"We have to do something about your teeth," Allie said to Weena.

"Me teeths fine! Me toothache's gone!"

"She had an abscessed tooth," Prof. Dr. Jordan said. "But the infection is gone. It's as if a magic bullet shot all the disease bacteria in her body."

"We should still take you to a dentist," Allie said. "Could you look up dentists, Marie?"

"Sure."

"Who's hungry?" a woman in white said, pushing a food cart.

Breakfast was a lamb chop with a fried egg on it, vegetables, coffee, and a vitamin pill.

Weena's mother and brother licked their lips.

"Let's give Weena some privacy while she eats," Allie said. "Have breakfast with us in the cafeteria."

✹✹✹

The cafeteria was at the end of a long corridor and around the corner.

The entire room was white — including the ceiling, walls, and tiled floor. Even the tables and chairs were white. To make matters worse, hospital personnel wore white, as did the cafeteria staff.

It hurt their eyes.

"I guess green surgical scrubs never caught on here," Derek muttered.

Clarice shot him a puzzled look.

They picked out breakfasts from steam tables and Derek paid.

"You look familiar," Clarice said to Allie. "I seen you somewhere."

"I have that kind of face."

Micah proceeded to inhale a stack of pancakes.

"After me Joseph passed away, poor Weena's all we got," Clarice said. "We love her so much and we need her."

We'd be in the street without the money from her three jobs, she thought, rubbing her face. *Her two other employers fired her for being sick.*

Weena makes a grand total of eighteen dollars a day, Allie beamed to Derek. *Appalling!*

"We'll pay her fifty dollars a day if she works for Mr. Moreau and us *exclusively,*" Derek said. *"And* while she's in the hospital. She might have to quit any other jobs she has."

Oh God, what will they make do for that kind of money? Clarice thought.

"Her duties will involve house cleaning and occasional cooking," Allie said. "Basically what she already does."

"How long is she ... allowed to stay ... in here?" Clarice said.

"Her health is the most important thing," Derek said. "She shouldn't leave a *minute* before the doctor says she's cured."

"Prof. Dr. Jordan thinks she'll have to be here for five days, so here's her salary in advance," Allie said, counting out $250 and handing it to Clarice.

Clarice stared in disbelief at the money in her hand.

"God bless you!" she sobbed, pocketing it. "We should tell Weena the good news."

After they left, Derek said, "You're thinking we're being generous, Marie."

"Yes."

"If we have servants..." Allie began.

"Everyone here either *has* servants or *is* a servant," Marie said.

"I guess we *have* to have them, or we'll look odd," Allie sighed. "I'm not comfortable with strangers poking through my stuff."

"Yeah," Marie said.

"If they're like Weena, it won't be so bad," Allie said. "She's sweet as a newborn kitten. The point is we have a *mountain* of secrets. Hell, we're from *another universe.*"

"Yeah, I guess."

"So we have to treat our servants *very* well and *pay* them well," Allie said. "We want them to regard working for us as the best job they ever had."

"It's also the right thing to do," Derek said.

"I talked Weena into doing her high school equivalency," Marie said. "They mail you the course materials and you take an exam at the Board of Education."

"Good idea!" Allie said. "You can study with her and learn about this world."

"Me thoughts exactly. Oh no! I'm beginning to talk like her!"

"You should sneak her one of those pills every day, Marie," Allie said.

"Sure. I'll visit her, and we'll study together."

Carrying a tray of food, an exhausted-looking man — all in white — staggered over to the seat next to them and collapsed into it. He stared into space for a moment and then examined his food.

Derek scanned him and learned he was a surgeon at the end of a seventy-two hour rotation.

"What really happened to Eakins?"

"We exiled him to another timeline," Derek said. "Incredibly, he's still alive."

"Why didn't you do that in the *beginning?*"

"We're not about to overturn a free and fair election," Allie said. "Not until he decided to murder Derek's hometown."

"You have *superpowers*," Marie said. *"Why didn't you fight him?"*

"And fight his *fifty million* followers?" Allie said. "You should talk, Marie! You *volunteered* for his campaign."

The doctor sitting next to them looked up, puzzled.

"I ... I ... I thought he'd ... bring ... change. Will we ever be able to go back?"

"Sure," Allie said. "After the orgy of hate and violence comes the hangover. Remorse. Non-Indigos like you and your dad will be welcomed back with open arms. They'll *beg* the Pincuses and the Williams family to return. I don't think they'll ever welcome Indigos back. We're just too powerful ... and scary. Especially if the US winds up as a dictatorship."

"When?" Marie said.

"Ten, fifteen years."

"But ... but," Marie sputtered. "By then we'll be settled here. I might be married with kids. We won't want to go back."

Derek sighed, shut his eyes, and scanned Mr. Michalis at Halifax Fused Glass.

Following the recipe Derek had given them, he'd worked through the night creating a small glass bowl.

Its properties astounded him.

Wearing protective gear, company executives watched him pack the bowl in ice and pour boiling water into it — without it breaking.

When Mr. Michalis used molten lead, the bowl didn't explode as expected — it only broke into three large pieces.

Raoul Argent, the company's president, examined the contract they had signed with the Indigo Concern.

This is what we've been looking for! he thought.

Chapter 27

After destroying fifty more Archy spaceships, Trask and Chloe stowed their spacesuits.

"So Mercouri *did* go to Disney World after all," Eldon said.

❋❋❋

They teleported to restrooms in the Magic Kingdom — between the *Merchant of Venus* and *Auntie Gravity's Galactic Goodies.*

Outside, the heat, humidity, and the crush of sweaty tourists took their breath away.

In front of them, tiny spaceships on metal arms attached to a rotating hub drifted in a circle between spinning planets — the *Astro Orbiter* ride.

Riders could raise or lower their spaceships.

"Mercouri's in *Space Mountain,*" Chloe said. "Wanna go?"

"No way! I throw up on roller-coasters. The *Astro Orbiter's* more my speed."

"Says the man who planned to fly a rocket to *Mars?*"

"I would've undergone *very rigorous* astronaut-training," he sighed, his mood plummeting. "The last six months ... flushed those plans down the crapper."

The boy in him still yearned to be an astronaut, to fly atop a shuddering exuberant pillar of fire that would leave his adoptive father awestruck — at long last willing to deem Eldon tough enough — and, perhaps, worthy of the time and money they had wasted raising him.

Chloe hugged him fiercely.

"Mercouri will pick up a package in the post-ride show," he finally croaked. "His ride's pulling into the station."

❋❋❋

They teleported into a room inside *Space Mountain* and watched Mr. Mercouri glide by on a moving walkway.

People stared as they stepped onto the walkway.

They saw us materialize! Chloe beamed.

"Transporter's working again," Eldon smiled, wrapping an arm around Chloe.

"Supposed to be Eldon Trask?" a teenage boy sneered. "You don't look *anything* like him! So *lame!*"

"After all those hours in makeup?"

A man in gray sweats and a red baseball cap set a black attache case on the walkway and melted into the crowd.

Mr. Mercouri spotted the case and picked it up.

A quick scan showed that the man — Jeff Pollack — had been paid $1000 to do this. He had no idea what was in the case or who'd paid him.

He assumed it was drugs.

"It's so strange!" Eldon said.

"What?"

"I can read the mind of the man who *handed* the briefcase to Pollack. Just because he physically met him. How's that *possible?*"

"They said our powers would increase over time," Chloe said.

Mr. Mercouri elbowed his way through the crowd and left.

"I can scan the man who contacted *him,* too. I can trace each link of the chain."

"Where does it end?"

"With Walter Fegelein," Eldon said. "Head of Obsidian Security."

"A *security company?*"

"They mostly do legitimate business. For a hundred million, though, they'll do *anything.* Even 'neutralize' Space Ventures."

"Who hired them?"

"Fegelein doesn't know, which bothers the *hell* out of him."

"Why?" Chloe said.

"He doesn't like working for an unknown. He'd like to know who can drop fifty million as a retainer."

"So would I."

The moving walkway disgorged them outside Tomorrowland's *Carousel of Progress.*

"Want to see the *world of the future,* honey?"

"Sounds overwhelming," Eldon laughed.

※※※

Back in his office, Eldon called Cape Canaveral.

"I fired Mr. Mercouri," he told them.

"You know that?" he continued. "Good. I received an anonymous tip."

He listened.

"Yes," he continued. "Mercouri will show up on site with forged credentials."

"The name on them?" he added. "Gary Johnson. He's carrying a bomb."

Trask hung up.

"Are we in the clear?" Chloe said.

"They'll be on the lookout and contact Patrick Air Force base."

"We should go there," Chloe said.

"I've got meetings all afternoon."

"I'll go then," Chloe said.

"Don't get cocky! Let the Canaveral people do..."

"I got a totally *batshit insane* request!" the director of Vehicle Assembly — Allan Jesperson — shouted, bursting through the door.

"I couldn't stop him," Susan apologized.

"That's OK," Trask said.

"Remove a Mars Lander's *fuel tanks and engines?*"

"Yes," Eldon said. "We're researching a new technology. How soon can you do it?"

"I suppose I can chuck them into the *trash* in an hour or so."

"Good! Don't throw them in the garbage. Is the fuselage that holds the fuel tanks vacuum-rated?"

"It could be," Jesperson said.

"Do it, and put seats for passengers in it with a monitor at each seat. There's room for twenty seats, maybe."

"What kind of seats?"

"Airline-type seats," Eldon said. "Or like the comfortable seats in movie theaters. They don't have to withstand high G-forces."

"It sounds to me like you're turning my Mars Lander into an *amusement park ride!* Should I get *Buzz Lightyear* on the phone?"

"That's enough, Mr. Jesperson! And may I remind you, it's not *your* lander? Will you do it or not?"

He sighed deeply and nodded.

"Good."

He left.

Their faces almost touching, Eldon and Chloe devoured each other with their eyes.

The intrigue and confrontations, he began.

Are making me horny, she continued his thought.

You smell sooo sexy! he beamed, filling his lungs with her haunting aroma. *God, that's a phrase I'd never imagined uttering.*

His eyes went blurry.

Part of the weirdness of being us, darling. Can we do it on your sofa?

Only if we can be quiet.

Not an option for either of us.

They lay on the sofa making out until Lin Wong's theatric cough interrupted them.

Maybe Chloe's a honey-pot spy, he thought, puzzled by the room's faint medicinal odor. *She takes her work seriously.*

Chloe laughed.

❋❋❋

After two hours of meetings, Eldon and Chloe returned to their Oz-bedroom and ripped their clothes off.

They briefly teleported to the Sea of Desire — only to find themselves in the midst of a squall with thirty-foot waves.

Hurricane season had begun.

Dripping with seawater, they returned home and made love.

When they were done, they gathered up sheets, hauled the mattress back onto the bed, and collapsed onto it — sleeping for an hour.

Then they showered and dressed.

"Let's get married," Eldon said. "Right now. Vegas style."

"OK. Ever been there?"

"Not in this timeline. I'm never going back to Origin."

"Got a globe in your office, right?" Chloe said. "We can use it to locate Culinary Vegas from the spirit world. Derek and Allie did something like that when they went on their honeymoon."

***

In their spirit-bodies, they flew through the nearly empty Space Ventures factory — closed for the evening except for three unconscious security guards slumped in front of monitors.

When they reached Eldon's office, they found a North Korean intelligence officer named Gul Ran ransacking it.

Bastard! Trask said. *I want to punch his lights out.*

Just call Drax Security.

He'll be long gone by the time they get here.

Hit him with a stun gun, Derek said, joining them in his spirit body.

Eldon returned to Derek and Allie's place, picked up a stun gun, materialized behind Gul Ran, and stunned him.

The North Korean agent whipped around and kicked Eldon in the neck — which made a sickening crunch — knocking him down.

Eldon reset.

Momentarily confused, he spotted Gul Ran and decided he was the enemy. He charged the North Korean — as Derek appeared behind the agent and stunned him in the neck.

This time, Ran went down, flopping on the floor like a freshly-caught trout.

Derek vanished.

They tied the North Korean agent up with electric cords, and Eldon called Drax Security and the police.

Trask is a demon! Gul Ran thought. *I heard his neck snap. He should be dead — but he's fine.*

I reset from death! Eldon beamed at all Indigos in existence. *It must be done immediately — before you drift away.*

Excellent! Derek beamed.

So Culinary You could've saved himself? Allie beamed.

If he'd been a trained Indigo, Eldon replied.

It's as if Trask is carrying on a conversation with invisible people, Ran thought looking around the room.

Every time he worked his bonds loose, Eldon stunned him again and re-tightened them.

After ten minutes, police sirens sounded in the distance.

Chloe and Eldon spent the next three hours talking to police, the FBI, and Drax Security.

✷✷✷

Back in Oz, Chloe said, "You tried, honey. Someday, we'll have a proper wedding. With a big reception in the factory. Champagne for everyone"

They went to bed.

Chapter 28

The sun hung low over the horizon, and a sea breeze stirred Allie's hair as she, Andy, and Llewellyn chatted on her deck.

"We're at an impasse," Andy muttered.

"Have you guys made *any* progress?"

"We see thousands of linguistic patterns and understand a few words, but that's it," Andy replied.

"Eldon is busy with his company," Allie said, as Vittoria appeared in arms.

"Even he isn't an electronics expert," Llewellyn said. "He knows more than we do, but that's not saying much."

"He has the best people in the world working for him," Allie said. "Maybe we can take the Squidward equipment to Los Angeles and have them study it."

"Wendy could teleport the entire cave there," Llewellyn said.

"What the hell is that?" Andy muttered, pointing to a ribbon of light rippling across the evening sky. It had a head, small wings, small claws, and a long, sinuous tail.

"A *dragon-kite?*" Llewellyn said.

"No," Andy said. "It's alive. It has consciousness, too. Like a worm or bug."

"Tori's making it," Allie said. "She pitched her thoughts into the sky."

Tori giggled.

"Are her powers greater than ours?" Llewellyn said.

"No," Allie said. "She tried something that never occurred to me."

"Kids do the darnedest things," Andy laughed.

"I *see* what she's doing," Allie said. "Give me a moment. I saw this at a wedding, once."

The air at the other end of the deck shimmered and congealed into a man with an accordion, sitting on a chair. He began to play a rousing rendition of the *Tarantella Napoletana*.

"My goodness!" Llewellyn exclaimed. "A complete 3D moving image with sound! I love the *music* too — straight out of *The Godfather* movie."

"That wedding was like the one in the movie," Allie said.

"With FBI and gangsters?"

"Yeah. Grandpa, his six bodyguards, and..."

"I can't *believe* you guys are babbling on about music and weddings!" Andy interrupted. "You created a goddamn *Tulpa!* Tibetan monks claimed they could project their thoughts into matter like you just did. One, named Geshe Rinpoche, told me he'd created an entire caravan once. A hundred people ... yaks ... horses ... and their baggage."

"Ordinary humans have our abilities, then," Allie murmured. "Or can."

Vittoria yawned and vanished.

Her dragon vanished piecemeal, the center of its body fading first, then its tail and, finally, its head.

Birgit Fischer appeared.

"The human brain is the only organ whose *physical structure* is changed by *thoughts*," she said. "Thinking the right thoughts could modify brains the same way the God Virus modified ours. Maybe some kind of meditation or visualization."

"Probably starting in early childhood," Allie murmured. "When the brain is flexible ... and growing. The God Virus gave us a shortcut."

"My God!" Allie exclaimed. "When I was four, I had an imaginary friend named Gino."

"Really?" Andy smiled.

"We played games and sang songs. He always did what I wanted him to do. Mom caught a glimpse of him once and thought our apartment was haunted. I'm pretty sure he was a *tulpa*."

"Maybe there's a world," Llewellyn said. "Of standard humans with *all* our powers."

"If something *can* exist, it *does*," Allie said. "Somewhere."

"What would they think of us?" Andy said. "I wonder..."

"I just wanted to make an announcement," Birgit Fischer said. "Ian and I moved the Oz Institute of Philosophy. Want to see its new home?"

Allie's accordion-player turned into colored smoke that blew away.

***

The Institute now stood beside a churning river in a brooding landscape. A dense evergreen forest bordered an adjacent meadow, and a wall of snowcapped mountains soared in the distance.

It was early morning.

Trees shredded mist swirling through the chilly, pine-scented air — like steam from a witch's cauldron — or the breath of God.

"In Origin, this would be in the middle of Munich," Professor Fisher explained. "I wanted to occupy the opposite side of the planet from Destiny Beach."

"We're as good at moving stuff as Wendy," Ian said. "Isn't this place beautiful? A lot more rugged than the islands."

Eight woolly mammoths and a woolly rhinoceros grazed beside the river, as wolves howled a distant conversation.

A murder of crows flew overhead.

Swooping down like an avenging angel, a huge golden eagle snatched one in its talons and bit off its head — as the others swarmed around it and screeched in protest.

"The river is snow melt from the Bavarian Alps," Birgit said, pointing to the mountains.

"It's *alive* with fish," Ian said.

They all sensed something stalking them — a horse-sized smilodon slinking through the grass, its foot-long fangs gleaming in the morning light.

They teleported away when it pounced.

※※※

At midnight, Culinary Allie's mental screams woke Allie and Derek.

They went to her.

"Loretta's missing!" Culinary Allie wailed, between sneezes. "I tore the apartment apart and she's *nowhere* to be found."

"She's perfectly safe," Derek said.

"You know where she is?"

"Yes," Allie said. "You could find her easily if you get out of body."

"Don't you *get* it? My child's *missing!* I have no time for *Indigo bullshit!* Why the *fuck* did I let you idiots talk me into it?"

"I called the police," Culinary Derek said. "They're coming over."

"Indigo *bullshit* is the only thing that'll work," Allie said. "The police won't find her."

"If you can't get out-of-body, we'll bring her home," Derek said. "You should try, though. You have everything you need at your fingertips."

"I'll try lying down," Culinary Derek said.

"You're a *worthless piece of shit!*" Culinary Allie wailed. "Our beautiful Loretta's missing and you *lie down?* If anything happened to her, I'll never forgive *any* of you!"

"Yelling won't accomplish *anything,*" Allie snapped.

Tony started crying.

"They seem to know what they're doing, honey," Culinary Derek mumbled. "I'm trying to follow their advice."

He lay in bed and closed his eyes.

Allie shut her eyes.

Good, she beamed at Culinary Derek. *Now think of Loretta.*

***

They both found themselves floating above the chicken coop on Destiny Beach, where Loretta petted chickens.

Now try to see her as clearly as possible, Allie beamed to him.

He and Allie materialized.

"Daddy!" Loretta said, hugging him.

"Hi, sweety," Allie said. "I know you like to pet the chickens but they need their sleep. If they don't get their sleep, they'll be very tired tomorrow."

"O...K."

"Let's go home, Loretta," Allie said, leading her out of the chicken coop onto Destiny Beach.

"How?"

"Just lie down on the sand."

She and Culinary Derek lay side by side and closed their eyes.

Now think about home and your mommy.

***

They floated near the ceiling of the Evans apartment.

Derek and Culinary Allie were talking to a policeman in the kitchen.

Let's go into a bedroom.

They drifted through walls into the master bedroom.

Try to see things as clearly as possible.

They all materialized and fell onto the bed.

"What was that?" Culinary Allie said from the kitchen.

Culinary Derek and Loretta strolled into the kitchen.

"Say hi to your mommy," Allie said to Loretta.

Loretta ran into the kitchen where Culinary Allie scooped her up and hugged her.

"She was just hiding in a closet," Derek said. "Sorry to take up your time, officer."

They shook hands and the policeman left.

"Where was she really?"

"Petting chickens on Destiny Beach," Allie said, entering the kitchen.

"She went there on *her own?*"

"Yes," Culinary Derek said, joining them. "Teleporting is easy."

"Accessing the spirit world is your super-power," Allie said to Culinary her. "You have to be *calm* to do that — at least in the beginning."

"I'm sorry I'm not a *robot* like you people. I *apologize* for *loving* my kids!"

"We're not *robots!*" Allie shouted. "If you could've calmed down for a *fucking second*, you would've known *exactly* where she was. *We* did. That's why we weren't upset."

"When something goes wrong," Derek said. "Getting into the spirit world should be your *top priority*. Not running around and screaming."

"I'm sorry, but ... I don't know if I can be ... calm. Now I hear *your* thoughts. You're thinking this was a big mistake."

"Yes," Derek said. "We'll have to live with it, though. Things will settle down once you get used to being Indigos."

"To get off this subject," Allie said. "Did anyone sneeze at that policeman? I don't want this virus spreading all over the place."

"I did the talking," Derek said.

"Yeah, he shoved me away from the cop," she frowned.

***

"Come!" a farmer shouted at Eakins. "Quickly!"

They dragged him through a hole in the floor and down a tunnel.

"The Safety Service has heard of you," one explained. "They're searching farms in sector 15. Checking bar codes. They execute anyone without one. On the *spot*."

They passed a chamber with a man and woman feverishly making out and moaning.

The farmer winked.

They rut like livestock, Eakins thought. *They are livestock. Not like my sublime encounters, my experiences with God-blessed little ones. Will I ever see that world again? That magnificent life?*

Further down in the tunnel, Eakins huddled in the darkness most of the night.

Chapter 29

Raoul Argent, the white-haired president of Halifax Fused Glass, had a neatly trimmed mustache and wore a brown tweed jacket, a red and blue plaid cape, black pants, and an eight-sided purple velvet hat with a peacock feather in it.

His huge office was a book-lined study that occupied the building's top floor.

Looking up, Derek spotted its chandelier — an impossibly delicate glass sculpture of an orchid-bouquet, with tiny electric lights in its flowers.

He tried not to stare.

A thick Persian rug covered its parquet floor, and Mr. Argent's desk was made of glass tinted to look like mahogany.

Hondo Michalis, and the company's chief attorney, June Foster attended.

A secretary sat poised over an ornate brass manual typewriter.

"After perusing your borosilicate glass extensively, our scientists have concluded that its properties are unprecedented," Mr. Argent intoned. "In our concern's hundred year history, we have never encountered its like. May I presume to speculate that you intend to patent this invention?"

"Yes, you may. And I do."

"As representative of Halifax Fused Glass, I am prepared to offer you ten millions for your formula," Mr. Argent said. "This, of course, precludes your right to patent. How say you, Mr. Evans?"

A scan of Mr. Argent showed Derek he could hold out for more, but he wanted to conclude the negotiations quickly.

"I agree to your terms," he said. "There is one condition: We must be able to purchase glass objects from you at cost. Chimney shapes. I can give you detailed specifications."

"Done," Mr. Argent said. "Anything else?"

"If you ever discontinue this product, we request having the option to buy it back from you for the same ten million you paid."

"That seems eminently fair," Mr. Argent smiled. "Why would we discontinue it?"

In Origin, a company making Pyrex glassware had discovered ordinary window glass was cheaper to manufacture and switched to it.

"I have no idea, sir. Possible unforeseeable changes in your business? We need an assured supply of these glass objects for other projects."

"Very well."

June Foster dictated contracts that the secretary typed, her fingers flying over her typewriter's keys.

All parties signed.

Mr. Argent called a courier service to convey the money to the Indigo Concern's bank account.

They concluded the transaction with a toast.

Mr. Argent pulled out elegant crystal glasses and poured hundred-year-old brandy.

"To our future collaborations," he toasted, and they clinked glasses and drank.

The brandy was as smooth as ... glass.

"Out of curiosity," Mr. Argent added. "What were you going to name your glass product?"

"Pyrex?"

"God, man! That's far too short a name for such a momentous product. Pyrex sounds like an ... ahem ... *rectal* condition."

The attorney and Mr. Michalis chuckled.

"I assumed you would call it something like *Derek Evans Durable Glass,*" Mr. Argent continued. "Something with *resonance* ... with *poetry.*"

"So you will call it *Halifax* Durable Glass?"

"I prefer my original formulation. We have many applications in mind, both exotic and quotidian. It is advantageous to have a person's name attached to a product."

Quotidian? Derek thought, scanning Argent. *Oh — common, everyday uses. Kitchen cookware.*

"May we use your name, Mr. Evans? In return for a suitable emolument, of course."

"Yes. On the condition that the glass sold under my name uses my formula."

"Very well. What would you require as compensation?"

"You intend to create a line of glass cookware? My compensation would consist of your new household products. As they become available. When we get settled, I'll provide an address to send them to. We're searching for a house or apartment, and we'll need things."

Mr. Argent laughed loudly and nodded.

June Foster dictated a rider to the original contract, the secretary typed it, and they signed.

"May I take the liberty of asking whether you have acquired the services of a realtor?" Mr. Argent said.

"We haven't, yet."

"We use the Mobley-Westin Agency when we relocate executives to this fair city. May I give them your name?"

"Yes. Thank you very much!"

✳✳✳

Derek checked on Weena and Marie at the hospital.

Papers and books covered Weena's hospital bed and the tray beside it.

"It's makin me head hurt," she moaned. "Too much to remember."

"Now's the time to study," Marie said. "You have nothing else to do."

"I wish I was cleanin or cookin. It's so boring here."

"I'll make up flash cards," Marie said.

"Cards that *flash?* You are always sayin things I am not understandin."

Marie pulled Derek aside and whispered, "This place is *so strange*, like a weird ... cartoon. Have you noticed how there's almost no black people?"

"I haven't spent much time here. Why aren't there many black people?"

"They never had *slavery* here — or a *civil war*. Hell, *most* of our wars never happened here. There's a black guy in the room next door, but he's a businessman from Africa. A country called Nyasamon."

"Wow! Good luck with Weena."

"Yesterday, she broke into a broom closet and started mopping the floor. A nurse made her go back to bed."

Derek laughed.

"How did you *find* this ... this place?"

"Allie found it," Derek said. "She went into the spirit-world and let herself drift. Currents of space and time carried her here. Maybe she needed this place, or it needed her."

"I didn't understand a word you said."

***

Derek's next stop was Wall Street, where he hung out in a restaurant named *Sky Captain's Snug Harbor Gustatorium.*

It's like déjà vu, he thought. A year ago, he'd dined at the Origin's Boardroom Grill, where he picked up stock tips and filled the Indigo treasury. This place was more ornate and had many unique Columbian touches.

As waitresses in dark red and black uniforms served customers, glowing airships sliding on ceiling-mounted tracks lit the place.

Each had unique and exquisite details, making Derek think they were scale models of actual airships.

The tables were polished brass disks sitting on the heads of carved wooden gremlins — mythical beasts that inhabited the stratosphere.

Derek took one beside the windows.

Time to make money, he thought, wondering whether he had any calling in life beyond making money.

After all, Allie was a brilliant artist.

What am I? he wondered. In Origin, he had never had time to find out. As soon as they had become settled, they had been driven out.

Can't design computer games here, thought, recalling his career in Origin. *I'll have to invent computers first. Maybe I could create Columbia computer games — novels.*

You're the engine of our existence, Allie beamed to him. *For now. I think you'll become a scholar, later. And certainly, an inventor.*

Recalling Marie's comments, he mused that Columbia did have a flamboyant quality that made his home timelines of Origin or Culinary look cold and flat — even lifeless. Even the *villains* here had a theatrical quality. The psychic atmosphere had an odd and different "flavor" to it.

There must be profound differences in the way people think here. Will we fit in? Do we even want to — in this cartoonish world? Well — Allie does, and that's good enough for me.

Derek marveled at the amount of work that went into designing and decorating everything. It was as if this civilization directed its energy into art rather than war and science. The relentless ornamentation might get grating at times.

It's still not a paradise, he thought, considering Weena and her family's plight. If she passed her high school equivalency exam, she'd be the first person in her family to graduate high school.

A waitress in a Napoleon-style hat took his order.

This included coffee and — out of sheer curiosity — a *Queen Margot's Complaint.*

He opened today's *Scrutineer.*

A story entitled "A heroine for our time" caught his eye, with a black-and-white picture of Allie at the *Elegant Pony.*

Her biographical sketch came straight out of Renard's Allie-playbook: born in Knickerbocker, attended public schools until she went to Sacred Heart High School, then she earned a degree in Art and Design from Knickerbocker University.

Few of her former teachers remembered her.

Her travels through the Orient included the Chinese Empire and Tibet — spelled Thibet.

He beamed that at Allie.

Guess I've got to give Elaine Hickey her interview.

Derek closed his eyes and scanned everyone around him, including brokers, corporate staff, and government officials.

One obese, elegantly-dressed man in a corner was particularly interesting.

Then he peeked into the near-future.

The waitress interrupted his reverie by serving breakfast, which turned out to be spiced goose liver pâté spread on sourdough toast with a fried egg on top.

Although it was rich, Derek loved it.

When he finished eating, he paid and strolled down Wall Street to the *Sugarbaker and Weems Universal Brokerage Concern.*

✳✳✳

Oil paintings of the company's executives covered the reception area's dark walnut walls, giving it the appearance of a baroque library or sitting room.

An elegantly-dressed twenty-something lady sat at a walnut desk in the corner with an intercom and brass typewriter.

Her brass nameplate said "Mary Philpot, receptionist."

After Derek explained what he wanted, she buzzed a broker, and a tall, thin man in a skin-tight outfit with a long black cape named Henni Parvue came out.

He looked like Batman.

Mr. Parvue led Derek through the firm's main room — a huge open space with men wearing green eye-shades, scribbling in ledgers. Electro-mechanical stock tickers clicked and buzzed along the far wall.

Mr. Parvue's office had a window to the trading floor, darkly-stained wooden walls, a wooden desk inlaid with mother-of-pearl patterns, and an enormous map on one wall whose legend said "South Columbia." Minute details covered the map: roads, cities, and national boundaries.

An desk-lamp with four brass angels holding up ornate lightbulbs lit the room.

How odd! Derek thought. *The continent's southern tip is pinched off — making the Andes Range some five hundred miles shorter.*

One corner of the room had an elegant brass contraption with many gears and little balls that Derek realized was an *orrery:* a model of the Solar System with planets and their moons attached to brass arms. Turning a hand-crank caused the bodies to rotate and orbit the "sun."

Too bad you don't have a globe of the Earth, Derek mused.

"I want to short the Argentine Canal Concern," he announced.

"That's the hottest stock in existence! Since the Suez Canal opened, everyone's jumping on the bandwagon."

"Nevertheless, I believe the canal will never be built."

"The continent's southern tip is a maritime graveyard. There's a *desperate* need for a canal."

"A glance at a map shows how ridiculous the idea is," Derek said.

"This map?" Mr. Parvue said, pointing to the map on the wall.

"No," Derek said. "A *valid* map. Check with *any* public library. I believe the canal concern is a confidence scheme."

He didn't mention that he *knew* it was, having scanned its organizer — a man claiming to be Major Phineas Bennington-Smyth of the British Imperial Army. His real name was Morton Fish, and he planned to flee the country that evening.

The brokerage concern would loan Derek 20 million dollars worth of Argentine Canal stock, repayable in a week.

"When you sell this, you must tell buyers I am shorting it."

"We're legally obligated to do that anyway," Mr. Parvue said.

"And that I believe the concern is completely fraudulent."

"They'll assume you have a reason for shorting it. *Must* we tell them *that?*"

"Absolutely!"

"That may put a damper on things," Mr. Parvue said.

"Sell what you can."

In a week the company would no longer exist, so the loan of stock would *never* have to be repaid.

✳✳✳

As Derek rode a horse-drawn cab to Knickerbocker University, the heavens opened up with torrential rains.

"Hope the thunder doesn't scare your horse," Derek said to the shriveled old man who drove.

"Seen lots of frog-stranglers, Daisy and me," he replied. "Love em. They make the air fresh, like in the country."

They arrived at the university's main building, a massive red sandstone castle bordering a mist-shrouded expanse of green named Perkins Park.

Derek paid and ran through the rain into the building's lobby.

Its granite-lined atrium was three stories high, and a newspaper-vending machine stood beside two elevators.

Brass letters saying *Mihi cura futuri* adorned the opposite wall.

"The care of the future is mine," Derek murmured.

The place was deserted.

A wall-mounted campus map showed that the biology department was in another building.

Derek cursed.

"Hi sparkly dad!"

"Tony!" Derek said to Loretta's brother.

He sensed Culinary Allie's spirit floating in the air overhead.

Move close to the floor, he beamed at her. *And then focus on Tony as clearly as possible.*

She materialized several inches off the floor, fell, and Derek caught her.

"I managed to keep my cool this time," she muttered. "I feel awful about ... my meltdown last time."

"Forget it.

"It's incredible! All I had to do is *think* about Tony and *instantly* knew where he was."

"That's how it works," Derek said.

"Where *are* we?"

Derek explained.

"I'm still worried about the kids popping into dangerous places."

"Not likely," Derek said. "When you teleport, you always see where you're going. And you see into the future."

"I noticed that!" Culinary Allie said. "Kids were playing ball in the street and I *knew* their ball would break a window; I *saw* it. Then it *did* ... *exactly* the way I saw it."

"Professor Fischer tried to materialize *inside* a bonfire."

"Why?"

"An *experiment,*" Derek said. "The instant she *thought* of materializing, she felt unbearable pain. The kids couldn't put themselves in danger if they *wanted* to. The worst that can happen is ... awkward situations. It's sheer luck nobody saw Tony materialize."

Derek bought Culinary Allie a souvenir — a copy of the *Knickerbocker Scrutineer*.

When they were sure nobody was around, Culinary Allie and Tony returned home.

Down the hall, Derek found the school bookstore.

✳✳✳

It looked a bit like the bookstore at New York University, if more ornate. Signs listed required reading for various courses and books jammed ornately carved wooden bookcases.

In the back a young woman sat at a desk that held a tulle-covered top-hat and a sign "Klara Boston, Notary Public."

"Named after the city?" Derek chuckled.

"There's a city named Klara?"

"Uh ... never mind," he said. "Can I get something notarized? In the biology department."

"Not today you can't."

Derek fanned ten hundred-dollar bills in front of Klara.

"Even for a thousand dollars for ten minutes work?"

"Are you out of your *mind?*" she gasped.

"Want it or not?"

"OK," she sighed.

She grabbed an umbrella and her notary kit and muttered, "Let's get this over with."

As they left the store, she pointed to a stand full of umbrellas and said, "Going out without a *rain-shirm?*"

"Oh, OK," he said, buying one.

✳✳✳

Rows of petri dishes covered the lab's gray stone benches as refrigerators hummed in the back, and windows on the side wall looked out onto the park.

Rain rattled them like machine-gun fire.

Professor Stan Epstein was a short, bald, mustachioed man in a white lab coat.

"Ten thousand, huh?" he said, looking over Derek's contract and signing it. "OK, I'll bite."

Klara Boston notarized it, and Derek paid her.

"Nice doing business with you," she said, leaving.

"Throwing money around! My favorite kind of crackpot. What's your big idea?"

Derek explained.

"That's *hardly news,*" Professor Epstein sneered. *"Everyone* knows mold-contamination destroys bacteria colonies. Experts do, anyway."

"Why does that happen?"

"The mold secretes a poison."

"Mightn't killing bacteria be a *good thing?"* Derek said.

"You can't study them if they're *dead!"*

"What about treating infections?" Derek said.

"It's *poison.* If it kills bacteria, it'll kill *people."*

"Has anyone ever verified that?" Derek said.

The sneer left Professor Epstein's face, and he stared out a rain-drenched window.

"Someone *must* have," he whispered, shaking his head. "I mean, it stands to reason..."

"Sure about that?"

Epstein sighed and finally said, "What organisms do you want me to research?"

"Penicillium notatum and *streptomyces griseus."*

"Yes, I published a paper proving *streptomyces* kills tuberculosis," Epstein muttered. "I apologize for calling you a crackpot, Mr. Evans; you've done your homework. I still say you're throwing your money away."

"We'll save thousands of lives."

Chapter 30

A frantic Walter Fegelein spent an hour scanning his office at Obsidian Security for hidden listening devices — and found none.

Mercouri had been arrested.

Told you the Cape Canaveral people could handle him, Eldon said to Chloe, his spirit-body hovering near the ceiling with hers.

Walter Fegelein packed up his scanning equipment and sat at his desk.

There's a draft in this room, he thought, shivering. *They told me not to harm key personnel except for Trask himself.*

Very interesting, Eldon beamed to Chloe.

Trask is almost impossible to kill, Mr. Fegelein thought. *Whoever's paying for this will just have to accept the consequences.*

Mr. Fegelein brooded over how he could kidnap or kill key Space Ventures engineers.

How do we protect so many targets? Chloe beamed at Eldon. *We can't be everywhere at once.*

Easy, Eldon replied. *We kidnap him first.*
We'll never find out who he's working for.

I have another idea, Derek said, joining the conversation. *He has a wife and two children. I'll do what Frank Moses did in the movie* Red.

I loved that movie but it was a comedy! Eldon Trask said.

❋❋❋

In his spirit-body, Derek floated around the Fegelein home. Fegelein's wife, Phyllis and her two young sons, Max and Kenneth were in the family room, playing a game of *Chutes and Ladders.*

Max sobbed and screamed because he'd fallen down a "chute."

Can't win all the time, kid. It's a lesson you need to learn.

Fegelein's study was off-limits to the rest of the family, no doubt because he kept proprietary client-information there.

Derek materialized in it.

A large glass-top desk and chair on a plastic carpet-protector sheet dominated the room. The desk held a landline phone, a computer, several pads of paper, and a bottle of single-malt scotch. A glass case against one wall held sports-memorabilia including a signed football and jersey.

A darkly-tinted picture window opened to the back yard, and a large oil painting of flowers in a vase almost occupied the opposite wall.

It looked like a paint-by-number.

Wearing cotton gloves, Derek dialed the phone.

"Mr. Fegelein! We're *appalled* at the steps you've taken against Space Ventures Corporation. Its employees are *family.* I can't begin to tell you how upset we'd be if anything happened to our family. *Capisce?*"

"Huh?" Fegelein mumbled, staring at the caller's number.

It looked vaguely familiar.

My God! He's calling from inside my home. Inside my study!

It wasn't so much danger to his family that concerned him as it was someone finding documents in the safe behind the painting.

Derek hung up and pulled the painting of flowers aside to expose a large wall safe with a number pad. A scan of Mr. Fegelein revealed the combination to be 91631735.

Police sirens sounded in the distance.

The safe contained a fat manila envelope, which Derek took to Destiny Beach.

✳✳✳

With gloved hands, Derek spread the papers from Fegelein's safe on the table.

"I can't believe he kept it in his *house*," he said. "It won't be admissible in court, but it's still useful."

He stuffed it back into the envelope and Allie attached a handwritten note saying, "Important anonymous tips!!!"

Eldon grabbed it and vanished, reappearing a minute later.

"Detective Martens stepped away from his desk," he said. "He'll be shocked when he gets back."

"What about the North Korean who *killed* you?" Allie said. "Ran Gul?"

"They told him to get stuff on quantum teleportation," Chloe said. "He didn't have the *faintest* idea what that was."

"What's he doing now?" Allie said.

"Sitting in jail with his mouth hermetically sealed," Chloe said. "The police don't know his name or nationality. Oh my God!"

"Yes, I see it too," Eldon said.

"What?" Allie said.

"I read his boss's mind," Eldon said. "And *his* boss's mind, and so on."

"The whole North Korean intelligence organization," Chloe said, wincing and shutting her eyes.

"I know who Mr. Big is, what he's doing, and why," Eldon exclaimed. "He's Dennis Nelson, a Washington lobbyist. He's trying to buy Space Ventures for North Korea."

"He can't do that," Derek said.

"He's claiming the buyer's a Japanese company: Kinoshita Technology. He's really working for North Korea."

"Does he *know* that?" Allie said.

"Yeah, they told him. Even exporting to *Japan* violates export restrictions. He's busy swining and dining key congresscritters."

"If Space Ventures fails *spectacularly*," Chloe said.

"He gets it at a bargain price and tells everyone the technology's *garbage*," Eldon said. "So why the fuss about exporting it? Congress should *thank* the Japanese for taking it off our hands."

"Kinoshita Technology," Allie began. "Does it exist?"

"On paper," Eldon said. "It's a one-room apartment in a seedy neighborhood. The Dobutsuenmae district of Osaka. Dennis Nelson visited it briefly where the North Korean agents explained their true plans."

"They want a space program that badly?" Derek said.

"That would be icing on the cake," Eldon said. "They mainly want to deliver their nuclear weapons. With my technology, they could hit anyplace on Earth. Their own rockets have an annoying tendency to blow up."

"They could reach New York and Washington," Chloe said.

"What'll they do now?" Allie said.

"They've given up on grabbing the whole company," Derek said.

"They're referring the matter to their *Abductions Division*," Chloe growled.

"Their *what?*" Allie said.

"Like ... like *raw sewage,* images of their their 'organization' flow through my brain," Chloe moaned. "They've been abducting people for decades."

"Picture a young Japanese couple spending their honeymoon at a beach resort in Ibusuki," Eldon said. "They take a romantic moonlight stroll — and two zodiacs full of commandos pull up and snatch them. Drag them away to a ship hovering outside Japanese territorial waters."

"That actually happened," Chloe said. "That couple spent the next twenty years working in a prison camp."

"What did they do there?" Allie said.

"Translations," Chloe said. "Writing propaganda. North Korea would love to add our engineers to their stable of slaves."

"They've admitted abducting eleven Japanese," Eldon said.

"They *admitted* that?" Allie said.

"The real number is two hundred and sixty-nine," Chloe said. "Right now, their prison camp has twenty-one survivors."

"Japan's practically in their back yard," Eldon said. "Snatching my people will be much harder."

"I guess that puts a damper on having your people look at the Squidward equipment," Andy muttered, joining them.

✲✲✲

After meeting with representatives of Liquid Gases Unlimited, Eldon stuffed random papers into an attache case and carried it out onto his factory floor.

Originally designed to house Boeing 747 fuselages, the building took up four city blocks under a brightly-lit fifty-foot-high ceiling.

He walked past its three-story Mission Control center, with its computer servers and rows of monitors and the Blue Mars Restaurant that occupied the factory's center.

Then he passed a row of twenty gleaming fifteen-foot-tall Zeus rocket engines. The Mars Lander section was around the corner from there.

"Your *amusement park* ride's ready," Allan Jesperson growled.

The lander was a fifty foot long cylinder ten feet in diameter that tapered to a point at its nose.

A prominent Space Ventures logo on one side punctuated its polished white surface.

"Let's check it out," Eldon said.

They entered a hatch at the lander's rear and found themselves in a cylinder with a floor and rows of large seats sitting on a newly-installed deck.

Recessed white and blue led-lights cast a soft glow over everything.

"I got the seats from a supplier for movie theaters. They recline and have cup-holders. I was able to fit twenty-five of them in here after throwing out the *useless crap.* Like *engines* and *fuel tanks!"*

"Excellent," Eldon replied, ignoring Jesperson's barbs.

"I'll have the monitors installed in two days."

"What about power?"

"We're plugged into the factory at the moment, but we have a bank of batteries for internal power."

"Install a Pincus generator as soon as possible," Eldon said.

He walked to the cylinder's opposite end and opened the

hatch to the cockpit. This was originally meant for crew quarters and had space for a pilot and up to seven crew.

Oxygen and water regenerators lined the walls and there were sleeping tethers for weightless crew members.

The far end of that contained the cockpit with seats for a pilot and copilot — and the only windows in the entire machine.

"Here's what we're going to do," Eldon said. "Hide this lander with the large Reveal Curtain. Unplug us from factory power, and tell me when you're done. We're going to take it for a spin."

At press conferences, Eldon had always believed in the Dramatic Reveal. He would announce a new product like a capsule or rocket — hidden behind a thick black curtain and, at the right moment, have it lifted away — often to applause.

The large Reveal Curtain was easily big enough to conceal the Mars Lander — indeed it had been used at last year's presentation of the original Mars Lander — the one now *on* Mars.

Mr. Jesperson left.

The lights went out briefly and then came on again.

Fifteen minutes later, Mr. Jesperson reappeared.

"Pick a seat in the passenger section," Eldon said, looking through the cockpit windows.

The black Reveal Curtain hid the factory.

Will someone spot for me, he beamed at the other Indigos.

No huhu, brah, Travis replied. *You got da kine rocket covered.*

He teleported to a beach on the north shore of Oz's Spice Island — its version of the Hawaiian island of Lanai.

Green replaced blackness out the cockpit windows.

The lander shuddered in time to a booming sound from outside.

Eldon found Mr. Jesperson in a reclined seat near the rear entrance.

"Let's look outside," Eldon said.

"Yeah, sure."

***

Eldon opened the hatch.

Cool Trade Winds whistled against the open hatch, whipping sand and sea spray into their eyes.

Speechless, Mr. Jesperson stared at the beach and pounding surf.

The cockpit faced away from the water toward a dense jungle of palms and plumerias.

"I parked perpendicular to the beach so we don't go rolling into the ocean," Eldon said.

"Um..." a dazed Mr. Jesperson mumbled, his jaw hanging.

"Sorta wish I'd brought swim trunks. I guess we've got to head back ... before anyone looks behind the curtain."

"Hah?"

Eldon shoved a dazed Mr. Jesperson back into the lander and secured the hatch.

***

Chloe chased people away from the curtain-shrouded area, and the lander returned — with a pile of gravelly beach sand.

"That's the quantum drive," Eldon told Mr. Jesperson, handing him a to-do list. "What you've experienced today is confidential at the highest level. *Strictly* confidential!"

Mr. Jesperson stared at the list.

"Could you ask someone to sweep up this sand?" Eldon asked Mr. Jesperson. "And paint the ship's new name on the side: *QS Schrödinger.*

"Hah?" Mr. Jesperson muttered, staring at the sand.

"Also," Eldon said. "An old New Yorker magazine had a cartoon showing a man sitting in a veterinary clinic. The doctor comes out and says 'About your cat, Mr. Schrödinger. We have good news and bad news.' Find it and make a big poster."

They pushed their way through the Reveal Curtain.

"We should rescue those poor people," Chloe said. "The abducted ones."

"We have to protect our own first. An abduction team landed this morning at LAX. From Tokyo."

"They can't kidnap anyone until their container-ship from Wonson arrives," Chloe said. "In four days, give or take."

Chapter 31

"Looks like Disney's Haunted Mansion, only newer and a lot bigger," Allie said. *Do we really need to live in a house that's like a small town? She's thinking we'll need a staff of twenty.*

"More like the Biltmore estate," Derek muttered.

"Mrs. Gofols did die in the house but those rumors are *completely false!*" the realtor, Mrs. Gervase, snapped. "I don't care what this ... Disney person says."

"I never said they weren't," Allie replied, realizing that Mrs. Gofols had died after battling brain cancer for two years.

The house overlooked the Hudson River in Tarrytown — still named that in the Columbia timeline. The house overlooked the Hudson River in Tarrytown — still named that in the Columbia timeline. With brick walls the color of honey, it was a sprawling Victorian gingerbread mansion with two satellite houses, stables, a carriage house, a greenhouse, and gardens.

It included 200 acres of rolling meadows and forest.

They had considered buying a twenty-room apartment in Knickerbocker, but couldn't handle the pollution and noise. Tarrytown was thirty minutes from the city on the Hudson Railroad. And, of course, they could teleport.

It was a clear, sunny day — something almost unheard of in the city.

I can't believe Mr. Parvue sold all $20 million worth of the stock! Derek beamed. *The suggestion that "Phineas Bennington-Smythe" was a fraud incensed Mr. Weems, who bought most of it himself. He wouldn't hear of checking the map.*

Will Parvue get in trouble for selling his boss garbage stock? Allie said.

Weems insisted, over his objections.

Mrs. Gervase took them on a tour. The basement had a restaurant-grade kitchen, an industrial laundry, a servants' dining room, the cook's apartment, and a coal furnace. The house's West Wing had many servants' apartments.

All the door-handles were polished brass hands, so one had to shake a hand to open a door.

The apartments are clean and cozy, Derek beamed.

Probably better than where Weena's family lives now, Allie replied.

The first floor had a main sitting room, a formal dining room seating twenty and served by dumbwaiters, a ballroom, and a solarium connected to a greenhouse full of exotic plants.

The solarium gets filtered sunlight, Allie beamed. *Perfect for painting.*

They visited the library, next.

It had darkly-stained walnut shelves with many empty spaces, and a rolling ladder on brass rails. Ornate carvings of animals topped the ladder's sides and a huge antique globe stood in a corner. A wooden pillar entwined with a dragon supported a stained glass ceiling with images of the sky, clouds, and exotic birds — fifteen feet above the floor.

"There's a skylight above the ceiling that provides illumination to the room," Mrs. Gervase said.

Ornate brass lamps around the room provided more lighting.

Three brown leather easy chairs surrounded a reading table with an wooden inlaid image of unicorns cavorting in a field.

These people give me the creeps, Mrs. Gervase thought. *They never say a word. Do they like the place or not?*

The second floor had an exercise room and children's playrooms.

"These portraits on the walls," Allie said. "Are they Gofols family members?"

"Yes," Mrs. Gervase said. "The house has been in their family more than a hundred years. Their family tree has withered over the last decades. Now it's barely a twig."

The third floor had "sleeping chambers."

Our guest-quarters could easily sleep fifty, Allie said. *It's a hotel!*

"Naturally, there are hidden passageways to the sleeping chambers," Mrs. Gervase said.

"Naturally?" Allie said.

"Yes, inside the walls."

"Why?" Allie said.

"So servants can start fireplaces in the mornings without disturbing you — of course."

Goodbye privacy! Allie beamed.

"It's a beautiful house," Derek said. "But it's a bit more elaborate than we had in mind. We were thinking of an apartment in the city. Or a much smaller house."

Like our house on Oz, he thought.

"*An apartment?*" Mrs. Gervase said. "*For someone of your station?*"

She sincerely believes our living in an apartment will raise eyebrows, Allie beamed.

We can always go to Oz for clean air. I suppose we should buy it, though. Commuting will be easy.

"How much is it?" Derek said.

"Five million dollars for the estate and its contents. It's greatly reduced because the heirs want a quick sale."

Scanning her, Derek and Allie learned that the "heirs" in question consisted of an estranged wayward son named Edgar who was buried in gambling debts. And that the house needed extensive repairs. And that they *were* afraid it was haunted.

"We'll take it," Derek smiled. "I'd buy it for the library alone."

Derek became aware that trading of Argentine Canal stock had been suspended, and the Knickerbocker Prosecutor's Office had issued warrants for Phineas Bennington-Smythe's arrest.

"We should uh ... water the greenhouse plants," Allie mumbled. "I don't want them to die."

"You have a grounds keeper to do that," Mrs. Gervase said. "Mrs. Gofols operated with a skeleton staff of five and a nurse. They're living here and would love to stay on. You'll want to hire more, of course."

"Oh," Allie said. *It looks like I'm to the goddamn manor born!*

You foresaw this, Derek said.

Yes. I saw this and Oz. I guess it's our destiny.

These two love their staring contests, don't they? Mrs. Gervase thought.

Allie turned her back on her and Vittoria appeared in her arms.

"Where did *she* come from?" Mrs. Gervase said, when Allie turned around again.

"She's good at making herself inconspicuous when she wants to," Allie said.

They piled into the Mobley-Westin Agency's steam-powered car, and Mrs. Gervase drove them to the agency's Tarrytown office — a two-story building on Main Street, between the Lyric Theater and the Majestic Hotel.

They spent the next half hour signing papers as an attorney notarized them.

A secretary played with Tori.

They all marveled at Tori's silvery eyes — since she was too young to wear contacts.

Afterward, Derek and Allie excused themselves and teleported back to the mansion with Tori.

❋❋❋

The servants drifted back to the house an hour later. Mrs. Gervase had told them to stay away whenever she showed it.

The house had a cramped "business office" with an old-fashioned roll-top desk and four chairs. Ledger books covered the open desk and stacks of yellowing paper occupied a table beside it.

They met with the butler, a Mr. Jerrold Holmes and his wife, Charlotte. He was a tall, bald, forty-something man with a British accent and a military bearing. She was, maybe, ten years younger with an apprehensive, careworn face. She pushed two thick ledger books in front of her, staring at Tori.

Strangest eyes, she thought. *A bit mongoloid. She seems to radiate happiness, though. We could use some in this miserable place.*

She and her husband said nothing.

"You've been doing the books?" Derek said to them, who nodded faintly.

Charlotte had taken a mail-order course in bookkeeping.

"Mrs. Gofols let the bookkeeper go two years ago," Charlotte said.

A quick scan disclosed that Mrs. Gofols's finances had declined along with her health, and the house had been run on a shoestring for years.

Current staff had remained out of a sense of loyalty — and because leaving would require finding other living quarters.

"What's a normal salary for a bookkeeper?" Allie said.

Charlotte quoted an amount.

"Do you mind if we put you on the payroll as the house bookkeeper?" Derek said. "For that salary?"

"Oh!" she said, pushing a wisp of light brown hair from her eyes. "Yes, sir! I mean, I don't mind."

He wrote a check for a million dollars to the household account.

"See that all employees receive missing back wages," he said. "I'm guessing there's a *lot* of that. While you're at it, give yourself back pay for the two years you've worked as the bookkeeper."

Charlotte stared at the check in disbelief and sighed.

"I noticed blank spots on the walls where pictures hung," Allie said.

"W...we had to s...sell paintings," Charlotte mumbled. "To make ends meet."

"I assume the same is true of the missing books in the library," Derek said. The library had originally contained many rare first editions.

They nodded.

"Well done!" Allie said. "You kept the place going. Could you have the walls repainted or re-papered so it isn't noticeable. I have a lot of paintings I'll want to hang. I'm an artist."

She took a blank sheet of paper and ball-point pen, and did a two-minute lightning sketch of Jerrold and Charlotte — with photo-realistic detail.

"My word," Charlotte murmured.

"The roof looks rather old," Derek said — knowing that it leaked in spots. "Please have it completely replaced and repair any water-damage beneath it."

"There are bedbugs in some of the servants' rooms," Charlotte mumbled.

Jerrold frowned at her.

"Bedbugs?" Allie exclaimed.

"Treat the entire house for them," Derek said. "Replace all the mattresses and the beds that aren't antiques."

"Put people up in the hotel in town," Allie said.

"Use the finest quality mattresses for *all* the beds," Derek said. "Ours and the staff. And upgrade the electrical wiring. I'm an inventor and will need a lot of electricity."

"OK," Jerrold said.

"Are you British?" Allie said, asking out of politeness.

She and Derek already knew Mr. Holmes had been a captain in the Caledonia Dragoons, and had been dismissed in disgrace when he'd eloped with Charlotte — who was the Duke of Edinburgh's daughter.

Why was that disgraceful? Allie wondered.

"Yes, We were originally from the British Empire. We're naturalized citizens now."

"College-age children?"

"Yes, a son, Albert," Charlotte said. "He has been accepted by Miskatonic University but..."

"Excellent!" Allie interrupted. "Since you're our employees, we'll pay his tuition and living expenses there."

"What?" they both exclaimed.

"Tell us the amount and where to mail the check," Derek said. "And tell our other employees about this benefit."

Charlotte jumped up and left, returning a moment later with a scrap of paper with the information.

Derek wrote two more checks.

"That's almost my *yearly salary!*" Jerrold said.

"We'll be raising that too," Allie said. "The point is: Employees' children go to school. We also want the younger children to attend public schools."

"There aren't any younger children at the moment," Mr. Holmes said. "Did you *really* capture the Black Bart gang? *Singlehandedly?*"

"Ah, yes."

Our lives are about to become extraordinary, Mr. Holmes thought.

"Are you two staying at the Majestic?" Charlotte said.

"Uh ... we'll be traveling," Derek said. "I'll check in on you from time to time."

Mr. Holmes raised his eyebrows.

"Anything more?" Mr. Holmes said.

"Not at the moment," Derek said.

"Want a lift to the station?" Mr. Holmes said.

"Oh ... OK," Derek said, beaming, *It's hard to sneak away without servants noticing.*

After a fifteen-minute ride to the railroad station, Derek and Allie waited until Mr. Holmes was out of sight. Then they went into restrooms and teleported away: Allie and Vittoria to Destiny Beach, and Derek to Sugarbaker and Weems.

✳✳✳

Derek stepped out of the restroom and ran right into Henni Parvue and his boss Fortescue Weems. Mr. Weems was a stocky elderly man with a white mustache and goatee — reminding Derek of a well-known purveyor of fried chicken.

"I'm sorry my suspicions seem to have been justified," Derek muttered, regretting profiting from a crooked scheme.

Could he offer Weems some of his money back without looking guilty?

"That *lying swag-bellied nikum!* He claimed he was from my old *regiment!* He knew things, too. Anecdotes ... our regimental motto ... people's *names*. He gave me his word of honor as a *gentleman*."

A quick scan disclosed that Mr. Weems was a retired major from the British Imperial Army.

Do they all come to the US when they leave the army? Derek wondered.

"Come here to gloat have we?" Mr. Weems glared at Derek.

"Not at all, sir. I've come to invest."

"In what?" Mr. Parvue said.

"The Knickerbocker Solid Valve Concern."

Derek had learned that electronic vacuum tubes were called *valves* in Columbia. A group in the Knickerbocker University Physics Department had discovered *solid valves — transistors* — and formed a small company.

"Solid valves?" Mr. Weems sneered. *"Artless bat-fowled baggage,* if you ask me! An electrical engineer told me they'll *never* work."

"I respectfully disagree," Derek said. "They'll change the face of electronics. Of the world, for that matter."

"The Solid Valve Concern is a penny stock," Mr. Parvue said. "There are, maybe, five million dollars worth of shares in existence."

"I'd like to buy them all," Derek said. "If you invest with me, you won't regret it, Mr. Weems."

"Not bloody likely!" he chuckled, leaving. "You'll lose everything."

This windbag deserves everything he gets.

"His ego's badly damaged," Mr. Parvue said. "Why *would* a respected engineer say they'll amount to nothing? If you don't mind my asking?"

"These inventors are *physicists*. They've developed theories engineers never heard of. Yet. You want in?"

"Oh, I don't know..."

***

Derek visited Professor Epstein next.

Jugs of milky liquid had replaced the petri dishes on his stone benches, and a smothering, moldy stench filled the air.

It turned Derek's stomach.

A tall, thin man in a blue shirt and wearing a leather apron accompanied the professor.

"Speak of the devil!" Epstein said. "We were just talking about you! Meet Simon Wilkins from the Chemistry department. He's helping me purify the ... mold-stuff."

Derek shook his hand.

"Early results are encouraging," Epstein said. "But it's maddeningly difficult to purify."

"We just get trace amounts," Professor Wilkins said.

"OK," Derek said, hesitating before speaking. According to Wikipedia, it had taken researchers in Origin *twenty years* to perfect penicillin — with thousands of false starts and blind alleys.

The Second World War had been a big motivator.

"Try growing it in corn-steep liquor," Derek said. "Mixed with lactose rather than glucose."

"Corn-steep liquor?" Professor Epstein said.

"The cloudy, gelatinous fluid you get from grinding up corn in water," Professor Wilkins replied. "Used as animal feed and a precursor to corn syrup. We can buy it in bulk."

"Rather specific for a random hunch," Professor Epstein muttered. "Any more suggestions?"

Derek summarized five other main points, trying to sound casual and — most of all — trying not to arouse suspicion.

He didn't succeed.

It's as though you've done the research yourself, Professor Epstein thought. *What do you need us for?*

Good question, Derek mused. "Discovering" penicillin on his own would've required a well-equipped lab, extensive lab-experience, and hundreds or thousands of hours work.

"Will you try my ... suggestions?" he finally said.

"Of course, Mr. Evans," Professor Epstein said. "What do we have to lose?"

Besides — you probably already know they'll work.

"Maybe we could even mutate the mold with Roentgen Rays," Epstein added. "And get new strains."

Roentgen rays? Derek thought. *Oh, they're x-rays.*

"Good idea!" he said, glad he didn't have to suggest that too.

He wrote Epstein a check for $500,000.

✱✱✱

After giving their new "address" to a secretary at Halifax Fused Glass, Derek checked on Renard Moreau.

His ears popped as he materialized in a gleaming metallic corridor with a row of open windows on one side. Moist sea-air blew though the windows as propellers droned in the distance.

"Ah," Renard said. "Mr. Evans!"

"Hi," Derek said, looking around in confusion. "Where are we? On a train?"

"Look out the windows."

A thousand feet below, the ocean glittered in the late-afternoon sun.

"The *LS Lorelei*," Renard said. "En route to Paris. Takes two days but it beats the hell out of flying in a sardine-can. We're pitching the Butaflor process to the head honchos at *L'Étoile Perfume*."

"We?"

"Me and Professor Larry Morgan from the Chemistry department. I'd introduce you but he's in the smoking room. Can you believe an airship floating on *hydrogen* has a *smoking room?*"

"Maybe it's better you don't introduce me."

"Oh, yeah," Renard laughed. "How's the penicillin thing going? The whole university's buzzing about it."

"Epstein and his partner eat, sleep, and *dream* penicillin. I guess your perfume project's doing well."

"I uttered the words 'butane' and 'essential oils', and Morgan figured out *everything*."

"Really?"

"My hardest job was convincing him they weren't *already* using that process. I had to *drag* him to the *Elegant Pony*, and he almost fainted."

"I guess master perfumers aren't chemists," Derek said.

"Hey, I'm headed to a wine tasting down on A-Deck. Join me!"

"Thanks, but I've got to get back."

✳✳✳

"What the *fuck* were we *thinking?*" Allie sobbed. "Buying a god-damned *decaying palace!*"

Derek hugged her.

She, Grace, and Taka sipped iced tea on their deck at Destiny Beach in the early evening.

The sea was unusually still as Norton stalked a seagull.

"Sounds like a money pit," Grace said.

"We can handle that," Allie said. "It's the *people* I'm worried about. We're *responsible* for them."

"They've muddled along for years," Derek said. "At the moment, all they really need is money."

"How can you forget?" Allie wailed. "My art gallery had three young students and interns. And people *threatened those poor girls' lives!"*

"Columbia's not Origin, honey," Derek muttered. "We've got to get over this ... if we're ever going to open an art gallery ... anywhere."

"Maybe we *shouldn't!* I want my art gallery *so much* but ... but..."

Tori appeared in her arms.

"You told Marie that Columbia was a good world," Derek said. "Was that all bullshit?"

"No..." Allie sighed, hugging Tori. "I even see some people knowing ... about us and everything still being ... OK."

"What are those servants doing now?" Grace said.

"They're at the Majestic Hotel," Derek said. "Throwing a party in the dining room. A reporter from the *Tarrytown Tattler's* covering it."

"How big is *dese* palace *kine?"* Taka said.

"They're hauling away eighty mattresses and fifty-two beds," Derek said.

Taka let out a low whistle.

"Look, honey," Derek said. *"If* we have to flee... Which is *not going to happen* but *if*... we can always deed it over to the staff. And they turn it into a resort. We won't leave them in the lurch."

"A resort needs a swimming pool," Allie murmured.

"We'll put one in," Derek said. "Hell, *we* could even swim in it sometimes."

"You have a whole ocean to swim in," Grace muttered, shaking her head.

"I know, I know," Allie sighed. "I'm a *city bitch.* I'm sorry I'm not more like Wendy and Travis."

"They and the Brocklesbys are always hiking and exploring with that professor lady and her husband," Taka said. "They even take the *keikis* with them. Oz is heaven for them."

"You're an artist, honey," Derek said. "You need people to see your work."

"If you don't want your palace, *I'll* live there," Kurt said, joining them. "I can appreciate having servants. In more ways than one."

Grace glared at him.

Chapter 32

"So much for anonymous tips!" Eldon muttered, opening his eyes and leaning back in his desk-chair. "Police won't *touch* the Abduction Team. Their travel-documents are perfect, down to the holographic strips. They speak perfect Japanese, too."

"What do we do?" Chloe sighed.

"Kidnap the kidnappers, I guess," Eldon said. "Wait a minute! Colonel Kim Il Chol is skulking in Fegelin's study, planning to kill him. The wife and kids are out shopping."

"He's their team commander. How'd he get into the house? The police are watching it, aren't they?"

"I'm scanning the area. Nope. No police van, no nothing."

"After you dumped the *mother-lode* on Martens's desk?" Chloe said.

Eldon shut his eyes again and scanned Detective Martens.

"His captain told him to shred it."

"What? Is he *in* on it?"

"Yes," Eldon said. "He's part of a well-organized, world-wide conspiracy: People with their heads up their asses. He got burned for tainted evidence in a case last year. Now he won't touch anything that isn't signed and notarized. Preferably with video."

Chloe grabbed a burner-phone and teleported to De Moines, Iowa, from where she gave Detective Martens an anonymous tip.

"I may have saved his life," she said, returning to the office.

"The guy who caused Culinary me's *murder?* Who's planning to kill our *engineers? That guy?"*

"I ... I just had to," she stammered. "I'm sorry."

He hugged her.

✺✺✺

Chloe and Eldon hovered near the study's ceiling in their spirit bodies.

Suddenly cold in here! Kim Il Chol thought, checking his watch.

The approaching police sirens didn't disturb him; he was confident he'd disabled the house's three security systems. Two had been in plain sight and the third had been cleverly disguised as a fiber-optic video hookup.

The police sirens disturbed the hell out of Mr. Fegelin, as he opened his front door.

They're getting closer! They got the documents from my safe!

He ran back to his car and drove away, intending to go into hiding with his wife and children — or at least lay low until they figured out what to do.

A police car pulled up.

They're stopping! Kim thought. *There couldn't have been a fourth alarm system!*

He checked his silenced pistol and crouched beside the door.

Noting the open front door, the Officer Rick Alvarez checked in with his dispatcher. He and his partner, Samantha Cather, left the car and warily approached the house.

They scanned the living room, and Samantha shouted "Clear."

Then they approached the study door.

With all their might, Eldon and Chloe *willed* Kim Il Chol to drop his gun and surrender to the police.

His response was to chamber a round.

Watch out! Chloe mentally shouted at the two police. *He's waiting behind the door with a gun. Kim Il Chol!*

"Kim Il Chol?" Rick exclaimed, drawing his gun.

"I heard it too," Samantha said, doing the same. "Weird voice in my head."

The police know my name? Kim thought. *Fuck! Fuck! Fuck!*

His eyes darted around the room, looking for a way out. Besides the door, the only possibility was the large, darkly-tinted window to the back yard.

The three shots he fired at it made star-bursts but didn't break it — the glass was as bulletproof as the manufacturer had promised.

"Shots fired!" Rick said into his radio.

Kim threw himself against the back window, which began to crack.

Once more, and I'm through.

"Freeze!" Rick shouted, as the two burst through the door.

Kim dropped his gun and put his hands behind his neck.

When Officer Cather started to cuff him, he snatched her wrists, bent down, and flipped her over his shoulder. Then he backflipped, jammed his feet into her midriff, and kicked, launching her against Officer Alvarez — who went down like a bowling pin.

All in under two seconds.

Kim bounced to his feet, leaped over the stunned police, and fled.

More sirens sounded in the distance.

※※※

"Officer Cather has two broken arms and a couple broken ribs," Chloe said. "But nobody died."

"Kim's travel-documents won't save him now," Eldon said.

"Too bad he got away," Chloe said.

"He *thinks* he got away. The minute he stops running, we tip off the police."

※※※

They visited Derek in Oz.

They materialized in a lush rain forest on a hillside beside whitewater rapids. Birds screeched around them.

"Where are we?" Chloe said, looking around.

"Eldonia, of course," Wendy said. "In Culinary or Origin, this would be in Australia."

"I'm... uh... very honored," Eldon began. "But you really shouldn't..."

"You have no say," Wendy said. "We live here and..."

"*We* make the maps!" Birgit cut in.

"Tough broads," Ian chuckled. "They named England after me."

"Is anything named after me?" Chloe said.

"Chloe," Birgit said. "New Zealand to you."

"What the hell is *that?*" Chloe said, pointing.

Snorting like a pig, a brown, furry, elephant-sized creature ripped ferns from the ground and chewed them.

"Oh," Birgit said. "That's a wombat."

"Who are they named after?" Eldon said.

"That's their actual name in Culinary," Birgit said. "Where they're the size of small dogs. Here, they're bigger."

"Eldonia also has seven-foot-tall kangaroos," Wendy said. "And carnifexes."

"Carnifexes?" Chloe said.

"Marsupial lions," Birgit said. "Not as bad as smilodons but still apex predators."

"Where's Allie?" Eldon said.

"In Knickerbocker," Derek said. "Scouting locations for her art gallery with Marie Moreau. And bed-shopping with Charlotte Holmes."

"That *house!*" Eldon muttered. "It's like the Grand Budapest Hotel!"

"It's a bit much," Derek admitted. "It'll be nice in the end. Restoring it will cost at least double the purchase price."

"What about having your people look at the Squidward equipment?" Andy said.

Birgit winced.

"Llewellyn's getting a lot of work done but I'm spinning my wheels," Andy continued.

You need to relax," Llewellyn said. "Think of this as a vacation."

"I don't take vacations! I'm an archaeologist!"

"I can prove the *Riemann Hypothesis!*" Llewellyn exclaimed. "And it's not even my field of mathematics. I see why it's true, anyway. The hard part is breaking it into thought-atoms."

"Thought-atoms?" Derek said.

"Words. Propositions, theorems."

"Yes, you'll be famous someday," Andy said. "What about our Archy friends? We shouldn't turn our backs on them for long."

✳✳✳

Derek lay on a chaise lounge on the deck and went out-of-body.

He thought of Katalluwana and Kef.

"The two planets in the main habitable zone are infested but the vermin do not appear to be *sentient,*" Katalluwana said.

The third star in the system of three was a different story.

It was smaller than the other two, red, and orbited the other two like a distant planet. And it had its *own* planet, closely orbiting it.

"It's like our *home!*" Kef said. "Yet it's covered with vermin — even *sentient* vermin."

"Yes," Katalluwana said. "There are manufactured hives, although these disgusting-looking creatures don't appear to have space travel. Otherwise, this world is almost identical to ours."

Disgusting looking? Derek thought, scanning them. *Oh, they look like giant millipedes. Pretty disgusting, I guess. So Alpha Centauri has intelligent life.*

"These creatures are trying to cleanse *each other,*" Katalluwana said. "How bizarre!"

Their telescope showed what looked two groups of millipedes battling each other with artillery.

"Our world never swarmed with so many varieties of vermin," Kef said.

"Of course it did. Ever wonder why the Grand Fleet is so large?"

"I assumed it had to be."

"Our first cleansing was of our *own* world," Katalluwana said. "The Fleet accommodated our queens, consorts, and a million of our most prominent people. We rid our world of vermin."

"We killed the billions who *couldn't fit?*" Kef said. "The

courage, the dedication to *purity.* Those were glorious times, indeed!"

"We should notify the high command. Not only is this world infested, it's suited for colonization."

"We still haven't located the ones who triggered the sentinel. Our supply of communication modules is limited."

Communication modules? Derek thought.

Maybe they're quantum-entangled photon-pairs, Eldon said, joining him. *They carry a fixed number of them that limits how many messages they can send. The messages would be instantly received — even over light-year distances. Receiving replies would also use these things up.*

Katalluwana sent the message.

Derek and Eldon returned to their physical bodies.

Chapter 33

"We're at an impasse with the Squidward stuff," Andy said. "I need to explore, and not Oz. I need human settlements, *artifacts!*"

"*Squidward!*" Birgit muttered. *"Mein Gott!* I despise that name. We should give them a *proper* name. Using the Linnaean taxonomy or an extension of it."

They sat in front of a blazing fireplace in Ian and Birgit's living room. The two had moved their house next to the Oz Institute of Philosophy.

"I know a place," Wendy said, cuddling her children. "It's depressing as hell but it has lots of ruins. I call it Deathworld. I seed-bomb it every once in a while."

"Seed-bomb?" Andy said.

"Always bringing things back to life," Travis said, hugging Wendy.

"Don't you have your hands full?" Andy said. "Two kids and all the farming you do."

"Seed-bombing only takes a few minutes."

"OK, let's see it!" Andy said.

"I'll tag along," Llewellyn said.

Liz appeared with baby Kile.

"I'd *love* to babysit my grandkids," she said. "I mean, the *keikis.*"

"Mom," Wendy said. "You're upset."

"Not as much as your father. They're making everyone sign oaths of personal loyalty to President Eakins. If he doesn't sign, they'll fire him."

"Maybe it's time to move," Travis said.

Liz groaned.

※※※

In their spirit bodies, straight lines and rectangular objects told them they were in an artificial place.

They materialized in total blackness.

"Where are we?" Andy said, her voice echoing.

"Cold!" Llewellyn said.

Wendy switched on her flashlight.

This did little to answer Andy's question. The beam reflected off massive polished steel pallets of ... yellow metal bars.

"Are those...?" she said, clouds of her breath swirling around her face.

"Gold bullion," Ian said. "Some three hundred eighty *billion* dollars worth. We're in a vault in a place called Fort Langlands. This world's version of Fort Knox."

Andy let out a low whistle.

"Are we going to get in trouble?" she said.

"No," Ian said.

"Federal Hudsonian Republic," Llewellyn read, inspecting one of the gold bars.

Ian switched on a small box the size of a paperback book. It ticked slowly and a meter registered.

"Radiation's barely noticeable here," he announced.

They walked to a massive open circular vault door, as Travis hefted the sack of seeds.

Four clothed human skeletons huddled in a corner — two adults and two children. Piles of food wrappers covered the floor around them.

"They probably took refuge down here and starved to death," Wendy said, her breath steaming.

"Refuge from what?"

"You'll see," she said, opening the steel door. "We could teleport to the surface but it's probably better to just walk up the stairs."

"We could rig up a Pincus Generator and get the elevators working," Ian said. "Not sure it's worth the trouble."

"Why am I panting like a dog?" Andy said.

"Oxygen levels are low," Birgit said. "Everything flammable on the surface was burned. The black clouds of soot cut off photosynthesis. No plants left to make oxygen."

They staggered up three flights of stairs in a concrete shaft, exited into a dusty hallway, and waited to catch their breath.

Wendy led them down the dark hallway until they reached a deserted office.

It had a stationary bicycle rigged up to cylindrical metal device with wires connecting it to a console on a desk with a microphone.

"That's a transmitter and receiver," Wendy said.

"How do you know?" Andy said.

"Because the sign says transmitter. A toggle switch has options to transmit or receive."

"My theory," Ian said. "One person used the bicycle to run that generator. Then another tried to raise someone on the radio. Probably the two adults."

"Who did they try to contact?" Andy said.

"*Anyone*," Ian said. "Any*where*. When they got too weak, they crawled back into the vault to die."

Andy sighed.

They left the office and continued down the hallway past deserted offices, until she reached a glass door.

They looked out onto blackness. Ian's flashlight revealed a deserted parking lot containing a single car with broken windows — all covered with gray and black snow.

More fell from a pitch-black sky.

"I suggest we reset when we get back," he said, as his Geiger Counter screamed.

Wendy and her sack of seeds vanished.

Ian pushed open the door against a snow drift and let in the acrid stench of burning rubber combined with a sickening sweet smell.

"It smells like this everywhere," Ian said. "Top of the rockies, the Hawaiian islands. Everywhere. Carbon dioxide levels are very high too."

"The plants love the carbon dioxide," Wendy said, popping into view with an empty sack.

"You're dropping seeds *here?*" Llewellyn said.

"Give me some credit! I go to the tropics to drop seeds. It's above freezing, but it still rains black mud."

✱✱✱

They decontaminated in the Institute shower and reset.

"We haven't touched the gold," Ian muttered. "It just seems ... tainted, somehow. If we're ever desperate we could, I guess. We scanned the whole planet looking for survivors."

"You can't even locate a satellite," Andy said.

"Living things glow in the spirit world," Wendy said. "Much

easier to find than that satellite. Deathworld has no glow I could detect."

"It must've had insects after everything went to hell," Ian said. "Something stripped the flesh off those bones."

"They *decomposed,*" Wendy said. "Didn't they?"

"No. When I made detective — thirty years ago — I attended a workshop at the U of Tennessee. They have a body farm outside Knoxville."

"Body Farm?" Birgit said.

"It's amazing how well I remember that workshop," Ian said. "As if it was yesterday. If you wrap a body in a very fine metal mesh — I mean fine enough to keep out insects — it just turns into a mummy."

"So Deathworld has killer insects," Travis said.

"Or had them," Ian said. "Maybe they ran out of things to eat and died."

✻✻✻

They teleported back to Ian and Birgit's living room.

"What's *wrong* with me?" Wendy growled, taking her babies from Birgit. "Derek lets his soul drift through the spirit world and comes to Oz. Allie does it and finds Columbia. When I do it, I wind up in a *graveyard!*"

"You'll bring em back to life, *ke aloha,*" Travis said.

"Eventually," Birgit said. "In a couple centuries, parts of it could become a garden of Eden. If we plan correctly. It might be better to dump buckets of tropical seawater into Deathworld's ocean. Phytoplankton produce far more oxygen than land plants."

"What about the radiation?" Andy said. "It'll take fifty thousand years for it to fade."

"The rains will wash most of it underground," Birgit said.

"Deathworld is not *inherently* more radioactive than Oz. Every bit of radioactive material was originally mined from the ground. In five hundred years, large areas on the surface should be safe."

"What about the place in Africa?" Andy said. "In Oz."

"It's fused glass," Birgit said. "The radioactivity couldn't be washed away."

"Every day, we take time to scan Deathworld," Ian said. "In our spirit-bodies. If we find any survivors, we'll rescue them. Take them to Culinary or here."

"So there's a mystery for you," Birgit said. "It was a nuclear holocaust, but how did it begin? Could it have been avoided? Was it the Archies? The Archy planet probably exists in that timeline too."

"I should wait for warmer weather," Andy said.

"That won't happen for a while," Birgit said. "Nuclear winter. The clouds are just beginning to dissipate. When they're gone, it'll get very hot indeed. The ice caps will melt completely."

"So it'll be like *Waterworld?*" Andy said.

"That movie was *nonsense!*" Birgit said. "Coastlines might move a hundred kilometers inland. That leaves thousands of kilometers of dry land."

"Won't coastal cities ... be inundated?" Andy mumbled.

"What coastal cities?" Ian said.

"Oh."

✱✱✱

Andromeda teleported to the Chicago condo she shared with Llewellyn and picked up a heavy winter coat.

Thus prepared, she lay in their bed, went out-of-body, and revisited Deathworld.

In her spirit body she explored the base and finally found a building with embossed letters that were visible in the spirit world: The Marsden Memorial Library.

She materialized and turned on her flashlight.

Black snow had drifted through the broken front door and down the main hallway.

A yellowed cardboard sign celebrated "National Library Week, May 9–15, 1978."

Andy stumbled down the hallway, past several skeletons in military fatigues and others in civilian clothes and entered a room with a plaque that said "Story Time."

She waved her flashlight.

Tiny tables and chairs filled most of the Story Time room and peeling posters of cartoon characters hung off the walls. One series of tattered pictures showed the proper way to brush teeth.

Yellowing construction-paper snowflakes covered the windows.

"Oh *shit*," she moaned, developing a splitting headache. "I *had* to go exploring. *Fuck me.*"

She fled down a dusty hallway and entered a door marked "Reference."

Two skeletons and a pile of ashes with partially-burned books occupied a corner on the right.

The far wall had a rack filled with decaying magazines and newspapers.

Gasping and feeling lightheaded, she grabbed a magazine called *Technology of the World* and a newspaper, *The Daily Ustonion.*

She carefully turned the magazine's crumbling pages to an article entitled "H-bomb swarms: the key to final victory."

She teleported to the Oz Institute and reset.

"You *crazy bastards!*" she sobbed, collapsing to the floor. "How *could* you?"

Llewellyn appeared and hugged her.

※※※

Andy, Ian and Birgit pored over the magazine and newspaper.

"Radiation's not a problem," Ian said, waving the Geiger counter over the reading materials.

"It looks as though there was at least one atomic war," Birgit said, reading the newspaper. "And they were planning another much bigger one."

"We need to go back and grab everything we can," Ian said. "Maybe there are encyclopedias or history books left."

"They burned a lot of stuff," Andy said. "It's so depressing there."

"You've studied ruins before," Birgit said.

"Yes — *exotic* cultures that died *thousands* of years ago," Andy said, tears running down her face. "They had their day in the sun and faded. Deathworld committed *suicide*, and it's neither ancient nor exotic. Makes me feel more like a cop investigating a blood-soaked crime scene than an archaeologist."

"I've seen my share of those," Ian sighed. "You never get used to it."

"That story-time room put the hook in me. When I was a kid, I went to a place just like that library. I *loved* story time. They read us *The Secret Garden* and *A Little Princess*. The Oz books."

"We should still learn what we can about those people," Birgit said.

"We'll all go," Wendy said, popping into view. "We each grab a book or two. We can get it done in a couple trips. I think I know why Deathworld drew me to itself."

Chapter 34

"Who's the bigger beef-brain, Tom?" Professor Janice MacCallan said. "The one who reads a map and becomes a millionaire. Or the one who doesn't and doesn't?"

Derek stood at the door of Willie's Boozer — a small establishment at the edge of Perkins Park and the Knickerbocker University campus. Fifty yards away, a steam calliope serenaded a carousel with many laughing children and parents.

It was a rare sunny and clear day.

"Is this the stockholder's meeting for the Solid Valve Concern?" Derek said to the three seated at a table by the door.

"Yes," Janice said. "And you are?"

"A map-reading beef-brain. Derek Evans."

"All hail our new overlord," a stocky man in sweats laughed, shaking his hand. "Tom Veltins."

"Janice MacCallan," a birdlike, fifty-something woman with piercing blue eyes said. Her ratty purple top hat sat on the table beside her.

"Angus Fornaester," the third person said. Fornaester looked to be in his twenties.

"Does the ... uh ... concern ... uh ... have a president and vice-president?" Derek said.

"Of course," Janice laughed. "On permanent assignment in the Hawaiian Kingdom."

"Maria," Tom Veltins sang out. "Be a *lamb* and bring me another ale."

"I'm nobody's lamb, you rump-fed strumpet," the bartender muttered.

Nevertheless she brought over a mug of ale.

Derek ordered one as well.

"These solid valves," Derek said. "Valves make me think of water. Since they transfer resistance, maybe we should call them *transistors.*"

"Transferring resistance?" Janice smiled. "You read my paper."

"Um ... yeah."

"Transistors?" Angus Fornaester said. "I like the sound of it."

"Transistors it is," Janice said. "Changing the concern name might be difficult."

It turned out the three had only built a single transistor — in order to patent it. They hoped to license the technology to other companies that would actually manufacture them and products that use them.

"Nobody believes they'll work," Janice concluded. "Despite my research papers and charts."

"You should actually *build* something," Derek said. "A transistor radio, for instance."

"Sounds like work," Tom Veltins muttered.

"One problem is germanium," Janice said. "It's not called a rare earth element for nothing."

"You should have plenty of money now," Derek said.

"Thanks to you," Janice said. "The problem is not cost, it's availability."

"Try silicon," Derek said. "Purified in an electric furnace. It's dirt cheap."

"It *is* dirt!" Janice chuckled.

"It's in the same column of the periodic table," Fornaester said. "So it should be a semiconductor too."

"I'm finished grading papers," Janice said. "I can make a couple more transistors and pegboard up a radio. I know someone in electrical engineering who'll help."

Indeed, Derek realized she was having an affair with a Professor Wick Newcastle in that department. Although Professor MacCallan's husband had passed away two years ago, Professor Newcastle was still married.

"What's the plan?" Tom said. "We make radios and hawk them on street-corners like *sausage-vendors?*"

"The *Elegant Pony* owes me and my wife a favor," Derek said.

"Wait a minute!" Angus said. "Is she the one who..."

"Caught the Black Bart gang?" Allie said, coming from the restroom at the back with Marie and kissing Derek on the cheek.

Where the hell did they come from? Angus thought. *Have they been hiding back there all along?*

"Is there really a Vulcan Death Grip?" Janice said. "It sounds phony."

"Yes."

"Demonstrate it for us!" Janice said. "On Tom here. He'd *enjoy* it!"

Tom stood and prepared to flee.

"I'd *pay* to see that," the bartender said.

"No!"

"We found the most *awesome* place for an art gallery!" Marie gushed. "Right on fifth avenue!"

Culinary me and her kids are outside riding the carousel and having ice cream, Allie beamed at Derek. *I gave them local money.*

I love this city! Culinary Allie beamed. *I hate the name Knickerbocker but this strikes me as a charming place to raise children.*

Wait until you smell the pollution, Derek beamed back.

Maybe my Derek can open a gustatorium here. God, what an awful name for a restaurant! Of course, ours would be a Ristorante.

"Meet three KU professors," Allie said to Marie. "From the physics department. You might take classes from them someday."

They nodded at Marie.

"I'm probably majoring in art," Marie said. "I might have to take some required physics courses."

"The world always needs artists," Allie said.

"No one ever says the world needs physicists," Tom whined.

"Here's a physics question," Derek said. "Have any of you heard of the formula ee equals em cee squared? Cee is the speed of light."

"Of course," Angus said. "It disproved the theory of hyperbolic space-time."

"It *disproved* it?" Derek said.

"Crazy theory!" Janice said.

Derek scanned her and learned that a mathematician at Miskatonic University named Nielson Pohl had proposed it twenty years ago — essentially Einstein's theory of special relativity.

A physicist named Milhous Pendergast had showed that it

implied Einstein's famous equation — which everyone regarded as a fatal flaw. After all, what could be more implausible than converting matter into energy?

Professor Pohl will be pleased to meet me, Derek thought.

"Dad's taking me on his next trip to Paris!" Marie said. "I can't wait to ride an airship!"

"It's a *rare* experience, my dear," Tom intoned. "Lounging on tubular aluminum lawn furniture, listening to an aluminum piano ... played, no doubt, by an aluminum pianist."

"I heard they have wine tastings," Derek said.

"Yes," Tom continued. "From waxed cardboard *milk-cartons* and served in *paper cups.* Barbaric! I suffered for two days — *twice. To* and *from* Vienna."

"Your martyrdom's the stuff of legend," Janice said.

"Well, we've got to run," Allie said.

She and Marie left.

"That Marie seems bright," Janice said. "I've taught classes where I say 'who understood what I just said?' Nobody raises their hands. Then I ask 'who *didn't* understand?' And nobody raises their hands. Then I ask 'who *neither* understood nor *didn't* understand?' Still no hands raised. Cows at a fence."

"Ever wonder where the sun gets its energy?" Derek said.

"I've wondered," Janice said. "Why?"

"Thought experiment," Derek said. "Smash three hydrogen atoms together to form one helium."

Angus shut his eyes for a moment and said, "That doesn't work. A helium atom weighs slightly less than three hydrogens."

"Multiply the missing mass by cee squared and you get a *lot* of energy," Derek said, standing. "I've got to run. Nice meeting you guys. I'll keep in touch."

"Wait a minute!" Angus said. "What could smash hydrogens together like that?"

"Gravity?" Janice said. "The pressure in the sun's core is extraordinary."

"There are other ways to fuse them, too," Derek said. "Or coax them together."

He left.

***

"Decorum will not permit me to answer," Allie smiled, as Derek joined her in Perkins Park.

"What do you mean? Oh my God, dad's with a *woman?* What's her name?"

"Not now, Marie," Allie said. *"TMI!* Maybe when they're having breakfast tomorrow. Or after they land in Paris."

"We're not voyeurs," Derek said.

Marie made a face.

***

In their spirit-bodies, Derek and Eldon hovered around the Archy fleet.

They materialized.

Like a cloud of fireflies, thousands of space ships swarmed over the genocidal fleet.

They've been in mothballs so long, Eldon said. *I'd be surprised if one in a hundred actually flies.*

The Archies were outstanding engineers, once, Derek said. *Just one of these ships could plasma Oz.*

Derek and Eldon set about destroying more dormant space ships. At the thirtieth, a laser blast burned through Derek's space suit and he barely managed to teleport back to the Space Ventures factory.

With blackened skeletal hands, he removed his helmet.

Charred skin fell of his face in strips and he was blind in his right eye. The pain on his blackened arms was almost unbearable, and his legs crumbled beneath him.

He reset.

His eyes darted around in momentary confusion as he spotted the charred pile of tissue on the floor in a pool of blood — and his memories returned.

Eldon appeared.

"OK, so they know about us," Derek muttered.

"They still don't know *who* we are, though," Eldon said.

✻✻✻

They returned to the fleet in their spirit bodies.

"What do you *mean* we're under attack?" Lord Enro said. "The planetary defense systems are silent."

"Their battle-cruisers are *minuscule,* Excellency — even smaller than our *physical bodies.* It was sheer luck that we hit one at all."

"Are we fighting *intelligent microbes?*"

"They can't be much larger, Excellency. We're unable to determine how creatures that small could have well-developed brains."

"It is a mystery. Since even *your people* don't seem to have well-developed brains! How do they destroy our space ships?"

"They rip them apart by ... unknown means, Excellency. Their weapons are extraordinarily powerful. We have been debating..."

"*What?*"

"Perhaps it would be wise to postpone Cleansing that distant world. We'd be leaving our home world wide open for attack."

"Very well, but continue activating the fleet."

Chapter 35

Chloe and Eldon paced his office.

"Marjorie and Aaron know we lied," she said. "They've spent every spare moment studying quantum mechanics. They could teach courses on it."

"The hazards of having geniuses working for us. I'll call a meeting."

✳✳✳

Eldon handed out non-disclosure agreements to the department heads: Ray Cristóbal, Marjorie Corcoran, Aaron David, and Gene Krupa.

Nora Weinberg appeared at the door.

The president of Space Ventures was a statuesque blond with a commanding presence who wore a black skirt and jacket covered with constellations from the night sky.

You aren't the company's president? Chloe beamed in disbelief.

Of course not. I just own it. Nora negotiates launch contracts, deals with the media, and personnel issues. A hell of a lot better than I could.

"I asked Nora to attend this meeting," Eldon said. "It affects her in a big way."

"Where's Lin?" Marjorie said.

"He won't be attending," Chloe said. "For reasons that we'll explain later."

"So you're the mysterious Chloe I've heard so much about," Nora said. "Shame on you, Eldon! Why did I have to hear about her from other *employees?*"

"I'm sorry," Eldon said. "I know I should've introduced you first. We've had our hands full lately."

"Apology accepted. I agree with the 'hands full' part; what happened with Mercouri is absolutely mind-boggling."

"Eldy isn't the greatest communicator," Chloe smiled.

"Why these NDA's?" Ray said. "We already signed forms to not disclose company technology."

"These bar you from disclosing anything discussed at this meeting to anyone *not present*. Even people in the company."

"Especially not to Lin Wong," Chloe said.

One of the company's attorneys, Walt Masterson, explained the agreements and penalties for violating them.

"We will not discuss anything illegal," Eldon said. "If you refuse to sign, it won't be held against you."

"You just won't be privy to the information we'll share," Chloe said.

They all signed.

Mr. Masterson witnessed the signed contracts, packed them in an attache case, and left.

Eldon summoned his secretary

"Please give Susan your cell phones," Eldon said. "You can retrieve them after the meeting."

They complied, and Susan left.

Eldon pushed a button on his desk and a curtain outside the window to the factory floor lowered.

"As several of you have figured out," Eldon began. "Our statements about quantum teleportation were lies."

"We rescued Greg Jones from Mars using alien technology," Chloe said.

They all gasped.

"We know how to use it, but only have a vague idea of how it works," Chloe added.

"We'll reverse-engineer the fucker!" Gene said. "Just show it to us."

"You're looking at it," Eldon said. "Chloe and me."

"Travel," Chloe began, and teleporting across the room, continued, "Is easy for us."

"Holy *shit!*" Marjorie exclaimed.

"Yeah," Eldon muttered. "Holy shit indeed. I believe teleportation is instantaneous."

Eldon launched into his tale, beaming, *I'll keep the lies to a minimum. Hell I might be able to pass a lie detector test.*

"One day," he said. "Aliens from another quantum timeline appeared on our doorstep."

Another quantum timeline? Marjorie thought. *This gets better and better!*

"What's a quantum timeline?" Nora said.

"I'll explain later," Marjorie said.

And Eldon told the story of Derek, Allie, Dr. Pembroke's experiments, and how they had offered Eldon and Chloe the opportunity to become Indigos.

"How does teleportation work?" Gene said. "Did they explain it?"

"Sort of," Chloe said, spinning a long story about the spirit world.

"That's not *science*," Ray said. "It's religion!"

"Nevertheless, that's all we've got," Eldon said.

"You two are telepathic?" Nora said.

"At times," Chloe said. "That *one ability* has saved this company and your *lives*. Possibly millions of others as well."

Eldon explained the North Korean plot to acquire the company.

A stunned silence followed.

"Wait, wait, wait!" Nora said, shaking her head. "I've been in meetings with Isoroku Kinoshita himself. I haven't committed to anything, but I find it impossible to believe he's a North Korean agent! He's a refined gentleman who knows his business. What motive could North Korea possibly have?"

"Attack US with nuclear weapons from a base on Japanese soil," Eldon said. "By a company that is ostensibly Japanese."

"This ... story is so *bizarre*," Aaron said. "You're asking us to accept too many unbelievable things. The soul exists? Your teleporting... It could be just a clever illusion. I'm sure the *Cirque de Soleil* knows how to do that."

"Maybe it'll be more believable if I tell it from over *here*," Eldon said, teleporting across the room.

"Stop that!" Aaron said. "I refuse to accept any of this. I'm leaving."

"We're sorry to see you go," Nora said. "Is there anything I can do to change your mind?"

"No."

"You're still bound by the nondisclosure agreement," Eldon said.

"Don't worry! I have no intention of repeating any of this ... this *insane crap* to *anyone*. I'll be tendering my resignation. This company has gone light-years off the deep end."

He left.

"That went well," Chloe sighed.

"Let's go for a ride," Eldon said. "I'll show you things beyond the *Cirque's* wildest dreams."

"I've never heard anything so outlandish!" Nora muttered. "This better be good, Eldon!"

"It's good."

The three remaining department heads and company president followed Eldon and Chloe out onto the factory floor.

※※※

"Last chance Aaron," Eldon said, as they passed him. "Something that will convince even you."

He frowned and shook his head.

"Strange!" Chloe said.

"What's so strange," Nora said.

"He feels there are two terrifying possibilities. *One,* we've lost our minds and the company's imploding. *Two,* we're telling the truth — which frightens him *more."*

"You read his mind?" Marjorie said.

"Uh, yes."

Now, the QS Schrödinger had a metal shell around it with an airtight door.

"Good," Eldon said. "It's space-ready now."

They went inside.

"Make yourselves comfortable," Chloe said, gesturing to the rows of seats.

Eldon went into the cockpit and shut its door.

※※※

What a strange feeling! Nora thought. *A flash of... ecstasy. Almost erotic.*

"What's going to happen?" Marjorie said.

"It already has," Chloe said, opening the back hatch.

A dark howling cloud swirled over a white-encrusted world, as a brisk, rancid wind whistled in the open hatch.

"Shit!" Eldon said. "I forgot about the passenger pigeons."

The three department heads peeked out of the Schrödinger's hatch and looked around.

"Look, folks," Eldon said. "I can take us to a less smelly place."

"Where are we?" Marjorie finally said.

"A timeline we call Oz," Eldon said.

"A different *quantum timeline?*" Marjorie whispered.

"Again, what the *hell* is that?" Nora muttered.

"A different parallel universe," Eldon said. "The Indigo homeland."

The QS Schrödinger's next stop was Destiny Beach.

***

When Chloe opened the hatch, the humid air — like warm scented oil — assaulted their senses.

Waves thundered into the shore.

The department heads stumbled out the hatch.

Wearing shorts, flip-flops, and an aloha shirt, Derek waved to them from his deck and said, "Aloha."

"That's ... that's *Diamond Head,"* Nora said, staring at the crater.

"Join us on the deck," Derek said, pointing to several chairs.

They sat.

"Want some lemonade?" Taka said.

Eldon introduced them to her.

"Thanks," Nora mumbled, taking a glass.

Marjorie looked out at the sea and numbly watched Wendy and Travis play their game: One would teleport high into the air and throw a ball that the other had to catch before it hit the water.

Then Tony and Loretta joined them, squealing with delight.

A pod of dolphins clicked and whistled encouragement and, when the ball hit the water, a dolphin would pop it back up to them.

"It's a game they made up," Derek said.

"Huh?" Marjorie muttered.

"They call it Teleball. In the new rules, the dolphins can be on teams with them and get points for popping the ball up."

The four Space Ventures employees numbly stared.

Swirling clouds rolled in and misted them for a moment.

Dressed in a lacy white blouse, burgundy ankle-length skirt, burgundy waistcoat fastened with a brass chain and tulle-covered top-hat, Allie appeared.

"Greetings," she said. "I'm the Alessandra that Eldon told you about. Call me Allie."

She removed her brown contact lenses as Marjorie gaped at her.

"C ... c ... cosplay?" Marjorie stammered.

"I came from a place where people normally dress this way," Allie said. "A timeline we call Columbia. Excuse me while I slip into something more suitable for this steambath."

"What do you people do at Eldon's company?" Taka said.

They replied.

"I see," Taka said. "No, actually I don't. What's a cryo...genic rocket?"

"The most powerful rockets use liquid oxygen," Gene said. "Since it's very cold, they're called cryogenic."

"Hypergolics use two fuels that spontaneously combust when mixed together," Marjorie said. "A hypergolic rocket can be turned on and off a hundred times, easily. And very precisely throttled. A cryogenic rocket gets you to orbit and hypergolics fine-tune it."

"Oh," Taka lied.

"GPS satellites need millimeter-accuracy in orbit," Marjorie continued. "Or cars will crash all over the place. You need hypergolics for that."

"Are you an Indigo?" Gene asked Taka.

"No," she said. "I'm just an old farmer. They offered to make me an Indigo but ... I don't know. Too old."

"How did you wind up here?" Marjorie said.

"In Origin, they were coming to kill me," Taka said. "So Wendy and Travis moved my farm here."

"Your *whole farm?*" Gene said.

"Most of it. My house is at the end of the beach."

"Wendy's our champion teleporter," Derek said.

Wendy appeared, making the Space Ventures people jump.

"Nice to meet you guys," she smiled, wiping sweat off her brow. "Gotta feed the *keikis*."

She collapsed into a chair and Kaiulani and Roger appeared in her arms.

"Keikis?" Gene whispered to Marjorie.

"Babies in Hawaiian," she replied.

"Hope you aren't offended by bare breasts," Derek said.

Wendy opened her blouse and the *keikis* nursed.

"Maybe we should head back," Eldon said.

***

The department heads and president staggered out of the QS Schrödinger and returned to Eldon's office.

Eldon called Maintenance and asked them to clean bird-droppings off the ship.

"We'll have many more discussions and ... visits ... to other places," Eldon said.

"How many timelines are there?" Nora said.

"An infinite number!" Marjorie said.

"True," Eldon said. "But we've only visited a few. There's *Oz,* which you've seen. There's *Origin* where Derek and Allie came from. The timeline we're in is called *Culinary,* for various reasons."

"The food's better?" Gene said.

"Sure," Chloe laughed.

"Then there's *Pembroke,*" Eldon continued. "It's like North Korea but not as warm and fuzzy."

"North Korea?" Nora said. "What's going on with them?"

"The FBI arrested their abduction team," Eldon said, shutting his eyes. "Their ship is ready to dock in the port of Los Angeles. The *Kobe Maru.*"

"Japanese?" Marjorie said.

"In name only," Eldon said. "They have a second abduction team aboard the ship."

"Who are they going to abduct?" Marjorie said.

"You guys," Eldon said. "And Aaron. They plan to put you on the ship take you to North Korea. They'd like to abduct us too, but that's physically impossible."

Marjorie gasped.

"Don't worry; we have your backs," Eldon said. "All of us do. Wendy even offered to teleport the entire *Kobe Maru* to another timeline."

"Burner phone," Chloe explained, pulling out a cell phone and calling the FBI. She gave them an anonymous tip about the *Kobe Maru* and disconnected.

Then she pulled out the phone's batteries and threw it away.

"Usually I teleport to some faraway place to do this."

"Then it's finished," Nora said.

"If they take our tip seriously," Eldon said. "They've ignored them in the past. Some of them, anyway."

"Until tomorrow, then," Chloe said.

Chapter 36

"I've got to be the dumbest asshole in the *universe!*" Derek moaned.

"Why?" Allie chuckled. "I'm sure there are assholes dumber than you. In other timelines, maybe."

Taka laughed.

"The way we destroyed those Archy spaceships," Derek said. "I left myself wide open by floating outside. We have to teleport *inside* a spaceship and take the whole damn thing away. I know just the place."

"What are you talking about?" Kurt said.

"The creatures who want to drop H-bombs on our *heads!*" Grace said.

Wendy appeared holding two pies, and Birgit followed with two more.

"*Zwiebelkuchen*," Birgit said. "Onion pies. From your wonderful onions, Taka."

"We could take the Archy ships to another timeline," Chloe said. "Like Culinary."

"*No!*" Derek said. "Archies exist there too — probably.

Archy ships might send signals to those Archies. Then they'd come and attack Earth."

Wendy, Derek, and Eldon donned space suits and Derek went into the spirit world.

***

He visualized the conch shell he'd discarded long ago and found himself beside it. Derek's space suit's light illuminated it, slowing rotating the utter blackness.

The others materialized.

You weren't kidding about getting away from it all, Eldon beamed.

This might be a timeline where the universe never formed, Derek said.

We've left the Milky Way galaxy, Eldon said. *That much is clear.*

Where are the stars? Wendy said, appearing in a space suit.

Every star you see in the night sky is part of our home galaxy, Eldon said. *The Milky Way.*

The Milky Way? Wendy said. *Isn't that the band of light across the night sky.*

Our sun is on our galaxy's rim, Eldon said. *The glowing band is our galaxy's main body.*

We're not at the center? Wendy said.

No, Eldon said. *At the center, the stars are so thick and close, the night sky would be a solid glowing dome. As bright as day.*

Wow! Wendy said.

Uh, Derek ... pal, Eldon said. *Did you look around when you came here last?*

I kind of panicked, Derek said. *There's nothing to see, though. Emptiness — everywhere. I don't think matter even exists in this ... place.*

About that, Eldon said. *Rotate your space suits, folks.*

How? Wendy said.

Use your maneuvering jets, Eldon said.

They pushed buttons on chest-keypads and tiny jets rotated their space suits. Wendy had trouble controlling hers and went into a spin. Eldon showed her how to stop spinning by activating counter jets, and they finally faced ninety degrees from their original direction.

Then they saw it.

Like a glowing diamond mandala, a spiral galaxy carpeted the otherwise-unbroken blackness, its pale white light punctuated by scattered red and blue dots.

We must be light-years away! Wendy said.

More like millions of light-years, Eldon said. *At least ten.*

Another, smaller galaxy lay off to one side — a bar of light trailing spirals from its ends.

The big one looks like Andromeda, Eldon continued. *But it could be the Milky Way. No one has ever seen our galaxy from the outside.*

Andy Cole has to see this, Derek said.

I can see it through your eyes, Andy said. *So that might be my namesake? My parents would've given their right arms to see this.*

Most galaxies — like these two — have about a hundred billion stars, Eldon said. *And forty billion like our sun.*

Really? Wendy said.

Every single one of those stars has planets orbiting it, Eldon continued.

Every one? Wendy said.

So we're looking at, maybe, eight billion Earth-like planets, Eldon continued. *There are trillions of people down there —*

loving, hating, struggling to survive. Can you feel their life-force?

Yeah, Wendy said. *I do feel energy coming from down there. A warm glow.*

Out here in the void, you can feel it, Eldon said. *Down there, it's background noise.*

So Eakins's stupid speech could've been valid, Wendy said.

What? Derek said.

When he said we were aliens from another galaxy. We weren't, but could've been.

It's so strange, Eldon said.

What? Wendy said.

We may be the first sentient beings to see this.

Huh? Wendy said.

Intelligent beings evolve on planets orbiting stars, and stars lie inside galaxies, Eldon said. *None of them can see galaxies in the void, like this.*

No one else ever developed the ability to travel here? Derek said. *Pretty arrogant, isn't it?*

Yes, Eldon said. *And Chloe would add that God has seen it.*

❋❋❋

In the next hour, they transported twenty Archy spaceships to the conch in the void.

None of them had Archy's in them, although one had been loaded with oxygen, and its systems were active.

We could go inside and take off our spacesuits! Wendy said.

The oxygen levels would kill you, Derek said. *We have to figure out how to bleed most of the air out. That would probably set off alarms.*

Maybe we could hold our breath, Wendy said.

The pressure would kill you. Or knock you out at least.

***

In his spirit-body Derek visited Lord Enro, and the others followed.

To the ones activating a genocidal fleet, Derek beamed to all the Archies in his entourage. *We will not sit idly by as you prepare to commit unprovoked murder!*

You're talking to them? Wendy said.

They know we exist and that we're attacking them, Derek said. *They may as well know why.*

"I heard a voice in my mind!" Lord Enro roared.

"So did I, Excellency,"

"Communication with sentient vermin is forbidden!" Lord Enro said. "With the death penalty!"

"It speaks directly into our minds. At least we know why they are attacking. They have altered their tactics, Excellency."

"I don't understand?" Lord Enro said. "Unprovoked murder? What do they *mean* by that? Murder is when we kill *each other.*"

"They seem to regard cleansing as a crime," Commander Kalf said.

"We're just killing *vermin,*" Lord Enro said. "That's not a crime; it's a necessity."

"They are demanding we regard vermin as equivalent to ourselves, Excellency."

"That's *insane!* The alien mind is beyond comprehension!"

"They're making our ships disappear," Commander Kalf said.

"Where do they go?"

"We haven't detected the ships' homing signals," Commander Kalf said. "We assume they no longer exist."

"How are they doing this?"

"There are no signs of radiation, electromagnetic or otherwise. The ships simply vanish."

"That's impossible!" Lord Enro said.

Wendy teleported into an unoccupied space ship floating beside the one containing them — and teleported it to Conch Point.

This stunned Lord Enro.

"What, Excellency?" Commander Kalf said.

"Out that portal." he said, pointing. "A ship vanished before my eyes!"

"A suggestion, Excellency," Commander Kalf said. "These creatures have extraordinarily advanced technology..."

"Vermin do not *have* technology!" Lord Enro interrupted. *Is there no limit to your blasphemy?*

"We have to renounce future Cleansings. We have an enemy with formidable capabilities and ..."

"Cleansings are vital to our civilization!" Lord Enro said, thinking, *Are you trying to get me killed?*

Get him killed? Derek thought.

"We haven't had cleansings in a million cycles," Commander Kalf said. "In that time no one has attacked us.

"You're flirting with a pain amplifier session!" Lord Enro said. "Is that what you want?"

"No, Excellency."

"How many ships are ready to fly? Right now."

"Three."

"Launch *immediately!* At the planet with the ancient sentinel! How long will it take?"

"Two cycles impulse power to exit our system, and..."

What's impulse power? Wendy said.

Rockets, Eldon replied.

"Two cycles flying around our *solar system?"* Archy One said. *"Why?"*

"We have to be *far away* before engaging the hyperdrive, Excellency. A nearby planet-mass can cause it to explode."

"OK, OK. What's the flight time after that?"

"Eight more cycles, Excellency," Commander Kalf said, thinking, *You're sending them on a suicide mission! Surely you know that.*

"Excellency," Commander Kalf continued. "You should lead this raid *personally.* It would inspire the others."

"I'm not a military person. And I have important business back home. I'm taking the next shuttle down."

❉❉❉

They returned to Destiny Beach, where Allie was painting Taka's portrait as Wendy watched.

"You have such a marvelous face," Allie murmured.

"Just a old farmer's wrinkled face," Taka smiled.

"Every line, every wrinkle tells a story … of a long life … lived well. Your face is the history of a moment."

"So much for exploring the solar system with an Alcubierre drive," Eldon muttered. "Incidentally, the Archy's will attack us with nuclear weapons in a few months, or so."

"You're taking it rather well," Allie said, looking up from her easel.

"I'm not fleeing!" Wendy shouted as Kaiulani and Roger appeared in her arms. "This is *our* land; it will not be *taken* from us! It's for our *keikis."*

"We have two cycles before they engage their hyperdrives," Derek said. "Wish I knew how long a cycle was. The ships haven't even left orbit yet."

"Will they have Archies in them?" Wendy said.

"They'll surely have crews," Derek said.

"I can't believe they're attacking at all," Allie said, shaking her head. "They must know their chances are nil."

"It seems to be political theater," Derek said. "Lord Enro needs to show he's doing something."

***

An unusually intense rally at Agri-Unit 243 left Eakins exhausted and wondering whether it had all been worth it.

My evangelical-preacher background has kept me alive so far, but how much longer?

Peasants — he really couldn't think of a better term for them — in shapeless gray sacks thrust babies at him for his blessings.

Their lives are barely worth living but they breed like rabbits.

Eakins saw a familiar face.

"Tung," he smiled.

Four men accompanied Tung. Although dressed as the others, their husky builds, catlike movements, and shaved heads marked them.

Soldiers.

Shit! I knew this day would come.

"We'd like to speak to you in private," Tung said, ushering Eakins into a cramped fertilizer storage room.

"From the ... Safety Service," Tung said. "I trust them with my life. They know ... everything."

"Freedom awaits," Eakins mumbled.

One by one, the four men repeated that phrase, shook his hand, and introduced themselves: Hank, Meran, Norris, and Loble.

"I apologize for not introducing them to you earlier," Tung said. "But we had to be sure."

"It is a profound honor to meet you, my lord," Hank said. "You're an inspiration to us all."

"Another man appeared in the City of Delight," Tung said. "Without a neck-barcode, like you."

"The authorities assumed he *was* you," Meran said. "And they executed him. He was heaven-sent to distract the safety service in their manhunt."

"So ... why ... ?" Eakins yawned.

"Why are we here?" Tung said. "We are here to give you a message. Your magnificent phrase Freedom Awaits will become reality."

"We're planning a *Great Push,*" Norris said. "It will change the world, and you will be its spiritual leader."

A push? Eakins thought. *What the fuck am I getting myself in to? Some kind of half-assed revolution?*

"I ... I ... I don't know what to say," Eakins mumbled. "I don't know how to lead a ... a push."

"Of course not," Tung said. "That's our job."

"Our supporters number in the tens of thousands," Norris said. "Millions will flock to our banner."

"We have planned this for years," Tung said. "Before the miracle of your purified neck, despair haunted our days."

"Then Heaven sent you to us," Meran said. "Now our plans are reaching fruition and, when the time is right..."

"We'll *strike,*" Tung said. "You've shown us Heaven's glorious mandate. Success is assured."

"This is overwhelming," Eakins mumbled. "I don't know what to say."

"We just wanted to give you the message," Tung said. "You look weary, my lord. You should try to get some rest."

"Your time will come," Meran said. *"Our* time will come. *Freedom Awaits!"*

Chapter 37

"This place is so *backward!*" Marie said. "They have *black and white* TV with clunky *picture tubes.* No internet! Don't get me wrong; this place is growing on me. I could live here."

It was nine in the morning at the Kensington Coffee Shoppy across 23rd street from the Knickerbocker Board of Education building.

The place had a black and white tiled floor, a brass coffee bar, and a odd glass display case filled with decadent pastries. Each of the case's shelves was blue glass, supported from the one beneath it by brass figurines like mermaids except that — instead of fish tails — they had eight long tentacles curled in patterns that struck Derek as vaguely obscene.

Octamaids?

The one other patron sat at the place's far end, sipping coffee and hiding behind an unfolded newspaper.

Dense rolling fog obscured their view of 23rd street and its light traffic.

"Look, Marie," Derek said. "People here just as intelligent

as in Origin. They have the same ideas and philosophical outlook on life."

"You made a *fortune* by knowing a *map* was bogus!" Marie said. "That would never work in Origin."

"There's no Internet here, and the fake maps were elegant and professional-looking," Derek said. "Checking it would've involved taking a cab to a public library and going through an atlas. I admit, not doing that was sloppy, maybe even irresponsible."

"The man behind the con was excellent," Allie said. "He knew his victims and appealed to their sense of honor."

"Appealing to people's honor?" Marie laughed. "That would never work in Origin."

"People here are less cynical," Allie added.

"Wars make people *smarter,*" Marie insisted.

"No," Derek said. "Leonardo da Vinci existed in both of our timelines. His notebooks depicted many modern inventions like the airplane, helicopter, and submarine."

"So?" Marie said.

"None of them would've worked," Derek said. "Not *one!* The airplane had too small a wingspan, the helicopter didn't have enough power, etc. Making things *function* is grueling antwork. As Edison said, it's one percent inspiration and ninety nine percent perspiration."

"Wars make people do the perspiration," Allie volunteered. "Imminent death is a fantastic motivator. World War I perfected fixed wing aircraft. World War II perfected atomic power and weapons, computers. The Cold War perfected rockets and satellites."

The man at the end of the place lowered his paper and stared.

"OK," Derek murmured. "We should cool it."

Weena and her family appeared.

"Ready?" Allie said.

"Oh, I feel sick," Weena moaned, running to the ladies' room.

"She didn't get a bug's whisper o' sleep last night," her mother said. "Afraid she'll shoot into the brown, she is."

"I'm sure she'll do fine," Allie said, beaming to Derek, *Poor Weena's throwing up.*

"Today's the history part?" Derek said.

"Tomorrow is Social Studies," Weena's mother nodded. "And Friday is math. Math scares her more than a lion's roar. Saturday, they give out diplomas to people who passed."

Weena rejoined them and she and Marie left for the exam.

They feel nervous around us, Allie beamed to Derek.

"Allie and I have some business to conduct, but we'll be back in an hour," Derek said. "Feel free to order food and drink. Our treat."

"Thank you, sir!" Clarice Fion said.

Derek went to the restaurant's owner and gave him $500 to cover anything the Fions ordered.

Derek and Allie crossed 23rd street, entered the Board of Education Building, found restrooms and teleported: Derek to Knickerbocker University and Allie to her art gallery.

※※※

Professor Janice MacCallan's lab at Knickerbocker University was a large airy room with stone-topped work-tables and windows that opened onto a grimy courtyard. Bookcases covered one wall, and huge coils of wire lay in a corner.

"How did you find me?" Janice chuckled. "This building's a labyrinth. Children have wandered in to emerge decades later as adults."

Derek laughed.

"Here's your transistor radio," she said.

Professor MacCallan pointed to a three-foot square lacquered mahogany slab with an array of copper posts extending from its surface. Each post had copper clips on its end. She had threaded a thicket of wires and electronic components to the clips. On one end, two cylinders with attached knobs hung from three wires each. On the other, a speaker hung from two wires.

She ceremoniously clipped a nine-volt battery to one end of the contraption.

Then she turned one knob and static came from the speaker. Turning the other knob tuned into a station playing music.

"Jeffrey's Morning Serenade," she said. "It took us *hours* to get this stupid thing working."

"The devil's in the details."

"I'll have to remember that phrase," she chuckled. "It's surely true."

"Now we have to simplify the circuit as much as possible and create printed circuit boards."

"Print a *circuit?* How does one do that?"

Damn! Derek thought. *They were perfected in World War II.* He tried to explain.

"Clever idea," she said. "I suppose we could just glue wires to a board."

They spent the next fifteen minutes discussing their next move: Professor MacCallan would simplify the circuit and come up with procedures for manufacturing transistors — ones a non-physicist could understand.

Derek would ask his broker to find a company capable of doing the work.

Janice changed the subject and said, "Have you considered going for your Ph. D. in physics?".

"Uh ... no."

"You really should. I think you'd do extraordinarily well."

A quick scan showed that she had three Ph. D. students: one was finishing up and the other two were floundering and would likely drop out.

Do it! Allie beamed. *You could discover quantum mechanics.*

I'd be a phony. I don't want that.

We need quantum mechanics to explain how Pincus generators work.

"OK," Derek said. "What do I have to do?"

Professor MacCallan clapped her hands and smiled.

"There are some forms to fill out," she said. "I'll arrange for you to take qualifying exams. I'll give you a list of topics and books."

They spent next the half hour signing papers at the Registrar's Office.

"You won't regret this, Mr. Evans! Not one bit!"

❊❊❊

A quick scan of Professor Epstein revealed that he'd produced a sizable amount of his "*penicilium arcanum*," and was testing it on terminally ill patients at the KU Medical Center.

Derek teleported to the woods outside the Gofols House in Tarrytown and approached it.

Seven large trucks covered the front lawn, and a crew of twenty hammered away on the roof.

A strange feeling came over him as he glanced at bushes beside the house.

The bushes bathed in sunlight suddenly seemed like part of the most transcendent painting imaginable. Every leaf in every bush aroused impressions of every plant that ever *had* or ever *would* exist. Images spiraled through his mind of grasslands on other planets and forests of intelligent trees.

The workmen on the roof elicited images of pyramids going up, cities sprouting up like plants, uncanny cities under the sea, and cities in space.

Sobbing, he leaned against the house.

He contacted Allie.

It's like the William Blake poem, she beamed back. *If the doors of perception were cleansed, everything would appear to man as it is, Infinite.*

We seem to still be changing as our new genes are expressed, he replied.

At least it was pleasant.

Yes, he said. *It was one of the most beautiful moments of my life.*

"Are you unwell, Mr. Evans?" Jerrold Holmes said. "You bear a most eldritch countenance."

He's ill. I knew these new owners were too good to be true.

"Fine!" Derek replied, wiping tears from his eyes.

"Fine?"

"I am well," Derek corrected. "Thank you for inquiring."

"As you can see, this place is a whirlwind of activity," the butler said. "Would you like to peruse the books?"

"Oh, OK."

The butler led him into the estate's cramped business office where Charlotte Holmes was making notes in a ledger book.

"Take a look," she said.

Derek rapidly flipped through thirty pages and slammed the ledger book shut.

If you couldn't be bothered to read it, why make the pretense? Jerrold Holmes thought.

"I noticed," Derek said. "On the bottom of page 11, you

purchased a new commercial washing machine and drier. Why did the drier cost so much more than the washer?"

"Um ... uh, it was a more expensive model," Mr. Holmes stammered, thinking, *Did he just memorize the whole damned thing?*

"Oh, I see, it was a Worthington rather than a Metro. And you installed a new walk-in ice-shronk. I noticed on page 23, Mr. Maitland was sent to the local hospital with a bacterial infection."

"Yes," the butler said. "He's the groundskeeper and he was planing wood and got a huge splinter. The nurse managed to remove most of it, but it got infected. They did minor surgery and managed to disinfect it."

"I noticed you list no renovations to the staff quarters," Derek said. "Are they in perfect condition?"

"Far from it," Jerrold laughed.

"Well, I want renovation to *all* of the rooms. This is our staff's home too, and I'd like them to be happy here. Happy employees are productive ones."

"Very well, sir."

Ah, his military background shows through, Derek thought.

"You've gone far above and beyond the call of duty for a butler, Mr. Holmes," Derek said. "Give yourself a thirty percent raise. From the day we bought the house."

He wrote a two million dollar check to the household account and asked Mr. Holmes to look into installing a swimming pool and a separate building to become Derek's workshop.

"While you're at it," Derek continued. "This office is cramped and depressing."

"Depressing?" Charlotte said.

"Puts you ... uh, into the morbs."

"Oh," she sighed deeply and rubbed her face. "I suppose it does."

"Build an addition to the house, or a separate building to house the business office," Derek said. "Bigger, with many large windows. We may make this the Indigo Concern's financial headquarters."

"Very well, Mr. Evans," Jerrold Holmes smiled.

"This is a magnificent house. Much larger than we need, although we have family and friends who will want to visit. It's a work of art, and I'd love to see it restored to its former glory."

"Before I forget, Sir," the butler said. "A crate arrived today from the Halifax Fused Glass Concern."

"They didn't waste any time," Derek murmured. "Let's see it."

Jerrold Holmes led him outside, to the carriage house.

A huge shipping crate lay in a corner of the cavernous room.

"They said they'd ship their latest products to me," Derek said. "Glass cookware."

"*Glass cookware?* It that possible?"

"Yes," Derek said. "It should be possible to cook and bake with it."

Jerrold took a crowbar and pried some wooden slats from the crate.

Wood shavings spilled out of it, and Derek spotted ornate liquor bottles buried in them.

"Oh my God!" Derek said. "This is the finest cognac I ever tasted. Do you and your wife drink?"

"Uh, yes, Sir," he replied, thinking, *The only thing that kept us sane these past two years.*

"Take some!" Derek said, handing him two bottles. "We should have a toast!"

✳✳✳

Jerrold Holmes and his wife met with Derek in the servants' dining room.

Framed painting of landscapes adorned its power-blue walls, and a long table seating twenty dominated it.

The smell of linseed oil hung in the air.

Charlotte Holmes produced three brandy snifters and Derek toasted.

"Bless this house and all who live or work in it!" Derek said.

They drank.

"To the future!" Derek added.

Then he checked his watch and said, "Oh, I've got to get back!"

After Mr. Holmes drove him to the train station, he rejoined Allie and the others at the Kensington Coffee Shoppy.

***

Teenagers and one old lady filed out of the Board of Education Building across the street.

Eventually, Marie and Weena joined them in the coffee shoppy.

"Either we both passed or both failed," Marie said, after they compared notes on the answers they had given.

"You took the exam too?" Derek said.

"Yeah," Marie winced. "Dad set it up. My name on it is *Maude Frickert!* Do I look like a Maude Frickert?"

Derek laughed.

"Your father's lady friend," Allie said. "The one he met on the *LS Lorelei?*"

"I'm *all ears!*"

"You have such a funny way of talkin!" Weena laughed. "Do they talk like that in France?"

"Uh, sure."

"She's the Baroness Anastasia von Durfee," Allie said. "She has a palace in the village of Durfee, in Germany."

"She's a *princess?*"

"Sort of," Allie said. "Her castle's in need of repairs. She came here to sell family heirlooms, but it fell through."

"We've been spendin your money long enough, Mr. Evans," Clarice Fion said. "Weena needs a good night's sleep."

They left.

"Professor Janice MacCallen really likes you," Allie said.

"She has the *hots* for Derek?" Marie giggled.

"She finds him attractive," Allie said. "Who wouldn't? But, there's more to it than that."

"We fascinate her," Derek said, blushing. "All of us. Even you, Marie."

"She senses we're different in some way," Allie said. "A breath of fresh air. She'll try to be your mentor, Marie. Then she'll try to pump you for everything you know about us."

Marie laughed.

✸✸✸

Derek and Allie went to bed in Destiny Beach.

"One of these days, we should sleep in our new house," Derek said. "You know, the one that's like the Grand Budapest Hotel."

"I'll keep that in mind," Allie chuckled as they drifted off to sleep.

Mental screams woke them at three in the morning. It was Wendy's daughter, Kaiulani, having a nightmare:

> At her twenty-first birthday party, all eyes were on sweet Isabella Thuyssen. Standing in an enormous living room, she sipped a cocktail and savored

its heady aroma. Daddy had paid more than ten million to acquire genuine wines and liquors for her soirée.

Isabella's gown was a diaphanous Bellacqua, covered with ronchi gratings that diffracted light, sending rainbow-waves of color rippling up and down her body every time she moved.

The new air-filtration system worked beautifully: guests said the air smelled like the countryside before the Three Wars.

All was perfect.

Outside the sealed French doors to the balcony, glittering mile-high buildings pierced the night — part of Hudsonia's largest city, Newport.

Elegant ladies, men in tuxedos, and men in immaculate black-and-silver military dress-uniforms sipped cocktails, chatted about "a final push to victory," and chuckled at little jokes.

Light flared.

Brighter than a thousand suns, it dissolved the apartment's walls in flame.

Screaming, screaming, screaming.

Isabella watched and smelled the flesh burn off her arms, exposing bone that disintegrated.

Blackness.

Sweating profusely, Derek beamed calming energy to baby Kaiulani, as Wendy tried to follow his lead.

Kaiulani finally drifted into a dreamless sleep.

"Wendy's kids are from Deathworld," Derek said. "They lived all their past lives there."

He beamed the dream to Eldon who replied, *Thanks for sharing!*

Sorry!

Guess I'm up for the duration, Eldon said. *No way am I getting back to sleep.*

"So Kaiulani was a young heiress," Allie said.

"And Roger was a army colonel named Jason Muller," Derek said. "He lost contact with the high command, and supplies ran low. Soldiers deserted all around him, and he didn't stop them. He gathered his wife and two children and fled. They holed up in the nearby Fort Langlands vault with all the food and water they could scrounge."

"Isabella's death was terrifying," Allie sighed. "But Muller's was desperation and heartbreak. He was among the Earth's last living humans."

We have to give them a proper burial, Wendy said. *Deathworld is ours, now. A hell to the Indigo heaven that is Oz. We'll breathe new life into it — for the children's sake.*

What kind of life could they possibly have? Derek beamed at the others.

A peaceful one, Wendy said. *They crave peace as others crave oxygen.*

Chapter 38

A bleary-eyed Eldon led the department heads through the QS Schrödinger.

"We'll need a cargo hold with a robot-arm and..." he yawned.

"Oh my God!" Chloe interrupted.

"I feel it too," Eldon said.

"What?" Gene said.

"Something's going to happen," Eldon said. "I'm not sure what. Impressions... of an explosion?"

"It's *him*," Chloe said, pointing to a burly man in a Space Ventures uniform and red baseball cap.

He was slowly walking away.

"Sir, would you come over here, please?" Eldon said. "We need to speak to you."

The man fled.

"Security!" Eldon shouted. *"Stop that man."*

Two security guards gave chase, and the strange man pulled out a pistol, fired, and wounded one of them.

"I should've handled it myself," Eldon muttered.

He teleported to a point in front of the fleeing man and tripped him.

The man twisted on the ground and fired at Eldon's head, which exploded into bloody mist.

Chloe screamed.

Eldon reset and kicked the man's gun away as Derek appeared with a stun gun and subdued him.

Ray and Gene ran over and helped tie him up with their belts. Chloe followed.

"I ... I saw your head..." Nora exclaimed.

"He missed," Eldon said. "That's our story, and we're sticking to it."

"Bullshit!" Nora insisted.

"We Indigos can regenerate ..."

An explosion cut him off, knocking them all to the ground.

Eldon and Chloe's ears were ringing, so they reset.

"Are you alright?" Eldon asked Gene, Ray, and Nora.

Several smaller explosions rocked the building, and Eldon ran inside, choking on the smoke and fumes.

He found the wounded security guard, now covered with blood and teleported him to Cedars-Sinai Medical Center emergency room.

He dropped him off and returned to the others.

After taking a deep breath, he and Chloe ran back into the burning factory.

Police and ambulance sirens sounded in the distance.

Fire seared Eldon's face as he tried to reach the Hydrazine Storage Facility. It was hopeless.

He and Chloe managed to pull two other injured workers out of the factory as three police cars pulled up.

"We caught this man running away seconds before the explosion," Eldon said. "He shot one of our guards."

Four fire engines and three ambulances pulled up.

"We've got hydrazine, liquid oxygen, and RP-1," Eldon said to the Fire Marshal, who discussed this with his men.

"How many inside?" the Fire Marshal asked.

"It was the end of the day, so people were beginning to leave. There might be twenty, including three night watchmen."

They all stayed there during the three hours it took the Fire Department to bring the fire under control.

✷✷✷

"We take our eyes off him for a *couple hours* and he pulls this shit," Eldon said.

"You know who's responsible?" Ray said.

"The bomber's name is Philip Makayo," Chloe said.

"You know his *name?*" Gene said.

"You don't get the telepathy thing, do you?" Chloe said.

"The man pulling his strings is Dennis *asshole* Nelson," Eldon growled. "The lobbyist we told you about. He's trying to keep this deal going. The North Koreans are backing out."

"The Coast Guard boarded their ship," Chloe said. "And they'll probably impound it. This time, the authorities are verifying everything with the Japanese government."

"Nelson is already telling people the explosion proves we're a slipshod operation," Eldon said.

"Makayo hasn't said a word," Chloe said. "They've got him on trespassing and assault with a deadly weapon."

"Nelson's not long for this world," Eldon growled. "Maybe Makayo too."

"I shouldn't be hearing this," Nora said.

"I'd *love* to kill him," Eldon said. "But that presents a problem."

"If we kill someone and it's not self-defense," Chloe said. "We lose all our powers."

"We'll exile Nelson to another timeline," Eldon said. "A nasty one, like Pembroke ... or even Deathworld."

"Deathworld?" Marjorie said.

"A radioactive graveyard," Chloe explained.

Please don't send him to Deathworld, Wendy beamed.

"Oops!" Eldon said. "Wendy vetoed Deathworld. Pembroke it is."

"It's like you're having constant conversations," Nora said. "Are you like the Borg in the Star Trek movies?"

"The answer is yes and no," Chloe said. "We're part of a kind of ... group-mind, but we're also individuals. We could go against Wendy but don't want to. We love her."

"I should've done this *days* ago," Eldon muttered, heading for a men's room.

"Constipation?" Nora said.

Chloe laughed and shook her head.

***

The next morning, Eldon accompanied Hans Jurgen, the Fire Marshal, as he and two assistants inspected the ruined factory.

An acrid smell of smoke hung in the air as rainwater dripped on them through holes in the roof.

"It began here," Hans said, pointing to a ruptured cylinder.

"Supercooled liquid oxygen storage," Eldon said.

"Tests for explosives were negative," Hans said. "What makes you think it was sabotage, Mr. Trask?"

"A phony employee running away and *shooting* a security guard. Test for TATP. I'll pay for it, if necessary."

Eldon scanned Hans.

The south Los Angeles congressional district's representative had urged Hans to bar Space Ventures from using liquid oxygen.

"Industrial accidents happen all the time, Mr. Evans," Hans said. "Liquid oxygen is classified hazardous H281. The supercooled stuff is far more dangerous. It can form oxygen *crystals*."

Slimy parrot! Eldon thought. *Repeating what they told you, word for word.*

"Humor me!" he snapped. *Makayo made the goddamn TATP in his refrigerator! I just hope there are traces of it left here. Maybe the FBI will find it in his room.*

Hans made a call.

***

Nora Weinberg's office was largely undamaged.

Framed photos of five successful launches shared space with crayon-drawings from her three children on two of its walls. Her desk had pictures her family on their last Hawaiian vacation. The third wall had a seascape and her framed degree from NYU's Stern School of Business.

They took seats around her desk.

A knock on the door caught everyone's attention. It was a middle-aged Asian man in a gray pinstripe suit.

"Ah, Kinoshita-san," Nora said. "This is a rather bad time."

"I wanted to offer my most profound condolences on this tragic event. I have *extremely* good news for you."

"Look, Colonel Shin Jun *Jin*," Eldon growled. "My president *said* it wasn't a good time."

Kinoshita-san gasped, staring at Eldon in shock. Then he clutched his chest and fled without another word.

"What the *hell* just happened?" Nora said.

"He got his cover blown to atoms," Eldon said. "He spent *years* developing it."

"So the Korean ... thing is ... is real?" Nora said.

"He's going to LAX, hoping to book a last-minute flight to Tokyo," Chloe said.

"The Japanese don't know about him," Eldon said. "Yet."

"You used telepathy?" Nora said.

"Well, *yeah.*"

"Why the *fuck* would they *bomb* us?" Nora growled. "It makes no sense."

"Kinoshita-san would've explained if we'd let him," Eldon said. "This so-called industrial accident proves we can't safely handle liquid oxygen. We'll be barred from using it."

"That shuts me down!" Gene Krupa said. "We're done for. You *know* they'll decide that?"

"Telepathy, Gene," Eldon said. "They're urging the fire marshal to rule that way. Dangling carrots in front of him, even."

"Where do we go from here?" Nora said. "That's the real question."

"We clean up," Eldon said. "And build more ships like the Schrödinger, a fleet of them. With cargo holds, air locks, and robot-arms. They don't need liquid oxygen. And I want to offer families of the dead full salaries and benefits for thirty years or so. I'll cover it out of pocket if necessary."

"My God, Eldon!" Nora said. "Chloe's turning you into a *mensch!* Just a month ago, you lectured me on how employees were expendable bio-machines. We'll dig up the money somewhere."

Chloe hugged Eldon, and said, "If need be, we have the Indigo treasury to draw on. Some three hundred billion in gold."

Marjorie whispered, "With a *b?*"

"I hate to bring up reality, but..." Nora said. "We have a Mars launch *next week.* It takes *nine months* for stuff to get there."

"Chloe and I could get supplies there in nine *seconds.* No launch pad, no nothing."

"About that," Ray said. "Mars has an orbital speed of 23 kilometers per second."

"Ah yes," Eldon smiled. "And Earth's is roughly 30. And they're both rotating on their axes. You're saying if we went back to where the Mars base *was*, we'd wind up in empty space, right?"

"Yes."

"Then it's a good thing we don't key off *physical locations*," Eldon said.

"In the spirit world, things have *unique identities*," Chloe said. "Every object, person — every *thought*. We can go to *that object, wherever* it is. If you moved the Mars base a million light-years away in a random direction, we'd find it."

"People and objects are the building blocks," Eldon said. "Space and time are secondary. In fact, we have trouble *locating* precise points in space. I can launch satellites but I'm not sure where they'd end up."

"We'd have to eyeball the Earth from the spirit world," Chloe said.

"So you could put the 300 million dollar Thaicom satellite in a crap orbit and *lose* it?" Nora said. "We're supposed to launch *that* next week too."

"No," Eldon said. "If I put it in the wrong orbit, I'd bring it back for another shot. A new era of space travel: Glitches are annoyances rather than catastrophes."

"We were a technology company," Nora said. "And now we're a company that runs on *magic?*"

"If the wand waves..." Chloe began.

"CGI!" Marjorie interrupted. "We can hack up a 3D visualization of the Earth from a satellite's orbit. That might help you eyeball things."

"Magic *plus* technology," Eldon said.

"If you get it to within two percent accuracy," Marjorie said. "My hypergolics can fine-tune it."

"Thailand is paying us a 61.2 million for that launch," Nora murmured. "If you pull it off, we won't have spent a hundred *bucks* to do it."

Chloe shut her eyes and said, "The fire marshal has concluded his investigation. We are free to enter the factory again."

"Assess damage to your departments," Nora said. "Gene, you're the new acting Avionics head. Look into making a simulation of the Earth viewed from our planned Thaicom 15 orbit."

The department heads left.

***

Two men appeared at the office door, introduced themselves as FBI agents Polhamous and Sedgwick, and displayed identification. Mr. Polhamous was a middle-aged white-haired, trim man, and Mr. Sedgwick looked like a black teenager.

Both wore nearly identical black suits.

The Men in Black, Chloe thought.

Eldon smiled.

They questioned Nora, Eldon, and Chloe for about an hour. The three simply described what they had seen — minus Eldon's head exploding.

"Sure looks like sabotage to me," Nora said. "What are your thoughts?"

"I'm sorry, ma'am," Agent Polhamous said. "We can't comment on ongoing investigations."

The FBI agents left.

"Yeah," Eldon said. "They're sure as shit it *was* sabotage and that Philip Makayo *was* responsible. They may take the death penalty off the table if he cooperates."

"They have mountains of circumstantial evidence," Chloe said.

"He hopes Nelson will rescue him," Eldon said.
"Nelson can't even rescue himself," Chloe growled.

※※※

A tall dark-complected Asian man appeared at the door and tapped on its frame.

"I apologize for intruding on you at this horrible time," he said in a mellow, unaccented voice. "But our satellite has arrived at the Port of Los Angeles."

"Ah, Mr. Chaiprasit," Nora sighed, introducing him to the others as Thaicom's technical liaison.

"You want to know where to send it," Eldon said.

"You must've read my mind," he smiled.

"Ship it here, to the factory. If we fail to launch on time, we'll return your satellite to you, intact. And I'll pay a penalty of 600 million dollars."

"What?" Nora shouted.

"I'll pay out of pocket."

"That's an extraordinary proposal, Mr. Trask," Mr. Chaiprasit said. "I've heard rumors of your new technology, of course. We all have. I'll have to discuss this with my people in Bangkok."

He left.

"I'll have legal draw up a contract," Nora sighed. "I hope you know what you're doing, Eldon."

※※※

Wearing hard hats, Eldon, Chloe, and Nora toured the wrecked factory.

It was noon.

"The damage seems to be confined to the cryogenic rocket section," Eldon said, pointing to ten wrecked rocket engines.

"We need a large vacuum chamber," Eldon added. "There!"

He pointed to a the test chamber for their early Manticore space capsules — a massive steel twenty-foot-tall cylinder that was fifteen feet in diameter. Years ago, it had been built to test the space capsules' integrity in a hard vacuum.

It was undamaged.

"We put the satellite and me in there and pump it out," he continued. "Then I teleport to orbit. Put impressive-looking electronics around it with massive power cables and flashing lights. We'll call it our quantum chamber."

Chapter 39

Martin Gorman, the Director of Human Resources, approached Nora.

"We've gotten three calls from an Andrea Martinez," he said. "She's a babysitter for Erin Maloney. Her mother didn't pick her up yesterday."

"Who was her mother?" Nora moaned.

"Theresa Maloney. Here's her personnel file."

Nora scanned it and let out an agonized sigh: Theresa had worked in the cryogenic rocket division.

It contained a photo of a blond thirty-year-old woman and listed her address.

"What do you know about her?" Eldon said.

"Not much," Martin said. "She had two years of college and dropped out ... started here as a receptionist. When we offered our 3D printing course, she passed it. We promoted her."

"Who does she list for 'in case of emergency'?"

"Her eight-year-old daughter, Erin."

"Send a car for them both," Nora said. "Contact area hospitals, too."

***

An hour later, Mr. Gorman pulled up in a company car. A middle-aged Hispanic woman and a young, light-skinned black girl stepped out.

In pink jeans and a white blouse with flowers on it, she carried a Hello Kitty back pack.

She had a beautiful but sad face.

"You must be Erin," Chloe said, hugging the girl.

"Mom was 'sposed to pick me up but she didn't come. Where's my mom?"

"We don't know honey," Chloe said. "We're looking for her. She might be sick."

Why does everyone pretend I don't exist! Theresa Maloney's spirit screamed. *Why can't I hug you?*

"I can't keep her any more," Andrea said. "I got four kids of my own."

"She's here," Chloe muttered. "Theresa's spirit. You don't have to check hospitals."

"Sure about that?" Nora said.

"Yes," Chloe sobbed.

"We'll care for Erin," Eldon said.

"Ms. Maloney was supposed to pay me fifty dollars."

"Here's a hundred," Eldon said, pulling out his wallet and handing her cash.

She doesn't deserve that much. She barely deserves fifty.

Andrea left with Mr. Gorman's secretary in the company car.

What do you remember, Theresa? Chloe beamed to her.

I was at my workstation. There was a bright flash. Then I was home, but I couldn't touch anything. My hand just went through things.

Someone set off a bomb in the factory, Eldon said. *It killed you.*

Are you sure, Mr. Trask? Theresa's spirit said. *I feel better than ever. I don't think I ever felt so healthy and alive.*

I'm sorry, Theresa, Eldon said. *Scan us, and you'll see we're telling the truth.*

Scan you? What do you mean by that?

Read our minds, Chloe said. *It's something you can do now*

"You guys..." Nora said. "You're staring into space."

"We're talking to Theresa's spirit," Chloe said.

"You see spirits?" Erin said.

"Did you watch any Harry Potter movies?" Chloe said.

"Uh huh. I saw the *Sorcerer's Stone.*"

"Eldon and I are wizards, like in those movies."

She thought for a moment, pursed her lips and said, "I know wizards aren't real! I'm not just a dumb kid!"

"You're right about the Harry Potter wizards, honey," Chloe said. "But we're different. Your mother's spirit is here with us."

"Where?" Erin sobbed, looking around. "I want my mom!"

"I know, honey," Chloe said hugging her.

I can't be dead! I'm all Erin has!

What about her father? Chloe beamed.

He's Alan Mercer, a senator from New York. On the Senate Intelligence Committee.

You're a Russian spy? Eldon beamed.

Not any more, I guess. My handlers thought being a single mom would help my cover. I was supposed to blackmail Mercer, but my handlers reassigned me to Space Ventures.

Any other relatives? Chloe said.

I was raised in a Tax Police Orphanage in Moscow.

"A *what?*" Eldon exclaimed. Then he realized that it was an orphanage that trained children to be members of a special police force going after tax evaders. The police force was their only family, and commanded their fanatical loyalty.

'Theresa' had done so well in school, they sent her to the Moscow State Pedagogical University. After she graduated, the SVR recruited her.

"What's going on?" Nora said. "Talking to yourself?"

"Theresa's real name is Natalia Makarovna," Eldon said. "She was a Russian spy."

"What?" Nora said. "Are you sure?"

"Yes," Eldon said.

"How could you let that happen? Nora said. "You're telepathic!"

"I'm not a peeping Tom," Eldon said. "I avoid looking into people's minds. It's kinda like stumbling across someone sitting on the toilet."

For God's sake someone take care of Erin! Theresa/Natalia said.

A gray-haired woman walked up to them and introduced herself as Cora Dreyfuss, a social worker.

"Your Human Resources manager called me," she said. "Apparently, this young lady's mother is missing."

"My mom's coming for me!" Erin said. "She's just late!"

"Well, young lady," Cora said. "Until she comes, we'll put you under the care of a nice foster family."

"No!" Erin screamed.

"Nonsense..."

"She can stay with us," Chloe cut in. *We owe her that much. At least!* Eldon beamed. *I feel responsible for her. I should've foreseen the bombing.*

Just because you have super powers doesn't mean you're responsible for everything that goes wrong in the world!

"We have plenty of room in our home," Chloe said. "We'll see that she gets to school on time. Walgrove Avenue School, Mrs. Sepulveda's class."

"How did you know that?" Erin said.

"We're wizards."

"Are you related to her?" Cora said.

"No, but we can provide for her," Chloe said.

***

They took their self-driving car to Erin's apartment in West Los Angeles.

"Mom's not dead!" Erin chanted over and over again as Chloe hugged her.

They arrived at the Wyvern Estates — a six story white stucco building with scattered glitter embedded in its walls and in its front sidewalk. Each apartment had a tiny balcony, some of which sported potted plants.

They entered the vestibule and regarded the row of mailboxes.

"2B," Chloe said.

"No surveillance cameras," Eldon muttered, looking around. "How cheap can they get?"

"We don't have a key," Erin said. "Mom was gonna pick me up."

Chloe vanished.

Erin's jaw dropped.

"Told you we were wizards," Eldon murmured.

The door buzzed, and they went up to Erin's apartment.

It was a neat two bedroom apartment with a tiny kitchen. Erin's bedroom was a disaster area — with clothes on the floor, an unmade bed, and toys strewn about.

Eldon found a beautiful doll-house in the corner and set it on the bed. Then he went through the closets and stacked clothes on hangars next to it.

"We'll just pile stuff on the bed and teleport it," he said.

"Just take a couple things," Chloe said. "Stuff she'll need for tomorrow, and we'll leave."

"Nooo! Mom's working late! We have to stay here for when she comes home!"

"OK," Chloe said. "We'll stay."

Erin ran to the kitchen and clattered around with pots and pans.

"Got to make dinner!" she said. "Fry the hot dogs first until they're brown..."

"Need any help?" Chloe said.

"No! I cook dinner when mom works late. I cook scrambled eggs in the morning and make her coffee, too."

"You're a very good daughter," Eldon said. "Your mom must be very proud."

"When the hot dogs are brown! We put baked beans in!"

She continued in the frantic manner and then ran out to the dining area with chipped melamine plates.

Then she spooned the mixture of hot dogs and baked beans on the plates.

"Thank you," Eldon and Chloe said, tears running down their faces.

As they started to eat, Erin shouted, "Save some for *mom!* She'll be hungry when she gets home! She'll be *so hungry...*"

Erin broke down and sobbed uncontrollably, and Chloe rocked her in her arms.

After fifteen minutes of crying, Erin bawled, "She's just *dead,* isn't she?"

Smoke poured out of the kitchen as the baked beans on the stove burned.

Eldon dealt with it.

Chapter 40

"I put the three Archy ships at Conch Point," Wendy said, lounging on the deck at Destiny Beach and petting Norton.

The Trade Winds were blowing again — a steady bracing gale.

"You went *alone?*" Travis said. "Honey, you should've brought someone along. Me or Allie."

"I know," she said. "It just made me so *angry*. Those things trying to attack our home. Our *keikis*."

"What are they doing?" Derek said.

"Stewing in their juices. Trying to figure out where the hell they are."

"They don't know?" Derek said.

"They don't believe what their computers tell them," Wendy said. "Some of them are doing space walks to see for themselves."

"You found a place to hide?" Travis said.

"Those ships are *huge,* with so many nooks and crannies. I found a giant ventilation duct and worked from inside it."

"Someone's coming," Travis said.

Chloe and Erin appeared on the deck, and Erin's eyes were tightly shut.

"You can open your eyes now, sweetie," Chloe said.

Erin looked around warily, and Eldon appeared.

"Welcome to Oz," Wendy said.

"Aloha," Travis said.

"I brought your bathing suit," Chloe said. "Want to go swimming?"

Erin said nothing.

"You don't have to," Chloe said. "We can just hang out."

"Mom used to take me to Santa Monica beach," Erin muttered. "When she didn't have to work on weekends. She said you were a real prick for making her work nights and weekends."

"Yes, I was a ... major prick," Eldon muttered. "Before I became a wizard."

"You're just agreeing with me 'cause you feel sorry for me," Erin muttered.

"I'm *not* automatically agreeing with you," Eldon said. "I really *was* a prick. I'm a different person now. A better one, I hope."

Allie appeared and hugged Erin.

"Sweet, brave soul!" Allie said, beaming to them all. *She radiates such pain.*

"She sits on the throne of grief," Chloe murmured. "We can only kneel before her."

She is so old and independent for her years, Allie said.

A spy's latchkey kid, Chloe said. *We'll let the authorities continue to think Theresa was American.*

If they know she's Russian, Erin might get deported, Eldon said.

She was born in America! Allie said.

Children of foreigners in this country on official business are citizens of their parents' country, not the US, Eldon said. *For instance, children of ambassadors.*

It's complicated by Erin's father being American, Chloe said. *He risks twenty years in prison if he steps up.*

Erin staggered out onto the beach, sat, and stared at the sea.

"We have a hearing next week," Eldon said. "Family court. If they make us her guardians, we'll adopt."

"How could they possibly turn us down?" Chloe said.

"We're not married," Eldon said. "Our attorney thinks *you* should become her guardian, Chloe. Unfortunately, you don't exist in that timeline."

"Oh," Chloe muttered. "Well then, let's get married. We'll go to Vegas like we planned."

"Did I hear *Vegas?*" Kurt Howland smiled, strolling up to the deck. "I'd love to attend your funeral ... uh, wedding."

"He's driving Taka and Grace crazy," Allie muttered.

"This *place* is driving *me* crazy!" Kurt said. "I'm *dying* here. This place might be paradise but, frankly, it can go fuck itself."

"There's always that nice park bench," Derek growled.

"Don't be ridiculous. We both know you're not taking me back there."

"Wanna bet?" Travis muttered.

※※※

Erin sat in the sand, staring at the roaring surf as two dolphins swam by squeaking and whistling. She imagined they were calling to her.

"Sorry your mommy died," Loretta said, popping into view.

Erin stared at her in shock.

Loretta kissed Erin on the cheek and said, "We have *chickens*. You can *pet* them."

"Are you a ... wizard *kid?*" Erin said, noticing her silvery eyes.

"Uh huh."

A dolphin squealed at them.

"That's Squeetz. He asked who you are. I told him. He said you could ride on him. If you want to."

Erin stared at her.

Chloe appeared and said, "Honey, Eldon and I are going to get married, and we'd love it if you came. You don't have to if you don't feel up to it."

"You're getting married?"

"We want to adopt you, and the lawyer thinks our chances are better if we're married."

"You're getting married just for me?" Erin said.

"We were going to get married anyway, honey. We just moved up the date for you."

"Do I need a new dress?"

"No, honey. What you're wearing is fine. Someday, we'll have a fancy reception and get you a new dress."

"You want to be my *new mom?*"

"Yes, if it's OK with you."

If we adopt her, we have to make her an Indigo, Chloe beamed to everyone. *She can't be a part of our lives if she can't teleport.*

Do we have a right to take her out of the human race? Allie said. *She might have a perfectly happy life as she is.*

We don't know that, Chloe said. *She's a girl without a country. Neither Russian nor American.*

OK, Allie said. *She would make a wonderful addition to our Ohana.*

✳✳✳

They materialized in a ladies' room that had white walls adorned with shiny red hearts.

They stepped out into a huge room lined with shiny white curtains and with rows of chairs that faced a podium at one end.

Eldon was talking to a man in a black suit and black hat who had a black attaché case chained to his right wrist.

"One of the Blues Brothers?" Chloe said.

"I'm Maxim Ivanoff," the man said. "An ordained minister. I have other costumes available. Elvis. A pirate. A Roman gladiator. Captain Kirk."

"No, you're fine," she chuckled.

"We really don't need this big a venue," Eldon told the man. "It's just the three of us."

"The *hell* it *is*," Derek boomed, coming out of the mens' room.

Allie came out of the ladies' room and handed Chloe a small package wrapped in ribbons.

"Wedding rings," she explained. "From the *Elegant Pony*. We had them sized to Derek and me."

The rings turned out to be golden, sapphire-eyed dragons biting their tails.

They fit.

One by one, all the Indigos in existence — and Taka, Grace, and Kurt — exited restrooms until the chapel was packed.

Erin hid behind Chloe.

"Who are these *people?*" the Reverend Ivanoff muttered. "Where did they come from?"

When everyone was seated and quiet, he performed the ceremony.

Afterward, a photographer took photos of everyone and the Reverend Ivanoff presented Eldon and Chloe with a marriage certificate.

"Well, this was a moving ceremony, Trask," Kurt said. "But I'd love to play in the casino. Any chance you'll stake me?"

"*Please* let him go," Taka said.

Eldon wrote Kurt a check.

"I can't cash this," he said. "I don't exist in this timeline."

"A version of you probably does."

Derek ducked into the mens' room and ten minutes later, returned holding two gold bars.

He offered them to Kurt.

"That's more like it," he said, taking the bars. "I'll figure out how to turn them into cash. It has been nice knowing you guys. Please — be strangers."

He left.

"I'm thinking we'll regret this," Chloe muttered.

***

They all teleported to Culinary Derek and Allie's *Ristorante Alberto*.

Colorful paintings of villages on Italy's Amalfi Coast covered the walls — the work of Culinary Allie. A row of steam tables ran down the room's center, and a separate table had buttered popcorn and champagne.

"Sorry for the buffet service," Culinary Derek announced. "I didn't have time to hire more wait-staff."

"Are we in another world?" Taka said.

"No," Travis replied. "New York City."

"I always wanted to see New York," Taka said.

"We can stay a couple days," Wendy said.

One by one, the people introduced themselves to Erin and hugged her.

"So happy to have you in our family, young lady," Culinary Derek said to Erin.

"Who are you?" she replied.

"I'm Derek."

"But *he's* Derek too," she said, pointing to the other Derek.

"I know," Culinary Derek laughed. "It's confusing. You see, I'm from *this* world, and he's from *another* one. There are copies of us in different worlds."

"Huh?"

"Did you ever have trouble deciding something?" Allie said, joining them. "And then you made a decision?"

"Last week, mom asked whether we should go to the beach or Griffith Park," Erin said, and then sobbed, "I miss my mom."

Chloe and Eldon hugged her.

"She's been through so much," Chloe said. "We should take her home."

"We teleported her stuff to a room in our house," Eldon said. "It's beginning to look like a home now."

We apologize for bugging out of your wonderful party, Chloe beamed to Culinary Derek.

They left.

✳✳✳

Eldon got Hawaiian pizza and chicken wings, and set it on his kitchen's granite island, next to the built-in oak-veneered Sub Zero refrigerator.

They started to eat and drink.

"If there are Dereks in different worlds. Could there be one where my mom is *still alive?*"

"Probably," Chloe said.

"Probably? *Really?*"

"Now you'll ask us to take you there," Eldon said.

She eagerly nodded.

"The trouble is, we can't," Chloe said. "There are too many worlds. It would take forever to search them."

Erin's face fell.

Then she said, "But *Derek* found another Derek."

"Yes," Chloe said. "He found another copy of *himself.* That's not so hard to do. Even though *we* couldn't find another copy of your mother, *you* could."

"But I'm not ... uh ... a Indigo."

"If we manage to adopt you, we'll make you one," Eldon said.

Erin's face lit up.

"It takes about a week," Chloe said. "What do you say to spending a week in Oz?"

"Yes!"

"So what did you do with your mom in the evenings?" Chloe said.

"I washed dishes and then watched TV," Erin said. "Sometimes I did laundry."

A scan of Erin showed that her mother often drank herself into oblivion in the evenings, sometimes muttering that Erin had ruined her life.

It also showed that Erin liked playing hearts.

Eldon vanished and reappeared ten minutes later waving a deck of cards.

They played cards for the next hour and put Erin to bed.

"Shall we retire to the bedroom, Mrs. Trask?" Eldon said, with a theatric bow.

"I thought you'd never ask."

"Oh my God!"

"What?"

"I just thought of several timelines where Erin's mother is probably still alive."

Chapter 41

"I've never seen so many people," Taka muttered, on the corner of 8th avenue and 44th street. *"Swarms* of them ... like ants."

They had exited the Majestic Theater, after seeing a performance of *Phantom of the Opera.*

People scurried to and fro in the light rain, jostling them and shouting for taxis over the incessant din of car horns and police sirens. Like portals to Hell, manhole-covers and gutter-drains spouted clouds of billowing steam.

It was five in the evening.

"This city wears you down," Travis agreed, as Kaiulani appeared in his arms and started bawling.

Grace carried a calm Roger.

"New York reminds Kaiulani of Newport," Wendy said. "PTSD."

"I feel like crying too," Taka said. "And I *wasn't* in Newport. We should go to Maui. In *this* timeline"

"You're willing to meet another you?" Wendy said.

"I've been thinking about what I'd say to her," Taka said. "Yes, I'm ready."

The six of them ducked behind a garbage dumpster in a stinking alley and teleported to their suite at the Hotel Pierre.

Travis went down to the front desk, announced that they would be checking out, and settled their bill.

"Will we have to stay the night?" Grace said.

"No," Wendy said. "We can leave right now."

※※※

They exited Kimo's, a restaurant on Front Street in Lahaina and walked along the road that bordered Lahaina Harbor. A small fence separated them from the rocky seawall and the ocean.

At 11:30 in the morning, it was sunny, hot, and humid.

When they reached Canal Street, an elderly man in an aloha shirt, shorts, and a wide-brimmed hat stared at Taka in shock and nearly fainted.

"You don't have to worry about what to say to the other you," Wendy said.

"She died a week ago," Travis said.

"What will happen to her farm?" Grace said.

"Good question," Wendy said. "Did you have a will?"

"No. My attorney was always hounding me to make one, but I never did."

"I'm getting an idea worthy of my brother," Wendy said. *"Maybe* it'll work. Who was your attorney?"

※※※

"He can see you now," the receptionist said, staring at Taka.

Trade winds whistled through the north wall's louvered windows, and an enormous marlin mounted on a wooden plaque covered the wall opposite the door.

A shocked Joe Shimura, Esq. greeted them. He was an elderly Japanese-Hawaiian man in a gray suit sitting behind an enormous *koa* wood desk.

"Meet Chihiro Ogino," Wendy said. "Taka Matson's identical twin sister."

"The only sister she ever mentioned was someone named Grace," he said. "Who died in a car accident on the mainland. Oregon, somewhere. Do you have documents to prove your relation to Taka?"

"No," Taka said.

"She has da same DNA-*kine*," Travis said.

"That would be probative," Joe said. "Will you submit to a DNA test?"

"OK, as long as it doesn't hurt."

Joe laughed and made a call.

Travis paid three hundred dollars in cash.

Fifteen minutes later, a thirty something man came to the office and swabbed Taka's inner cheek.

"We should have results in three days," he said.

"If the test is positive," Joe said. "As Taka's only living heir, you'll inherit her farm. Where can we reach you?"

"We'll contact you," Travis said, taking his business card.

They left the lawyer's office — a single-story building on Waine street with a large parking lot. They were in a suburban neighborhood of small homes with lawns, palm trees, and shrubs.

"We can go shopping here," Travis said. "Anytime."

"How can she be dead and I'm not?" Taka said.

"This timeline is five years out of sync with Origin," Wendy said. "In the future."

"So I'll be dead in five years?"

"You don't know that," Grace said. "How did she die?"

"I'll scan *da kine* lawyer," Travis said, shutting his eyes.

"OK," he continued. "That Taka died of pancreatic cancer." Taka groaned.

"You don't *have* to die!" Wendy said. "Now that you *know* it's cancer, you can catch it very early."

"Maybe you should just sell the farm," Grace said. "Why spend your last days growing onions."

"It's not just *onions!* It's a way of life. It's about ... field hands from all over the world. Kids backpacking across Hawaii. Last year we had a German divinity student who even traveled to Africa. It's about Christmas and Thanksgiving *luaus,* too. People come from all over the island. From other islands even. We have Easter egg hunts for the Lahaina kids."

Chapter 42

"Angelic boy," Eakins yawned, stroking Jonah Whitely's silky black hair.

Life was taking its toll: intense rallies, travel in manure wagons, sleeping in unfamiliar places.

He'd stayed with the Whitleys three days, now, and the plan was for him to remain here another week.

He had hoped this bit of stability would help.

This is the classiest hovel I've seen so far, Eakins mused. *They have four rooms.*

The Whitley's lived in an apartment that was part of a complex of steel shipping containers welded together, with doors and windows cut into their sides.

"Stop annoying our guest," Jonah's mother yelled from the kitchen. "Get some water from the well."

"I'm showing him my kitty!"

"Now!"

"Wanna hold my kitty?" Jonah said, handing Eakins his black and white tabby and running out of the room.

"Jonah could become *your* pet," the cat said in a faint, tinny voice.

Eakins jumped up, sending the cat hissing and fleeing the room.

I'm losing my mind!

✳✳✳

They all gathered around the dinner table: Joss, her husband, Garry, Jonah, and two other guests, an elderly man and a young woman.

Joss introduced those two as Dr. Edwards and his daughter Millie.

"We pray that all good come to our savior and lord," Joss said, as all but Eakins bowed their heads.

"We have real mashed potatoes!" she announced. "And *cauliflower!* I grew it in secret."

They passed steaming dishes of vegetables and mashed potatoes around, reserving the meat for Eakins.

"Jonah's cat is very..." he began.

"It's a *miracle,*" Joss exclaimed. "You *never* see stray animals, yet this cat appeared in our midst. A few days before your blessed arrival."

"Never see stray animals?" Eakins said.

"Of course not, my lord. Not with all the kwash going around."

"The Hankels have it something awful," Dr. Edwards said.

"They all look pregnant," Millie said.

"That's horrible!" Joss said.

"I scrounged peanut butter for them but not nearly enough," Dr. Edwards muttered.

"If Jonah hadn't spotted that cat," Joss sighed. "It would've landed in *our* cooking pot."

Shit! Eakins thought. *I could be eating cat or dog? Doesn't anyone live well in this disgusting world?*

✷✷✷

Eakins tossed and turned in the lumpy bed, thoughts of Jonah running through his mind.

The cat jumped onto his chest.

In the same tinny voice as before, it said, "Be silent. We know all about the coming push and are prepared for it. Its chances of success are nil. We need to know its ringleaders and timing. If you cooperate, you'll be rewarded. If you don't, we'll put you back in a Starvation Chamber — where you belong."

The cat jumped down and left the room.

If they know everything, what do they need me for?

He thought, again, of Jonah.

My God, what a reward that would be! If I help them, why would they keep their side of the bargain? They wouldn't need me anymore.

Chapter 43

Three days of frenetic activity by factory employees and outside contractors had cleaned up the factory and patched the roof.

The Cryogenic Propulsion Division no longer existed.

A large flatbed delivered the Thaicom 15 satellite to the factory, and workers wrestled it inside.

It stood fifteen feet high and ten feet wide and bristled with antennas and folded solar panels, looming over the factory floor like a grim sentinel.

Marjorie's group began to install sixteen small rockets on it to fine-tune its orbit.

Other factory workers had set up rows of chairs and a small podium for a memorial service.

With tears running down her face, Chloe stood before the solemn crowd. Babies cried and mothers tried to comfort them.

Some of the injured attended in wheelchairs.

Chloe spoke.

> Four days ago, we suffered a sucker-punch to our guts. We lost thirteen beloved brothers and sisters.

> They were true pioneers, working at jobs they loved — on the forefront of humanity's future.
>
> I didn't know them personally, but I have faced death and known grief.
>
> How shall we weep for them? How will we face the gaping holes left in our lives?
>
> It reminds me of John 12:24.
>
> On the eve of his crucifixion, Jesus said, "Verily, verily, I say unto you, Except a corn of wheat fall into the ground and die, it abideth alone: but if it die, it bringeth forth much fruit."
>
> The spirits of the fallen are among us now, in this very room, visiting from the place where dreams are born.
>
> They live eternally — forever upheld and maintained by the infinite creativity, the inexhaustible vitality of God.
>
> For me, this is not an article of faith; it is a direct experience. It can be one for you if you open your hearts.

After these remarks, she invited spouses and children of the fallen to share remembrances of their loved ones.

> I'm organizing a support group for all of us. If you and your children need counseling or anything else, counselors will be there for you.

The service concluded with a catered banquet where Chloe circulated and chatted with family members.

"Quite a woman you've got," Nora said to Eldon.

"Helping people is her life's calling," he said. "She used to be an Episcopal minister."

"You're a *massive* bundle of surprises! And I can't believe you got married without telling *me!*"

"It was a Vegas wedding," Eldon said. "We moved up the date so we could become Erin's guardians."

Erin looked up at him.

"That means we'll be taking care of you," Eldon said. "It's the first step to adopting you."

"Once... once, mom said she wished you would adopt *her.*"

"A lot of people wish that," Nora chuckled.

"Why?"

Nora laughed.

"You'll understand when you're older," she said.

"After tomorrow's launch, we're going away for at least a week," Eldon said. "In Oz."

"What about Erin's ... apartment?"

"I had Drax Security pay the rent on it for a year and remove perishables. They also towed Theresa's car to one of their secure lots. They'll get replacement keys."

"Oh, before I forget," Eldon said, handing Nora a piece of paper. "I looked up every skirt and pawed through every underwear drawer. Here's a list of spies on our payroll."

She examined it in shock.

"What can I say?" Eldon shrugged. "Everyone wants a piece of us. Oh, you might want to check the network router room in building 3E. Skip Picchinini — uh, the third shift night watchman — keeps an inflatable woman there. He uh ... *plays* with it. Every night."

✳✳✳

That afternoon, in a small ceremony in the San Fernando Valley, they interred Erin's mother.

Through a layer of smog, Chloe could make out a black SUV

parked about a mile away. Like ghosts, two men stood beside it and watched, sunlight glinting off binocular lenses.

Please don't tell Erin I'm here! her spirit beamed at them. *It'll only upset her.*

We'll make her into an Indigo, Eldon replied.

Then I can speak to her myself.

Chloe delivered a short eulogy.

"You sound like a priest," Erin said.

"I used to be one, honey."

"I'm going to have a mom who's a *priest?*"

"Yeah, so you better watch out!"

To support her cover-story, Theresa and Erin had attended the Church of the Good Shepard a few times over the last year.

✳✳✳

They had a quiet dinner in a tiny, elegant Pasadena restaurant named *Sign of the Dove*.

"When can we start looking for mom?" Erin blurted out.

"A couple days at least," Eldon said. "It takes a while for you to become an Indigo. Then we have to teach you how to use your super-powers."

"Another thing, honey," Chloe said. "You may find someone who *looks* like your mom and *sounds* like her, but who's a different person."

"But the two Dereks are *the same!*" Erin said.

"No," Chloe said. "They get into fights all the time. Remember when Allie asked you about going to the beach or the zoo?"

"Huh?"

"At the party," Chloe said. "When you got sad, and we went home."

"Oh."

"When you decided to go to the beach, you split into *two people*," Chloe continued. *"You* went to the beach and the *other you* went to the zoo — in a different world. The one who went to the zoo likes zoos more than you do."

"She's *almost* the same as you," Eldon said. "But not *exactly* the same. When people make *big* decisions, the two versions are *much* more different."

"What decisions?"

"Like where to live," Chloe said. "Or whether to have children. Many of these other versions of your mom will also already have a daughter named Erin. You might be able to become her sister."

"I don't know about that," Eldon muttered. "Since she's a spy, her Russian handlers are watching her constantly."

"What's a Russian handler?" Erin said.

"Her spy bosses," Chloe said.

Erin grew very quiet at this revelation.

Chapter 44

The next morning, Eldon stepped out of a restroom near his office at the Space Ventures factory.

Media vans and reporters thronged the parking lot, and Dusit Chaiprasit greeted Eldon with a handshake.

"Amazing how you avoided the gauntlet," Mr. Chaiprasit chuckled. "It's almost like you quantum teleported yourself."

Eldon stared at him sharply.

"Take it easy, sir," Mr. Chaiprasit said. "I'm on your side. I can't wait to see history made. The deal you offered us is a win-win for Thaicom."

Marjorie, Nora, and Gene Krupa awaited Eldon in the Avionics Lab.

"Where's the *fam?*" Nora said.

"Chloe's taking Erin shopping."

"OK," Gene said, pointing to a computer display. "We've rigged up a simulation of the Earth's appearance from the proper orbit."

Eldon stared at the slowly-scrolling image and tried to memorize it.

"It's centered at Florida," he said.

"Our tracking facilities are still down," Marjorie said. "So we're using NASA's. Is that a problem?"

"Shouldn't be. Guess I better suit up."

"We left at least one foot of clearance all around and five feet on one side," Nora said, referring to the Thaicom-15 satellite in the vacuum chamber.

"Start pumping the air out of it in five minutes," Eldon said.

Eldon left the lab and strolled across the factory floor, passing the enormous vacuum chamber now containing the satellite. Someone had painted "Quantum Teleportation Chamber" on its side and covered it with thick cables and flashing lights.

He ducked into the now-deserted Space Suit Development lab. As expected, the lab personnel were on the factory floor to watch the "launch."

Eldon donned a space suit and teleported into the vacuum chamber.

The air pumps' throbbing faded as the air thinned — leaving an all-insulating vacuum.

"Dear lord," he muttered. "Please don't let me fuck up."

"What was that?" Nora's voice crackled on the radio.

"Uh ... I said the quantum chamber's ready to go."

"That's what I thought you said."

He went out-of-body and engulfed the satellite.

You're taking part of the chamber wall, Wendy said. In their spirit-bodies, she and Derek watched him.

He made an adjustment.

Now you're missing one of the antennas, Derek said.

He made another adjustment.

Looks good, Derek and Wendy said.

He soared through the vacuum chamber walls and the factory roof.

Below him, the Earth looked like a translucent glass surface, lightly etched with an image of the California coastline.

Pulsating colors throbbed around him — the spirit world's teaming energy and life.

He soared higher until his purview took in the entire globe.

He imagined the globe rotating until Florida appeared below him.

He materialized and scanned Marjorie.

Holy shit! she thought. *It's halfway to the moon!*

"Oops!" he said to no one in particular.

Eldon went out of body and imagined his spirit body was a giant sphere that enclosed the satellite.

Much easier when I don't have to worry about a chamber around it.

Then he descended until the image of Florida matched the remembered computer simulation.

He materialized and scanned Marjorie.

Fuck! she thought. *It's at the right altitude but it's not orbiting. It's dropping like a rock.*

Eldon went out of body again.

This time he was more careful, taking pains to make the Earth image scroll by at the same rate as the computer simulation.

He materialized again.

I can work with this orbit, Marjorie thought.

❇❇❇

Eldon teleported back to the Space Suit Lab, took off his suit, and rejoined the others in the Avionics Lab.

Marjorie didn't look up from her workstation, computing orbital elements and shouting instructions to her team.

"91 second burn on 2, then 15 on 10, at my mark," she said. *"Now!"*

"You pulled it off," Nora said. "It was amazing to watch."

Dusit Chaiprasit rolled in a cart with a two magnums of *Dom Perignon* and rows of champagne glasses.

"Congratulations!" he said.

"You had champagne standing by?" Eldon said, wishing the cart included buttered popcorn.

"If you'd failed, it would be a consolation prize for the six hundred million you'd owe us."

Fifteen minutes later, Marjorie reported, "Orbit is *nominal*."

"Great work, Marjorie. I did a pathetic job of placing it."

"This launch was not as dramatic as usual," Gene said. "Boring, even."

"When three hundred million dollars of electronics are involved, boring is good," Mr. Chaiprasit said. "It was fascinating to watch the satellite going to different locations. It was as if you had trouble *finding* the right orbit. Is that the Heisenberg Uncertainty Principle?"

"You know your quantum mechanics," Eldon smiled.

"I'm from *Aerospace Perspectives*," a middle aged man said. "Care to describe your new technology?"

"No," Eldon said. "It's a company secret. Besides — Marjorie's the real hero of this operation. She guided the satellite into its proper orbit. Why don't you interview her?"

"Well *thank you*, Mr. Trask," Marjorie frowned.

Nora pulled Eldon aside and said, "They won't buy that *proprietary* bullshit forever. Especially if the military becomes interested. And they will."

"I hope my fumbling around discourages them. Who wants a *random* weapon? Makes me wonder whether I did the right thing — telling you guys about us."

"What was the alternative?"

"Return Greg Jones to Mars and lie, lie, lie."

"They'd know you were lying," Nora said. "The technical people, at least."

"Yes, but they wouldn't have anything concrete they could put their finger on. We'd do business as usual — under a smoldering cloud of suspicion."

"Another timeline?"

"Yes, a strange one. I'd use my precognitive ability to prevent launches from failing, arousing *more* suspicion."

"You have that ability?" Nora said.

"To some extent," Eldon said. "It doesn't always work in time — like with the bombing. Eventually the truth would come out — badly."

"What about our Mars astronauts," Nora said.

"Obviously there won't be a launch this week," Eldon said. "Mr. Jesperson has a lengthy to-do list for the QS Schrödinger that shouldn't take more than two weeks. We have plenty of time to build more of them, too. We'll send our people to Mars quickly — and in *style*."

Mr. Chaiprasit approached them and said, "Just got off the phone with Bangkok. The solar panels deployed, and the satellite passed its self-test. Southeast Asia thanks you."

Eldon gave him a thumbs-up.

"Oh, by the way, Eldon," Nora said. "On the news, last night. A lobbyist named Dennis Nelson seems to have vanished into thin air. From a restroom in the *Pentagon,* of all places."

"It would be logical to assume he's on the lam," Eldon said.

"Logical?" she smiled. "Yes, I guess it would be."

Chapter 45

"What a strange dream!" Erin said to Chloe and Eldon.

They had arrived at Destiny Beach Saturday morning, and Allie had briefly popped in from Columbia to initiate Erin in the Indigo Ohana — a solemn ceremony, where Erin had sworn to use her powers for good.

Then Eldon, Chloe, and Erin had spent the day waiting for the pill to take effect and, by nine, Erin had developed a scratchy throat and went to bed.

"It's not a dream, honey," Eldon said. "We're in the spirit world."

Mom! Erin shouted.

Hello, kitten, Theresa's spirit said.

I missed you so much!

I missed you too, kitten. Now as much as you miss me, because I've never been far away. I look in on you every day. I miss being able to hug you.

I'm gonna find you, mom!

Please don't, honey. You'll only find heartache and disappointment. You'll disrupt other people's lives too.

I have to find you!

No, honey, Theresa said. *God, I wish I'd been a better mother to you.*

You were a good mother. I ruined your life!

No, kitten. Having you was the best thing I ever did. I'll be here for you as often as I can. I'm so busy, now.

Busy? Eldon said.

The newly dead review their lives, Theresa said. *Everything they did ... everything they might've done ... and how it affected others.*

"*Might've* done?" Chloe said. "You mean timelines?"

Yes, Theresa said. *All of them. Watching a billion timelines... It's an overwhelming experience.*

"So there *are* other copies of you!" Erin said.

More than grains of sand on the beach, kitten. Many of them aren't pretty, though. Some of those lives are downright awful. I asked Eldon and Chloe to take care of you. They'll be wonderful parents. All of the Indigos will be your family.

"I don't *want* them. I want *you*, mom."

Help her! I have to go.

✳✳✳

On Sunday, Erin developed a mild fever and sneezing fits. Eldon and Chloe taught her to teleport, and they all went to Volcano Island to watch the glowing lava fountains.

The heat felt good on Erin's skin.

They spent the rest of the day at Derek and Allie's house, playing cards and teleporting short distances. In the evening, Erin wanted to watch TV.

Chloe explained that TV signals and the Internet didn't carry over to different timelines, and Eldon picked up a bunch of DVD's and a Blu-Ray player from Matrix Video in Culinary Los Angeles.

"You don't really need a TV though," Chloe said. "What's your favorite movie?"

"Spirited Away," Erin said.

"Go into the spirit world," Chloe said.

She did that, and Chloe met her there.

"Now imagine that movie playing," Chloe said.

A crystal-clear image appeared before them of the opening scenes of *Spirited Away*.

"It's like having a TV in my head!" Erin exclaimed. "It's *better* than TV!"

They all watched her movie for a while and went to bed.

✳✳✳

Erin's symptoms cleared by Monday, and the three of them went for a morning swim — with a pod of dolphins following them.

"They're *talking* about us!" Erin said.

"You're hearing their thoughts, honey," Chloe said. "You can talk to them too."

They dried off, showered, and got dressed.

Llewellyn strolled over and joined them.

While Chloe fed Norton and cleaned his cat box, Erin got eggs from the chicken coop.

"They're still warm!" she said, holding up three colorful eggs. "Do the colored eggs taste different?"

"No, honey. The difference is only on the outside."

"That's what mom said about people."

Erin made everyone coffee and pancakes.

"Wow!" Erin said to Llewellyn. "Your thoughts are strange! They hurt."

"I solved a famous math problem. I just have to find a way to put it into ... words ... and equations."

"Where's Andy, these days?" Eldon said.

"Exploring timelines," Llewellyn said. "She can't just sit around doing nothing."

"Archies are *bugs* who want to *kill us?*" Erin exclaimed.

"Don't worry about it, honey," Chloe said.

"You're a *very good* cook, Erin," Birgit said. "I'll show you how to make German pancakes. Thin and stuffed with apples or jam."

"We need to work off this breakfast," Chloe chuckled, after they had loaded the dishwasher.

"Our jogging days are over," Ian said, as he and Birgit vanished.

"I need to clear my head," Llewellyn said, joining them.

They all jogged barefoot to Taka's farm at Destiny Beach's other end — half a mile away.

Chloe pointed out the Pincus's empty house along the way.

✳✳✳

Gasping and sweating, they staggered onto her lanai to find the house deserted.

"Why do we have to jog?" Erin said. "We can just teleport."

"To keep in shape," Eldon said. "I'm ready to throw up, which tells me I should jog more."

"Taka's visiting *our* world with Wendy and Travis," Chloe said. "Honey, ask her if it's alright to help ourselves to stuff in her fridge."

"How?"

"Imagine you're talking to Wendy, who's sitting next to her," Eldon said. "She'll pass your message on to her."

Erin shut her eyes for a moment and then said, "Taka says it's OK. We shouldn't go into her bedroom or anything."

"See, Erin," Chloe said. "Indigos don't need a phone to

talk to each other. Next experiment: look at the world through Wendy's eyes."

"*What?*"

"Just imagine you can see through her eyes. She gives you permission."

"They're sitting at a table in a restaurant next to the ocean. They're eating hamburgers and popcorn. I can even look through *your* eyes and see *me.*"

"You don't need a mirror," Chloe laughed.

"Indigos rock!"

They stepped into the kitchen and found iced tea in the refrigerator.

After refreshing themselves, they cleaned up and teleported back to the Evans house.

Llewellyn returned to her house and lounged in the hot tub.

✳✳✳

Ian and Birgit reappeared holding a laptop between them.

"Little experiment I want to try, Erin," Birgit said, booting the computer.

"Focus on the screen, *mein Liebling,*" she added, hitting the enter key. Images rapidly flashed on the screen for a few minutes and then stopped.

"How many images did you see?" Birgit said.

"It was too fast! It looked like one thousand, two hundred and thirty one."

Birgit typed something on the computer and that number appeared.

"Sehr gut!"

"I was *right?*"

"Now, what was the five hundred and first image?"

"I don't know," Erin said. "Uh ... a boy walking a dog?"

Birgit typed 501 into the computer, and the image Erin had described appeared.

"The program varies the images at random," Ian said. "Even the number of them. So she can't just read our minds."

"You are a true Indigo, my dear," Birgit said. "You do not need to go to school. You could learn more in a week here than in several years at school."

"All my friends are there!"

"Of course they are, honey!" Chloe said. "We wouldn't stop you from going to school."

❋❋❋

The four adults spent the rest of the day teaching Erin to teleport rapidly — and to reset.

"She's learning this a *lot* faster than I did," Eldon muttered.

"The bad guys *killed you!*" Erin blurted out to Eldon. "The ones who killed mom."

"Can't keep secrets from her now," Ian chuckled.

"Yes, they killed your world's Eldon, and I took his place. Then they almost killed me, too ... well, they *did* kill me. Then I reset. When you can do that, it's almost impossible to kill you."

"I wish mom could of done it," Erin sobbed, and Chloe hugged her.

They spent the evening playing a card game called *Wizard,* and went to bed.

❋❋❋

On Wednesday, Culinary Allie and her children arrived along with Ed and Heidi Brocklesby.

Tony and Loretta taught Erin the game of Teleball, and the three played it with five dolphins.

After an hour, they all landed on the deck, and Culinary Allie served lemonade and cookies.

Erin grew quiet.

"You feel guilty," Chloe said.

"I'm having fun, and mom's *dead*," she muttered.

Don't feel guilty, kitten, Theresa's spirit said.

Mom! Erin beamed.

Being dead isn't painful; living is much harder. You like being in the spirit world?

Yes!

Well I live here all the time, kitten. And I love watching you play. And I will love watching you become a young woman.

I want to be with you, mom!

You will, someday. You place is in the world, now. Your destiny is to make it beautiful.

Were you really a spy?

Yes, kitten.

What was it like, mom?

Exciting at first, then sad and very lonely. I have to go now. Be good.

"We're going sightseeing!" Ed Brocklesby bellowed, beckoning with an exaggerated wave.

"Are you coming?" Tony said to Erin, as he, his sister and mother joined Ed and Heidi.

✽✽✽

They teleported to a pine forest under an ultramarine sky, their breath steaming in the chilly air. Pushing through a wall of trees revealed a vast canyon at their feet.

Although smaller than the Grand Canyon, it was breathtaking — with red- and orange-stained white rocky walls, and a waterfall at one end that fed whitewater rapids running through it.

Some twenty feet away, steam billowed from a hole in the ground.

"Where are we?" Culinary Allie said.

"In our world, it would be Yellowstone Park," Ed replied.

"Someone *lives* here!" Erin said.

"You feel it too," Heidi murmured.

"A sadness, a haunting stillness," Birgit said, joining them. "A spirit lives here. It lacks physical form, but is drawn to this valley."

"A little like Glinda," Birgit said. "But Glinda seems to love us even if it can't communicate very well. The one in this valley isn't even aware of us."

"Why is it sad?" Loretta said.

"It radiates feelings that *seem* sad to us," Birgit said. "They might mean something completely different to it. Its thoughts are so alien they don't translate to anything we can understand."

"It's more alien than *actual* aliens?" Heidi said.

"You're thinking of the Archies," Birgit said. "Yes, as strange as they are ... we have more in common with them than with this Earth spirit."

They spent the next two hours viewing mud volcanoes, brilliantly colored hot springs, and geysers. Twice, they had to teleport out of the way of charging smilodons and bears.

✳✳✳

After breakfast, Thursday, Derek and Allie appeared on the deck and hugged Erin.

"How'd you like to visit another world, Erin?" Allie said "We'll go shopping there."

"OK."

"Oh God," Chloe murmured, staring at her hand.

"What?" Eldon said.

"This happened to me the other day," Derek murmured. "I worried about turning into an Ek, but it didn't happen."

"An Ek?" Eldon said.

"Someone in a timeline we call Ek for Ecstasy," Derek said. "The God Virus turned out ... differently there. It made people into grinning zombies, starving to death in their own bodily wastes."

"I'm seeing the face of God," Chloe breathed with a dreamy expression. "This grain of sand ... contains the ... the *entire universe.* It's part of God's mind ... in ... in trance ... pretending to be inanimate matter."

"That grain of sand?" Eldon said.

"Any particle, however small. And if you could destroy all of existence, *everywhere* ... except for this *one* tiny *grain of sand.* The universe would regenerate itself."

"Mom! Are you OK?"

"You called me *mom,"* Chloe smiled, hugging Erin. "I'm fine, honey."

"The masks come off sometimes," Derek said. "And you glimpse things as they really are."

"Like Neo at the end of *The Matrix?"* Eldon said. "What happens if we're like this *all the time?"*

"I could've snapped out of it anytime," Chloe said. "I didn't want to. It was a beautiful experience."

"The one *living* Ek we met felt that way too," Derek said. "He was emaciated, so we offered him food."

"What did he say?" Chloe said.

"Nothing. The sound of our voice enraged him, our very *presence* did. He wanted us to leave, so we did."

"What I felt was *not* the same! You guys didn't irritate me at all. If anything, I felt *closer* to all of you then ever before. And consciousness is the key to everything. Conscious ... stuff can *mimic* inanimate matter but the reverse is impossible."

※※※

After a day in Columbia, the Trask family returned to their Los Angeles house.

"That place was so cool," Erin said, of *The Elegant Pony*. "And that man thought I looked like an *Egyptian Princess!*"

"That's what we'll tell people when we're in Columbia," Chloe said.

"Why do we have to lie?"

"They wouldn't understand us, honey. The only place we don't have to lie is Oz."

"I love playing Teleball with Tony and Loretta."

"I love watching you. If you played it here, people would be absolutely terrified."

Eldon rummaged around in the study and called Drax Security.

"Someone has been going through our stuff," he announced.

"They aren't here now," Chloe said.

"I know, but it pisses me off. What are we paying them for?"

Chapter 46

"Hope you had fun on your *vacation!*" Nora growled. "All Hell has been breaking loose here. We've been hounded by an alphabet soup. DARPA, the CIA, the NSA. When I said I didn't know where you were, they threatened me."

"They have no legal basis for that!"

"I *know*. Creeps ran black ops on us when you only had *superior* technology. What'll they do now that it's *exotic?*"

"We'll deal with them," Eldon said.

"The NSA wants us to launch a spy satellite for them next week."

"OK," Eldon said, shutting his eyes. "Interesting!"

"What's interesting?"

"The main thing it will be spying on is *us*. It'll be loaded with test equipment designed to image our quantum chamber. Millimeter wavelength scanners and the like."

"They'll see your space suit!" Nora said.

"Yes. So we make a space suit that doesn't look like one. A featureless cylinder with some life support. No windows, arms or legs. No seam, even. Put the cylinder in the vacuum chamber and I teleport into it and transport stuff."

"How do you see without windows?"

Eldon just stared at her.

"OK. No windows."

"Line it with lead too, in case they use backscatter X-rays. Postpone the launch until it's ready."

❋❋❋

In a space suit, Wendy floated near the Archy space ships at Conch Point.

The Archies' computers had told them it would take more than a billion cycles to fly home — and they finally believed them.

In short, they were as good as dead.

Fleet commander Gref had issued directives on rationing food and oxygen — putting inessential crew into medically-induced comas.

"We should *all* do that," the flagship's captain said, conferring with Gref in his quarters. "And not just comas. It's more humane than slow death."

If you jettison your atomic weapons, we'll return you to your home, Wendy beamed to all of them.

"I heard rumors that our adversaries are telepathic," Gref said. "I never believed them."

"How do we fight creatures who know our plans as soon as we do?"

"More to the point, how do we fight creatures whose technology is so advanced?"

"That kind of talk can get you executed back home," the captain said.

"We are far from home," Gref said. "That much is painfully clear."

"To the aliens who brought us here," he added. "What assurances do we have that you'll keep your side of the bargain?"

You simply have no choice. You have two cycles to respond.

"My first command will *not* involve *surrender to vermin!*" Gref said.

She teleported home.

※※※

Derek ran into a haggard Professor Janice MacCallan in the hall outside her office.

"What *happened?*" he exclaimed.

"I have a tiger by the tail, Mr. Evans," she croaked. "I can't let go."

He scanned her.

She was exploring his suggestion regarding nuclear fusion powering the sun and hadn't slept or eaten in three days.

"I got time on our Babbage," she added, waving a printout. "I can correctly compute the sun's energy output to within *one percent*. Unprecedented!"

Another quick scan revealed that a Babbage was a mechanical computer. Knickerbocker University had the third largest in the world, with almost a million brass gears and powered by a 5000 horsepower steam engine.

"You're here for the transistor stuff," she muttered, waving him into her office.

She shuffled through piles of papers on her desk, pulled out two sheafs, and handed them to Derek.

"This is for manufacturing transistors, and this other is the simplified circuit for transistor radios," she said. "Superheterodyne, with a minimum of components. It works on a pegboard, so it should just work."

"Thanks," he said. "Allie designed a spiffy case for it."

"Spiffy?"

"Elegant. Attractive."

"You'll have to excuse me, Mr. Evans," she yawned. "I have to get back to work. This might be one of the most groundbreaking papers of my career. I will definitely mention you."

"You don't have to."

"Of course I do. It's also a big boost for the theory of hyperbolic space-time. I'm going to contact Nielson Pohl at Miskatonic."

"You look like you could use some sleep."

"I'll sleep when I'm dead!"

At this point her head slumped down onto her desk.

"Professor!" he said.

He shook her but she didn't respond.

"Damn it! Relativity's not worth *dying* for!"

He dragged her out of her swivel chair and hefted her. She was surprisingly light.

Carrying her in his arms, he staggered down the hall and passed the department secretary.

"What have you done?" she shrieked.

"Professor MacCallan has collapsed," he said. "I'm taking her to the University Medical Center. Please contact her family."

He knew Professor MacCallan had a daughter in Seattle.

"Oh, my God," the secretary wailed, dialing a number on her desk phone.

"I have a cab waiting," he shouted, ducking around the corner to a deserted hallway.

He teleported to a hallway near the Emergency Room.

※※※

He walked into the main room, and several nurses ran over with a gurney.

"This is Professor Janice MacCallan of Knickerbocker University. She collapsed in her office. I understand she had been working on a project for three days without eating or sleeping."

He signed papers and offered to cover her medical expenses.

"Derek Evans?" Doctor Marks, the admitting physician, said. *"The* Derek Evans? The one in the penicillium arcanum project?"

Derek realized that injectable medicines were called arcana.

"Yes. Professor MacCallan might need some of that ... stuff."

"What is your relation to the patient?"

"A business partner. The physics department secretary is trying to reach her family."

With no success, so far, Derek thought, scanning her.

"I'll spare no expense. I want her to receive the best of care."

"All our patients receive that, Sir!" Dr. Marks frowned.

"Fancy meeting you here!" Professor Stan Epstein said, clapping Derek on the back.

Derek explained what had happened.

"Your casual suggestions on growing penicillium increased our yield ten thousand-fold," he said.

"Good."

"We put out a radio advertisement asking people to send us moldy food. A rotten cantaloupe from Kings County won the prize, further doubling our output."

"Fantastic!"

"You seem to have your fingers in a great many pies," Professor Epstein said. "Rumors are flying about that you have a radio that runs on only nine volts."

"Professor MacCallan built a working prototype. We're gearing up to mass-produce it."

"Hmm."

"She's a patient here and might need some of your arcanum."

Professor Epstein would consult with Janice's doctors.

Deciding that there was nothing more he could contribute, Derek ducked into a restroom and teleported back to Professor MacCallan's now-locked office.

***

Papers, books, and notebooks covered her cluttered desk. One yard-long brass ruler-like object puzzled Derek. It had two sections, one that slid against the other. Fine hairline markings covered both sections with rows of tiny numbers beneath them, and a sliding glass cursor with built-in magnifying glass attached to the outside of both.

A slide rule!

It struck him as extraordinarily elegant: A primitive mechanical device — indeed the most primitive possible — powered by mathematics alone, by logarithms.

The craftsmanship is extraordinary. It must be her most prized possession.

He found the two sheaves of documents he'd dropped earlier.

Then he found her notes on nuclear fusion — a ring-bound notebook — and leafed through it.

What he had thought would be a simple back-of-an-envelope calculation turned out to be quite complex.

There were three types of hydrogen that could fuse into two types of helium. Each reaction produced a different amount of energy, and one had to account for the proportions of each. Furthermore, some of the helium atoms fuse into heavier ones, releasing more energy.

Professor MacCallan had complicated equations estimating "weather conditions" in the sun's interior.

He let out a low whistle.

She had performed these calculations on a slide rule and a glorified adding machine. What could she have accomplished with a real computer?

"Don't you dare die on me, professor," he whispered.

❋❋❋

Following his broker's advice, Derek teleported to the Midland Chemicals Concern. There, he met with its Chief Technical Officer and explained how to manufacture transistors and how to test them.

He ordered ten thousand units.

In like fashion, he contacted the Electrical Magic Concern regarding manufacturing his radio circuit boards, and verified they would fit in the plastic cases Allie had designed.

Chapter 47

"OK," Chloe said. "This is a world where your mother *probably* didn't die."

They stood on the sidewalk at Galaxy Boulevard, beside a shuttered and deserted Space Ventures Factory.

Eldon appeared.

"The factory looks so desolate," he said. "I can't believe I refused to contact the company here. What kind of ... of *me* lives here?"

Eldon tried his cell phone and was surprised to learn that it worked in this timeline.

He called a taxi, and they took it to the Wyvern Estates.

※※※

In the lobby, they were unable to find a Maloney listed on the mailboxes.

Eldon pushed the button for the building superintendent, Sam Franklin.

Sam came out.

"Hello squirt," he said to Erin. "I have your stuff in storage. Want to get it?"

Erin broke down in uncontrollable sobbing, and Chloe hugged her.

They all had scanned Sam.

After Space Ventures had been "sold" to Kinoshita Technology, the then-unemployed Theresa/Natalia had started drinking heavily.

Now, she was in prison for driving drunk and killing a pregnant woman in a hit-and-run accident.

If her identity as a Russian spy was discovered, she would get a longer prison sentence.

Social Services had put this timeline's Erin into foster care.

"Are you the foster parents?" Sam said.

"Yeah," Eldon lied.

"Keeping her stuff in storage costs lots of bucks," Sam began.

Eldon counted out ten hundred dollar bills, saying, "Keep her stuff until she's ready to look at it. Obviously not today."

They walked around the corner and, when they were sure no one was watching, they went home.

※※※

"I *hate* her!" Erin sobbed.

"Don't hate her, sweety," Chloe said. "She had a wonderful daughter."

"How could she put me in foster care?"

"She didn't put you there," Eldon said. "She's in jail, and someone has to take care of you. That copy of you, anyway."

"Try to scan the other you," Chloe said. "Is she OK?"

"Yes," Erin said. "Her foster parents are treating her nice."

"That's wonderful!" Chloe said.

"She's very sad though."

"I'm worried about what happened to *my* people in that timeline," Eldon muttered. "You know — the department heads, the engineers."

"We can't fix *every timeline*," Chloe exclaimed. *"Down that road lies madness!"*

"But I *know* about this other timeline," Eldon said. "I can't look away."

✳✳✳

Eldon returned to the shuttered Space Ventures factory and took a cab to the Zyber LAN Internet Cafe in Los Angeles.

It was a large, dark room with purple walls filled with rows of computers and gamers hunched over them. Some looked as though they hadn't bathed in days.

The din of ray guns and swords clanging against magic shields irritated him, but this place offered perfect anonymity.

"What's your game?" an attendant asked. "We have them all."

"Just want to surf the web."

"Sign this!" he said. "They almost shut us down last year."

It was a legal disclaimer stating that Eldon would not view or download pornography.

Eldon, signed it, found a free computer, and logged in.

A careful check of social media and job sites seemed to show that his employees were doing alright. Most of them had found jobs at other aerospace companies.

"So getting my hardware and technical notes was enough," he murmured to himself.

Next, Eldon composed a long email to the FBI, Homeland Security and the CIA claiming to be a North Korean agent named Kim Il Chol and listing everything he knew about that agent from his own timeline.

He described North Korea's plans for the Space Ventures hardware and said his contact in Washington was a lobbyist named Dennis Nelson.

"Bastard!" a familiar voice growled. "You'll destroy us."

Eldon quickly hit the enter key, sending the emails.

The man standing over him was a version of himself. Although he was the same age, his face's bitter lines made him look years older.

They stared at each other.

"The *only* way to survive is to keep a low profile," the other Trask muttered. "Not get involved."

"If I hadn't, you'd die in New York along with everyone else," Eldon said.

"We've sensed approaching disaster and are moving out of the New York area. The authorities will ignore your emails, so you've saved *no one.*"

"Hey," one teenage gamer said. "Aren't you the *rocket man?* I thought you disappeared. Now there's *two* of you?"

Chloe charged out of the Ladies' Room.

"Huh?" Eldon said.

"I'm from this timeline," she said. "Give *me* the message. Allie and I know the CIA director's secret email account. We planned to warn him about the coming disaster. Now we can be detailed and specific."

"Thanks," Eldon said, beaming his email to her.

"You do this, Chloe, and it's over between us," the other Trask growled.

"Then we're through, Trask. I'm quite frankly fed up with your paranoia and selfishness. We all are. You're willing to sacrifice millions of people to keep our secrets. If you ever want to be a part of our lives again, you'll have to *earn* it."

"In my world, we're *married* and..." Eldon moaned.

"I wish you and *your* me all the best," Chloe interrupted. "And Erin, too. Don't worry about *this* world's Erin. We'll be her guardian angels. I suspect her mother's Russian handlers have written her off."

Eldon entered the mens' room and returned home.

❋❋❋

"I have got to be the most screwed-up person in the universe!" Eldon muttered, pacing in their kitchen. "All these other versions of me are so neurotic! Paranoid, obsessive-compulsive..."

"I'm glad I got the semi-OK version of you," Chloe smiled.

"They'll help the me in that world?" Erin said. "And my mom?"

"Looks like it, honey," Eldon said.

Erin smiled.

"It all makes me think of God," Chloe breathed.

"Huh?" Eldon and Erin said.

"My whole life, the image I had of God," Chloe murmured. "It was a cartoon. The real God is so much more complex. Creating all these different versions of us. That's the only way he could really understand us and our ... history. The universe doesn't just expand. It *multiplies* itself from one eye-blink to the next."

Andromeda Cole appeared.

"Sorry to startle you guys," she said. "Hi Erin. You probably don't remember me."

"Yes I do."

"What's up?" Eldon said.

"I need your help," Andy said. "It's important."

Chapter 48

Eldon followed Andy and materialized in a small, neat hotel room with large French doors leading out to a balcony.

To the left of the doors, the wall held a flat screen TV, and the opposite wall held a framed antique map in German. A backpack filled with dusty old books covered the table.

It was night.

A TV news program showed loud demonstrations in front of a building flying the Canadian flag with a caption "Washington, D. C." under it.

Andy turned off the TV.

"Where are we?" he said.

"The Seaside Hotel in Swakopmund, Namibia," she said. "In the Origin timeline. I've spent the last week here, scanning ... places."

"What do you think of Origin?"

"Depressing as hell," Andy said. "Educated Americans are fleeing, mostly to Canada. Andy and Llewellyn fled to Germany. Llewellyn's at Göttingen and Andy's at the Pergamon Museum. The government said 'good riddance to garbage'."

"They need *some* educated people," Eldon said. "To keep technology running."

"They're beginning to realize that. The sane approach would be to entice the scientists back. So, naturally, they didn't do that. The *same people* who said *good riddance* did a 180 and accused Canada and Europe of *kidnapping* people."

"*Canada?*" Eldon laughed.

"People believe it; morons do, anyway. Even after scientists go on TV and say they left voluntarily. There are angry demonstrations all over the US."

"Wow."

"Every day, I have to go out for an hour so the staff can make up the room. I'd take a book and eat in one of this town's charming restaurants and cafés. Reading and hobnobbing with South *'Ifricans* on holiday."

"What are those books?"

"The history of ... Deathworld. Radioactivity's minimal on them. Terrifying reading."

Eldon strolled out onto the balcony and basked in a cool sea breeze blowing across a sandy beach. In the distance to the left, a pier jutted out into the ocean with what looked like a restaurant on the end of it.

Below, people chatted and sipped cocktails under flickering torches.

"Don't you wonder why I picked *this town* to explore Origin?" Andy murmured.

"The Squidward chamber? That's impossible!"

"Of course it is. Nevertheless..." Andy shrugged. "I had a general idea where it *should* be but it still took a week of out-of-body searching to find it."

"How did you know it existed in this timeline?" Eldon said.

"I didn't. Lewellyn has a major research project going, and now I do as well. I couldn't just sit around and vegetate."

"What happened to the Squidwards? Where are the *ruins?*"

"*Aboveground* ruins would have vanished ages ago," Andy said. "A hundred thousand years is a long time."

"Why don't they *rule* the world? On Oz, humans were their *pets.*"

"*That's* why I need your help."

They lay on the king-sized bed and went out of body.

✳✳✳

Andy played her flashlight on the Squidward chamber's walls.

"Pretty much the same," Eldon muttered.

They followed the dusty corridor until they almost tripped over a Squidward skeleton — with an axe splitting its skull.

"Now that's different," Andy murmured.

They reached the electronic equipment at the tunnel's end.

"It has been smashed!" Eldon said.

"I was thinking we could transport this whole place to Oz," Andy said. "Maybe you can locate its ... disk drives or something."

"Disk drives? My *esteemed* Professor Cole..."

"I'm full of shit?" she chuckled.

"Yes. Storage technology has varied wildly over time, in *human* computers. I doubt this stuff uses *anything* we'd recognize. It would take years of intense study."

"Damn."

"We'll have to do the archeology thing. What do you think happened?"

"I'm guessing Planet of the Apes," Andy said. "Or Planet of the Humans. They tried to domesticate early humans and it backfired."

"Our ancestors were probably a *lot* more ornery than dogs," Eldon chuckled.

"A lot more useful, too. The Squidwards probably used them as servants and laborers."

"Why did you come to Origin?" he said. "To check up on your counterparts?"

Then he knew.

Andromeda had assumed they would teleport the Squidward chamber to Oz to study it. She wanted the Culinary copy of it to remain intact so she could mount an expedition to "discover" it. Finding ancient aliens would be the archaeological discovery of the millennium.

They picked their way down the rubble-strewn hallway and found another hall branching off to the right.

"This wasn't here in the Oz version," Andy said.

About twenty feet further, the hall opened up to a large room.

Three more Squidward skeletons with cracked skulls lay on the floor next to a large brown-stained rock.

At the room's far side, they found a human skeleton wielding a knife that appeared to be stainless-steel, with a wicked-looking serrated edge.

"Cro-magnon," Andy said.

"It sure as *hell* didn't manufacture that knife," Eldon said. "Maybe Cro-magnon stone implements were copies of Squidward tools and weapons."

"Yes..." Andy said.

They teleported to the moonlit surface.

"Nothing here but sand dunes and a couple birds," Andy said. "Nobody should object to our excavating it."

"It bothers me that humans got tool-making from Squidwards. I'd always thought we discovered it on our own. I guess we owe them, though — and even owe those Archy-*fucks* for chasing them here."

"Why didn't they follow them here?" Andy said.

"I'm sure they tried," he said. "It's a big galaxy with ... billions of stars. The Squidwards of Oz were just unlucky. If humans ever venture into interstellar space, we risk running into Archies."

"And genocide," she muttered.

"And genocide. *Damn!* It means we can't just wash our hands of Origin. We're the only ones who can protect these people."

"We have to maintain an outpost here," Andy said.

Across a dry riverbed, Swakopmund's lights glittered like jewels as a car sped by on a raised highway to the right.

Fog rolled in from the sea.

※※※

In an out-of-body state, Wendy visited the Archy ships at Conch Point.

In Gref's ship, the three leading officers with weapons were no match for the hundreds of enraged crew armed with wrenches, hammers, and cutting torches who charged down the main corridor.

The officers retreated to the control room and sealed it.

"That door won't hold for long," the captain said.

"I will *not* lose control of my ship," Gref said. *"Vent* it!"

Open vents to space? Wendy thought. *Why would a space ship even have that feature?*

"We should listen to our crew," the captain said.

Gref relieved the captain of his duties, promoted the XO to captain, and repeated his command.

"We must record it with the Third God's Representative," the mate told him.

What the hell is that? Oh, it's an AI program that actually runs everything.

The former captain tried to block them, and Gref shot him dead.

His promotion made official, the new captain issued the order, and oxygen howled from the ship's vents — sucking many crew members with it.

Running on auxiliary power, the Control Room remained sealed.

Crazy bastards! Wendy beamed. *You've murdered your crew and lost most of your oxygen.*

"We'll die with honor," Gref replied.

Ah! One ono idea kine!

She beamed messages at the fleet's other two ships describing what had happened and what she intended to do.

Then she teleported to the Space Ventures factory in Los Angeles, donned a space suit, and returned to Conch Point.

She scanned Gref's flagship and its officers.

Sure enough, the ship's atomic weapons lay two decks below Engineering. She engulfed that half of it with her spirit-body and cut it away from the rest.

Then she teleported the remaining half — a coffin, except for its control room — back to the fleet orbiting the Archy planet.

As twenty shuttles swarmed around the ship-fragment, Wendy returned home.

Chapter 49

"Perfect!" Allie exclaimed. "They match this house's architectural style beautifully."

Jerrold Holmes had hired the Ferrignano Architectural Concern to design the new office building, Derek's workshop, and the swimming pool — and they had provided detailed scale models made of painted balsa wood.

"When can construction start?" Derek said.

"I can't *wait* to work in my new office!" Charlotte exclaimed.

"The Drake Building Concern can start in two days," Jerrold Holmes said, showing Derek a typed bid on the job.

"The price looks reasonable?" Derek said.

"Yes," Jerrold said. "I think so."

Derek wrote Jerrold a check.

❋❋❋

Allie spent the afternoon hanging her paintings as a group of servants followed and watched.

"They're like strange and beautiful dreams," one twenty-something maid named Mabel said.

Allie hung a four-foot wide painting of Destiny Beach over the library's fireplace.

"It reminds me of the Kingdom of Hawaii," Jerrold said. "Honolulu, I think. I was on a ship from Bombay to San Francisco that stopped there."

Hawaii's a kingdom here? Allie thought.

"Of course, Honolulu has buildings along the beach," Jerrold continued. "And the royal palace."

"I don't know what *Ruth* will make of these paintings," an older maid named Edith muttered.

"You mean the ghost of Ruth Gofols?" Allie said.

"I apologize, Mrs. Evans," Mr. Holmes snapped. "I *strictly forbade* staff from mentioning this nonsense!"

"Ah, Mr. Holmes," Allie said. "If ghosts concern our people, we must deal with them. I consider myself an expert."

"Of course, madam," Jerrold muttered, thinking, *She's going to use psychology.*

***

At Allie's suggestion, they retired to the solarium.

Sunlight filtered by the glass roof and the branches of blooming orange trees bathed Allie's easel and paints in a soft glow.

The easel held her work in progress, a portrait of a maid named Bernice.

Allie sat in front of it.

"Gather around me," she said.

The servants retrieved chairs from the servants' dining room and set them in a circle around her.

"Doesn't it have to be dark to have a séance?" Mabel said.

"Not at all," Allie said. "You must think of Ruth Gofols. You knew her and have a bond with her. Ask her to join us."

The servants all closed their eyes and their lips moved.

"I will enter the spirit world," Allie said, closing her eyes and holding our her hands in the lotus position.

What a bizarre spectacle! Jerrold thought.

"Is Ruth here?" Edith moaned.

"She is indeed."

"Is she angry with us?" Mabel said.

"Not at all. She is ashamed and haunted by guilt."

"Guilt?" Mabel said.

"She feels terrible about how she treated you all. Especially what she did to you, Edith."

How does she know about that? Jerrold thought, thinking of when Mrs. Gofols threw scalding coffee in Edith's face and said her retarded son should be drowned. *Did she interrogate the staff?*

"I knew you was sick and dyin," Edith said, tears running down her face. "You didn't mean it."

"She needs you to forgive her," Allie said. "All of you."

They all earnestly muttered their forgiveness.

What a manipulator! Jerrold thought. *Are we going to have theater whenever there's a personnel issue?*

"Oh my God!" Allie exclaimed.

"Another spirit?" Mabel said.

"No. *Living* people. Edgar Gofols and two other men approaching the house from the North Woods. Croaker Connelly and Cut-eye Corb. Jerrold, please call the police."

Jerrold didn't move.

I'm not participating in this charade! I wish I didn't need this job so badly.

"Someone, please call the police," Allie frowned.

Mabel ran to the study, tried the landline phone, and shouted, "It's dead!"

"They plan to kidnap Derek and me, and plunder the house," Allie said.

"If you say so," Jerrold murmured.

Gunshots rang out in the distance.

"Derek subdued Cut-eye," Allie said. *You bastards will ruin everything!*

How far are they going with this insanity? Jerrold wondered.

The blurry image of two men appeared outside the solarium's glass.

"Open up!" one shouted.

The other fired a pistol at the wall, shattering its glass and making the servants scream.

The two entered.

Edgar Gofols was in his mid-twenties with long brown hair, and haunted, bloodshot eyes.

His stained and tattered tweed suit had been elegant once. He held a pistol in his right hand and wiped his nose on its sleeve.

Croaker Connelly was a mountain of a man wearing blue pants, a gray sweatshirt and work-boots.

"My God!" Jerrold exclaimed. "Mr. Gofols! What are you...?"

"Getting what's rightfully mine. Materkins had a shitbucket more than the stinking million I got. It barely covered my gambling debts."

"Mrs. Gofols was almost bankrupt when she died!"

"Enough talk," Croaker said. "Where the hell is Cut-eye? I thought he was right behind us."

"Ever the loyal dog, you are, Holmes," Edgar muttered. "I should kill you!"

"We're the ones you want!" Derek shouted from the door,

waving a gold bar. "We're wealthy beyond your wildest dreams."

The Tarrytown Police are on the way, Eldon beamed to them.

"Give it to me!" Croaker said.

Derek complied, and Croaker weighed the ingot in his hand. "By *Jove's* incandescent *asshole,* this is *solid gold!*"

"We have tons of it," Allie said. "Leave these people alone, and we'll take you to the gold."

"No so fast," Edgar said. "We have these comely whores to entertain us. Not to mention the new lady of the house."

"Look, you addlebrained coxcomb!" Croaker shouted. "Money is why we came and what we're after."

"What *you're* after. I'm after teaching these strumpets respect. They *rejected* me. *Me!* Heir to the Gofols fortune."

"Give me that thing," Croaker snapped, reaching for Edgar's pistol.

Edgar fired.

The servants yelped as a stunned Croaker gazed at the spreading bloodstain on his sweatshirt and collapsed.

"That's enough," Derek said, running toward Edgar.

The servants wailed and covered their eyes.

Edgar fired four more times at Derek, who reset each time, and finally pummeled Edgar to the ground.

Jerrold stared at Derek in open-mouthed shock.

"Perhaps we should tie him up," Derek murmured.

"Yes, of course," Jerrold said, jumping up and binding Edgar with a thin hose.

Police sirens sounded.

Derek and Allie pulled Jerrold out the door into the hallway.

"The four times Edgar shot me, he missed," Derek said.

"He didn't, though," Jerrold said. "And he didn't fire blanks. I saw bullet holes appear, *behind* you."

"He missed," Derek insisted. "That *must* be our story."

"*We'll have to leave,*" Allie wailed. "It's all *ruined*. Whenever we try to build something nice, it gets *ruined!*"

"Leave?" Jerrold said.

"Abandon this house and my art gallery. *Permanently!*"

"*Abandon* it?" Jerrold said. "Did you really *say* that? It's ... it's *madness!*"

"Please, Jerrold," Derek said, hugging Allie. "I'm begging you. Stick to our story. I'll explain later."

"I will."

✳✳✳

After speaking to the police for an hour, the four of them met in the library.

Derek and Allie had filled one section with art books, and Jerrold had purchased a batch of books from an estate sale, including a twenty-volume Oxford English Dictionary and a thirty-two volume Encyclopedia Imperica.

Derek locked the doors.

"You saw something remarkable today," Derek said. "One of our many secrets."

"If these secrets come out, we will *have* to leave," Allie sobbed. "As we've done before."

"But *why?*" Charlotte said.

"Suppose you had a magical ability to rob a bank," Derek said. "And it became common knowledge."

"You'd never dream of doing it," Allie said. "You're people of honor."

"So what is the problem then?" Jerrold said.

"You'd be a prime suspect every time a bank was robbed," Allie said.

"And others would want you to rob banks on their behalf," Derek said.

"I see," Jerrold said. "They threaten you."

"Since you're invulnerable, they threaten your family ... friends," Allie said. "And *employees.*"

Jerrold pondered this for a moment.

"So you remain anonymous," Jerrold finally said. "They don't know who the people with magic bank-robbing powers are."

"The superman tactic," Derek said. "There are children's stories of someone named superman who does that — for precisely those reasons. Unfortunately it can be defeated."

"Picture a barbaric dictatorship," Allie said. "That can commit brutal acts with impunity."

"I grew up in a small fishing village," Derek said. "Government officials announced 'Do our bidding or we'll destroy this town. Everyone in it, men, women, and children.'"

"They don't have to threaten family and friends," Allie said. "Everyone on Earth is a hostage."

"That's horrible!" Charlotte exclaimed.

"Will those monsters track you down?" Jerrold said.

"No," Derek said. "We're only worried about people *here* finding out about us."

"How can you be so sure?" Jerrold said. "If it's a government, it has vast resources."

Derek sighed.

"OK," he finally muttered. "I guess it all had to come out. That government is on another world."

Jerrold and Charlotte stared at them in silence.

"Al... Albert," Charlotte stammered. "Thinks there might be ... other planets. He ... he even thinks we could build rockets to visit them."

"I know someone he'd love to meet," Derek smiled. "No,

these aren't planets in outer space. They are other *versions* of the Earth."

"It's the most bizarre claim we've made," Allie said. "And, ironically, the easiest to prove. We can *take* you to another world."

"If you consent," Derek said. "Just a short visit."

Allie alerted the others on Oz.

"Do you?" Allie said. "Consent?"

After a long pause, Jerrold said, "If it will clear things up, I'll go. Charlotte stays."

"I don't know what it'll clear up," Derek smiled. "It'll be interesting, though."

✳✳✳

They stood on the deck on Destiny Beach.

"It's warm," Jerrold said, his eyes firmly shut. "That sound..."

"Maybe you should look around," Derek said.

Jerrold opened his eyes and stared, open-mouthed, at the breakers crashing into the beach.

"Welcome to Oz," Ian and Birgit said.

Jerrold nodded at them and they shook his hand.

"You look like you need a drink," Derek said.

He vanished and reappeared with a Mai-Tai that he put into an astonished Jerrold's right hand.

"It's mostly rum and pineapple," Derek said.

"Pineapple?"

"This fruit," Ian said, holding up a pineapple.

"You mean *ananas*," Jerrold mumbled, sipping his drink.

"Please," Derek said. "Sit."

Jerrold sat and looked around, stunned by the light and humidity.

"My God, Mrs. Evans!" he finally mumbled. "This is your painting!"

"Yes," she said. "This place inspired several of them."

"Oh, Charlotte's getting upset," Derek said. "We should go back."

✻✻✻

They returned to the library.

"You vanished into *thin air!*" Charlotte sobbed, hugging Jerrold and spilling his drink.

"That was the most extraordinary ... experience," Jerrold mumbled. "One minute I'm here, and the next in a tropical paradise. Just like that painting."

"We can take you there anytime you want," Derek said. "You could even vacation there. The point is that the barbarians cannot possibly find us here. Hell, they don't even believe multiple worlds exist."

"Will you keep our secret?" Allie said.

"Yes," Jerrold said. "I daresay no one would believe me if I tried to divulge it."

"We've kept secrets before," Charlotte frowned. "For Mr. Gofols senior and his beef-brained son."

Derek realized that the old man had had at least two affairs with young chambermaids during the time Jerrold and Charlotte had worked here. One had produced an illegitimate daughter.

"We claimed that world for ourselves," Derek said. "For people like us. We call it Oz."

"There are more of you?" Jerrold said.

"A handful," Derek said. "They mostly live there and in another world."

"What about ... the people who already lived in Oz?" Charlotte said.

"There weren't any," Derek said. "The human race never evolved there. A matter of concern to us..."

"What do you need... of our world?" Jerrold said.

"Need?" Allie said. "I don't know about need, but it's beautiful. Plain and simple. We want to live here."

"Our world beautiful?" Charlotte chuckled. "That's a new one."

"It is beautiful! It attracted me like a magnet. The magnificent art... the culture... the people. It's more civilized than ours... in so many ways."

"It still has its share of criminals," Derek said. "Croaker Connelly. Edgar Gofols. The Black Bart Gang."

"My God, Mrs. Evans," Jerrold breathed. "So that's how..."

Allie nodded.

"What will we do?" Charlotte said. "Now that we know?"

"Why should anything change?" Derek said. "Just run the household as you've done so brilliantly in the past."

"Apropos of that," Jerrold sighed. "I should prepare for dinner. Mr. Maitland bagged a wild boar in our vegetable garden this morning. It promises to be a rare treat. Will you be dining here?"

"Yes," Allie laughed. "For once. Would it be possible to get buttered popcorn with dinner?"

"Popcorn?" Charlotte said.

"When you heat dried corn kernels in oil until they explode," Allie said.

"You mean kindercorn," Charlotte said. "We can make that."

"And champagne?" Allie added.

"I'll send Bernice into town for it," Jerrold said. "The Tarrytown Zymurgium might not have the best, though. I'll order some from the city."

As he left, Jerrold stopped and said, "What you said about spirits. Are they real?"

"As real as you and I," Derek said. "We can see them."

"One last question," Allie said. "May we invite some friends for dinner?"

"You're asking *permission?*" Jerrold laughed. "You *own* this house, or did you forget?"

"Oh..." Allie laughed, slapping her forehead.

Birgit and Ian appeared in the library's far corner.

Ian shook Jerrold's hand and said, "Will you two be joining us?"

"Please," Allie said. "You and Mrs. Holmes are burning up with questions. And it's such a relief that our secret's out now."

Chapter 50

"Mrs. Simes sneaks in to Mr. Peterson's office," Erin smirked, eating scrambled eggs at their kitchen island. "He's the gym teacher. Then he calls her his dirty girl and then they *do* it. On his *couch. Every single day.*"

"*What?*" Chloe exclaimed.

"What an education," Eldon chuckled, shaking his head.

"You're too *young* to know ... about that!" Chloe frowned.

"They don't think anyone knows about them, but all the other teachers do. They whisper behind their backs. Mrs. Simes thinks her son is from the gym teacher."

"We *have* to pull her out of that school! *Eldon!*"

"*Nooo!* My *friends* are there."

"We can't insulate her from life," Eldon said. "Granted, she picks up things a *lot* faster than other kids. And *more* things."

"In science class, Mrs. Feldman told us about ecology," Erin said. "So Birgit talked in my head. With pictures of Easter Island in Oz. It's covered with trees. Then she showed me *our* Easter Island. It doesn't have any trees, 'cause people chopped em down. Just statues."

"What happened?" Chloe said.

"When there's no trees, people couldn't make canoes and go fishing," Erin continued. "They couldn't even sail away."

"What did they do?" Eldon said.

"They starved and ate *each other!*"

Eldon let out a low whistle.

"I told the teacher about it," Erin said. "Not about Birgit talking in my head, but the other stuff."

"What did she say?" Chloe said.

"She said nobody likes a know-it-all."

"What?"

"She thought it," Erin said.

"Erin's getting getting a first-rate education — even *at* school," Eldon said. "I tell her about algebra, sometimes, although I won't be able to today."

"That's OK. Llewellyn's gonna teach me calculus. My home room teacher said I'm a rich bitch. And I am lucky my mom died."

"She said that?" Chloe roared.

"She *thought* it."

"Lots of dumb things run through people's minds, honey," Chloe said. "It only matters when they *say* something with their *mouth*. Or *do* it. You thought about killing Shari yesterday. Would you actually do it?"

"No!"

"See what I mean? Time to go now, honey. Kids are drifting in to your home room."

Chloe and Erin vanished.

Eldon teleported to the Space Ventures factory and bought a deck of company playing cards at the gift shop.

Then he lay on a couch in his office and spent the next hour scanning people and places.

***

In their spirit-bodies, Derek and Eldon drifted through a small, sad prison.

Local time was 2AM.

Elderly guards patrolled two corridors fronting fifteen cells each, with massive steel doors. Every thirty minutes, they opened peepholes, spied on their prisoners — and yawned.

Easy duty.

Eldon, Derek, Allie, Ian, Wendy, and Travis combined into a gestalt — a being with one mind and six bodies.

In ghostly choreography, pairs of them materialized in three prison cells and teleported prisoners and their cots to a dimly-lit and deserted park.

The Kinkaku-ji temple grounds in Kyoto.

Across a lake, spotlights illuminated Japan's shimmering Golden Pavilion, making it hover in the dark like a child's dream.

With inhuman precision, the three pairs made six more trips — each lasting less than two seconds — and transported the remaining prisoners to the park.

The gestalt dissolved.

Allie went back to her art gallery in Knickerbocker, Derek to the university, and others to Oz.

Eldon stayed behind.

He returned to the prison and dropped an ace of spades from the Space Ventures card-deck onto a prison-cell floor. Then he went to the park and put the rest of the deck next to a sleeping prisoner, a middle-aged man named Takashi Yamanouchi. He also stuffed a report on Colonel Shin Jun Jin/Isoroku Kinoshita — showing where authorities could find proof of his crimes — under Takashi's pillow, almost waking him.

"Welcome home," Eldon whispered.

A cool breeze rose, making some of the sleepers stir on their cots. They remained sleeping, though, and would shortly awaken to freedom and new lives.

A night-watchman spotted the proceedings and shouted into a walkie-talkie.

Eldon returned to the Space Ventures factory.

※※※

For the first time — in any timeline — Eldon entered the *Blue Mars* restaurant at the factory floor's center.

Clear Plexiglas panels muffled some of the factory-din, and a black Plexiglas dome over it held tiny lights simulating stars and a spotlight simulating the sun — the cosmos over Los Angeles at the exact moment Space Ventures had been founded.

It had been Culinary Trask's one flight of whimsy.

He took a table and ordered coffee.

As he sipped and tried to make sense of the morning, he spotted Nora Weinberg walking to her office.

"Ah, Nora," Eldon said, waving her over. "I have a proposition for you and your family."

"Just the man I want to see!" she said, joining him. "Authorities have raised *grave* concerns about our launching satellites from inside the factory. It's in the middle of LA, after all."

"Understandable. We can launch from Vandenberg or the Cape. In fact, it might be better to get our own island."

"You look kind of ... odd, Eldon."

"I feel beyond odd. I just had the strangest experience of my life. We moved against North Korea."

"No! You can't start a war with North Korea!"

"They waged war against us *before* we did anything. We just rescued people they'd abducted from Japan. The survivors, anyway."

"OK..."

"Breaking into a maximum security prison terrified us. So we did something ... unprecedented. I became an aspect of someone else's personality."

"Who?"

"A person who no longer exists. Six of us formed him, her, or it and plucked twenty-one people from a prison in less than a minute. We were a well-oiled machine, teleporting *instantly* and *flawlessly*. With *no need* for spotters. I suppose all of us got our start as personality traits of other people. Before our souls became full-fledged people. It's the nature of souls ... to constantly grow and develop."

"I didn't understand a word you said, Eldon."

"Doesn't matter," he smiled. "We were easy on them. We could've sent three of their top officials to Pembroke. That would've been less risky than what we did."

"Do the Japanese ... know?"

"Yes," Eldon said. "I left a calling card."

"You did them a solid," Nora said. "As my uncle Jake would've said. Still, getting revenge is bad business!"

"They killed me *three times*," Eldon growled. "The first time was heartbreaking and the second ... was so blatant. And the third killed Erin's mother."

"Three ... times?"

"Haven't you wondered why there aren't two of me? One from Origin and one from here?"

Nora gasped.

"Remember when I fired Mercouri?" Eldon said. "It happened about an hour before that meeting. Poor bastard went out to look at his dried up garden, and a sniper shot him in the head."

"You're... an *impostor?*"

"Up until I was sixteen years old, I was the *same exact per-*

son as your Eldon Trask. I was to become his long-lost twin brother, Jefferson. He was searching for fake parents for me."

"I can't wrap my mind around this. Why aren't you running the company in Origin?"

Eldon showed her the video of Eakins's speech.

"They threatened my employees with prison or worse. They blew up my private plane and killed my pilot."

Nora grew very quiet for several minutes.

"Do *I* live there?" Nora said. "I ... I mean a ... version of me?"

"You fled to Canada," he nodded. "You're the president of Ariston Productions, a Vancouver-based movie company. You're having the time of your life."

She mulled this over and frowned.

Eldon sighed and added, "You love working there so much you wonder why you didn't make the move years ago. Your life will be fantastic unless the US invades Canada."

"Why would they do that?" Nora said.

"They wouldn't *here,* but all bets are off in Origin. You saw the video."

"How do I know this isn't a lie? Or *yet another* lie?"

"Please! I can't run this company without you. I couldn't manage a *nap."*

Nora consulted a news app on her phone.

"The Japanese have shut down a temple in Kyoto due to a 'gas leak'."

"They're keeping a lid on things."

"Well," Nora growled, standing. "I've got a shitty day ahead of me. Going to meetings and working for a *stranger* who *lied* to me."

"Guess you don't want to hear my proposition."

"Staggering insight! Must be your *telepathy* at work."

She left.

"She reached her bizarreness limit," Chloe said, sitting across from Eldon. "Your revelations today were the last straw. Kind of ironic because she liked you better than the other Trask."

"Maybe she'll cool off."

"Maybe," Chloe said. "She's doing a web search on Ariston Productions."

"Shit!"

"You used a bad word!" Erin said, materializing beside her.

Luckily, the place was almost empty, and no one noticed.

"Your teacher lied about you being *disruptive?*" he said.

"Uh huh," Erin said. "Mrs. Feldman said Pluto used to be a planet, and then it turned into a *star.* She asked me about it. I said it didn't turn into anything. They just changed the *name* to a dwarf planet."

"She calls herself a *science* teacher?" Eldon exclaimed.

"The principal backed her up," Chloe said. "The thing is, they have kids who really *are* disruptive. They pick on other kids and steal lunch money. And they suspend *Erin,* of all people. The principal's hoping we pull her out of school."

"Let's get out of here," Eldon sighed.

They went to restrooms and teleported three thousand miles away to Florida's Disney World.

***

They materialized in the Magic Kingdom and, this time, located the main gate, and paid admission.

Eldon had to call his credit card company to explain that he was in Florida now.

The clerk overheard him, stared at Eldon and the name on the credit card, and summoned his supervisor.

He turned out to be a heavyset short man in a gray suit named James Meehan.

"We'd love to take a photo of you and your family," he said.

"Oh, OK," Eldon replied.

A photographer appeared and snapped their picture.

"How long are you staying?" the Mr. Meehan said.

"A couple hours," Eldon said.

"Take this complimentary VIP pass for you and up to ten guests," Mr. Meehan said. "Good for a week. We can even get you complimentary accommodations. We hope you'll stay longer than a few hours."

"Thanks," Eldon smiled. "We'll think about it."

Erin and Chloe went on the Space Mountain ride, while Eldon waited by the post-ride show and stewed over his confrontation with Nora Weinberg.

He scanned her.

She had contacted a friend in the Los Angeles police department who told her the bullets on Eldon's patio matched a sniper rifle belonging to a man they had arrested in the Stardust Dreams Motel — a professional assassin wanted by Interpol and a half dozen police and intelligence agencies.

So the phony Eldon didn't murder our Eldon, Nora thought.

"You suspected *me?* Maybe you *should* haul ass to Canada!"

"Stop scanning her or I'll *belt* you!" Chloe said, joining him. "This is our day off!"

They all got hot fudge sundaes at Auntie Gravity's Galactic Goodies.

Afterward, they strolled through the Harry Potter attraction and the world of Avatar.

"That's not a *real* volcano," Erin frowned, when they went to Volcano Bay.

They went to Destiny Beach.

While Renata looked after them, Erin, Tony and Loretta played Teleball over the water that fronted the beach.

❋❋❋

Eldon and Chloe transported twenty more Archy spaceships to Conch Point.

The Archy's in the two stranded ships detected their presence and beamed, *We've complied with your demands. We jettisoned our cleansing devices.*

So you have, Eldon replied.

Eldon and Chloe sent them back to the Archy planet.

❋❋❋

At five, Chloe beamed Culinary Allie, *What do you want to do for dinner?*

We're hosting a big wedding party. The whole place is booked.

Come with us and bring the kids, then.

They all went to a Cinderella-themed restaurant in Disney World.

"Eating here feels like cheating on Derek," Culinary Allie laughed.

"I can't believe that school wants Erin out," Renata said. "You're filthy rich."

"We are?" Erin said.

"Yes, honey," Chloe said. "They don't feel our wealth benefits *them*. And they envy her."

"I could ask the mayor to yell at the principal," Eldon chuckled. "They'd hate her even more, but they'd keep their mouths shut. Or we send her to an expensive prep school where they'd tolerate a smart kid. Or we home-school her in Oz."

Chapter 51

"Get me the hell out of here!" Professor Janice MacCallan muttered. "I have work to do."

"No, mater," Janice's daughter, Doris, said. "The doctor said you have extreme neurasthenic exhaustion."

"In other words I'm tired."

Doris and her husband, Milbert, had flown in from Seattle. She was a thirty-something, bird-like woman — clearly her mother's daughter — in a burgundy outfit, and he was a stocky man with a bushy mustache and forest-green cape.

The contrasting colors hurt Derek's eyes.

"Your work will keep," he said. "They have people covering your classes, too."

"Are you two staying at my apartment?" Janice said.

"A Mr. Willoughby said it was faculty housing," Milbert said. "For faculty *only,* not family."

"That bat-fouled *swine-banger!*"

"Mater!"

Although he wasn't sure why, this shocked Derek almost as much as it did Doris.

"We looked for a hotel room but everything's booked," Milbert said.

"Except for places that rent by the hour," Doris muttered.

"The Great Whig Convention," Janice sighed.

A quick scan disclosed that the Whigs were a political party, and that they were holding a nominating convention — for their presidential candidate.

"Then we ran into Mr. Evans at school," Doris said. "He invited us to stay at the Gofols House. Better than the finest hotel."

"I'll reimburse you, of course, Mr. Evans," Janice said.

"Nonsense. It's nice to have guests in that big, empty place. Too bad you guys have to take a train to get into the city."

"It's a delightful ride," Doris smiled. "We have our morning coffee, read the paper, and watch the beautiful Hudson River rolling by."

"I wish Seattle had a paper like the Scrutineer," Milbert said.

"I'll never miss the pollution," Doris muttered. "You should consider moving out west, mater."

"Seattle's not *The City!*"

"To change the subject, Professor MacCallan," Derek said. "A thousand transistor radios went on sale this morning. The *Elegant Pony's* charging $30 apiece."

"That's insane! No one will pay that much for a dumb *radio*."

"Portable radios cost at least that," Derek said.

Although they existed in this timeline, portable radios contained fragile vacuum tubes that needed massive batteries to power them — which meant they weighed at least fifty pounds and came in their own suitcases.

"But who uses them?" Janice said. "Police and the military. Not a big market."

Derek scanned the store manager to learn that the radios had almost sold out — in an *hour.* The Scrutineer was covering the event and buying units for its star reporters, including Elaine Hickey.

"They'll be collectors' items," he said. "At $30, we clear a profit even after the Elegant Pony takes its cut."

That profit paled in comparison to the sale's effect on the Knickerbocker Solid Valve Concern's stock. A quick scan of Henni Parvue revealed that it had quadrupled in value since the stock exchange had opened this morning and was continuing to rise.

"Once we mass-produce them, our costs will plunge and we can lower the price," Derek said. "I'd also like to study making transistor calculating machines and televisions."

"Oh God," Professor MacCallan groaned. "We'll become *business people?"*

"Tycoons," Derek replied.

"There are worse things you could be, mater!"

※※※

Eldon met Nora Weinberg in her office.

"You may be angry at me but *I'm* angry at *you,"* Eldon muttered. "In *every* timeline where I *don't* contact the local version of me, he vanishes without a trace. He's murdered and the body's disposed of. The company vanishes soon afterward."

"I have no way to verify that, do I?"

"Of course you do," Eldon snapped. "I can take you to a dozen timelines where you can Google the company. Culinary Eldon's spirit *begged* me and Chloe to keep things going."

Nora sighed deeply.

"Look," she said. "For the sake of argument, let's suppose you're telling the truth. Sometimes you're just so *strange,* so thoroughly alien."

"You've contacted Ariston."

"I can't believe how welcoming they are. They want me to fly up for an interview. *Tomorrow*."

"They're trying to raise venture capital from Hong Kong-based businessmen for a video game division. They think your star-power will clinch the deal."

"So that's what's going on," she smiled.

"You believe me?"

"I guess so. What ... what did you do with ... his body?"

***

Eldon, Nora, Chloe and Erin stood next to Culinary Eldon's grave in Oz.

Clouds drifted over the Grand Canyon, casting moving shadows over its painted pillars as a light breeze blew.

"I can't imagine a more magnificent location," Nora sighed, looking around. "He didn't have family or friends, and I felt sorry for him. That's a beautiful grave-marker, made with love. I apologize for suspecting you."

Allie had carved a six-foot-high granite obelisk with her inscription in English and hieroglyphics.

"She composed that ... long ago," Eldon said. "Culinary Trask deserved it a *lot* more than the pharaoh Amenemhat III."

"Oh my God," Chloe moaned.

"I'm afraid we have to return you to your office and do more crazy alien stuff," Eldon muttered to Nora. "We have to rescue someone."

***

At 3 AM in the Origin timeline, two stealthed Black Hawk helicopters at treetop level flew south from Vancouver, British Columbia.

It had been a successful mission.

They had been told they were rescuing kidnap-victims. Their CO had known what to expect, though — immediately breaking out zip-ties and blindfolds.

"They never got the memo," the pilot quipped. "You know — about Canadians kidnapping them."

"Cut the line-chatter, grunt."

As they crossed the US border, they climbed to two thousand feet.

Thirty minutes later, they landed at the Joint Base Lewis-McChord, near Tacoma, Washington.

The prisoners were hustled into a large conference room and their blindfolds removed. At 4AM, the fluorescent lighting made them look like red-eyed cadavers. Nora Weinberg and her husband Caleb were haggard and five-year-old Ben and seven-year-old Jonathan sobbed. As the guards started to remove their zip-ties, a tall white-haired civilian in a blue suit stopped them and said, "Leave them bound and turn off surveillance. And give us privacy."

"Yes, Sir."

"I am Jackson Walters," he said. "Executive assistant to President Knox. If you interrupt me with questions or comments, I'll have you gagged. This is neither a legal hearing nor a negotiation. You have two options: A. you willingly left the US with technical expertise vital to our space program — and committed treason. Or, B., you were kidnapped by Canadian commandos and will publicly state that. There is no option C."

"I worked for a *movie studio,*" Nora protested. "We didn't give information to any foreign..."

"No questions or comments!"

As Mr. Walters was about to call guards, Allie popped into existence and zapped him in the neck with a stun gun.

As he fell, Derek appeared and caught him as Chloe wrapped

a blindfold around his forehead. Derek flipped him face-down and zip-tied his hands behind his back as Wendy gagged him.

Derek dropped a business card on his back bearing the caption, "Renard Moreau's Army."

Less than three seconds had elapsed.

The Weinbergs stared in open-mouthed shock as the Indigos teleported them to Destiny Beach.

❋❋❋

As Derek untied them at the Pincus house, Eldon appeared.

"I thought you were *dead*," Nora sobbed, hugging him.

"What the hell just happened?" Caleb said.

"We'll answer all your questions in the morning," Derek said. "You should get a good night's sleep. You're totally safe here."

"A lot of answers are in this book," Allie said, handing Nora a paperback.

"Science-fiction?" Nora said, turning it over and examining it.

"Not as fictional as it looks," Eldon said.

They spent the next two days explaining things to the Weinbergs and giving them a tour of Oz and Culinary.

❋❋❋

Culinary Nora knocked on Eldon's office door.

"Busy?" she said.

"You accepted the job with Ariston," Eldon glared.

"I guess I deserve that," she sighed. "At least I don't have to deal with ... aliens. Except in computer games."

Eldon nodded.

He knew they had offered her a beautiful house overlooking English Bay — free and clear — and a job for her husband.

"They want me to start immediately," she added. "So I won't be able to train my replacement."

"I'd like you to meet with her for a day or two. That should be OK with your new employers."

"Found someone already?" Culinary Nora exclaimed. "You didn't waste any time."

"Should I have?"

"I suppose not. Who is ... *she?* I know everyone even *remotely* qualified for this job."

***

On Allie's deck, the two Nora Weinbergs silently stared at each other for several minutes.

"I don't *have* a twin sister!" Culinary Nora exclaimed.

"You do now," Eldon said. "Her DNA's identical to yours. At least until we make her an Indigo."

"I'm hurt you didn't offer me that."

"You shut me down before I had the chance. Would you have accepted?"

"No."

"Becoming an alien frankly scares the *shit* out of me," Origin Nora muttered. "But I don't *ever* want to be trapped again. We were looking at life imprisonment or worse."

"I ... I ... I'm not calling you a liar," Culinary Nora stammered. "But I just can't believe you."

"Uncle Eitan was always spouting that crap," Origin Nora growled. *"I don't believe it, but I believe you believe it. Bullshit!"*

Culinary Nora smiled.

"Living in unbelievable times has opened my mind. I'm not keen on running Space Ventures, though. Was your rescue contingent on that?"

"No," Eldon frowned.

"After we become Indigos, we'll be kidnap-proof. President Knox is blaming *Canada* for Eakins's death and talking about invading."

"They already convicted Moreau for it," Eldon exclaimed.

"Canada took us in as refugees. I need to stand with my friends there. We'll fight alongside them if we have to.

"Claiming you were identical twins would've been awkward," Allie sighed.

"Guess you'll have to *work* for a living, honey," Chloe said, hugging Eldon. "I'll help."

"It's time Pete Eakins returned home," Allie said, shutting her eyes briefly. "In fact, it's *precisely* the time for that."

✻✻✻

After dinner, a disheveled Tung appeared at the Whitley's door.

"I need to see you, my lord," he said to Eakins. "In *private.*"

"Of course, my son."

They went into the room where Eakins slept and he shut the door.

"What's the problem, son?"

"No problem. I need your blessing — to survive the night."

"Whatever for?"

"The day, the very *hour* is upon us," Tung said. "We'll awaken to a new world tomorrow. *Freedom Awaits.*"

Tung knelt at Eakins's feet, his forehead pressed to the floor.

"I bless you and your compatriots in your *hour of glorious destiny.* In the name of Mishak, Schmedrik, and *God ♪ on ♪ high.* May your weapons fire true and find their mark."

"I also ask for a blessing for another."

"Of course, my son. Who?"

"Doron Mezvinsky."

"May Mezvinsky's weapons fire true and to deadly effect," Eakins intoned.

"No, my lord. He isn't a soldier. He's a physician. Sacred Leader's *personal* physician."

Wow. Is he going to poison him?

"What am I blessing him to do?"

"It's a secret."

"Can't give a blessing unless I know what it is for," Eakins said. "You can trust me, my son."

"Of course. Doron will sabotage the security systems in Sacred Leader's palace. We'll break in and disable the Safety Service's network and atomic weapons."

"Bless this courageous patriot in his *divinely-ordained* mission. May it succeed *brilliantly* with no risk to himself."

Tung sighed deeply and breathed, "Thank you, my gracious lord! We'll build a statue of you someday. Future generations of schoolchildren will learn of this meeting and your part in it."

He stood, shook Eakins's hand one more time, and ran out.

Eakins went into the kitchen.

"Mrs. Whitley, have your seen Jonah's cat?" *What the hell's her first name? Joss?*

"Not today, my lord. Jonah said the cat likes to stay in a muddy spot behind the containers. It's *always* tracking mud all over the kitchen. I swear, it's going to land in my cooking pot one of these days."

Eakins left

✷✷✷

"Here, kitty, kitty," he said, squeezing between shipping containers and thinking, *I can't believe the fate of an empire hinges on a fucking cat!* "I've got a treat for you."

Derek appeared.

"You!"

"Want to go home?"

Eakins mulled that over.

"A trick?" he finally said.

"I'll take you straight to the Oval Office. Or do you want to stay here and play prophet?"

"At home I was a *real* prophet. They were going to replace the *Statue of Liberty* with me!"

Chapter 52

Eleven Indigos — all the adults except Culinary Renata (who watched the children on Oz) — formed a gestalt, and it scanned many people, places — and futures.

A scan of the White House staff disclosed that its security and surveillance systems were controlled from a locked room in a sub-basement one hundred feet deep. Derek popped in there and verified that the room was empty and everything was turned off. President Knox had replaced the Secret Service with The President's Own — thugs who disliked surveillance.

We cannot put people in Pembroke, tonight, the gestalt concluded. *It would alert the government there. We've interfered with that world enough.*

At nine PM, nine large black armored Cadillac Escalades stood in the curved White House driveway next to the Beast — the President's heavily-armored car.

Members of The President's Own occupied each vehicle's driver's seat in shifts — so they were never left unmanned. In three cars, prostitutes serviced the drivers.

Seven more bodyguards lounged on sofas and a card-table in

the White House's West Sitting Room. Some drank and watched TV, and others played cards. Three watched a stripper gyrate in the Yellow Oval Room.

President Knox sat at the Oval Office's desk and rubbed his eyes.

At that instant, Derek teleported Pete Eakins into the office and left, while Allie appeared in a corner and recorded the two with a camera.

He teleported to an alley on H street NW and called the police from a burner-phone.

Henderson Knox stared at Eakins in open-mouthed shock.

"You wouldn't believe where I've been," Eakins said. "A nightmare to end all nightmares."

I'll issue a standing order to annihilate Boothbay Harbor if I ever disappear again. Derek and Allie won't dare touch me.

"You're tracking mud on the carpet," President Knox murmured, standing and drawing his pistol.

"Put that cannon away before you hurt someone! Blustering *idiot!*"

"You're already dead, you know," Knox said, hefting the pistol in both hands and fumbling with it. "Moreau murdered you. Then Canadian commandos."

"I died twice?"

"We changed our minds," Knox shrugged, adding in a whisper, "You should *not* have come back."

He fired.

This threw Knox back into his seat and flung Eakins several feet.

A bodyguard named Giorgio ran into the room and looked around. As he turned his head, Allie deftly flitted to new positions, staying out of everyone's line of sight.

"You shouldn't fire that thing in the office, Mr. President.

The bullet-holes show up on TV. That's what your firing range..."

Then he noticed Pete Eakins on the floor.

"President *Eakins?*"

Pete Eakins's mouth moved and quivered but no sound came out.

"No," Knox said. "An impostor who attacked me."

"I'll call the police."

"No police! Keep the staff away. Tell them all to stay upstairs. Get rid of the bitches. And tell the men to start the cars. We're going for a drive."

"What?"

"Do it! That's a direct order! And then help me drag this ... piece of shit to a car."

Giorgio left.

***

Bodyguards ran from the White House, entered the parked SUV's and armored car, and dismissed the prostitutes.

The moment all the car-doors shut, Indigos popped into back seats, teleported the vehicles to a predetermined location, and left — in less than a second.

Derek placed a five-gallon gasoline-cannister prominently labeled "Flammable" — but full of water — beside the door.

***

"Who's back there?" one bodyguard said. "I thought we got rid of the whores."

"What are you talking about?" his companion muttered.

"I thought I saw someone ..."

"Where the hell is the *White House?* We were parked next to it a minute ago."

They exited their cars and looked around. They were in a pitch-black muddy field with a two-lane country road running beside it.

"No service," one bodyguard said, trying his cell-phone.

"No radio either," another said. "Just static. AM, FM, the whole dial."

They returned to their vehicles and slowly headed to the road.

The Beast got bogged down in the mud, so they abandoned it.

A mile down the road, they encountered a defunct railroad crossing with a sign that said *Pocahontas County Visitors Center.* Another sign said *Greenbriar River Trail* and *A West Virginia State Park.*

A building next to it had a sign with the word *Marlinton.*

They drove further, entering a small village. They passed the *Pocahontas Opera House,* turned a corner and drove aimlessly until they found themselves in the village's center.

They passed a drugstore and bank, and the lead car stopped in front of a small cafe.

"Maybe someone can tell us what the *fuck* is going on," a bodyguard named Baldwin said, leaving his SUV.

He entered the cafe.

A jukebox blared Linda Ronstadt singing *Blue Bayou,* as a twenty-something blond waitress in a uniform served three people seated at tables and a man at the counter wearing a leather jacket bearing a Swift Worldwide Trucking logo.

The waitress's name-tag said "Penny."

"Where are we?" Baldwin asked her.

"Marlinton."

"I know that. Where the *fuck* is that?"

"There's no call to use cuss words," Penny frowned, as the trucker stood — ready to defend her.

"Look, *bitch,*" Baldwin said, whipping out a Glock 19. "I'm one of the *President's Own!* I can rape and murder you in front of these witnesses and there isn't *thing one* anyone can do about it."

The trucker sat.

"I ... I ... I didn't understand the question," Penny sobbed.

Sorry we inflicted these assholes on you, Allie thought.

"Why the *fuck* don't we have cell-phone coverage?" he shouted

"We're in the National Radio Quiet Zone," an elderly patron volunteered. "Cell-phones are illegal. Radio stations too. They even buried the power lines. All because of the radio telescope."

"I know my way around DC! There's no radio telescope..."

"Washington?" the elderly man said. "That's two hundred miles away. At *least.*"

Baldwin pondered this a moment.

Then he spotted a land-line phone receiver beside the cash register.

He checked it for a dial-tone and shouted, *"Out!* Everyone out!"

He fired his gun at the ceiling three times for emphasis.

"Next shot goes into a person!"

The patrons, waitress, and cook fled.

Two other bodyguards with drawn guns entered.

"What are you doing?" one asked Baldwin.

"Calling the White House and the DC cops."

"No! Remember when Eakins's bodyguards ghosted after he vanished? They killed them all."

"OK," Baldwin said, hanging up. "Canada or Mexico?"

"Mexico's further but it's easier to disappear there."

"Gotta disable the cars' GPS's," Baldwin said.

"Lazy-eye Luiz was the king of car thieves. Won't take him ten minutes."

"We might make it. If we stick to back roads and drive in shifts."

※※※

"OK, Mr. President," Giorgio said. "Gotta put the body on a tarp or something and drag it out. Don't want to leave a blood-trail."

Pete Eakins had died by now.

"Just get four guys to carry him," Knox said.

Giorgio left and called out to the others.

He returned, breathless, and said, "I can't find them."

"They're by the cars, you jackass."

"The cars are gone too."

"They left without us?" President Knox howled.

Giorgio found a painter's tarp.

They rolled Eakins's body onto it and dragged it out to the west portico — as Allie recorded everything.

There, they found Derek's gasoline-cannister, doused the body, and unsuccessfully tried to set it on fire — as police sirens wailed in the distance.

Allie returned to Oz.

※※※

On the Institute's computer, Birgit spliced Allie's many video segments into a single "movie" and put it on a flash drive.

Allie teleported with it to a locked terminal-access room in the National Security Agency.

She logged onto the system with President Knox's user id of 'god' and password of 'HoneyBadgerDont1*Care'.

A screen came up requesting a number for two-factor authentication. A random number would be sent to Knox's secure cell-phone — ensuring that even *with* his id and password, hackers couldn't use Knox's account without *physical* possession of the phone.

Knox's phone buzzed.

"This *better* be those assholes! The President's Own, indeed!"

The phone's screen displayed '1663942052'.

"What? I'm not on the system."

Allie scanned him, typed the number into the terminal, and the *President's Control* screen appeared.

Police cars pulled up to the White House's West Portico.

"What happened, Mr. President?" one policeman said. "We got a call about shots fired at the White House."

"Uh ... uh. Someone ... uh ... attacked us."

In the National Security Agency, Allie clicked on the *'Mandated Viewing'* button and uploaded her flash drive's video.

Then she clicked on *'Immediate Release',* logged off, and teleported to Oz.

In seconds, more than a hundred million cell phones in the US received the video — and wouldn't function until someone viewed it.

The Indigo gestalt dissolved.

Epilogue

The President's Own made it as far as Brownsville, Texas where police arrested them after a brief shootout.

Someone had tipped them off.

President Knox was impeached, tried, and acquitted by a single vote. All but one of the senators who had voted to acquit refused to comment on their reasons. One stated that Knox's murder of Pete Eakins was "unproved": the video was obviously fake, and the testimony from police officers, FBI agents, and forensic pathologists were all lies.

Although he remained in office, Knox's approval rating was less than ten percent, and his effectiveness was nil.

Plans to replace the Statue of Liberty with a five-times larger one of him were shelved — along with the plans to invade Canada.

Congress passed a series of laws that severely curtailed the president's power, and reversed Renard Moreau's conviction.

Renard Moreau's 'army' had become folk heroes.

Someone named Chuck Malliozzi claimed to have served in it and published a tell-all book.

There were plans to make it into a movie.

❋❋❋

Wendy sent a thousand-mile-wide asteroid hurtling toward

the Archy planet and issued her ultimatum: the planet with the sentinel and neighboring star-systems must *not* be cleansed or colonized — or *else*.

The bluff worked.

She teleported the asteroid to Conch Point.

The Indigos of Oz had become unseen guardians to Alpha Centauri's warring millipedes.

The Williams and Weinberg families spent a week in Oz, training in the use of their Indigo powers.

Rosa Williams had finally consented. Now they could visit family in Origin anytime they wanted.

Giggling and squealing with delight, the Indigo children pitched glowing thought-forms into the sky over the beach: cartoon characters, fireworks, and mythical animals.

As they sat before a roaring bonfire on Destiny Beach, one evening, Eldon pointed out a star visibly moving relative to the others.

Eldon shut his eyes, scanned several Archies, and said, "A de-orbit burn. Lord Enro ordered the sentinel satellite destroyed. He's erasing all evidence of our existence."

They watched for another fifteen minutes as the star picked up speed, until it flared brightly and vanished.

"Enro's afraid," Allie murmured. "If the Archies know we exist, future generations will feel compelled to attack us."

✱✱✱

In Culinary, Eldon Trask became the president of Space Ventures and gained a great deal of respect for the job Nora Weinberg had done.

Their competitors lobbied heavily and managed to get Space Ventures barred from using quantum technology to launch satellites on American soil — declaring it "unsafe."

Eldon searched for an alternative.

One morning, a fifty-something Asian man in a blue pinstripe suit appeared at Eldon's office, introduced himself as Heisuke Kato, and bowed.

Eldon bowed.

A scan revealed that Kato-san was the deputy director of the *Kōanchōsa-Chō,* the Japanese intelligence agency — and that he had flown to Los Angeles solely for this meeting.

"Here," he said, handing Eldon a deck of cards. "In the interests of returning misplaced objects to their rightful home. We couldn't find the ace of spades, though."

"I misplaced it ... to the north."

"I see. You might be interested in learning Kinoshita-san fell from his balcony to his death."

"Accidents happen."

"Some even have an air of inevitability."

Eldon realized why the Japanese had handled it this way: Kinoshita had been wired into their political and corporate establishments in countless ways. The alternative would have been decades of trials and scandals.

"I understand you are barred from using your technology on American soil," Kato added.

Thus began a series of negotiations that resulted in Space Ventures purchasing bizarre and uninhabited Hashima Island — with its many decaying buildings and abandoned coal mines — as its main launch site.

Eldon and Chloe celebrated by taking a long-overdue honeymoon in Taormina, Sicily with Erin. It was a week of long, languid mornings on their balcony overlooking the sea, afternoons spent sightseeing and watching ancient Greek plays, and romantic dinners.

Erin took a few side-excursions to Destiny Beach, where she played Teleball with Tony, Loretta, and her favorite dolphins.

In New York, Culinary Derek converted their restaurant to vegan cuisine — having visited a farm and hearing the animals' thoughts. He invested heavily in artificial meat.

Andromeda and Llewellyn shocked their colleagues by taking a leave of absence from the University of Chicago and traveling to Africa.

Using Indigo gold, they founded the Swakopmund Mineral Exploration Corporation and purchased land south of the town for a "diamond mine" — planning to uncover something that would change the course of human history.

Who knows? Maybe they would even find diamonds.

✷✷✷

In Columbia, Derek celebrated his success on the stock market by donating ten million dollars to the Water Street Mission — Professor Doctor Jordan's charity clinic where he volunteered three evenings a week.

It was the first of many charitable contributions.

Derek's parents, Liz and, Thomas, teleported themselves, baby Kile, and their entire house to a secluded area of the Gofols Estate — in the North Woods. The Indigos set them up a Pincus Generator and a well and septic tank.

Derek introduced them to the staff and said they would be frequent visitors.

Although they didn't need the money, Thomas would attempt to get a teaching certificate, and Liz would give private piano lessons.

They might even operate a school *in* the Gofols house for servants and their children.

Renovations complete, Derek and Allie held a housewarming party, inviting the mayor of Tarrytown, executives and staff from Halifax Fused Glass, Professors MacCallan and Epstein, and the two Moreaus: Renard and Marie. The entire Indigo Ohana also attended — now including the Weinberg family from Origin, and the Williams family. The Culinary counterparts wore simple disguises — wigs and a bit of makeup.

After the banquet, everyone moved to the ballroom and danced to a band called *The Three Tulpas* that played Broadway show tunes, Beatles songs, and Italian *tarantellas*.

Allie sat beside them, silently cursing the no-shows Jerrold had hired.

"Their music is so new, so exotic!" Mr. Argent remarked. "I didn't recognize *anything* they played."

"They're from Tibet," Allie smiled.

Mr. Argent shook the accordion player's hand and resumed dancing.

At nine, several guests left to catch the last train to The City.

The others eventually drifted upstairs to their assigned bedrooms.

At two in the morning, Allie yawned, verified that only Indigos were present, and made *The Three Tulpas* vanish — instruments and all.

Never again! she beamed to the others, teleporting to her bedroom.

In the morning, Derek and Allie hosted a "survivors' breakfast" that ran into the afternoon — fending off inquiries from guests who wanted to book *The Three Tulpas.*

"You have a whole new career, Allie," Derek had laughed. "If the art-thing bombs."

"Oh shut up."

The National Journal of Physics rejected Professor MacCallan's masterpiece because it relied on the "thoroughly discredited" theory of hyperbolic space-time — in other words, *relativity*.

In disgust, she threw herself into the business of developing transistorized calculators and televisions.

"We could even build an *electronic* Babbage machine," Derek said.

"It has been tried," Professor MacCallan said. "At Miskatonic, they built one with some seventeen thousand valves. The trouble is, valves burn out. Its computations were lightning-fast, but it would fail after an hour or so. Then they'd have to take it apart and crawl around looking for the bad valve."

"Our transistors will be a *lot* more reliable than vacuum tubes, I mean valves. They'll make electronic computers practical."

Professor MacCallan looked at her rejected paper and sighed.

"Someday, those beef-brains will eat their words," Derek said.

"Someday, I'll be dead."

Wait until I show you a Pincus Generator, he thought but didn't say.

Derek and Marie began their studies at Knickerbocker University in the spring semester. Derek passed his Qualifying Exams and became Professor MacCallan's Ph. D. student. He would do his thesis on the Photoelectric Effect — studied by Einstein in Origin.

Although Renard and Marie could return to Origin, they loved Columbia and Anastasia von Durfee too much for that.

The End

Some terms

Hawaiian

Vowels in Hawaiian words are pronounced individually so Kaaawa (a wonderful beach on Oahu's windward side) is pronounced kah-ah-*AH*-va, and Koolau (as in the Koolau mountains) is pronounced *KOH*-oh-lau, where the last syllable rhymes with wow.

> *Ohana* — a Hawaiian word for an extended family or tribe. I lived in Hawaii for three years and encountered this concept firsthand. When I shopped and bought steaks and wine (in Hawaii, liquor is a "food"), the checkout clerk (a *complete stranger!*) would comment: "Red meat is not good for you, and you drink too much."
>
> No one is a stranger.

Some of the characters — i.e. Travis Howland and Wendy — speak Pidgin, sometimes.

- *"Alii,"* pronounced "al-*LEE*-ee," were the nobility under the old Hawaiian monarchy.

- *"Auwe,"* pronounced "ow-*WAY*" is an expletive meaning "Oh no!" or "Damn!"

- One of the most common phrases is *"da kine,"* meaning "that kind of" or "something like that." Generally this refers to something vaguely similar to something else that the speaker doesn't want to nail down.

  Often speakers like to be vague about things that are actually specific. For instance Travis might say "I have one idea *kine"* meaning I have something *like* an idea, when in fact he has *precisely* an idea.

- *"kama'aina"* means someone who has lived in Hawaii a long time.

- *"ke aloha"* means beloved. *"aloha"* by itself means love or affection (used to say 'hello' and 'goodbye').

- *"keiki"* pronounced KAY-kee. It means "child." It is one of many Japanese words widely used in Hawaii.

- *"lanai"* mean "porch." This word for porch is often used in California, too.

- *"luau"* a traditional Hawaiian feast.

- *"No huhu"* means "no problem" or "no worries."

- *"Not!"* by itself means "it can't be" or "no way!".

- *"okole,"* pronounced oh-KO-lay is the part of the anatomy on which the sun doesn't shine.

- *"one"* is often used in place of "a".

- *"ono"* means "good" and "some ono" means "fantastic." It's also a kind of fish.

- *"pau,"* pronounced "pow," means finished, done for. Servers in restaurants ask if you are *pau* before taking your plate.
- *"pilau"* pronounced pee-LAU, where LAU rhymes with pow. It means filthy and disgusting.
- *"pilikia"* means trouble or complications.
- *"talk story"* means "have a conversation" or "chew the fat."

Columbian

- *"ananas"* is pineapple
- *"arcanum"* is an injectable drug.
- a *"gustatorium"* is a restaurant.
- *"ice-shronk"* is a refrigerator
- to be *"in the morbs"* means to be depressed or sad.
- *"kindercorn"* is popcorn
- *"mater"* is mother. *"pater"* is father.
- *"nikum"* is a con-man.
- a *"rain-shirm"* is an umbrella
- *"Roentgen rays"* are x-rays.
- a *"Zymurgium"* is a wine-store

Acknowledgements and notes

I'm grateful to Christian Ivan Tors for his descriptions of the town of Swakopmund in Namibia.

I am grateful to the internationally renown actress and comedian, Jana Marie Backhaus, for commenting on and correcting some of the German used in the book.

I'm also grateful to Jeffrey Popyack for being a *(very thorough!)* beta test reader and making *many* helpful suggestions — in grammar and *content.* He asked whether timelines ever merge. My thought on this: They probably do, but people never notice it. When two timelines come together, they must become *identical* — so everyone's memories must agree.

I'd also like to thank Eva Thury for helpful suggestions.

The *Kauai 'o 'o* is an extinct Hawaiian bird whose haunting song can be found on
`https://www.youtube.com/watch?v=obrM8K-UDsc`.

The exchange with Professor Epstein is fictional but represents a basic truth: great discoveries often come from noticing what is sitting in front you.

When Alexander Fleming discovered penicillin, it was *well known* (and mentioned in textbooks at the time) that molds and certain bacteria secreted substances that killed other bacteria.

Researchers in the field were trying to *grow* bacteria, and had no interest in *killing* them. Fleming's contribution was in showing that the poisons bacteria and molds use might be harmless to humans.

He discovered this by accident: he had a bad cold and his nose dripped into a bacteria colony on a petri dish. The bacteria died where the drop hit — showing that the human body can tolerate substances toxic to bacteria.

"The drip heard round the world."

North Korea's kidnapping of Japanese civilians from beaches has been well-documented.

The National Radio Quiet Zone actually exists and is as described. Power lines are buried a minimum of 4 feet deep. The Green Bank Observatory is the world's largest fully-steerable radio telescope. It is so sensitive that an electric heating pad in a pig pen disrupted it.

In the early days of electronics, vacuum tubes were called *valves* — which accurately describes how they work. The epilogue's "electronic Babbage machine using valves" actually corresponds to the ENIAC, one of the first electronic computers ever built.

Albert Einstein won the Nobel Prize in physics for his work on the Photoelectric Effect — experiments easily implemented using Columbia's technology. Although this work paled in comparison to his theory of Relativity, the Nobel Committee was reluctant to award the prize for a theory.

Made in the USA
Lexington, KY
17 December 2017